Alice
in
Bed

A NOVEL

JUDITH HOOPER

COUNTERPOINT

Library of Congress Cataloging-in-Publication
Hooper, Judith, 1949-
  Alice in bed : a novel / Judith Hooper.
        pages cm
  ISBN 978-1-61902-571-4 (hardback)
  1.James, Alice, 1848-1892—Fiction. 2.James, Henry, 1843-1916—Fiction. 3.James, William, 1842-1910—Fiction. 4.Mental illness—Fiction. 5.Intellectuals—Great Britain—19th century—Fiction. 6.Intellectuals—United States—19th century—Fiction. I. Title.
  PS3608.O59458A45 2015
  813'.6—dc23

        2015009409

Cover design by Rebecca Lown
Interior design by Domini Dragoone

COUNTERPOINT
2560 Ninth Street, Suite 318
Berkeley, CA 94710
www.counterpointpress.com

Printed in the United States of America
Distributed by Publishers Group West

10 9 8 7 6 5 4 3 2 1

Arm yourself against my dawn, which may at any moment cast you and Harry into obscurity.
  —ALICE JAMES IN A LETTER TO WILLIAM JAMES, 1891

HENRY JAMES
3 BOLTON ST., W.
NOVEMBER 4TH 1885

TO WILLIAM JAMES
Dr. Garrod, here in London, says that all of Alice's troubles stem from
Suppressed Gout. I don't know quite how this relates to her seasickness
aboard the Pavonia but she seems grateful for a diagnosis, any diagnosis.
She is still v. weak and nervous, prone to fainting and fits, and bereft
without Katherine, who has taken Louisa to Bournemouth for her lungs.
I have engaged a Miss Ward, a "gentlewoman in reduced circumstances,"
as a companion for her. A. likes her well enough and says she is collecting
her sayings for "A Golden Treasury of Miss Ward." She is still unable to
walk—I know not what the future holds.

HENRY JAMES
3 BOLTON ST., W.
MAY 9, 1887

TO WILLIAM JAMES
Alice and Katherine left last week for Leamington, Louisa having recov-
ered sufficiently to sail back to Boston, an event that has done wonders
for A's morale. After another contretemps—including a long frighten-
ing spell of unconsciousness—her doctor here recommended the Royal
Leamington Spa. Let us pin our hopes on those hygienic waters.

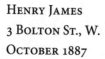

HENRY JAMES
3 BOLTON ST., W.
OCTOBER 1887

To WILLIAM JAMES

Alice's determination to remain on in Leamington for the winter rests on all sorts of good reasons & at any rate is fixed. Her isolation there combined with her weakness seems rather pitiful but mainly to us—she doesn't think so. She misses Katherine but elle en a pris son parti. That she has been able to do it is proof of her strength. Of that sort of strength she has much. I miss her greatly here, as a communicant & talker.

PART ONE

~ ONE ~

THE STREETS OF BOSTON AND CAMBRIDGE ARE RUNNING
through my head again, and it is as effortless as dreaming. From 13
Ashburton Place, on Beacon Hill—where our family moved when I
was fifteen—my feet lead me down steep cobblestone streets, polished
by last night's rain, the gold dome of the state house hovering behind
and above me like a plump, gaudy moon. I pass hitching posts and
dray carts, hear the clop-clop of hooves on cobblestone, the knife man
chanting *Knives sharpened*.

I can slow it down and make out individual blades of grass, a
chink in a stone wall, a button missing from the dress of an elderly
lady on a park bench, the flies settling on the face of the horse pulling the milkman's wagon. Perhaps in the absence of an outer life, the
inner life shines brighter. My brother William ought to study this in
his psychology.

With a throng of people I huddle at the intersection of Charles Street
and Beacon to wait for the horse-cars. When they arrive, bells tinkling, I
mount the steps behind a lady wearing a ghastly confection of marabou
feathers and satin rosettes on her head and breathe in the familiar odor
of dirty straw and old clothes, mingled with breezes from the river. If it
is winter I look out upon a river glazed with ice, bluish in late afternoon;
if it is summer I count the white sails of sailboats. In Cambridge I dismount at dusty Harvard Square, shaded by its great elm, with four roads
radiating out to Boston, Watertown, Arlington, and Charlestown, like
choices laid out in a fairy tale.

My nurse left a half hour ago to do the marketing and has not yet returned, which most likely means she has met someone and will come back with news from the neighborhood. I hope so, as her reports are my sole contact with the wider world for weeks at a time. Possibly she has *not* met anyone but has simply been caught up in a long queue in the bakery; there is no way of knowing.

While I wait, I slip back into the past again. I walk several blocks to Mrs. Agassiz's school, at the corner of Quincy Street and Broadway, across the street from Harvard Yard. I sit at a scuffed wooden desk in a third-floor classroom, inhaling the odor of wet wool, chalk dust, and beeswax. I watch the way the girls shift in their seats while Mr. Agassiz, the great natural historian and the husband of Mrs. Agassiz, lectures us on glaciers, on which he is the world's greatest expert. Despite the fact we are only girls, we are being taught by esteemed Harvard professors of mathematics, science, and Greek. (In Boston, even the maidens are supposed to be well-educated, although it is also true that an intellectual girl is assumed to be something of a pill and a poor addition to a social gathering.) Mr. Agassiz's younger daughter, Pauline, who is Swiss, is our French teacher, and all the girls are in love with her. As she stands at the blackboard or sits at her desk to read the *dictée* aloud, we study her clothes, mannerisms, features, hair, noting every new shawl, hair-clip, ribbon, or locket. She has black hair, black laughing eyes, a rosebud mouth, and a perfect dimple in one cheek. Her perfections make us all wish we were Swiss.

Owing to my childhood immersion in French, I am one of the best French students. I would have been happy enough at school if I could have sat at my desk all day worshiping Mademoiselle Pauline as she spoke of Chateaubriand and Victor Hugo, alexandrines, the three unities, and *explications de texte*. I would not have minded the other classes, either, though I could never warm up to geology or mathematics. My *bête noire* was the other girls, who had known one another since infancy and talked in a dense Bostonian code I could not crack.

Having been educated at home, largely in Europe, with only brothers for playmates, I'd apparently missed out on absorbing the crucial girlish pastimes. I mean autograph books, commonplace books,

secret diaries, coded letters, cat's cradles, Jacob's ladders, cootie-catch-
ers, blood oaths of eternal sisterhood. I might as well have been an
Esquimaux for all I knew of these female mysteries. Someone would
ask if I could do 'Double Flying Dutchman' and I did not even know it
was a maneuver in jacks.

My personality was well concealed under a mask of Well-
Brought-Up Young Girl. Inside the mask I was terrified. The rowdiness
of the girls on the omnibus and on the street frightened me. I lived in
terror of these self-confident Boston girls finding out that our family
did not summer at the Shore because my one-legged father could not
keep his balance on sand; that my parents had once lived in a Fourierite
commune in France; that Father had suffered a "Vastation" before I
was born, turning him into a mystic; that our family tree included a
gallery of tipsy, strange, and dissolute relatives whose lives were frequently cut short by madness or drink.

Despite our peculiarities and semi-foreignness, however, my parents were warmly embraced by the Boston Brahmins. Father seduced
Boston society with his charm and mesmerizing talk and was invited
to join the Saturday Club, mingling with the scions of Boston's old-
est families. We were quickly taken up by people like the Nortons,
the Childses, the Holmeses, the Fieldses, the Lowells, the Appletons.
Father especially doted on and flirted with the beautiful, learned, and
witty Annie Fields, wife of the editor of the *Atlantic Monthly*, who ran
the closest thing Boston had to a literary salon in those days.

If it hadn't been for my interesting brothers (William and Harry
effortlessly became part of Boston's *jeunesse dorée*, as did Wilky and
Bob later), I should probably have remained a nonentity in Boston. I
would study my face in the looking glass for protracted periods, analyzing its defects, hoping that time would improve the picture. I don't
mean to say that I was ugly; I was (I thought) a bland pudding of a
girl, lacking definition. A complexion without roses, hair a lackluster
brown, eyes nothing special, a mouth already hinting at a disposition
to turn down at the corners and look discouraged. All that would have
been workable if bolstered by charm, vivacity, and a pleasing personality, but these qualities seemed to elude me as well.

One rainy morning, while tugging off my galoshes in the school cloakroom, I overheard a conversation around the corner. A giggling girl was quoting from William Dean Howells's review of Father's latest book, *The Secret of Swedenborg,* in the *Atlantic Monthly.* In a stagey voice, she quoted a line from the review—*Henry James has kept the secret!*—sending her two companions into paroxysms of mirth. I did not understand why this was so hilarious—and then, suddenly, shamefully, I did. You could read the whole book, Mr. Howells meant, and fail to learn the secret of Swedenborg, because Father's prose was impenetrable. Although he was a good friend of our family's, the popular novelist was unable to suppress this deadly truth.

Until that moment I had not realized this about Father's books. I had never thought to read them myself, but I assumed they were very eloquent and wise, as Mother assured us they were. Separated from me by a row of wooden cabinets, the girls went on laughing hysterically, snorting through their noses. When they caught sight of me, one of them had the decency to blush while the other two gathered up their books and dashed into the classroom, arms linked, whispering to each other. My face burned. What I would have given for the gift of invisibility!

"The trouble with your looks, Alice, is that you have too much forehead." A casual comment, some months later, by Charlotte Dana. She meant no harm; she intended to be helpful, and advised curls in front. After that I became obsessed with the vast expanse of my forehead, which I saw gleaming from every reflective surface. My whole life would be marred by it, I foresaw; wherever I went, whatever I did, this great shiny dome would accompany me. Some years later, my brothers' great friend Oliver Wendell Holmes, Jr., who was never happier than when he could humiliate me, said, "Alice, one is simply blinded by your forehead. What a lot of knowledge you must keep in there." (Pretending it was a compliment. And to think we let this man make our laws!)

When I confided my misgivings about my forehead to my beloved years later, she said, "What are you talking about?"

"Well, look at me."

She studied me from every angle, then said, "Your forehead looks quite unremarkable to me." I saw that she was right. Either the rest of my face had caught up with my forehead, or it had never been as predominant as I thought. So ended that fixation.

Nurse's entrance cuts short this wool-gathering. I have become fascinated with her character, for she is, after all, the only other castaway on my desert island. Yesterday I asked her if I was different from English ladies, and she said, "Yes. Not so 'aughty, Miss." This morning she wears a secret smile, which must mean she brings interesting news from the street.

TWO

"These are from the Bradleys' yellow hen, Miss," she tells me, extracting four fat brown eggs from her marketing basket. "The brown hen is poorly and hardly lays now. They are thinking of eating it."

This leads to speculation about how many meals this indigent family might stretch out of one sickly hen. What I have been learning about the poor in England is a brutal revelation. One of Katherine's social worker friends told us there were thousands of families in London living in one room, subsisting on "sop," which is not a metaphor, as I first supposed, but consists of crusts of bread they get from the parish and soak in water. And these are the families of working men, carpenters and cabinet-makers, all crying out for work!

But there is other news today, and Nurse can hardly wait to impart it, I can tell. In the bakery where she buys our rolls, she conversed with a new neighbor who has just moved in upstairs in our lodging-house. "A young parson just starting out, Miss, very nice. He said he would like to call on you." The tip of her nose is red from the cold.

Oh dear. Unable to get about on my legs, I have become a sitting duck for parsons. And Nurse herself, a devout Anglican, is a glutton for church.

"Did you tell him I'm a sort of pagan from Boston?"

"Oh no, Miss." Blushing. She has.

"Very well, Nurse. So long as he doesn't get his hopes up."

Nurse (whose name is Emily Bradfield) was hired by Katherine three months ago, shortly after we moved from London to Leamington, K having foreseen that she would eventually be called back to America by family troubles (i.e., her sister Louisa). Her departure came to pass a short while later, in fact, not long after I received a particularly pitying letter from brother William (to be known hereinafter as the Quagmire Epistle). I told Katherine that if she had not been there, I might have gone out, just like a candle.

"Oh Alice, you *wouldn't!*" she said.

"Yes, I would. Being my eldest brother, William can make me feel that I exist or not. It was *very* fortunate you were here." I was only half joking.

When Katherine sailed home, I thought I would die of heartbreak. I can't go back to America—ever. Between us lies a large ocean, and it was seasickness that laid me low two and a half years ago, five hundred nautical miles east of Newfoundland. By the time we steamed into the docks of Liverpool, I could not walk or stand. When I do, even now, the world reels around me, and my legs collapse. Although I have seen many doctors—who have blessed me with the most varied and ingenious diagnoses—spinal neurosis, nervous hyperaesthesia, suppressed gout—the reason for my illness remains obscure, although everyone agrees I should not dream of taking on an ocean.

Our voyage had been perfectly lovely the first few days, or *would* have been if not for Louisa's possessiveness. Whenever K and I were playing shuffleboard on deck, count on Louisa to pop up with her hand pressed to her forehead like a dying nymph, and K would have to go tend to her whilst I remained in a swaying saloon, hemmed in by a crowd of missionary women on their way to convert the Far East. When we'd walk on deck in the evening, wrapped in woolen shawls in the frosty air, Louisa would chatter away about cousins and second cousins I did not know. Bostonians and their cousins! She suffers from consumption—though she seems an Amazon to me—and it is axiomatic to her that a sister comes before a friend.

At times during our crossing I thought of pouring out my sorrows in a letter to K, so distant did she seem when Louisa wedged herself between us. But that is ancient history now. (Incidentally, Katherine was the last person standing on our ship. She attributed her hardiness to my brother William's seasickness cure, which consists of a blistering patch behind the ear and has something to do with the semicircular canals of the inner ear. Don't ask me any more, but he has written papers on it for medical journals.)

WILLIAM JAMES
18 GARDEN ST., CAMBRIDGE, MASS.
AUGUST 9, 1887

To ALICE JAMES
Your card, and H's letters, have made us acquainted with your sad tumble-down, and I am sorrier than I can express. You poor child! You are visited in a way that few are called to bear, and I have no words of consolation that would not seem barren. Stifling slowly in a quagmire of disgust and pain and impotence! Silence, as Carlyle would say, must cover the pity I feel.

I can only encourage you by noting that the laws which govern these vague nervous complaints means that they usually disappear after middle life.

ALICE JAMES
11 HAMILTON TERRACE
LEAMINGTON, WARWICKSHIRE, ENGLAND
AUGUST 31, 1887

To WILLIAM JAMES
Kath. and I roared with laughter over your portrait of me "stifling in a quagmire of disgust, pain & impotence," for I consider myself one of the most potent creations of my time, & though I may not have a group of Harvard students sitting at my feet drinking in psychic truth, I shall not tremble, I assure you, at the last trump. I seem to present

a very varied surface to the beholder. Henry thinks that my hardships are such that I shall have a crown of glory even in this inglorious world without waiting for the next, where it will be a sure thing & my landlady says, "You seem very comfortable, you are always 'appy within yourself, Miss."

⌒ THREE ⌒

THE PARSON PRESENTS HIMSELF ON A WEDNESDAY: A HANDSOME young man with a wispy mustache. I watch his eyes avidly scan my poor sitting room, alighting in turn on the feeble watercolor of Mt. Vesuvius, the dreadful Nottingham lace, the lamp with its sticky mantle, Miss Clarke's porcelain shepherds and shepherdesses, wrapped in their shawls of mauve or grey dust. (So far the visits of the parlormaid have succeeded only in moving the dust around.)

He praises the view from my window and some features of the mantel, and I am struck by the fact that to fulfill his clerical duties he must substitute hearty enthusiasm for real connection, which produces a disagreeable impression of hailing someone across a great distance. Already the man is quite fatiguing and has only just arrived.

I invite him to sit in one of the wing chairs, and after Nurse brings in tea and scones (simpering like a lovesick girl), I explain that I am basically a pagan with Unitarian influences, but I am reading the Bible now with great interest. The Old Testament, actually. At this the parson brightens, like a traveling salesman invited to display his wares.

"Splendid, Miss James! Most people intend to read our Lord's words but never get round to it. I always say, you could die tomorrow, and then where would you be?"

I refrain from pointing out that the Old Testament surely cannot contain "our Lord's words." I explain that I was not in the habit of reading scripture and had no idea the Bible was full of so many abominations; indeed, when it comes to smitings, abominations, plagues, stonings, and the like, the Old Testament must have no equal.

"Ah yes, that is why we find the New Testament far safer, Miss James. Particularly for ladies." He is smooth as oil, this Roger Yardley. He has for the most part avoided looking directly at me, no doubt finding me quite hideous.

Nurse glides through the room again, now in her woolen cloak, carrying her marketing basket, eyes cast down in her angelic mode, one of her standards. I watch the cleric's hand slide into his Gladstone bag and emerge with a stack of tracts, which he places on the table between us. I read, upside down: *The Wages of Sin is Death*. (Shouldn't it be *are* death? And since everyone dies, isn't that an empty threat?) He asks if I'd like him to read to me, and I say, "Oh, no, thank you. Nurse is reading to me just now, from Tolstoy." He looks perplexed. Only after he leaves will I realize that he was proposing to read one of the tracts to me.

He and I lumber down several unpromising conversational paths. He asks me about the nature of my suffering, and I give a garbled account of suppressed gout, mind cramps, useless legs, attacks of panic, and am just about to describe the dreadful sensation of snakes coiling and uncoiling in my stomach that afflicts me just as I am falling asleep when I notice his glazed smile. In a flash, I see myself through his eyes: a boring invalid, full of peculiar fancies, pathetically grateful for a few kind words from a handsome young cleric.

How far I have fallen and how quickly, too! Six months ago, in London, I presided briefly over what Henry referred to as my "salon," and fashionable Londoners would call every Wednesday morning to sample my American drolleries. Even Fanny Kemble, the great actress, came, and her entrance never failed to be dramatic, owing to her breathlessness and pallor after the ordeal of my staircase. Although she was gracious and went around telling people about the "so very clever and droll Miss James," I felt self-conscious in her presence, having heard that American women made her think of white mice shrieking. William's friends from the Society for Psychical Research also came and discoursed amusingly about mediums and "beings."

Then my legs collapsed again, and I had to give up London for tranquil Leamington. (Tranquil is a kind way of putting it.) Katherine and I had a lovely two months here, until Louisa's lungs went downhill again and K was summoned home. And here I am, stranded in the Midlands, unable to walk, far from every soul I have ever known. (But I shan't sink into self-pity and become a bore even to myself.)

The parson has been talking about the weather and from there has managed to leapfrog nimbly to Nature, in which he naturally discerns the hand of the Creator.

"You have heard of Mr. Charles Darwin, I suppose?" I say.

"Naturally, Miss James." His jaw muscles work yeomanlike at his chewing.

"Then you must know that Nature is just one thing eating a smaller thing all the way down. Even the birds seem to spend most of their time trying to peck one another's eyes out."

"Miss James, I think you would be persuaded to change your mind if you were to read Bishop Paley. He gives this example: If a person who has never seen a watch were walking through a wood and came upon one, he would know immediately that it had been *designed* and could not have arisen by chance. So too with the human frame and the complex working of various organs, Miss James. Consider—" And he's off and running, don't ask me for details.

In an instant I see through him as if he were transparent. Underneath the religiosity lurks a ruthless ambition. This young cleric is prepared to claw his way to the top of the heap, and will spend the remainder of his life groveling before his superiors and condescending to his inferiors.

"The human eye, just to consider one organ, is too well designed to have arisen by accident," he is saying, adding more anatomical minutiae, which I'll spare you. A standard speechlet, I suppose. When he winds down, I say, "I wonder if your bishop ever went out into the woods and saw a wasp caught in a spider web. A torment worthy of Dante, I assure you. The wasp struggles, at first believing it will escape but becoming more tightly wrapped all the while in its sticky winding-sheet. The struggle is agonizing, lasting hours. When it stops struggling I am sure the wasp knows it will die."

With a handkerchief the clericule dabs at his nose, which (I have just now noticed) drips. His hands fumble with the tracts. His tongue darts out to catch a stray crumb from his mustaches. How quickly he is undone—by a supine female invalid.

"It is a pity to waste your theology on me, Mr. Yardley, when there are other invalids who would be more easily redeemed." He smiles thinly, fishes his gold watch from his waistcoat pocket, mimes surprise at the lateness of the hour, and takes off as if fleeing a pestilential city. Afterwards, I tell Nurse to toss out the tracts, which are no doubt crawling with microbes.

"If you don't mind, Miss, I'll give them to the Bachellers." The Bachellers are among the most miserable of Leamington's impoverished families. Mrs. B has had all her teeth pulled and unable to afford new ones, subsists on soup and sop. Mr. B is grotesquely crippled from a work accident and cannot work. There are nine or ten small Bachellers in various states of misery.

"I'm sure they'd prefer something more filling and sanitary, Nurse."

She clears the tea things briskly, without looking at me. I am afraid I am a continual disappointment to her. By early evening the duel with the cleric has ripened into a severe neuralgia. I am stretched out on my back like a dead Crusader, with the heavy velvet curtains drawn, thinking of the past, of Cambridge, of my dead parents, of poor Wilky, of William's small son—all our beloved dead laid out in the earth of the Mt. Auburn Cemetery.

WILLIAM JAMES
GARDEN STREET, CAMBRIDGE, MASS.
JULY 26TH 1887

TO ALICE JAMES
I am desolated to hear of your latest troubles. We hear much about Suppressed Gout even here on these shores; Dr. Beach says that if the poison could be made to come out in your joints, your nervousness would leave you entirely.

I think I have told you of Mrs. Leonora Piper, a Boston medium who has impressed me by minutely describing the illnesses of some of Alice's California relations, as well as the most embarrassing secrets of our household. Most mediums are fakes and rogues but Mrs. P seems to be the genuine article. She has brought some comfort to poor Alice (and me) after the death of our little Herman.

Would it be too much to ask you to snip a sample of your tresses (about two inches in length) and send it to me with your next letter, and I will let you know Mrs. P's "diagnosis." I know your skepticism about the occult, but what is there to lose?

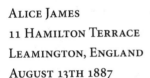

ALICE JAMES
11 HAMILTON TERRACE
LEAMINGTON, ENGLAND
AUGUST 13TH 1887

TO WILLIAM JAMES

I hope you will forgive my base trick about the hair. It came not from my head but from a deceased friend of Nurse's. I will be curious to hear what the woman will say about it. Its owner was in a state of horrible disease for a year before she died—tumors, I believe! I thought it would be a test of whether your prophetess was simply a mind-reader. If she were anything more, I should greatly dislike to have the secrets of my being exposed to the wondering public.

⟶ FOUR ⟵

IN A FIT OF BOREDOM (APPARENTLY I HAVE NO APPEAL TO THE Midland mind) I have been rereading George Sand's journal. I just came to an entry where, after being jilted—again!—by Alfred de Musset, she hacks off her hair dramatically and sends it to him. I could have told her not to bother. A bit later she confides, *At least I should regain my looks if I could stop crying.* Isn't that typically French!

Since my beloved sailed, I have lost track of the date. Days pass, then weeks, alike as peas in a pod. In a long letter from South Carolina, Katherine describes the sanitarium, its amenities, and the invalids themselves. How curious of fate to send us both to spa towns four thousand miles apart (ironically, in my case, as I am considered too feeble to take the waters of the famous Royal Leamington Spa). Her letters tell of Southern ladies prone to fantastic feminine vapors who refer to the Civil War as the War of Northern Aggression. *Being a Northern Aggressor myself, I simply pretend to be intermittently deaf. Such a pity the proper climate for consumption should lie so far below the Mason-Dixon line.* Her sweet references to our happier times get me through the next fortnight and her letter becomes quite dog-eared.

Winter has descended. My windows are sealed tight against the cold, and the horses in the lane become mired in a thick mud-paste some days. A few virtuous matrons have come to nibble at me but no one worth recording; they all seem like the tamest of tame Boston. I tried to explain this in a letter to William, but gave up the attempt. How can he imagine what it is like to live shut up in Nurse's little centimeter of mind?

It is almost a relief to fall into a faint around noon, as is my custom. This is usually preceded by an "aura" in which the paintings on my wall glow with an inner light and beckon me into another world. More than once, Nurse, tall and narrow like a Fra Angelico madonna, has appeared to me stretched like taffy, words streaming out of her mouth in a Gothic script. Naturally, I don't confide these visions, which might lead her to suspect me of witchcraft or insanity. When I come to, I generally ask her to read to me. She has a pleasant reading voice, almost musical. Sometimes we take up a novel; at other times I ask her to read to me from *A Short History of the English People* by J. R. Green, my favorite historian, whose widow attended my salon in London. Everything Nurse reads astonishes her ("War for a Hundred Years, Miss? That is too awful!").

This afternoon I ask her to read to me from the *Standard*. "You know the kind of thing I like, Nurse."

"Certainly, Miss. Tragic stories, debates in parliament, and news about Ireland." She begins several articles that do not prove interesting enough to continue. Then she reads the following gem:

An inquest was held on Thursday at Hull, touching on the death of Miss Amy Cullen, aged thirty-three. Miss Cullen, who resided by herself, was found dead in bed on Wednesday morning, having poisoned herself with vermin killer. It appeared that the deceased had been engaged to be married to a clerk named John Aston. On Wednesday he had requested her by letter to break off the engagement. On Thursday morning he received a letter from her—

"Shall I read the whole letter, Miss?"

"Please do, Nurse. I would be interested in hearing her reasons. If we are ever fully ourselves, surely it is in a suicide note."

Nurse reads on, in her high, clear voice:

Dear Jack,—you have done right in letting me know the truth. You cannot gauge the depth and intensity of that love which you thus carelessly fling away as a thing not worth keeping. Pride would forbid me saying this to you if I had not made up my mind not to live; but what I could not say living I can say dying, for, oh, my darling, I cannot live without you. After the one glimpse of heaven that you have shown me I dare not face life with the prospect of never seeing you again. By the time you have received this I shall be no more; but don't reproach yourself, dear . . .

And the letter continues in that vein, full of love and forgiveness toward "Jack," to whom the suicide bequeaths her grand piano. "What a beautiful sincerity and dignity," I say when Nurse reaches the end.

Nurse gasps. "But, Miss, he jilted this lady for another. Now the other lady will get her piano, too. That's not right!"

"I mean, Nurse, how happy and wise of her to go in the illusion of her sorrow and never learn that 'Jack' is a figment of her fancy, born simply of her rich and generous possibilities."

"I can't fathom what you mean, Miss. How could she be happy or wise and take rat poison?"

You cannot gauge the depth and intensity of that love which you thus carelessly fling away as a thing not worth keeping. No one means to carelessly fling love away, no one means to die from it either; they simply can't help it.

HENRY JAMES
34, DE VERE GARDENS, KENSINGTON W.
LONDON
SEPTEMBER 6TH 1887

TO WILLIAM JAMES
The manner in which Alice bears the dullness, isolation & solitude of Leamington is almost beyond my comprehension. She is very political and very sure of certain things—the baseness of the Unionists, &c. I don't think she likes England or the English very much. This is owing in large part to her isolation and the fact that she sees only women.

WILLIAM JAMES
18 GARDEN ST., CAMBRIDGE, MASS.
OCTOBER 7, 1887

TO HENRY JAMES
I am reading The Bostonians now. One can easily imagine the story cut and made into a bright short sparkling thing of 100 pages ... you have worked it up by dint of descriptions and psychologic commentaries into nearly 500—charmingly done for those who have the leisure and the peculiar mood to enjoy that amount of miniature work—but perilously near to turning away the great majority of readers who crave more matter & less art.

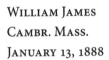

WILLIAM JAMES
CAMBR. MASS.
JANUARY 13, 1888

TO HENRY JAMES
The only experiment I should feel like seeing Alice try would be some mesmeric experiment or other, if a good operator can be got—if Edmund Gurney, for example, could recommend someone as a magnetizer.

⁓ FIVE ⁓

Nurse helps me to sit up and brings me my cup of tea on a tray. The cup trembles in my hand and a few drops splash onto my quilted bed jacket. The hours of the day will be dealt out like a pack of cards, always the same hand. Nurse will go out to do the marketing and bring back eggs from a nearby farm and buns from the bakery. Miss Clarke will bring up the post, straighten pictures, and talk about her nieces. She will try to find out who my correspondents are without revealing that she has studied the postmarks with a spy's single-mindedness. Nurse will return. The midday papers will arrive. The sky will grow cloudy. Perhaps it will rain. By noon I will be exhausted and will most likely "go off."

But this is my holy hour. Nurse pulls back the heavy velvet curtains and the morning light gushes over my quilt like a river, bright white some days, pearly or opalescent if the sky is overcast. For a short while the earth and the heavens are brand-new again, unspoiled, like the Garden of Eden or the pure light of infancy. My cup runneth over, compensating me for whatever horrors or tedium will inevitably come. And Nurse thinks I am an unbeliever!

Everything I think about is saturated with strong feeling now, as in significant dreams. Scenes of Cambridge, Newport, Paris, even fragments of New York City when I was an infant, flash through my mind. To an observer it looks as if I am immobilized, but I am a traveler with a spectral Baedecker, visiting all the places and the people I have known.

In 1866, when I was seventeen, our family moved from Boston to 20 Quincy Street, Cambridge, across the street from the Harvard president's house on the edge of Harvard Yard. When the wind blew from the Harvard direction, you could smell the row of privies on the far side of Mr. Eliot's house. Cambridge was a small, ingrown world then. On a stroll you might run into the legendary Mr. Agassiz, or Professor Sophocles, who had been teaching Greek for as long as anyone could remember, or Mr. Childs, who collected ballads, or Mr. Eliot, with his port-wine birthmark and brusque remarks. (In Cambridge when you spoke of "the president," you did not mean the President of the United States.)

George Ticknor (Harvard Professor of Modern Languages) famously compared Boston to ancient Athens, and the period just before our family moved there was referred to, without irony, as the Periclean Age. Bostonians took their city and its institutions seriously and were ravenous for culture. The poet James Russell Lowell's Harvard course on the English poets was repeated the next day in the afternoon for those who had not got there the evening before and printed in the newspaper the day after. There were dozens of Browning Societies in Boston, exceeded only by the number of Dante Circles; there were lectures on every subject under the sun, and so many of the city's grand dames were committed to Hegelism that it was rare to get through a Back Bay dinner party without hearing about "the dialectic."

Oratory was inculcated in the young in the belief that every young man of good family should be prepared to mount a pulpit and stir the citizenry with an exhortation of some sort. To hear Bostonians talk, you'd think that such institutions as the Saturday Club, Papanti's dancing school, the Ether Monument, and the water side of Beacon Street were on a par with Salisbury Cathedral, Versailles, and the Sistine Chapel, and a newcomer had best acquaint himself with them in a hurry.

Mr. Eliot's first cousin, Charles Eliot Norton, editor of the *North American Review* and future Harvard professor of fine arts, resided in baronial splendor on his estate, Shady Hill, north of Harvard Yard. It provoked considerable mirth in Cambridge that the two cousins had staked out antipodal positions on the great questions of the day. Pragmatic, scientific, and utilitarian, Mr. Eliot, a chemistry professor before becoming president of Harvard, declared on more than one occasion, "The most useless people we see are the Americans who live abroad without any profession or occupation but that of time-killer." His cousin, meanwhile, spent long periods abroad, preferring Italy to all other cultures. Of all parts of Europe Italy was the most decadent in Mr. Eliot's view. "Rome stinks," he was heard to say. Also: "Cathedrals are bad things, being costly and not well adapted to other uses when no longer needed for idolatry." Meanwhile, Charles Norton suffered daily, hourly, from the newness, crassness, tastelessness, ignorance, and barbarism of America.

It was to Charles Norton, his formidable mother, and his two cultivated unmarried sisters, Jane and Grace, that our family was principally beholden in those years. Charles was the Platonic idea of the pedant. An autocrat on intellectual matters, he was fond of saying that "two institutions—Harvard College and the New York *Nation*—are the only solid barriers against the invasion of barbarism and vulgarity."

If you conversed with him, you'd be subjected to utterances like, "Like Antonio in *Twelfth Night*, I can no answer make but thanks, and thanks, and thanks." He would confide over his after-dinner brandy, "What I have suffered most from in my life is the omnipresence of vulgarity." The real cause of his suffering, *I* thought, was that he lived cut off from his feelings and then blamed society for the hollowness he felt. He, of course, believed he was a deep thinker and never understood that he merely skimmed the surface of life.

Charlemagne, as I liked to call him, became the butt of Father's jokes, and the two remained in a genial state of war for years. I recall Father lifting his gaze to heaven and saying, "How that man does wither every green and living thing!"

For me, the great gift of the Nortons was that through them I met Sara Sedgwick. Until then, Fanny Morse had been my closest friend. I loved Fanny dearly, but I soon loved Sara more. She was, you might say, the best and the worst thing that happened to me in those years.

The four young Sedgwicks were orphans, left in the care of a pair of kindly British maiden aunts, the Misses Ashburner. When Susan Sedgwick gave her hand in marriage to the much older

Charles Eliot Norton, the two families became inextricably linked. Father could never accept the May–November union between Susan and Charles. "To think of that prim old snuffers imposing himself on that pure young flame!" he would say with a dyspeptic wince. "What a world!"

Charles was a man stricken with a perpetual melancholy, perhaps due to his belief that culture had been going steadily downhill for the past three or four centuries. Renaissance and baroque Venice was the apogee of civilization, and Tintoretto the greatest of artists. Although Charles's private art collection included several Tintorettos and other masterpieces, nothing could seem to console him for the absence of art museums, Gothic and Romanesque cathedrals, and even gentlemen (according to him) in America.

As we became friends, Sara and I read the same books, passing them back and forth with notes inserted in the pages, often in a private code. Like many eighteen-year-olds, we were affected in a deeply personal way by our reading and came to feel that we suffered from grave *ennuis*. These were triggered almost daily by the mind-numbing calls a woman had to make on infirm old ladies, distant relatives, and anyone who left a calling card in the brass bowl in your hall. Also by the Boston pieties, such as the habit of quoting other Bostonians (e.g., Julia Ward Howe, Miss Elizabeth Peabody, and Dr. Oliver Wendell Holmes) as if no one else in the world had ever produced a memorable utterance. Above all we scorned the syrupy cult of womanhood embodied in such magazines as *Godey's Lady's Book*, which Sara and I would sometimes leaf through, hunting for the most moronic passages.

We were gorging ourselves, meanwhile, on subversive French ideas. We savored the scandalous worlds of Flaubert and Zola, and quoted Baudelaire as other Bostonians quoted Mr. Emerson. Opium and absinthe poets, natural realism, decadence, corrupt men, fallen women, kept women, *cocottes*—things that did not exist, as far as we knew, in Boston—thrilled us. We idolized George Sand, a woman with a man's name who scandalized the bourgeoisie by smoking in public, leaving her husband, carrying on tempestuous love affairs with

Chopin and the poet Alfred de Musset, among others, and threatening suicide at the drop of a hat. Most glamorously in our eyes, she dared walk around Paris at night dressed in men's clothes.

"George Sand writes gracefully, but why, oh why, do they have to translate books about adultery and such things where any young person can get hold of them?" Mother said at supper one night when Sara and her sister Theodora were dining with us.

"You are forgetting, Mother, that we can read French. Sara has been very much corrupted by taking on *Les Liaisons Dangereuses* at a tender age."

Puzzlement clouded the maternal brow and Father unleashed one of his great belly laughs, pointing his fork in my direction as if to award me the point.

"Well, leaving them in French would at least make them *more difficult* to read," Mother persisted.

"Logic has never been our mother's strong suit," William remarked to Sara.

Father then said amiably that George Sand's latest book made his gorge rise. "I don't think I ever read a thing that reflects a viler light on her personal history. How bestial that woman must be, to grovel spontaneously in such filth." Such abrupt changes in the conversational weather were par for the course at our house, and visitors were often taken aback. Sara had become very still, looking from face to face to judge the gravity of the quarrel—if it was a quarrel.

William said, "Whatever you do, Sara, don't take our father seriously. No one does, you know."

Father laughed heartily at himself as he went back to cutting up his meat.

PART TWO

ONE

1866

"I THOUGHT TONIGHT WAS WORSE THAN USUAL. . . . WHAT DID you think?"

No need for Sara to explain that she was referring to the dinner party we'd just endured with four other families at Shady Hill, home of the Nortons, her in-laws. (Or, as she preferred to call them, her *out-laws*.) Over the past few years we'd reached the highest stage of young female friendship, marked by a private code of allusions and jokes quite indecipherable by and surely annoying to others. We were eighteen years old.

"Well, it was certainly *Nortonesque*," I said. "Grace was quite louche about the oysters, I thought."

Sara's laughter rang out like a bell at the notion of her tightly wound, perfectionistic sister-in-law, Grace Norton, being louche. (We would learn that she really was, but that came later.) It was hot and muggy, and we were stretched out on the Sedgwicks' back lawn in our nightdresses. "After twelve hours of wearing a corset, not wearing one is almost wanton," Sara said. She could be depended on to make this observation almost every time. "I could melt from sheer pleasure and end up as a little puddle near the azaleas."

"We ought to start a society, Sara. The Nightdress Society! Boston does not have enough societies; it needs *more*." Of course, it went without saying that Boston had more societies than it had inhabitants.

So we stared up at the heavens for a bit, exhausting the constellations we knew and arguing over whether the heavenly object above the crown of the beech tree was Jupiter or Mars. Sara insisted briefly that it was the North Star. When we fell silent, the cicadas and tree frogs were deafening. As a small child, I thought this was the sound of the stars twinkling, and I told Sara that this had been a holy thing to me, this tinkling twinkling from deep space, and how crushed I had been to learn the pedestrian truth. (I'd never admitted this to another soul.)

Sara went quiet and I could feel her taking it in.

After a while, I said, "It might not be *so* bad at Shady Hill, if not for the long, drawn-out ordeal of shaking hands with Charles. Why does he *do* that?"

"Oh, I think it is something to do with Italy."

"How so?"

Sara was prone to long, deep pauses, and we were in one now. Finally, flipping over onto her stomach, she pressed her face into the grass and inhaled deeply. It sounded like the wind sighing in the tops of trees.

"Well, Alice, I think I *can* explain the origin of the long drawn-out hand-shaking thing." Whereupon she sat up, and, clearing her throat dramatically, began to speak in the cadences of "Nortonese," our version of the hyper-affected speech of the Nortons. "It is widely believed," she said, "that this *barbarous* custom originated when Don Carlos was wending his way through his beloved Italy. Not infrequently, he was seized by an ungovernable passion to visit certain great noblemen, who waited breathlessly to be enlightened on Dante's *Paradiso* by this melancholy American of the lugubrious mustache. On one such occasion, through the scrim of rude hovels, Charles discerned the gaunt figure of a count—Do Italians have counts?"

"I believe so."

"—a count shaking hands with his peasants on Christmas Eve. Returning to his barren native shores and dejected at having no peasants on his own land, Don Carlos took up the feudal custom with his guests. And not just on Christmas Eve."

I was giggling helplessly now, as much at Sara's mock-ponderous delivery as at her words. Mockery was one of our favorite sports. We both felt that Charles had become very tiresome about Dante lately, and there was widespread fear that he might launch a Dante circle at any moment.

I picked up the thread. "It cannot be denied that he is a distinguished looking man, Lord of Shady Hill, Propagator of *Ruskinism*, Explicator of Dante, Devotee of Tintoretto-ism. . . . And yet, and yet, something spoils the effect. Can it be the manner in which the mouth and mustache droop when he quotes from the *Purgatorio*? That womanish rosebud mouth fringed by a drooping mustache—so reminiscent of a pond fringed by weeds!"

"Oh, stop, Alice! My stomach hurts!" Sara was rolling around on the lawn now, clutching her sides.

"Well, Sara," I continued, "the dinner guests, whose paws had been thoroughly caressed and massaged, with long melancholy Nortonian glances thrown in, bore up as well as could be hoped. But being crude Yankees, unfamiliar with the customs of fealty, they found it wearisome in the end. Certain guests, notably two maidens of that shire, slunk homeward afterwards and, taking refuge beneath a starry canopy, found solace in singing of the incomparable exploits of Charlemagne. The End."

"The End," Sara repeated, like the *amen* at the end of a prayer.

Our problem was not really the Nortons—even we knew that—although it was undeniable that they took art and themselves too seriously. The real problem was that we were eighteen, and our lives were beginning to feel like clothes we'd outgrown.

"It's impossible to imagine Baudelaire here, or Coleridge, or really anyone," Sara complained. "Cambridge is at heart just a small parochial village."

"Yes, it is sad. Could the Charles River inspire a decent hashish poem? Even with the Harvard crew sculling upon it?"

Unfortunately, our families were incapable of discerning that we were meant for finer things, for lives more intensely lived. What this life might consist of was hazy, but it consumed us in those days in a fever of yearning. Like the Jameses, the Sedgwicks were a brilliant family star-crossed by eccentricity, tragedy, madness, and early deaths, and perhaps that was one reason I felt free to confide in her about such things as "Father's Ideas."

"Isn't he a Swedenborgian or something?"

"Yes. It started when Father went to an English 'watering hole' and met a lady there who told him about Swedenborg. This was years before I was born. When I was very young I heard this as 'Sweden Borg' and assumed that 'borg' was Swedish for bog, and that Father had been to a very wet one somewhere in Sweden."

Sara laughed enthusiastically. "There *could* be religions that start in bogs, I suppose. Is he still a Swedenborgian?"

"No. He diverged. Now his religion is so exclusive it has only one member. Father."

As Sara giggled, a great relief fell over me. Father's Ideas had been a burden for me since early childhood, to be honest. I couldn't make sense of his writings, but William told me not to worry; no one could. Father had been disinherited in his youth by his father, the stern Calvinist patriarch known as "William James of Albany," and successfully contested the will. I'd already divulged this to Sara, along with other family secrets. That my Aunt Janet was a madwoman, several uncles drank to excess and were prone to spells, and my peculiar cousin Kitty James was in the habit of holding Bible study circles with the lunatics in her husband's asylum. "The husband is an alienist, whom we have never met because he is supposed to be afraid of people," I explained. (It was immensely consoling to me that some of the Sedgwick relations were equally mad.)

"Only of *sane* people, evidently!" Sara said, and this made me laugh so hard I snorted through my nose. "And yet," she added, "despite our questionable and probably degenerate ancestry, we are both extraordinarily sane."

"Yes, *astonishingly* sane."

I'd been enlightened on modern theories of Hereditary Degeneracy by William, the designated genius of our family. At breakfast he had a habit of reading aloud juicy sections of medical books tracing the downfall of a family from "unwholesome habits" in the first generation to slobbering idiocy in the fifth. Acquired characteristics were inherited, according to these authors, inevitably sinking a marginally sane family into mindless degeneracy in a few generations.

"Genius and madness are closely related, according to William. The more genius, the greater the odds of madness. I don't know how this works scientifically, but I'd venture to say that if any families are on the path to incurable degeneracy it would be the Jameses and the Sedgwicks."

Sara hooted at this, a little too loudly in my opinion.

"Shh, Sara! You'll wake your aunts!"

"Oh, don't worry; they're deaf. They are also quite sane, by the way. So how did your father lose his leg?" This was the sort of personal question that good Bostonians would rather die than ask, though they would be secretly desperate to know. In those days Sara was taking a stand against the Beacon Street niceties.

"A barn fire in Albany when he was twelve. I thought I told you. He dashed in to rescue the horses and his leg had to be amputated."

"Well, I suppose something like that could drive a person to Swedenborg. Have you seen the stump?"

"Of course. You can come over and see it anytime you wish. Father is not shy about putting it on display."

"What color is it?"

"Mottled, violet and white, more or less." I sighed, thinking of the twelve-year-old Henry James having a leg amputated without anesthesia and growing up under the Calvinist tyranny of William James of Albany. "Poor Father! He believed the end of slavery would usher in a new heaven and a new earth. But even with slavery abolished, the same old sinful world just keeps rolling along."

"How disappointing. That is why I try to have no high ideals."

And then Sara sprang to her feet and began to turn in a slow circle in the moonlight, arms outstretched, like a jewelry box ballerina. "Do you see what is *wrong* with this scene, Alice?"

"What?"

"Not a single light in any window. All the dull professors and their adoring wives asleep. It's like a spell, a torpor. Everyone in this house retires before ten o'clock—my aunts and Theodora, anyhow. We never know where *Arthur* is. Being a man, he can do as he pleases, while we have a dozen people at our backs. It is a very unjust world."

A perfect half-moon, with a sharp edge like a cookie cut in half, hung low in the east, encircled by a halo of milky blue.

"I know what, Alice. After we make sure my aunts are snoring like angels, let's visit Arthur's wardrobe and borrow some trousers and cravats and hats—"

"Oh, for heaven's sake," I say, not wishing to go down this road again. "Arthur's clothes won't fit us."

"We'll *adapt* them, you'll see, and then we'll cross the bridge into Boston and find out for ourselves what the world of men is like. Like George Sand. Don't you want to *know* what they keep from us?"

Maybe it was the light in Sara's eyes or the way she clutched me from behind and leaned into me, a sensation rendering me briefly speechless; at any rate, I submitted to another fruitless discussion of how to pass ourselves off as males of the species. I was of the opinion that the great George Sand had made up the whole thing. After all, the woman did make up stories as her profession!

Still tipsy from the Nortons' after dinner brandies, Sara got up and tried out a male swagger.

"You look like a drunken sailor on shore leave, Sara. A bizarrely feminine one. Anyway, where would we *go*? What would we actually *do*?"

"A tavern. We'll pop in and order a whiskey. Two whiskeys."

But how did you conduct yourself in a tavern? When you ordered a glass of whiskey, did you ask for a particular brand? Did you pay when you ordered or at the end? While Sara and I knew no end of sewing stitches, ordering a drink in a tavern was plainly beyond us. And then there was the problem of our voices. "Anyhow," I pointed out, "the moment we leave the house we'll be recognized by President Eliot, who always knows by some mysterious power what everyone in Cambridge is up to."

"Does he really?"

"Yes, he does. Father says he derives a secret joy from delivering bad news to people. You can be sure he'd lecture us about how young ladies are meant to behave, and bring us home to our families in shame."

The tavern idea was jettisoned, for now. We lay on the lawn in silence, slapping the mosquitoes that were landing on our bare flesh with increasing frequency.

Sara said, "Have you ever studied men's faces at a dinner party after they've gone off by themselves to smoke? When they rejoin the women, they look as if they'd returned from some dark and mysterious country about which they are sworn to secrecy."

We stared up at the night sky in silence for a while. Unlike Boston, Cambridge had only a handful of streetlamps then, and the stars were a splash of diamonds on black velvet. I felt a wave of irritation at them for being so far away and inaccessible.

"If you were a man, Alice, what would you do? I think I'd go live with the Bedouins. Flaubert says the vast silence of the desert is like the sea."

More drunken shouts erupted on Kirkland Street. A pack of young men nearby were howling like wolves. "Ah, the great scholars of Harvard," Sara sighed.

"I shouldn't like to go about on a camel, Sara. They are bad-natured, so they say." In truth, I didn't feel drawn to join the Bedouins at all, and despite growing up with four brothers, I suspected the real lives of men were as remote from women as the craters of the moon. Meanwhile, women were obliged to live inside safe little cages like parakeets.

We fell silent. What more was there to say? Our little fantasy of liberation had collapsed and could not be revived. When the mosquitoes became intolerable, we headed for the house.

The French doors always stuck in humid weather. Sara vigorously jiggled the handle while pushing against the door with the sole of her foot. This did the trick. Inside we wandered about the sleeping house silently, like assassins, grass clippings stuck to the soles of our bare feet. Sara stubbed her toe on a chair leg and at the same moment a mouse jumped down from a pantry shelf and sped across the floor. We grabbed hold of each other as if we were passengers on a sinking ocean liner, laughing and shushing each other.

In her bedroom, Sara charged around lighting candles and rummaging through drawers as I sat at her dressing table. My arms ached from holding them up to unpin the countless hairpins anchoring my plaits to my head, and I wondered how I should bear the next half century of pinning, unpinning, washing, brushing, combing, braiding, and coiling this uninteresting mass of hair. Just as I was picking up the hairbrush to begin my hundred strokes, Sara popped up in the mirror, smiling broadly and holding a green bottle in one hand and two long-stemmed glasses shaped like tulips in the other.

"Here is something I've been saving for the right occasion, Alice. Prepare yourself for a *bouleversement*." She looked like the cat that swallowed the canary.

"What is it?"

For answer, she uncorked the flask and poured the liquid into the two tulip glasses. I blinked at the startling green color, like melted emeralds or something else out of a fairy tale.

"Don't drink yet," she warned. "*C'est dangereux*." She dashed over to the washstand, returning with a pitcher of water. As she poured half a cup of water into each glass, she instructed me solemnly, "*Never* drink this straight, Alice." Mystified, I watched her remove a small sugar bowl from a compartment in her chest of drawers, spoon a half teaspoon of sugar into each glass and stir. Then she picked up one of the glasses and clinked the other glass with it.

"*Salut*, Alice! Aren't you going to drink up?"

"What is it?"

"We-ell, they call it *la fée verte*."

My eyes fastened on the bottle's label with its drawing of a female fairy with green wings. That the fairy looked friendly made me only slightly less apprehensive. (What can I say? I was a youngest child. During my childhood my brothers applied themselves to scaring me to death whenever possible.)

"Drink up now; ask questions later."

Well, why *not*? I picked up the other tulip glass and touched it to Sara's. She was now beaming like a goddess bestowing a boon. The glasses were Turkish, she informed me. I took a sip and was surprised by a mouthful of liquor with a licorice under-taste. I coughed and my throat burned.

Sara, behind me, was drinking with gusto.

"I would never have guessed you had a tavern in your bedroom, Sara."

"It's *absinthe*, Alice." Her warm breath was near my ear. She bent forward, rubbing her upper arms with her hands, and her eyes gleamed. "My brother gave it to me and swore me to secrecy. You know how Arthur is always trying to *épater les bourgeois*. Part of the mystique of being a journalist, I suppose."

"What is it made from exactly?"

"Anise! That's where the green comes from. But wormwood is the critical ingredient, I believe. And something else—fennel maybe. What *is* fennel?"

"Never mind that. The real question is how soon should we expect to go raving mad?"

Sara dismissed this with a wave of her hand. "Old wives' tale. The most we can expect is strange and colorful dreams, which I would not wish to discourage." I saw that Sara was naturally brave, but daily life provided few opportunities for female bravery apart from the gory mess of childbirth. Wishing *I* had a brave bone in my body, I kept my eyes fastened on the looking glass. Our eyes met for a moment in the mirror world, and I felt something pass between us.

"*C'est l'heure émeraude*, Alice. Would you allow me to brush your hair?"

I must have nodded.

"You would not believe how many poems have been written about absinthe," she said as she brushed. Not since the era of my French governesses had my hair received such single-minded devotion. "It's practically a cottage industry. *It seems when I drink you, I inhale the young forest's soul during the beautiful green season.* I forget the rest, but isn't that lovely? Oh, and this one, by a different poet. Poet*ess*, actually. *I drank till the solid walls of my own room appeared to me like transparent glass, shot throughout with emerald flame/Surrounded on all sides by phantoms.*"

The absinthe was evidently making her loquacious. "Phantoms? That doesn't sound very pleasant."

"Well, think of emeralds then." The green was draining rapidly from her glass, like a stage magician's trick. "Think of the verses we'll write under the influence, and with the money we make from our poetry, we'll buy more absinthe! A perfect plan, no?"

After an indeterminate period, I found myself falling into an unknown zone of myself. *La fée verte* was melting me by degrees while Sara ran her fingers through my hair and mock-seriously demonstrated different styles of hairdressing. Each touch of her fingers ignited a fleeting sweet-sharp explosion. I kept my gaze on the mirror. If I looked at her directly, it would break the spell.

She moved her hands to my shoulders and our reflections gazed back at us, the candle flames multiplied in the mirror and the silvered objects on the dressing table.

"*Voilà!* The Grecian look, Alice." She was referring to the hair arrangement she had erected with a scaffolding of hairpins, combs, and clips. "*Godey's* says it is a classic that is coming back in style." She took a step back to appraise her work. "Yes, I do think you bear an uncanny resemblance to Minerva."

Her eyes in the candlelight held pieces of flame.

"You must mean Athena, Sara, if it's a Grecian look."

"I stand corrected. What a mercy we only have one god to remember." She turned serious. "Do you think God could be a woman, Alice?"

"I never thought of that." I felt my mind sinking deeper. How had I never suspected there were so many layers to myself? For the first time I could recall I felt that I could do anything and face the consequences. This was a radical departure from my ordinary self, cautious and tortured by worst-case scenarios.

"Wouldn't that be a joke on them?" Sara was saying. "While I don't believe in God, I would love to see that happen." I wondered briefly what Father would do about a female God. He didn't think of God as a person at all and said the events in the Bible were meant to be metaphorical, not literal.

It was surprisingly easy to relax into the softness and deftness of Sara's fingers. I felt her warm, absinthe-laced breath on the top of my head and then the kiss she planted there.

"Oh! I almost forgot, Alice. Close your eyes and don't peek."

With my eyes shut, I felt the absinthe hissing inside my head, the cotton cloth of my nightdress brushing against my nipples, the moistness where my inner thighs met. Then my hand was resting in Sara's palm and her two fingers were pressing softly on the underside of my wrist where the blue veins came together like the Mississippi River Delta on a map. I opened my eyes and stared at my wrist and forearm, as if I'd never seen them before. The alabaster whiteness of my skin, the delicate hairs, each with its own follicle, the pale scar near my elbow from falling out of a tree in Newport. The perfection of the human body! Why had I never seen this?

"Smell, Alice!" Sara held her wrist up to my nose, brushing it lightly against my lips. I smelled roses and something else vaguely familiar, and then something remarkable happened. A pulse of electricity shot up from my toes to the middle of my body, hinting at a world of feeling and sensation of which I had but the dimmest notion.

The emotions that arose in me were strange and familiar at the same time, as if I were reliving something that had already taken place. Had everything already happened in reality and were we just re-dreaming it? Motionless as a caryatid, I kept my eyes on Sara in the mirror.

"I don't know what it is *exactly*. It was my mother's. For me it is exactly like falling into a poem by Rumi the Persian."

"Who?" It was an annoying quirk of all the Sedgwicks to refer to obscure books no one else had read.

"Oh, he's a Mohammedan who's written some shocking verses, which Aunt Grace, of all people, gave me, evidently failing to grasp a few of the metaphors. Have some more absinthe, Alice! You only live once." She refilled both our glasses, adding more water and sugar. I drank again, my eyes glued on Sara's in the mirror. As long as I kept my gaze there, my shyness and solitariness could melt away like snow in the sun.

Holding my gaze, Sara said softly, "Alice, would you like me to show you the seven places where a woman should wear perfume?"

There was evidently a great deal about being a woman I didn't know. My mother and Aunt Kate seldom bothered with scent and didn't seem to know about the seven places. My eyes were fixed on the mirror as Sara's fingers unbuttoned the first three buttons of my white cambric nightdress, gently dabbing the perfume on the first of the seven places. I almost forgot to breathe. After all seven places were anointed, Sara bent down, took my face in her hands and kissed me tenderly on the mouth. It took me by surprise, that lips should be so soft and pillowy, that a kiss could last so long, have so many different parts to it, and awaken such pleasure.

Freeing my hair from its restraints, she wound some of it loosely around her hand and buried her face in it. In the candlelight she looked as if she were made of spun gold. The next thing I knew I was being led by the hand over to her bed. Had I fallen into a dream or a dimension so real it made everything else seem fake?

Then I recalled that I'd been drinking absinthe.

Sara was lying on her back and, with a yearning expression, tugged at my hand to pull me down on top of her. Wrapping her arms around me, she murmured, "Mmmmm" next to my ear and licked my earlobe with a flick of her tongue. My mind stopped, immobilized like a stunned bird, while my body yielded to the sensations coursing through me. Sara was meanwhile applying herself to kissing my neck and the hollow of my collarbone until my toes curled with pleasure, and then her lips crept lower. When she reached her arms around me and clasped the small of my back, the heat of her touch dissolved something hard and unyielding inside me. My insides were thawing and liquefying like ice in the sun.

Then her hands were working their way down my spine, pressing and releasing, finding all the chords of my body and playing them. Later I would ask myself how Sara had acquired this expertise, and with whom, but for now my limbs were heavy and every part of me was surrendered—something that had happened before only in the best sort of dreams. My hand found the fullness of Sara's breast, and then I was feeling and hearing my own breath, and Sara's, quick and ragged as if we were climbing a steep mountain. Later I would not be able to recall how our nightdresses came off on their own, as if they were our chrysalises.

It went on for a long time, caressing and being caressed in ways I didn't know were possible. Cambridge, with its pontificating professors and their doting wives, Sara's nice old-maid aunts, my parents with their fixed routines, the Nortons and their perfect manners and formal dining room full of Tintorettos—all that fell away and vanished.

The next morning my life felt brand-new, sharp and bright as crystal, as if I'd never lived before. I hardly knew what to make of the mysteries unveiled to me during the night. It was puzzling that Sara was behaving as usual at breakfast, buttering her toast and methodically smearing jam on it as if our extraordinary night had not happened. It did not help to be hemmed in by Theodora, holding forth pedantically on a biography she was reading, and the Misses Ashburner, kind and pink-skinned, asking after my brothers.

When we were briefly alone at table, Sara, stirring sugar into her coffee, said, "I believe there *was* a man who drank absinthe and murdered his whole family. It was in France."

"Thank you for the timely warning, Sara."

"*Obviously* it had less to do with the absinthe than with the man's preexisting lunacy. We haven't murdered anyone, have we? Yet?" That lovely, wide, slightly insolent smile. Those grey eyes, with their shifting mysterious depths like the sea.

"That is hardly reassuring."

She shrugged and became preoccupied with her eggs. When I bade her good-bye, she barely looked up.

Over the next few days I noticed new things unfolding inside me, as if Sara's embraces had implanted a slow-acting drug. Frequently I found myself pierced by a desire so fierce it left me breathless. Natural beauty overwhelmed my senses. Even a passage in a book set off a series of paroxysmal shivers and I had to stop reading or "go off."

"What do you mean, you 'go off'?" Sara said when I mentioned it a few days later. We were out in her garden planting impatiens in the shade of the beech tree. The day was beastly hot. Flies droned over the flowerbeds. Sweat gathered on my upper lip; I tasted the saltiness with my tongue.

"I don't know, just that I—I pass out for a minute or two."

"Well, why do you do that?" Her tone was impatient. I wondered what I had done to displease her.

"I don't know." Sometimes I suspected the "going off" was a doorway to another world, but seeing Sara's closed face, I said no more about it.

At home, meanwhile, I felt like a stranger, or else my family had become strangers to me. At odd moments I felt Mother's and Aunt Kate's eyes on me and wanted to swat their glances away like mosquitoes. When I met their gaze, they looked away and pretended to be absorbed in some domestic task. I avoided undressing in their presence; my body held secrets now.

Sara had revealed to me the essential nullity of my sentimental education so far. I'd been living in my body as if it were an inert, unfeeling thing. Now I felt like Vasco da Gama or Cortez landing on a new continent, with still unnamed rivers, virgin forests, secret veins of gold. Being so sheltered, I was not entirely sure at this point that the transports of the Emerald Nights were not Sara's private invention.

Our rituals were repeated many times over the next few months, always, by unspoken agreement, at Sara's house, because of the privacy offered by the deafness and sleeping habits of her aunts. Our nights were electric, but none of the enchantment was permitted to touch ordinary daytime life, and thus remained a sort of dream, which was evidently how Sara preferred it.

No doubt Sara had always been capricious, but it hadn't caused me pain before. Now everything she did or said cut straight to my heart. One moment she'd say that I was her best, her truest, her dearest friend and we must make a pact not to marry anyone who would take us away from Boston and each other. (This was easy for me. I was not sure what women got out of marriage, anyway.) The next moment she'd be talking about Fanny Morse and her family and would say, "Aren't they the most wonderful family? Don't you wish you could be adopted by them?" When her family bought a sewing machine, Sara became preoccupied with the clothes she intended to sew with it—suits for Arthur, dresses for her aunts, Theodora and herself—and shut herself up for two weeks without seeing anyone, including me.

She would never speak or allow me to speak of what passed between us in the dark, although *la fée verte* always led us back to the same rapture, with Sara as passionate and tender as I could wish. One night, as we lay in each other's arms, our hearts slowing to a resting rhythm, I was stroking her hair and blurted, "Let's run away together!"

"Where would we run to?" Her tone was resigned.

I considered this. I had no money of my own, nor did Sara. But if I were ill, surely the funds would be found to send me to a hydropathic establishment in France or Switzerland, and Sara could accompany me. Perhaps she could be ill as well. But it did not take long to grasp that we would never be allowed to sail to Europe unmatronized. If I went abroad, Aunt Kate would come along and that would change everything.

As the weeks and months slid by, my happiness and peace of mind increasingly depended on Sara. But you could not set your clock by Sara, she was prone to such extreme fluctuations. Some days she didn't eat and other days she consumed five or six meals. She developed a sudden irrational interest in the French dancing master and speculated wildly about him. She went to Bar Harbor and acquired a passion for mussels, and then to New York City and returned speaking differently, while denying that she did. She surrounded herself with several people whom she'd previously dismissed as boring. She became acutely critical of George Sand, whom we'd previously idolized together. ("It's rather bad taste to threaten suicide so often; it should be held in reserve, don't you think?")

My state of longing now rendered me so jagged and raw that, in my lucid moments, I was compelled to admit to myself that I no longer enjoyed my friend's company as before. I was losing any objective sense of who Sara was since she had become everything to me. Was that what love did? I decided frequently to break things off, but her gaze always dissolved my resistance, her arms would reach for me, and my resolve melted. I now understood the lovesick heroines in novels whom I'd previously dismissed as stupid, silly, and weak.

By mid-autumn, it did not escape my notice—or my family's—that I was breaking out in symptoms of nerves. I "went off" while lacing my stays, when Father rehearsed his lecture on "Is Marriage Holy?" when the dressmaker pinned the sleeve of my frock. Occasionally I found myself lying on the floor with no memory of getting there. Within the family my going off became "one of Alice's things," just as dressing like a dandy was one of William's things and being minutely well-informed about the theater was Harry's thing. Jaunts to the country were proposed. Suspicions were voiced about certain types of weather, heavy meals, newspaper accounts of railway crashes, French novels, staying up too late, and excitement in general.

When I failed to improve, Aunt Kate mentioned the name of a great doctor in New York City and volunteered to accompany me there.

─ TWO ─

IT WAS IN SOME WAYS AN OLD STORY. I HAD CELEBRATED MY thirteenth birthday by "going off" and coming to with a vision of my family standing in a ring around me like trees around a clearing. I recalled my mother's face looking frightened, my father's concerned but mildly curious. My "fit" was traced to mysterious vapors associated with my first menstrual period, which had just struck without warning.

Since then my mind and body had been at war, like the armies of France and Prussia, enjoying fragile cease-fires but no lasting peace. Anything could send the caissons rolling toward the front again, blowing up bridges and shelling towns. When I tried to see back to how it all started, there was only a dense jungle behind my eyes.

Now, as our train chugged along the coast of Connecticut, I was suffering from a thick head-fog through which I could dimly make out the shapes of thoughts. I was unable to bring myself to eat anything or read or talk and merely watched fields of brown stubble, purple marshes, and glassy bits of the Long Island Sound glide past while Aunt Kate knitted and read Elizabeth Gaskell in the seat next to me.

By the time we pulled into New York City in a cloud of soot-flecked steam, my nerves felt like hot wires. Not wishing to set the seat ablaze, I stood up and fixed a dumb-ox stare at the blur that was Aunt Kate in motion: taking charge, locating our trunks, finding a porter and a hansom, giving directions to the coachman. Her omniscience about practical details—how many shawls to take in a carriage, how much to tip a porter, who were the best doctors in New York—was handy when you were off in remote zones of yourself.

From the cabriolet the dusky streets rolled by in a haze, as if I were dreaming with my eyes open.

I was taken to Broadway and Thirty-fifth Street, to a narrow row house with steep front steps (surely treacherous for invalids?) belonging to Dr. Charles Lafayette Taylor, an orthopedist. With his brother, Dr. George Taylor, likewise an orthopedist, he had devised the Improved Movement Cure, considered by Aunt Kate the most advanced treatment for nerves. The basic idea, if I'd grasped it rightly, was that nervous illnesses were the lamentable result of an imbalance between over-stimulated nerves and an under-developed body. To remedy which the brothers Taylor (creatures so much of the same mold I could scarcely tell them apart) applied their medicine. This consisted of orthopedic manipulation, Swedish massage, and deadly stretches of bed-rest. The first morning I was *rigorously* examined by the first Dr. Taylor, who expressed concern that my "nervous excitement" might have drawn too much energy into my nervous system, leaving other bodily functions "depressed." Were my legs and arms weak? Did I suffer from headache? Ever feel dizzy or faint? How about palpitations of the heart?

"Yes," I admitted, "and just as I am falling asleep, my stomach attempts to tie itself in knots, a sensation accompanied by a feeling of unspeakable dread." In fact, the chief benefit I was hoping for from this Manhattan adventure was some medical clarification of this malady of mine, but Dr. Taylor only nodded gravely as if he knew everything about me already.

The shops were smarter and the women more fashionable in New York than in Boston, a fact I confirmed each morning as I dragged myself up the three blocks of Broadway to Thirty-eighth Street, to the brownstone of the second Dr. Taylor. Every morning I wondered if I had it in me to be a fashionable New Yorker, and decided probably not. "I cannot reconcile myself to the peculiarities of my clothes," I wrote to Sara in one of many meandering letters. Carts, drays, omnibuses, carriages of all types plied Broadway, where crude sheds appeared next to marble palaces—all the sounds combining in a dull roar in my head like a waterfall.

The second Dr. Taylor had invented a machine for limbering the pelvis, expanding the chest, and kneading the abdomen, the features of which he proudly displayed to me. Tufts of grey hair sprouted from his ears; otherwise, the Taylor brothers were nearly identical, two nondescript balding men of middle age. This Dr. Taylor predicted that I should become "perfectly well" if I submitted to his daily exercises. A woman's nerves were more delicate than a man's, he explained, and susceptible to stronger impressions. It followed—though I may be forgetting some of the links in the chain of his reasoning—that a woman who "consumes her vital force in intellectual activities" was diverting it from the achievement of True Womanhood. This spelled tragedy, not just for her but for her children and her children's children—indeed, for the human race.

"The body is literally starved! It becomes perverted!" he warned, peering at me through a glass that magnified one watery blue eye. "I hope, Miss James, that you do not read excessively."

"Not *excessively*," I lied. If I read less, would I develop a keen interest in things like running a house, being married, having children, visiting the poor and comforting the sick? Perhaps I'd prefer to stick with reading. But since I was such a sorry specimen, I vowed to do my best to adhere to the Taylor program.

It was distressing to learn how many ways I'd been courting disaster. Not just by reading but also by walking on hard pavement, bathing at the wrong time of day, exposing myself to the damp, not drinking enough water, going to bed too late, not resting my eyes for an hour after reading the newspaper, eating fruits and vegetables at the same meal, and a hundred other things.

Apart from my unbridled reading, I become an exemplary patient. Living amongst aged and moribund people, I began to forget my youth, my rebelliousness, the sharp longings of the flesh. My body settled into a dormant state; perhaps I would hibernate next. I fed on the creamy fattening food served *chez* Taylor, and my cousin Elly Van Buren, who saw me over Christmas, wrote approvingly to my family that I was looking "fat as butter." My days were consumed with resting and cultivating the feminine virtues—patience, faith, self-denial, concern for others. Aunt Kate sent home glowing reports of my saintly patience and Mother wrote me weekly, praising my "ultra-spiritual qualities."

One evening a strange thing occurred with Aunt Kate; I hardly knew what to make of it. I'd just suffered one of my attacks, after which I was feeling cleansed and clear-headed, like the sky after a thunderstorm. Aunt Kate was by my bedside. Feeling nostalgic about her New York girlhood, she was telling me some old-timey stories when she suddenly exclaimed: "Did you know, Alice, that your father courted me first?"

"What do you mean, Aunt Kate?" She couldn't mean *that*.

"Well, your father came to our church in New York to give a course of lectures. He was already lecturing and still a young man. He could have charmed the birds out of the trees. I wish you could have known him then."

"Well, clearly, I couldn't have done so without violating the laws of nature."

She did not appear to hear me, so lost was she in this strange reverie. "We talked one day and he gave me a sort of *penetrating* look. You know what I'm talking about." I did. "He made some flirtatious comments about my bonnet. There was something about him; I can't explain it."

Oh dear, where was this going?

"He took to calling two or three times a week, sitting in the parlor with us. He met Mary, of course, and soon you could not tell which of us he was courting." She laughed in a queer way. "He was so *expansive* there seemed to be enough of him for two! But then our father—your grandfather Walsh—took Henry aside for a little talk, and after that he had eyes only for Mary. She was the elder sister, of course."

Did Aunt Kate remember to whom she was talking? Maybe she did, because a minute later, she seemed to shake herself out of her trance. "And what a beautiful and sacred marriage they have had!" she beamed.

For hours afterward I was so disconsolate I was unable even to swallow tea.

My aunt's confession reminded me that, not long before our family sailed for Europe in 1855, Aunt Kate was briefly and disastrously married to a Captain Marshall. Whatever went wrong was never stated, but she returned to us a few months later with sadder eyes, and we children were told never to mention the marriage. (In those days a distressing fact could be neutralized simply by not acknowledging it. Yet Father would say *anything* to *anybody*.) I don't recall meeting the Captain, though I must have. In my mind he assumed the shape of a swarthy sea captain who forced poor Aunt Kate to dance the tarantella for hours and then dragged her by the hair into his cabin. My imagination drew a blank at what might have occurred next—I was only seven years old—but I knew it was surely unspeakable. After that, our aunt stayed securely attached to the safe and the predictable.

After I'd been in New York for five dull, fattening months, a letter arrived from Mother startling me with the news that William had just sailed to Europe.

But he would *never* go to Europe without a word to me!

Well, apparently he had. Mother explained that he would spend the next two years studying physiology at the German graduate schools, and as it was a great opportunity for him, I ought not to *indulge in selfish regrets in the matter, but accept cheerfully that life is made up of changes and separations from those we love.*

I stared at the blue stationery and the familiar maternal script. The news was so inconceivable that for several days I half believed a second letter would arrive saying that William hadn't sailed after all. But no second letter came and William *was* gone and I had no choice but to bear his absence angelically. If you had feelings about anything they called it hysteria.

My health slid backwards for a while and I didn't return to Quincy Street until May of 1867, when the wisteria climbing one side of the house was in bloom. I found Harry stretched out phlegmatically on a divan in one of the parlors. His back was poorly again, he said, and our household was "as lively as the inner sepulchre." (A typical Harryism.) While other Boston families were packing up for a summer at the shore, we were condemned to stagnate in stifling Cambridge again, because Father refused to go anywhere. Cambridge was a social desert, he complained. The Nortons offered good conversation, but whenever you went there with Father you had to worry that Charles would hold forth on the superiority of European society, and this would inspire a blast of the paternal patriotism. Inevitably, Father and Charles would have to be separated and apologies made.

It was strange to be home. I'd lived so isolated in New York that it was almost as if I'd died and left the world; to be back in my old life made me feel like the ghost of myself. I was half surprised that people greeted me as if they knew me. Whenever I turned round, Mother was pressing something on me—rhubarb jam for my toast, a different newspaper. If I was in my bedroom, her knock would jolt me out of my daydream and force me to consider whether my bookcase needed dusting or I wished to have a baked potato with dinner. She'd want to chat about what day the laundresses were coming and whether the butcher was overcharging us. Why was I required to be interested in these domestic details, while Harry was assumed to have better things to do? I suppose the answer was obvious. He wore trousers and I a skirt.

Not that my parents weren't overbearing toward my brothers, too; their affectionate absorption in their five children was almost legendary. Father made the final decisions on the boys' careers. Steering William, his pride and joy, away from painting into science. Paying the fees to keep William and Harry, but not Wilky and Bob, out of the Civil War. Negotiating fees and terms of publication with Harry's editors. By holding the purse strings, our parents could veto any venture. Both casually opened and read any mail that entered the house, even when it was marked "private." There was no escaping them, and, of course, Aunt Kate, when she was present, was a virtual third parent.

Although Harry was in the law school, sightings of him with a law book in his hand were extremely rare, and whenever his (and William's) friend Oliver Wendell Holmes, Jr. held forth on legal topics, a perfect blankness would fall over Harry's features. His dissatisfaction with Boston's provincial dullness (as he saw it) was making him withdrawn and morose. He wrote to William—in a letter left unfinished on a table, which I read, naturally—*I am tired of reading and know it would be better to do something else. Can I go to the theatre? I have tried it ad nauseam. Likewise "calling." Upon whom? Sedgwicks, Nortons, Dixwells, Feltons.* I worried about Harry; mostly I worried that he'd flee to Europe, too.

In the first weeks following my homecoming, Sara was fond and loving, asking concerned questions about my health, laughing at my tales of the Brothers Taylor and the invalid hotel, filling me in on all the Norton atrocities I'd missed. I saw that she had really missed me; she even admitted as much. While I was away, she'd tried having heart-to-heart talks with Theodora, she said, but it was hopeless. She'd gone to a dozen or so plays and concerts and lectures with Fanny Morse, who, though delightful, of course, was too tame-Boston to conceive of a world that did not revolve around "the Shore," Beacon Street, and all the "dear people" of her acquaintance.

Sara was anything but tame; she was drawn to vivid, violent things—volcanic eruptions, Nor'easters, revolutions, shipwrecks. The details made her eyes shine. Pompeii was her favorite place in Europe. She could not stop thinking about the dogs struck dead alongside their masters, and all the people mummified in the act of eating grapes or patting the family dog or scrubbing the floor, their agony preserved for eternity. "It is almost indecent to look, they are so exposed. Your heart is pierced by pity. And yet isn't that its great appeal?"

"But how do you stop your mind from cramping around it?"

"What do you mean?"

"Nothing. Never mind." I made a mental note to steer clear of references to my mental cramps around Sara.

It was a mild July evening and, still in our clothes, we were lying on the lawn under the stars, holding one of our rambling conversations about everything. Whether we believed in God (Sara didn't; she'd given up on Him when her parents died), whether it would be worse to be blind or deaf ("Don't forget crippled," I said), what our deepest fears were. I told her about a girl at school I'd disliked so much I could think of nothing else; every day I felt my thoughts sharpening like daggers inside me. Later this girl went down in a shipwreck off the shores of Nova Scotia and I was aghast at my witchy powers. Since then I'd tried to police my mind and not think ill of anyone, but people who advised you to do this had no idea how difficult it was.

"Arthur says that you should never *try* to be good. You either are or you aren't. Or you are as good as you can be, given who you are."

"That's rather facile." It was irksome to have Arthur Sedgwick cited as an authority. In my view, Sara's brother was conceited, fancying himself too urbane for Boston, and never made the slightest effort to be cordial to me. In contrast, my brothers adored Sara—as did my parents, for that matter. It was rather amusing to hear them singing the praises of the corrupter of their only daughter.

Sara jumped to her feet. "What we need, Alice, is some absinthe!"

So we drifted inside and Sara headed for her secret cupboard.

"Wait, Sara! First you must ponder this gem from *Godey's Lady's Book*."

I dug the article out of my reticule and handed it to her. She read it aloud in a didactic old lady voice, the way we imagined the *Godey's* editresses would speak:

> *Quarrels are bad things and no one within his senses—his moral senses we should say—would advocate them, save under such provocation of insult as should be chastised if self-respect is to be maintained.*

"Ha, young Alice James!" she laughed. "This is *possibly* the most *fatuous* sentence ever penned by Woman or Man. Perhaps its significance can be discerned only under the influence of *la fée verte*. If you catch my drift."

She gave me a wink, then poured the emerald liquid into two Bohemian glasses, and we drank it in the flickering candlelight. She lit a joss stick (part of her new séance equipment) and whipped out her pack of tarot cards (which she kept wrapped in a special cloth of some talismanic significance) and laid the cards out in the "Celtic Cross pattern." She was wearing her seeress expression.

After some mystic discourse about pentacles and cups, the major arcana, the wheel of fortune, a hanged man and a hermit, and whatnot, she pointed to the magician card at the center of the spread, a man with an infinity symbol waving over his head and a wand in his hand, and said, "The card can indicate an interest in a scientific career or someone who is already in such a career."

"William! Does it say if this person is in Germany?"

Wrinkling her brow, she read from her book, "This card can indicate a career in which speech or writing is of great importance, a salesman, a speaker, a storyteller. . . ."

"Ah, Harry! And Father, of course. We've covered almost everyone in the family."

"Have you considered that it might be about *you*, Alice?" From her serious expression I saw that she wasn't joking.

"I'm no magician, Sara." The absinthe was making me giggle. "Maybe it's you."

Sensing my mood, and possibly losing interest in the tarot herself, Sara moved swiftly through the rest of the cards, telling me: "You will make a voyage overseas and this card indicates an older man who will appear in your life."

"Will he be on the ship? How much older *is* this man?"

"The cards aren't that specific."

"I don't think I fancy *old* men, Sara."

"Relax, Alice! I just said 'older.' You are always trying to control life and that just keeps life from happening."

Was that true? Was that why I was always waiting for my life to begin?

Sara made it plain that she considered herself a gifted spiritist, a talent she attributed to having nearly drowned in the ocean at the age of three. "I was sorry they brought me back. It was so beautiful being dead."

"Did your life flash before your eyes?"

"Yes, but it was a very *short* life."

For some reason, this caused me to collapse in gales of laughter.

"I'm serious, Alice."

"I *know.*"

I couldn't stop laughing, and this made Sara laugh, and then we were giggling and kissing and undressing each other, tugging on laces, undoing stays, peeling off stockings. When we'd flung the last of our clothing onto the floor, and Sara was stretching out her arms to me and I was feeling the tidal pull of her, rapid footsteps were suddenly pounding down the stairs, which terminated just beyond Sara's door. Sara quickly blew out the candle and I slipped like a sylph between the sheets, and we went absolutely still, holding our breath, our pounding hearts pressed together, like expert jewel thieves synchronized in the commission of our crime.

The footsteps were moving away now. "It's only Theodora," Sara whispered, sliding a hand to one of my breasts. "I recognize her tread. Don't worry. Her self-absorption makes her oblivious to others."

Then, with a sly smile, she kneeled over me, kissing me tenderly on the lips several times. Then she straddled me, with a knee planted on either side, and dreamily worked her way down my body, forbidding me to touch her at all ("You are my captive and I've tied you up"). After flicking her tongue in my ear, and demonstrating the concupiscence of the navel and the erotic zones of the feet, she applied herself to gratifying me in a new and intense manner. Tears streamed down my face from the pleasure of it; I had to hold a pillow over my mouth for a long time. How had Sara learned these things—from an exotic Oriental love manual? (The Sedgwicks seemed to have no end of obscure foreign books.) Would I ever get to the bottom of Sara's mysteries, pin her down finally? Did I wish to? Were the pleasures of the flesh just something for which she had a natural bent, like the tarot or the dreaming technique she'd told me about last week?

That conversation took place while we were blackberry picking in the Norton woods, acquiring dozens of tiny scratches on our violet fingertips. While picking a thorn out of her thumb, Sara confided two things, swearing me to secrecy.

"You know me, Sara. Silent as the tomb."

"Well, the first thing is that Susan"—Sara's sister, Mrs. Charles Norton—"is far more than Charles's muse, as you may have heard him nauseatingly refer to her."

"What do you mean?"

"I mean that she *writes* many of his articles, the ones published in the *Nation* and the *North American Review* and the *Atlantic Monthly*. She was always a talented writer, but no one outside the family knows this. How it works is that Don Carlos pens some pretentious drivel and Susan rewrites it. 'Edits' it, as they say. Whenever you read something good under his name, you can assume it's mostly Susan."

"Incredible."

"*Many* books by Bostonians were written by the authors' sisters or wives, you know. They say Francis Parkman's sister Lizzy wrote most of his tome on the French and Indian Wars while he was hysterically blind and couldn't read or write a thing. She had to translate a heap of French-Canadian documents. Took years. That's what I heard, anyhow."

"Are you saying that Susan must do Charles's intellectual work on top of bearing and raising his children, running the household, and catering to his over-refined nerves?"

"Exactly. She's a model wife, even declining to state her own opinions at dinner, in case you haven't noticed. When he was wooing her, she kept saying how brilliant and original his mind was. Now she finds his opinions insufferable, I believe. The other day she said, 'Charles's views, I'm afraid, are as immutable as Fanueil Hall.' And then she sighed in a tired way. My heart aches for her. She looks so ancient after five children, Alice! How can a person of eighteen have any idea what marriage will require? And then it's too late." Sara seemed on the verge of tears.

"Will she leave him, do you think?"

"With five children? No, she's caught! If they divorced, he'd get the children; that's how it works. Not that he actually *enjoys* his offspring but they are pleasant accessories to his greatness. Besides, Susan, like the rest of us Sedgwicks, is without a sou. She'd have to put arsenic in his soup to get away, but I am not sure that she is even aware of how unhappy she is. So it will just go on and on."

"Maybe it's just as well she doesn't realize she's unhappy."

"Maybe." She sighed again.

"So let's hear your second secret."

Whereupon Sara divulged that while I was in New York she had mastered a technique known to "Tibetan occultists" for becoming awake in one's dreams. Arthur had bought a queer book on the subject in a bookstall near the Seine, which she had lately been studying and putting into practice.

"I don't understand. It seems to me that either you are awake or asleep."

"No, Alice, you can be dreaming and aware of it. If you catch yourself dreaming, you can control what happens in the dream." Judging by her flushed face, the subject exhilarated her.

"Like what?"

"Oh, anything. You can ride an elephant or fly through the air. Nothing irrevocable can happen to you in a dream. You can't die, for example."

"Have you ever flown?"

"Yes. If you believe you can fly in a dream, you just do. You float up and glide. The feeling is exquisite, more beautiful than anything." I watched a dreamy look steal over her face, which I wished *I* had put there. Now I was becoming jealous of Sara's dreams; what follies love gave rise to!

Then I made the fatal error of telling Sara that just as I was falling asleep, I often suffered waves of ice-cold panic and a roiling sensation in my stomach. "It feels like snakes writhing and this is accompanied by an overwhelming fear—a fear of being *alive*. I can't really describe it."

When I glanced at Sara, I caught the scowl that flickered over her features.

"Maybe you ought to take a digestive tablet or something."

Clearly my night terrors and other problems were complications Sara preferred to ignore. I almost asked her if dream-flying was more beautiful than what we did in the dark, but you could not ask her such questions. In her aspect of *belle dame sans merci*, Sara made the rules and you had best follow them or she would pull away.

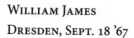

WILLIAM JAMES
DRESDEN, SEPT. 18 '67

TO THE JAMES FAMILY
I only wish I had that pampered Alice here to see these little runts of peasant women stumping about with their immense burdens on their backs.

TO ALICE JAMES
Looking back on what I have done in the way of study this winter it seems one of the emptiest years of my life . . . I am sorry to hear you are feeling delicate. I would give anything if I could help you, my dearest Alice, but you will probably soon grow out of it. How do the Cambridge girls get on?

~ THREE ~

Nothing much changed at 20 Quincy Street, meanwhile. Mother rushed around doing a thousand useful things. Harry read or daydreamed and then disappeared for hours on mysterious errands, which, unlike me, he was never expected to account for. Father, after taking the horse-cars to the post office in Boston and back every day, shut himself up in his study to write about Divine Nature. I had always taken it for granted that Father's Ideas were very "advanced." Hadn't Mother been telling us this since our infancy?

At breakfast one morning I was perusing the *Nation* and came across a letter to the editor by Henry James. It was evidently Father's response to a letter from a reader in a previous issue criticizing an essay by Father that had run in a still earlier issue. I scanned it while gnawing on my toast with rhubarb jam.

I conceive that you and I, and every other man, are directly or immediately created by God, and not indirectly or mediately through the race. I contend that God creates me not mediately through other men, but immediately by himself; that he, and he alone, gives me being at this moment. If I could confine myself to reacting along with all the world, in the beginning God created the Heavens and the Earth, no man's speech, I venture to say, would seem more frank than mine. But when I append a harmless benignant coda to my special performance in that concerto, importing that the "Heavens and the Earth" therein mentioned are not primarily the physical phenomena so designated, but the "Heavens" exclusively of the universal mind, I grow unintelligible. Why?

Why indeed? No matter how many times I read it, I could make no sense of this letter. Although no one felt moved to buy Father's self-published books, many people did flock to hear him lecture, their expressions cycling from delight to intense puzzlement. Father's Ideas were *so advanced*, Mother always told us, that most people could not grasp them, and that was why he often looked dispirited when he came home from lecturing. This did not discourage him, however, from continuing to lecture and to write about the Cosmos in the *Nation* and the *Atlantic Monthly*, whose editors were his friends. I wondered now if Father was spending his life pursuing a mirage only he could see.

One night Father gave a talk entitled "Society: the Redeemed Form of Man" to a small but devoted group at the Fields' house on Charles Street. Mr. Fields was editor of the *Atlantic Monthly* and his wife, Annie, ran the closest thing to a salon that Boston had to offer. Sara came with us, and afterwards we went home to Sara's house and whispered in the dark, loosely intertwined. Holding one of my hands in hers, Sara was caressing the flap of skin between my thumb and index finger, and it seemed to me at that moment that there had never been a sweeter gesture. How safe I felt with Sara—but only after darkness fell.

After saying all there was to say about Father's lecture, which puzzled me as much as it puzzled Sara, we went on to discuss our families and their peculiarities, and how we had been affected by these. Tearfully Sara said that she could scarcely remember her parents now. "I have a sort of fog in my head that blurs their faces. I know I loved them . . . maybe the loss did something dreadful to my brain."

"Amnesia?"

"I don't know. Something." She fell silent. After a minute or two, she said, "By the way, most of your father's talk flew right over my head. What's a Vastation again?"

"Oh, it was a thing that happened to him in England, when William and Harry were infants, before I was born. Father was sitting in front of the fire one day, happily digesting his midday meal when, completely out of the blue, he was struck by an 'insane and abject terror,' as he put it."

"Why?"

"No reason; that was the point. He went on to describe *some damned shape squatting invisible to me within the precincts of the room raying out from his fetid personality influences fatal to life.*" I made quotes in the air with my fingers.

Sara laughed delightedly and pulled me closer. "Ye gods! The way your Father talks!"

Yes, Father could talk, commanding a startling rhetoric full of exuberant and highly original invectives. People recalled his words years later and copied them into their memoirs. There was the time when, speaking at an Astor library event, he proclaimed, "These men do not live, and if books turn men into this parrot existence, I hope the Astor library will meet the same fate as the Alexandrian." And the time when, somewhere else, he observed, "I never felt proud of my country for what many seem to consider its prime distinction, namely her ability to foster the rapid accumulation of wealth."

And was there a Bostonian who did not know by heart his legendary jousts with Bronson Alcott?

Father: You are an egg half hatched. The shells are yet sticking about your head.

Mr. Alcott: Mr. James, you are damaged goods and will come up damaged goods in eternity.

I reminded Sara of this last dialogue now, and she brought my hand up to her face and softly nuzzled it. "You have a bit of the James gift of gab yourself, Alice. To be candid, I find it . . . stimulating."

This was a rare admission by Sara, who smelled of lily of the valley, absinthe, and tooth powder tonight and whose skin felt silky and electric at the same time. Her lips curved into a naughty smile. She was tender and droll as she kissed and sucked on each of my fingers in turn. It did not matter whether we used the word *love*; we were ruled by forces more potent and subtle than anything belonging to the daytime world.

I shifted my weight so that my thigh came to rest between Sara's legs, and she shifted to accommodate me. We were sensitively attuned to each other in this way. If only the rest of life could unfold so easily.

"To tell you the rest of the *fascinating* story, Sara—"

"What story is that again?"

"The story of Father's Vastation."

"Oh yes! I am very interested. I've never met anyone who had one before."

"So it's 1844 and Father is desperately broken down—on the verge of suicide for more than two years, according to him. In this sorry state, he betakes himself to the Malvern Spa in England, where he meets an English lady invalid to whom he confesses his troubles. She tells him that his travails sound like what Swedenborg called a Vastation. A dark night of the soul sort of thing."

Tenderly smoothing my hair and kissing my face and neck (tomorrow she would delete this from her mind, of course), Sara murmured, "Mmmm. Sounds like a *breakdown* to me. And I should know."

"Are you referring to your aunt who puts rocks in her dog's dish to make it eat more slowly?"

"Oh, there are *dozens* of mad Sedgwicks."

A shiver passed through me. Why had I never considered the possibility that Father had suffered a nervous breakdown? Only now did it occur to me that whenever Father told this story, as he did frequently, a pained look crossed Mother's features. There was another side to this story, and Mother and Aunt Kate had locked it up inside them so no one else would ever know.

But Sara's hands were fluttering over my body, and her lips were having their way with my breasts, and Father's philosophies flew right out of my mind.

I'm sorry to say that after five months in Cambridge, it was becoming apparent that Dr. Taylor's cure was *not* holding. I was successful at disguising this at first, but toward the end of August, the collapse of my scaffolding became evident to the household. The difficulty lay, I suppose, in my inability to assume the receptive attitude, that cardinal virtue in women.

It started just after I'd spent the weekend with Fanny Morse in Brookline. We'd been sitting at her dressing table brushing out our hair and braiding it for the night and discussing the Cambridge Bee that was forming under the leadership of Susy Dixwell.

Fanny said, "What a pity Sara will miss the first meetings but, of course, she can join when she gets back."

"Back from where?" I expected Fanny to say "Bar Harbor" or "New York."

"Why, Europe, of course."

That was the way I learned that Sara was to join the Nortons on their upcoming Grand Tour. For weeks, Grace Norton had suffered from a verbal tic that compelled her to cite Ruskin, Leslie Stephen, Carlyle, Elizabeth Gaskell, and the pre-Raphaelites at random moments. (Leave it to the Nortons to be on intimate terms with all of them!) Sara and I had been laughing about the Norton connections last week and Sara said nothing about her plans to travel with them. Now I learned that she'd been mentally packing her steamer trunks all this time, happy to toss me aside for a chance at the pre-Raphaelites.

Was I being unfair? Had I lost all proportion? I hardly knew.

Sara had so many ways of disavowing what we were to each other. When I told her about *La Fille aux Yeux d'Or* by Balzac, describing a love affair between two women, I thought she'd be intrigued. But her face snapped shut and she said she wasn't interested. How could a man know what a woman feels anyhow? she asked peevishly. Her private fiction seemed to be that whatever transpired between us in the dark was a momentary accident that kept recurring despite her best efforts.

When I confronted her about going abroad with the Nortons, she insisted she'd told me about it and was so adamant on this point that I half believed her. Not ten minutes later, she contradicted herself. "You can understand why I didn't want to tell you, Alice. You have such a tendency to over-react, to take things so deadly *seriously*."

"What 'things,' Sara? Us, you mean?"

This, like everything else I said that day, irritated her. "What do you mean *us*? There is no 'us.' In a few years, Alice, we will marry and we'll be occupied with housekeeping and children and what have you."

Really? Was that the future? We were at breakfast, and the muffin I'd been eating was stuck to my palate, dry as sawdust. I saw starkly at that moment that our relations were always conducted on Sara's terms. Endearments such as "darling" or "dearest" were permitted, if at all, only in the night-world, but as soon as we had clothes on we had to snap back into our public characters. If I accidentally smiled too yearningly at Sara at breakfast or addressed her in fond tones, I'd pay for it with a week's shunning. It was clear now, if not before, that I would never be happy as Sara's lover.

And since grand tours lasted for a year at the minimum, I would have to consider Sara dead and go through all the mourning associated with that. Because I was already losing her forever, or so it seemed to me, I dared for once to press her on the great taboo, the question of Sara and Alice.

"How can you say 'There is no us,' Sara, after our nights together? If you found it so trivial, you have hidden it well. But maybe you are just a liar. Perhaps everything is only a game to you."

A vein throbbed at her temple, and her voice trembled. Fixing her gaze on the milk pitcher, she explained that "what we do at night" was a momentary experience of the eternal, which afterwards scattered like mercury. You should never discuss it—*discuss* meant tedious and ponderous in Sara-world—because that made it dead. "The eternal is like water; it flows through your fingers, you cannot hold onto it."

I didn't know about the eternal, where it flowed. All I knew was that, whatever intimacies took place between us, Sara could be counted on to ignore me the next day. Most people (Fanny Morse, for instance) would probably live and die in the Boston virtues, never dreaming there were embraces that could make you weak in the knees. I sincerely wished I were one of the unawakened ones now. Sara was leaving me for a year, as if it were nothing. It was a bitter truth: the one who loves less (or not at all) has all the power, and this is why love is so painful.

After going through the motions of bidding good-bye to Sara's aunts, I set off down Kirkland Street, arriving at 20 Quincy Street a quarter hour later. I waved to old Mrs. Lowell, dead-heading the day lilies in her perennial bed, and went inside and waited for the tears to flow. Instead, I was dry-eyed, feeling nothing at all.

Perhaps this was the answer. Train yourself to be a Spartan mother to your emotions. If you *do* have feelings, for heaven's sake keep them to yourself. My spirits brightened at the prospect of becoming a different sort of person—healthy-minded, unemotional, detached. Whenever Sara came to mind, I dismissed her like an appointment that must be cancelled. I made a list of her annoying traits and consulted it whenever I felt stabs of longing.

It wasn't just Sara, either. *Everyone* disappointed me. Harry, who went around feeling superior to Cambridge, which he considered quite good enough for me—a mere girl, belonging to the domestic sphere. And William! Complaining in his letters from Dresden about not hearing from me and begging me to write. As if I could write in the state I was in! I still hadn't forgiven him for deserting me without even bothering to say good-bye.

His first letters from Germany were read aloud by Father on the verandah with the oil lamp hissing in the perfumed dark. They were passed around to family friends and read at gatherings, where everyone roared with laughter at William's depictions of the residents of his Dresden lodging house. The landlady who kept exclaiming *wunderschön* about everything. The "Hamburg spinster" who queried William about a *people we had with us called 'Yankees' about whom she had heard such strange stories and who seemed to be, if reports were true, of all the people in the world the very worst.*

His letters always made us laugh. I savored a sweet one to me in which he portrayed himself as a lovesick troubadour pursued by lovely women but remaining true to one woman, whose name he muttered under his breath—*the peerless child of Quincy Street, i.e. Thou.* Fanny Morse's brow furrowed at this and she asked me later, "Why does your brother write you love letters?"

"Don't be silly, Fanny." William always wrote these sorts of letters.

As the eldest in the family, William was forever dispensing advice to the rest of us, although he himself often appeared to be the one most in need of advice. In another letter he wrote:

> *Let Alice cultivate a manner clinging yet self-sustained, reserved yet confidential, let her face beam with serious beauty, & glow with quiet delight at having you speak to her; let her exhibit short glimpses of a*

soul with wings, as it were (but very short ones) and let her voice be
musical and the tones of her voice full of caressing, and every move-
ment of her full of grace, & you have no idea how lovely she will become.

"Very short wings!" I grumbled to Harry. "Like a mosquito, I suppose."
Harry laughed. "I believe William has just described his ideal woman." In fact, I had been quietly monitoring William's crushes from afar and had recently written him that Fraulein Schmidt, of whom he had written a bit too warmly, must be a bold-faced jay.

A week before their sailing date, the Nortons hosted a "last supper" to bid farewell to their friends. After dinner, everyone gathered on the piazza while Charles pontificated and Grace gazed starry-eyed at him. It was clear that the Norton sisters were on a crusade to correspond with every great (masculine) intellect in Boston and Cambridge, and were steadily extending their range to England. They considered themselves muses to men, if not scholars in their own right, and were equipped with a mysterious sense of a man's future greatness (which Sara speculated was an instinct similar to the navigation of migratory birds). Grace and Jane Norton did not have the slightest use for their own sex.

From the piazza, situated on the rise of a hill, we looked east, beyond the azaleas, to the tidal flats of the Charles. It was a magnificent view, changing color with the time of day, slowly fading through sunset tints of tangerine or salmon pink, through violet, mauve and indigo, to black. After sunset that night, there was no moon, and the only source of light was a smoking oil lamp at one end of the table. Sara and I were sitting at the other end, in darkness, where we could whisper to each other unmolested. (But while preserving an outward politeness, I was already striking Sara from my heart. In my mind she was as good as dead.)

Earlier in the evening Charles had announced, "Name me any American production in which any thought appears!" No one took up this absurd challenge, and I thought I saw Susan briefly roll her eyes but she reverted so quickly to her usual expression of Supportive

Wife that you could not be certain. Like many men who live inside their heads, Charles's emotions were of a crude and infantile cast, in my view. His interactions with his infants were especially painful to behold; incapable of spontaneity, he could only mime the gestures of a devoted papa. When it came time for the children to be put to bed, he patted each on the head awkwardly and smiled sadly, as if mindful of their inevitable future as heirs to a crude, disappointing culture.

Shortly after the eldest child had been rounded up and packed off to bed, sherry cobblers were served. Harry had been speaking reverently of *Madame Bovary*, whereupon Charles observed sanctimoniously that "irregular sex relations have no place in literature. The deeper passions are seldom those of illicit love." Sara was stifling her laughter behind her fist. I was thinking, What about Abélard and Héloise? when I felt something drop into my lap. I flinched and nearly bolted out of my chair, thinking of bats. But it was Sara's hand. Gripping my brandy glass with both hands to steady myself, I hissed at her. "Stop it!"

She did, but only for the time it took to remove her beaded shawl from her shoulders and drape it over my lap. "I noticed you were shivering," she whispered, and under the table her hand delved beneath my skirts and came to rest between my thighs. Say what you will, she was good. I could scarcely make out her face in profile, like a queen on an ancient coin, whilst in the enchanted underworld—under the table, under the shawl—her right hand was pressed up against my drawers, having its way with me. I am sorry to say that despite my best intentions her caresses could no more be resisted than a fever, and all the time she sat composed, occasionally making remarks pertinent to the general conversation. Reveling in her power over me, like a torturer.

At the other end of the table, meanwhile, Father was tormenting Charlemagne by insisting that the ancient Persians had a culture far more advanced than that of the Greeks at the time of the Persian Wars. Everyone had everyone else's number here, I thought. Grace Norton had subtle ways of reducing Jane to second-ranking sister and Susan to "not really one of us." Inclining her head toward me, Sara whispered something random about the Persians but in such a tender tone it became part of the waves of pleasure lapping through me. Bunching my linen napkin in front of my face, I had to pretend to be stifling an attack of sneezing.

Was this Sara's way of saying, "See what I can do to you? Won't you miss me?"

By now I just wanted her to leave and get it over with. But when she drew me into her bed two days before their party sailed, I succumbed helplessly, of course. How could I stay angry while Sara kissed me so thoroughly and ran her hands over my back and buttocks in a way that turned me to jelly? While my tongue traced the outline of her earlobe and inched down her neck toward her breasts, she was tugging at me with an aching desire written on her face. And then the boundary between us seemed to drop away and we melted into one rapturous, gasping person. I knew better than to mention this to Sara; it was the sort of thing she would scoff at, and I was doing my best to get over her. But the sweetness of it lingered for days.

⌒ FOUR ⌒

I WAS RELIEVED WHEN THE NORTONS FINALLY SAILED. NOW I could breathe more easily, put Sara out of my mind, get on with my new healthy, sane life. I had all sorts of plans. I threw myself into gardening, planting runner beans, lettuce, butternut squash, asters, and chrysanthemums. I spent hours watering and weeding and staking and pruning and fighting off insects. I liked the sight of the dirt in the creases of my palms, proof that I'd done something earthy and real for a change. Some days I tried being a social butterfly, attending teas and receptions and making bright, animated chit-chat. In the evenings I went to lectures and pronounced them "fascinating." I went to bed exhausted.

Harry, meeting me on the stairs, looked baffled. "What has gotten into you, sister of mine?"

"What do you mean, Harry?"

"Where is your stylish languor, your feminine vapors? Next thing we know you'll turn into Aunt Kate."

"What about you, Harry? How is the *law business* coming?"

"Fine," he said unconvincingly.

I gave him a jaunty little wave and continued on my way upstairs to help Mother muck out the attic. The next day we beat the carpets, and a few days later I let Fanny talk me into coming along on her home visit to one of her immigrant families, and tried to overcome the nausea that would strike me inside those fetid rooms. I kept telling myself I would get used to it, but who was I fooling? A single glance from Sara could undo in an instant all my emotional fortifications and bring me to my knees. In her absence even a stranger with the same way of tilting her head while she laughed could make me catch my breath.

I was distracted from this monomania, fortunately, by a visit from our Temple cousins, which had the added benefit of providing me with material for my next letter to William. I informed him that Minny—his and Harry's favorite of the girls—was not as interesting as she used to be. I attributed this to her being too much influenced by the last person she talked to, so that you never knew where you'd find her. I also described for him the view from my window of the Lowells' garden, where Effie Shaw was seated, looking as lovely as ever. She was the beautiful widow of the dead Civil War hero, Charles Lowell, and sister of Robert Shaw, another fallen hero. She regularly brought her small orphaned daughter to visit her in-laws. How I envied her! To go through life as the tragic widow of a war hero, mother of an orphan. Nothing more would be expected of Effie; she could rest on her laurels.

Clover Hooper sometimes came out to spend the day with Effie, and sometimes Clover and I would exchange a few words over the fence. *She still threatens to invite me to dinner,* I wrote William, *but has never been able to bring her mind to the point of doing so yet, although from what she says she encourages me to think that she tries very hard.* I did not tell William how hungrily I'd waited for the dinner invitation that never came. Nor that at a recent dinner party I'd overheard Mrs. Howells asking Clover, "What do you think of Harry James's *Galaxy* heroine? She reminds me of a great many people in general but no one in particular." To which Clover replied, "I think as usual the boy has chawed more than he can bite off."

A week after the Temples departed, Mother solicited my help in choosing new wallpapers for one of the parlors. We set out all the samples and stared at them from up close and across the room, but I could not find my way to an opinion. While pondering the wallpaper, Mother confided that she hoped William would not "waste his opportunity" in Germany, as a number of shares of real estate in upstate New York had to be sold to send him there. There had been, as I recalled, a slight unpleasantness about money—bad investments by Father, corrective action by Mother.

"Is it so very expensive?"

"Well, your father's *immortal work* certainly won't pay for it!"

This was a shock. I'd always assumed that Mother was a fond handmaid to Father's genius. She sat at his lectures beaming like a madonna, and was disappointed when his self-published books did not sell well (or, to be completely accurate, *at all*). To Father, this world was a shadow of the real, a sort of mass hallucination. He was always urging us children to pluck out the thorn of our egotism and recover our Divine Nature, and Mother endorsed this project one hundred percent. When, as children, one of us was yelling or pouting or pulling another's hair, she'd say, in an admonitory tone, "D.N., dear." Since we were educated at home, it was some time before I discovered that other families did not march to the drumbeat of D.N.

Now I wondered if, to Mother, Father's Ideas were only the hobby-horse of a lovable crank. Her pride in knowing how to stretch a dollar, her mania for order and her relentless housecleaning might be seen in a new light. Someone had to take care of business, she must have reckoned as a young bride. Father drifted here and there like a will-o'-the-wisp, charming roomfuls of people with his intoxicating talk, writing esoteric books and giving esoteric lectures, going off on mysterious journeys by himself, while Mother did the hard work of keeping the family going.

Efficient and energetic, Mother could probably have run a small nation—if nations were ever governed by those wearing skirts. To me she seemed equal to any task but one: managing French servants. How disturbing it had been, when we lived in a grand rented house on the Champs-Élysées during our childhood abroad, to hear the servants mocking Mother's accent and running circles around her, Françoise the cook whispering to Aurore, the head parlormaid, "Madame speaks French like a Spanish cow," Aurore observing, while hanging Mother's and Aunt Kate's nightdresses on the line in the courtyard, that "Monsieur has two wives like a Mohammedan." I was seven years old and knew almost nothing, but I had quickly and effortlessly picked up the French language. To see Mother cowed by the French was shocking, like discovering that God did not care whether people were good or bad.

***

Casting Sara out of my heart was proving more difficult than expected. By summer's end, I'd stopped calling on people or going on picnics, sails, rides, or walks. I said I was tired but it was really that nothing seemed worth the effort. I turned down Fanny's invitations until she was telegraphing me concerned looks whenever we met. The vegetables and flowers I'd planted went unweeded and unwatered. It required a Herculean effort to move myself from the parlor to the verandah. Aunt Kate made noises about the bad airs that came up from the marsh this time of year, and I said, yes, that must be it, but it was not.

I could not even eat a peach now because Sara loved them so.

One morning I woke up with my heart racing and a sensation that my breath was being sucked out of me. It was horrible, annihilating. For a few minutes I was unable to move, speak, or think. Was this what madness was? Aunt Janet loomed in my memory, trembling like a leaf in a gale and jabbering about a plot by the Albany newspaper to omit key ingredients from its recipe for pound cake. And my cousin Kitty James Prince with her God-dazzled eyes and her schemes for putting clothing on dogs and cats for the sake of decency. I would have to discontinue myself if I got like that.

At breakfast Mother and Aunt Kate asked me if I felt all right, and I said I did. Later I admitted that my nerves were troubling me, and that the world seemed blurry and far away.

Aunt Kate said, "Well, darling, I know just the medical man for you. Dr. Munro will put you right."

She went on to say that he had *completely* cured her nerves and back. "Now whenever I feel nervy or have lumbago or a neurasthenic headache or anything at all, I have a few sessions with the doctor, and I'm right as rain. The man is a miracle-worker!"

A few days later I was in his treatment room.

When I think of Dr. Munro, I see his hands, large and square, with springy copper-colored hair at the wrists. His treatment room was in his home on Beacon Street, a tall, narrow building of maroon brick across from the Public Garden. I rang the doorbell under the brass plaque with DR. EDWARD MUNRO on it, and a servant directed me down a murky corridor past portraits of stern, unsmiling Puritan ancestors. The first time I saw Dr. Munro, I was put off by his squint, which made you think of a troll you must meet and overcome in a fairy tale. But I knew that Aunt Kate's health had been improved by seeing him, and his manner was all benevolence.

He had me lie down on his table. He loosened my clothing, and then his fingers were traveling lightly over me. He was like a dowser of the body, sensing unseen nerve currents beneath the skin. Eventually his hands would locate a spot of particular significance: a place below one armpit, an area at the top of my hips, a spot near my clavicle, a place high on the inner thigh. While his touch frequently embarrassed me and made me twitchy, his gentle manner reassured me. When he reached a spot of interest, he would cock his head to the side, as if hearing secret music inside me. If I tried to speak, he would shush me and explain that he was "reading" me now.

He had a habit of popping peppermint candies into his mouth and humming. There were always a series of notes that *seemed* to be leading to a tune but never quite arrived, which was frustrating to me. He halted his humming to ask me personal questions about my periods, their duration and intensity, and to predict that I should greatly benefit from bearing children—the sooner the better. On the third or fourth visit, he became engrossed in a spot four inches below my navel that was apparently associated with "hystero-epilepsy," which I did not recall being told I had. What did it feel like to be hystero-epileptic? I could not bring myself to ask.

On the next several visits, his fingers inched into more intimate territory, not shying away from the triangle of my pubic hair, the junction of the inner thigh and the torso, the labia. Naturally, one had to expect this sort of thing from doctors, but this did not make it any less humiliating, especially as I sensed I was disappointing him continually with my tepid or flinching responses.

"Why are you so *nervous*, Miss James?"

"I don't know."

"Well, here we will teach you to relax,"—using the royal 'we' as usual—"and your life will become more beautiful. You will see."

Patting my knee paternalistically. Yes, I thought, life *would* be better if I could relax, but how did one do it?

My body stiffened, erecting invisible barricades against his fingers, and Dr. M would gently massage away my resistance. His benign clinical detachment made it possible somehow to divorce his hands from the rest of him, and, for a brief period afterward, I felt as if I had honey running through my limbs. I did not know what to think about this.

On my seventh visit, Dr. Munro clucked his tongue and informed me that my uterus was "tipped" and this could explain the enfeebled state of my nerves.

"But how would this have happened?"

"Oh, it could be the result of an old horseback-riding injury or a fall or simply a hereditary defect."

"I did tumble down a flight of stairs shortly after my thirteenth birthday."

"We hear that sort of thing *all the time*, Miss James," he said, brightening. "Don't worry; we can remedy this in short order." He strolled over to the wooden cabinets that took up most of one wall and drew something out of one of its drawers.

It was a shiny instrument of highly polished wood, with a handle and a rotating knob. He did something to it to make it purr, then rumble. He held it against my upper arm so that I could feel it vibrate. It seemed like an ingenious clockwork toy, and then alarm bells went off in my head. "What is it for?"

Dr. Munro smiled his gentle smile and said there was nothing to fear. Then he poked around with it a bit, finally laying the vibrating object against a part of my anatomy I'd always regarded as private. My body jumped as if electrocuted, and I barely suppressed a yelp, but I reminded myself that Dr. Munro was "the best in the business," according to Aunt Kate. Did that mean that Aunt Kate had experienced this vibrating wand business? This was something I did *not* care to picture. When the instrument vibrated against another very personal spot, it was painful at first, and then turned to a sort of pleasure, which, in a way, was worse. I cried out involuntarily, as had occurred before only during my Emerald Hours with Sara. It was mortifying to experience this in Dr. Munro's office, by mechanical means.

The doctor, however, congratulated me on having attained a "proper hysterical paroxysm."

"Is that a *good* thing?"

"Yes, it is, my dear. The paroxysms are the body's way of discharging hysterical energy. If you carry on with the wand, I predict you will be *completely* cured in no more than three months. You are fortunate, Miss James. Many ladies are unable to attain such a paroxysm."

"Oh?" I was completely at sea now.

"Yes, and they can be identified by certain facial features, which are monuments, as it were, to a lifetime of dissatisfaction. Fortunately, these patients can in many cases be re-educated—not in their minds but in their bodies."

"I see," I said, though I didn't.

Dr. Munro was willing—not to say eager—to prescribe a "wand" for home use if I felt so disposed. "Thank you. I don't think that will be necessary," I said politely. At the end of that day's treatment, I dashed down his brownstone steps, nearly bumping into Mrs. Munro on her way up. She was a plump woman in a squishy layered bonnet resembling a meringue, and I wondered if she ever consoled herself with one of her husband's vibrating wands.

A few days later I told my parents that Dr. Munro was not helping me, and they did not object to my discontinuing his ministrations.

At first I could not identify what the Dr. Munro episode reminded me of. Finally I recalled a strange conversation that took place years ago on the horse-omnibus that took the pupils from Beacon Hill to Mrs. Agassiz's school in Cambridge. I was fifteen, a newcomer at the school, and was sitting beside Grace Coolidge, a new nonentity like myself. On the omnibus there was always a great deal of horseplay, shouting, tossing of hats and muffs, songs with multiple rollicking verses that everyone but Grace and I and a few others knew. I had no idea how to approach these clannish Boston girls.

The driver pulled over to the side of the road twice that morning to reprimand the pupils for not "behaving like young ladies." From my seat, I could see the girls' shoulders heaving in silent hilarity.

When we pulled over for the second reprimand, Grace turned to me and asked, "Alice, have you ever heard of the 'local treatment'?"

"No. What is it?"

Well, she said, something dreadful happened to her aunt years ago and she swore on a stack of bibles that it was true. The aunt suffered from a form of hysteria known as "wandering womb" and went to a doctor for the "local treatment." This consisted of painful manipulations and injections in the "female areas" and at some point—Grace's voice dropped to a horrified whisper—the doctors placed leeches *inside* her and by mistake they crawled up into her womb.

"What do you mean, *inside her*?"

"You know, Alice!" She dropped her voice to a whisper behind her cupped hand. "*Down there.*"

The words "down there" immediately triggered a twinge down there in me. I crossed my legs; then finding that my thigh was pressing against "down there," uncrossed them again.

"How ghastly! Did she die?"

"No, but she was never the same afterward." The leeches weren't meant to be in the uterus, she explained, but one or two crawled up inside. The pain was "beyond imagining," she said. Her aunt, a spinster, became a lifelong invalid, queer in her mind and an epic hoarder of newspapers.

At the time I suspected that Grace made up this dramatic story to impress me, as mousy, unpopular girls are apt to do. (You have no idea of tall tales until you've heard the rumors that young girls circulate at school.) But after my sessions with Dr. Munro, I saw that such things could happen. It would start with casual questions, such as whether your periods were regular, whether you ever felt faint, and before you knew it, you'd end up with leeches in your womb.

I saw no more of Dr. Munro, but after my ordeal in his office, I did feel somewhat better, almost normal for a while. This was probably due to the sheer relief of being relieved of Dr. Munro's massages and his tuneless humming. Aunt Kate attributed my improvement, of course, to the doctor's skill.

WILLIAM JAMES

DEAR ALICE

Your excellent long letter of Sept. 5th reached me in due time. If about that time you felt yourself strongly hugged by some invisible agency you may not know what it was. What would I not give if you could pay me a visit here! . . . I stump wearily up the 3 flights of stairs after my dinner to this lone room where there is no human company but a ghastly lithograph of Johannes Muller and a grinning skull to cheer me . . .

1868

WILLIAM, MEANWHILE, WAS NOT IMPROVING AT ALL.

By the next steamer came a letter confessing that his health was actually very poor. His German servants were greasy and unclean, he wrote, and the thought of his breakfast plates being handled by them sickened him. And no window was ever opened in that land.

My servant here asked me in great excitement if I slept with the window open. She said there was a man in Weimar who slept with his window open and he became blind! Out in the street the slaw and fine rain is falling as if it would never stop—and the street is filled with water and that finely worked up to a paste of mud which is never seen on our continent.

Although permeated by melancholy, this letter was at least leavened by humor. As it happened, it was the last letter from Germany that would be read aloud to the family group. Subsequent ones were read silently by Father and tucked away like contraband. Harry and I knew from his expression not to ask.

When William arrived home in late autumn, I thought at first I was meeting his ghost. I wanted to shake him out of this trance or whatever it might be, because this was not the William I knew. Thin, hollow-eyed, and silent, he conversed without animation, shuffled his feet when he walked, complained of always being cold, even next to a roaring fire. When he held a teacup, the coffee splashed onto the saucer or the tablecloth, and it was heartbreaking to see how he tried to hide the tremor from the family.

"I don't know what's eating him," Mother said. "He looks *transparent*, as if you could poke a hole right through him."

Sorrow registered in her eyes before she snapped back to her default mode of taking care of business and pretending everything was fine. Being the only robust member of the James family was her cross to bear, as she shouldered the various illnesses, black moods, breakdowns, financial disasters, and heartbreaks of her children, whose temperaments were complicated and foreign to her.

"He keeps saying it is philosophical hypochondria," Harry said. "I can't make out what he means."

If you asked William what was wrong, you'd get a long laundry list. His back had "collapsed," his eyes were bad, his brain "moribund," he could not concentrate or remember anything. And, on top of all that, he suffered from "severe dyspepsia and chronic gastritis of frightful virulence and obstinacy." He took long walks in the cold and came back half frozen, pale and silent. He rarely joked now, and a humorless William was like an ocean without tides.

Mother had her theories. "He has too much morbid sympathy!" she complained to Harry and me. "The other day he was fretting about the servants having only one armchair in the kitchen. He wouldn't stop talking about it!"

Dejected at seeing his *wunderkind* so fragile and unhappy, Father blamed Darwinism and other atheistic doctrines.

At meals William was either silent as a wax figure or twitchy and combative, starting painful arguments with Father. "I have read your article on Swedenborg, Father, and I can't comprehend the gulf you maintain between Head and Heart. To me they are inextricably intermingled."

"Then you understand nothing, William. You are as dense as the pusillanimous clergy."

(The pusillanimous clergy were a favorite target of Father's bombasts.)

"Your theory of Creation is a muddle, Father. I cannot fathom what you mean by 'the descent of the Creator into Nature.' You don't explain it, and it seems to be the kernel of the whole system. You live in such mental isolation that I cannot help but feel that you must see even your own children as strangers to what you consider the better part of yourself."

Father's face clouded as he hacked at the roast with the carving knife.

When William remarked one evening that he was unable to decide what he should be, Father said, "Being is from God. A man cannot *decide* to be anything."

William grumbled under his breath, "A nice life, provided you can live off your dividends."

At Sunday dinner, hunched over his soup bowl, narrowly focused on keeping his spoon from shaking, William observed, "I am convinced, Father, that we are Nature through and through and that we are wholly conditioned, that not a wiggle of our own will happens save as a result of physical laws."

I failed to understand why men took philosophy so personally, as if their lives depended on it. William, compulsively philosophizing, seemed to me like a person who persists in taking a drug that everyone else can see plainly is making him ill.

Father had lured William into science in the first place so that he could use its methods to corroborate Father's theories of D.N. He even permitted him to go to Harvard, although he'd always insisted that colleges were "hothouses of corruption where it is impossible to learn anything." William's studies led him in the opposite direction, into a cold mechanistic universe, which was now tearing him apart.

In a household less metaphysical than ours such topics might have caused only minor perturbation. Here the father–son arguments raged loud and fierce, like the wars of the gods on Mt. Olympus. Father would say, "It is very evident to me, William, that all your troubles arise from the purely scientific cast of your thought and the temporary blight exerted upon your metaphysical wit. All scientists are stupefied by the giant superstition we call Nature."

According to Father's private religion, there was Nature and then there was Divine Nature. Only Divine Nature was real; "the world" was a sort of dream.

William would mutter, "Hmm, I wonder which of us is more stupefied by superstition."

Father would say, "The first requisite of being a philosopher is not to think but to become a living man by the putting away of selfishness from one's heart!"

"Not think? *Really*, Father?"

In an attempt to defuse the argument, Mother began to describe some gardens she had seen along Brattle Street, but no one took this up. Throwing his napkin on the table, Father shoved his chair back, scraping the floor, and limped into the other room.

"Oh, now you've upset your father!"

"It is equally true that he has upset me." William got up and climbed the stairs wearily, as if he were a hundred years old.

"Henry has pinned all his hopes on William," Mother remarked to Aunt Kate. "I don't know why William can't keep his ideas to himself. And now they are both missing dessert!"

"More for us then," I said, attempting to insert some levity into the near-daily wrangle. Mother glowered in my direction.

"Oh, I think they both rather enjoy sparring," Aunt Kate said.

William did speak excellent German; you could say that for him.

Then he astonished us all by reviving, like a plant that is given water. It seemed to occur overnight. He'd gone to bed wrapped in his usual listless melancholy and the next morning bounded down the stairs two at a time, and amused us by reading absurdities from the *Boston Evening Transcript*, such as a witness in a murder trial who testified that the corpse was "pleasant-like and foaming at the mouth."

He went out in bright spirits, wearing a jaunty hat, a colorful waistcoat and gloves he'd picked up in Europe—he'd always dressed like a dandy—and took long, brisk walks for miles. If you accompanied him, it was like walking an eager, inquisitive dog that was always straining at the leash. He took up the Lifting Cure that had helped

Harry so much and reported that his back was improving from day to day. He was suddenly full of praise for the "transparency" of American skies, without Europe's veils and mists.

The dinner table arguments became less rancorous. Father would say, "I suppose, William, you still put forward the absurd argument that thought has a material basis?"

With a mischievous grin, William would reply, "A study of the mind apart from the body is utterly barren, Father." Then Father would rail against scientists, and William would say, "Father, your ideas are untestable. It's only a matter of time, you know, until we prove that the higher mental operations, like the lower, are functions of the supreme nerve-centers, obeying the same physiological laws of evolution."

"Well, I pray you wake up to the enormity of your foolhardiness, William."

But it was clear from their faces that their arguments were sport again.

Buoyed by the improvement in his health, William picked up medicine where he'd left off and applied himself to studying for his M.D. exam. Every so often he'd call me into his room to examine a slide under a microscope, showing me how to focus the lens on the teeming micro-world under the glass.

"Can you guess what that is?"

I squinted through the lens. "Nothing good, I expect."

"That, young lady, is a polypus of the nose. Now—this one." He put in another slide.

"A hundred gnats entombed in a custard?"

"An inspired guess, Alice, but this is Nutmeg Liver. The patient died of phthisis. If I ever have a patient with this condition I will know what it looks like microscopically."

"Is there a cure for Nutmeg Liver?"

"Death is the only one I know of."

"Then what is the point, William?"

"Oh, Alice, I don't intend to *practice* medicine, you know."

But if he did not practice medicine, the vexed question of what William *would* do remained unresolved. Still, it *was* a relief to see him in high spirits again.

He passed his M.D. exam in March but showed no disposition to put up a shingle or seek patients. His mind had moved on. With a band of fellow truth-seekers he formed the Metaphysical Club, which met in the second-floor library of our house. Whenever I passed the room, arguments were flying like bullets, punctuated by bursts of masculine laughter. I was never invited in, which I did not mind, as I was not even sure what metaphysics was to begin with. Whenever the door was ajar, I heard strange things, as if from another world. I heard William say, "My father who looks at the Cosmos as if it had some life in it. . . . " I heard terms like "psychophysical parallelism" and "the thought-atom." I heard William say, "If God is dead, how long are we going to keep all we know from the public?"

Did William really think God was dead? Had He been alive until recently? Was I part of the ignorant public that either would or would not be kept in ignorance of His demise?

Suddenly, I found myself truly wondering for the first time about God (who previously was only a vague figure wearing the robes of *A Child's Illustrated Old Testament*). As I pondered the idea of God, I seemed to sink deeper into my being. Before, I'd felt that I was living my life "out there," in the world, but I saw now that all along the world had also been living inside me. Or the dream of the world, you might say. And there was a pure awareness in me that was not trapped inside the bubble of thought. Or so it seemed. This was as far as I could go, and I did not know if that made me a believer or an unbeliever.

Oliver Wendell Holmes, Jr.—called Wendell—was a founding member of the Metaphysical Club and a proud atheist. (Atheism was his only point of compatibility with his father, the humorous, epigram-spewing Dr. Holmes.) My brothers idolized him, but whenever I met him on the landing, I tried to make myself invisible. The man made me shiver, like an evil wind. One evening when he stayed for supper, Mother whispered to me, "Did you notice how he carries his manuscript about in that green bag and never loses sight of it for a moment?"

We had just slipped into the front parlor between courses, supposedly to look for candles. Mother and I had our secret signals, which none of the men ever noticed. (And they claimed to be the superior sex!) Wendell always made it clear he had no use for Mother or me, and addressed himself only to Will, Harry, and Father when he was at our house.

"What manuscript?"

"His thesis, Will says. He started to go to Will's room to wash his hands but came back for his bag, and when we were about to go to dinner—this was all before you came downstairs—Will said, 'Don't you want to take your bag with you?' and Wendell said, 'Yes, I always do at home.'"

"Maybe he is afraid his family will burn it." The Holmeses were a fractious family who for mysterious reasons all seemed to loathe one another. My comment inspired silent spasms of laughter in Mother, and I caught a glimpse of the carefree girl she must have been before we wore her down with all our tribulations.

I asked William one day if he disagreed with *all* of Father's Ideas. He said he'd "leafed through" a few of Father's books recently ("leafing through" was his preferred method of taking in information; he absorbed an astonishing amount this way). He concluded that Father's solution to the problem of evil was "philosophically unsatisfying."

"What is Father's solution?"

"Oh, that Nature is basically evil and Divine Nature is all good. It's essentially watered-down Hegel and the Hegelian solution is like the maudlin stage of drunkenness. In my opinion."

I should mention that a strict if unspoken economy of health held sway in our family. It boiled down to the principle that the sickest member should be permitted to use family funds to travel abroad to regain his (or her) health in the healthier European air. (All doctors agreed about the air.) The sickest James was now deemed to be Harry, with his persistent though ill-defined back trouble. Thus, three months after William's return, he sailed to Europe with a letter of credit and went directly to the Malvern Spa (where, years before, Father first heard about Swedenborg) to take the famous waters.

His letters began arriving, one or two a week.

After Malvern he was not sure that his cure was "clinched" and thought he might need to go back a second time. Despite his mysterious "dorsal infirmity," he sounded like a gay blade, describing a garden party he'd just attended with Grace Norton and Sara Sedgwick. It was held at the home of Mrs. Lewes, aka George Eliot, whom Harry went on to describe as *magnificently ugly, deliciously hideous, an ugly likeness of Mrs. Sam Ward of Boston.* This vision of Harry and the Nortons (and Sara!) conversing with the great George Eliot plunged me into a painful cognizance of my insignificance. In that brilliant society, why should either my brother or my friend spare a thought for me?

Harry's letters were read aloud at the Emersons' and the Howells', and everyone said how marvelous they were. I wondered briefly if I could write something equally marvelous if I had more access to the picturesque, before remembering that such egotism was unbecoming in a woman.

∼ SIX ∽

1869

By the time I turned twenty-one on August 7, 1869, every-one was commenting on my "great improvement," the roses in my cheeks, my being a "perfect sunbeam to father." This last was Mother's assessment in her weekly letter to Harry, which she gave as usual to Father to take to the post office in Boston.

A creature of habit, Father rode the horse-cars into Boston every afternoon to mail our letters and collect our mail, always returning with anecdotes. (I suspected that the anecdotes, more than the mail, were the point of the excursion.) A woman on the cars who looked just like a parrot, with bright beady eyes and a scarlet cape. The poet James Russell Lowell composing verses on the spot about the new transat-lantic undersea cable, then complaining, "I hate science. I hate it as a savage hates writing, because I fear it will hurt me somehow." A man returning from having a nasal polyp removed by Dr. Bigelow who said the doctor seemed entirely indifferent to his pain. The horse-cars were the social high point of Father's day.

I had just written to Nanny Ashburner: *I feel so well now that to feel any better would be superfluous.* It felt true when I wrote it, and I hoped it was. Nanny was Sara Sedgwick's cousin (through the British side of their families) and she had become my chief correspondent after she moved to England. Whenever I found myself at an awkward tea or a boring lecture, I consoled myself by recreating the scene for Nanny and, after a few months of this, the so-called life I was living felt less vivid and interesting, even less real, than my retelling of it. I was beginning to understand why Harry wanted only to be left alone to write to his heart's content; I felt the same desire, but because I was only a girl, no one, including myself, took my writing seriously.

And William: after a brief burst of renewal, his chronic weariness of spirit was back. You could see it in the pinched look of his face, his baleful silences, his slow and halting movements. Having dispensed with medicine, he planned to devote himself to psychology or perhaps philosophy. Meanwhile, he was making sporadic efforts to get on track with anatomy, disappearing into his room for hours with acrid chemicals, dissection knives, and microscopes. It was like having a mad scientist living in the house.

Mother harped at him about spilling solvents on the carpet and reminded him daily to lay a towel over his dresser scarf if he planned to set staining liquids there. He promised sincerely to take great care and unquestionably meant to, but it was a fact of nature that disorder erupted around William. Although he'd extracted a promise from Mother not to clean or even enter his room—which he'd taken to calling his "laboratory"—she was incapable of passing his door without an aggrieved sigh. One day she ordered a cleaning raid while William was spending the day in Milton, resulting in the destruction of two prize grouse wings he had set aside for some scientific purpose.

When William returned to find his room tidied and the wings missing, he flew into a rage. "Honestly, William!" Mother said. "The wings had insects crawling on them." She told him not to act like a spoiled child and added that Father said the other day that he was "a bit of a shirker" and sometimes regretted having paid the fee to keep him out of the war. From the landing, I saw the shock on his face, as Mother vented her frustrations. Wasn't it time he figured out his life? Look at Harry! He had already been published, and *he* was not diverted into a different career every time he read a new book, et cetera.

"Harry James, angel, hero, martyr," William mumbled under his breath. Mother turned her back and walked briskly downstairs, casting a dark look at me, whom she considered too soft-hearted about William. When she was out of earshot, I said, "You know, William, she *always* quotes Father whenever she wants to say something unpleasant about us. I don't believe Father says half the things she claims he does."

"Who knows?" he said in a choked voice, and disappeared into his room like a phantom.

Harry's latest letter confided that he'd been to Malvern a second time, but was not certain that his cure would hold. Meanwhile, he wrote from Oxford:

> *I thought that the heart of me would crack with the fullness of satisfied desire. As I walked along the river, I saw hundreds of the mighty lads of England, clad in white flannel and blue, immense, fair-haired, magnificent in their youth, lounging down the stream in their punts. The whole place gives me a deeper sense of Englishness than anything yet.*

I wondered if I would ever have a deeper sense of anything but Bostonness.

William, too, suffered from Harry's letters. They reminded him of how he'd squandered his chances, and suggested that shy Harry might be better at making his way in life than he, the supposed genius of the family. It remained a sad fact that however much he brooded over the question of what to do, his thinking only spun him in circles. He was obliged to admit finally that Harry's Lifting Cure was not working for him. Upon quitting it, he took a series of questionable patent medicines that left him sicker than before. He bought a battery from someone at the Massachusetts General Hospital and electrified himself religiously. This was supposed to help his nerves, but no one could detect any improvement.

On one of his better days, he and I took a walk in the Norton woods, and who should appear on the footpath like an evil toadstool but Jane Norton. She droned on in her usual manner about a book on Madame de Sévigné. As the footpath was just wide enough for two abreast, I was obliged to hang back behind them. To my relief, Miss Norton had a tea date and left after ten minutes.

"Did you see how she *blocked* me, William? It was a choice between walking through the poison ivy or walking behind, like an Oriental wife."

"Sorry, Alice. I'm not very perceptive these days." A brooding silence. "You know, don't you, that my nineteen months in Germany were a waste of the family funds. An utter failure."

"But your German improved, and didn't you learn masses of physiology?"

He went silent, frowning at the ground. Then he said, "Until recently, Alice, it was thought to be impossible to determine the rate of transmission of a stimulus along a nerve. Then this German genius, a man called Helmholtz, figured out how to measure this time with the greatest accuracy in the sciatic nerve of a frog. Do you know what that *means?*"

"I have no idea."

"Well, it was like discovering the atom of consciousness."

While he was in Germany, he explained, he took an overnight train to Heidelberg to hear Helmholtz lecture. "When I got there, the university was empty; there were no lectures. I'd arrived during a vacation! The closest I got to a German physiologist during my time in Germany was a brief glimpse of Wilhelm Wundt"—whoever *he* was, I thought—"up on a dais, mumbling from his notes in German, while students copied down every word in huge notebooks called *Hefts.*"

"Hefts?"

"Yes, a peculiar German invention. It was abominably clear that my brain and eyes would never permit me to sit for hours taking notes in German. Nor, due to my dorsal infirmity"—a malady as mysterious in William as it was in Harry—"could I stand for eight hours a day dissecting frog nerves in the laboratory."

"Yecch, William! You *like* to do that?"

"Yes, actually. Eventually I broke down completely and made my halting, shuffling way to the Teplitz spa."

"Where is that, in Germany?" I saw that William was filling me in on what occurred after Father stopped reading his letters aloud.

"In Bohemia. Unfortunately the *Kur* left me weaker than before. I tried it again a few months later, with identical results. Later, I went to Divonne to see if a French watering-hole would suit me better. It didn't, alas." He sighed.

"But why go *three times,* William, if it did you no good?"

"Oh, I told myself it would work *this time* because the temperature of the water was different or because I was having cold rubs or sponge baths or wet packs. The doctors always act as if the *Kur* is a sure thing, you know."

"The Doctors Taylors in New York were like that, too! On the whole, doctors seem to have an unreasonable optimism about their dark arts."

William agreed that that was true. Then, in a spasm of self-disgust, he was ticking off on his fingers all the careers he'd abandoned. It was an impressively long list. He quit painting (on Father's insistence) to study chemistry, then quit chemistry to study comparative anatomy, then quit anatomy to study natural science. Then, "after the great Amazon expedition of 1865 with Mr. Agassiz exposed my incapacity in that field," he turned to medicine. Just short of an M.D., he was lured to Germany by the promise of physiology. And all he'd ended up with, he said, was "a handful of monstrous compound words in German."

I wished I could think of something wise or helpful to say. I didn't know why he didn't just practice medicine since he already had the degree, but that seemed the wrong thing to say. I longed to tell him how desolate it had been at Quincy Street while he was gone. If he left again, I'd be left alone with the old people, and eventually I would lose them, too, and end up completely alone, a nervous, twitchy woman with an enormous library, like Miss Anna Ticknor of Chestnut Street. But, of course, I didn't say this, either.

No one bothered to tell me, in the course of our peculiar, insulated childhood, that sisters and brothers could not marry, and it amused our family to pretend that I would wed William. It was a joke, of course, only I did not get it. From my infancy onward, William was celebrating my supposed beauty and charms in a courtly manner, addressing me in letters and poems as Sweetling, You Lovely Babe, *Charmante jeune fille*, and "the sweet lovely delicious little grey-eyed Alice who must be locked up alone after receipt of this letter." He would claim that I was breaking his heart when I failed to write back to him promptly. He made sketches of me captioned "the loveress of W.J." and penned sonnets and odes to me in French and English, once inviting the family into the parlor to hear him perform his *sonate* to Alice. *The moon was mildly beaming/Upon the summer sea,/I lay entranced and dreaming/My Alice sweet, of thee . . .*

When my childish heart formed a picture of being loved and adored, it was the picture William painted. To understand this, you would have to grasp how magnetic William was; men as well as women would follow him with their eyes across a crowded room. And I was just a little girl.

I did not learn the truth about brothers and sisters until I was nine, when Mary Tappan said, "You've got bats in your belfry, Alice. Brothers and sisters can't marry. Their children would be two-headed monsters and put in a circus!" The magnitude of my folly was revealed to me at one stroke. But perhaps a part of me persisted in believing that in some queer way William and I *were* married, not literally but in our inmost hearts.

Christmas found William glum and saturnine, shivering inside three or four layers of clothing. He'd stopped joking about absurdities in the *Transcript* or anything else. He'd hunch over his dinner, cutting his meat into microscopic pieces, speaking little.

In January, our cousin Minny Temple came to visit, looking thin and drawn, but she was not too ill to provoke an unpleasant scene at dinner by arguing with Father. Eyes ablaze, she insisted that his solution to the problem of existence—surrender to Divine Nature—was "ignoble and shirking." Father turned crimson and denounced her. From where I sat I could see Minny's hand in her lap wadding her napkin, but she did not back down or apologize. I had to admit she was brave.

Our six Temple cousins were the children of Father's sister Catherine, who had died of consumption within weeks of her husband. The orphaned Temples were being raised by their childless aunt and uncle, the Tweedys, who receded ineffectually into the background over the years, as if overpowered by the vitality of their young wards. Mother always said they had "grown up by the side of the road like wildflowers." In Newport the girls went barefoot, with their hair hanging loose and their skirts hitched up, and I had come upon them more than once "practice-kissing" one or another of my brothers.

"People who kiss their cousins have babies with two heads," I would say, hearing Elly and Kitty snicker as I walked away.

After dinner that fateful evening in January 1870, Minny went to sit in the library with William. I joined them, thinking I'd enjoy a little chat with my cousin, but they hardly bothered to make conversation with me. Nor did they try very hard to disguise the fact they were waiting for me to leave. But wasn't it my home, too, and wasn't William my brother? Something in me was determined to thwart their desire to be alone together, so I sat in the library for some time, staring into the flames, picking at my cuticles, immovable as a boulder. Inside my heart a Medean rage smoldered. In the morning it was painfully obvious they'd stayed up all night, burning through six or seven large logs. What had they talked about all night long? Whatever it was, Minny hurried away at the crack of dawn, and William was behaving queerly. A letter arrived from her ten days later, and he stopped taking walks and seeing people and simply stayed in his room, emerging only for meals, eyes glassy, hands tremulous. What had Minny *done* to him?

One day when the door was ajar I saw him sitting before his looking glass sketching. It was a self-portrait, very well done, but his face looked hollowed out by grief. It was almost as sad as the sketch he did five years earlier of Wilky lying in our parlor at Newport, delirious from his war wounds.

In early March came the telegram informing us that Minny was dead, of consumption. William closed in on himself completely, and Mother delivered his meals on a tray, left outside his door. The food was seldom touched.

Minny Temple
Pelham, New York
January 15th '70

To William James
. . . the unutterable sadness & mystery that envelops us all—I shall take some of your chloral tonight. Don't let my letter of yesterday make you

*feel that we are not very near each other—friends at heart. Altho' prac-
tically being much with you or even writing to you much would not be
good for me—Too much strain on one key will make it snap—& there is
an attitude of mind, (not a strength of Intellect by any means) in which
we are much alike—Good-bye*

⌒

JOURNAL OF WILLIAM JAMES
MARCH 1870

*Death sits at the heart of each one of us; some she takes all at once; some
she takes possession of step by step, but sooner or later we forfeit to her
all that nature ever gave us. Instead of skulking to escape her all our days
and being run down by her at last, let us submit beforehand.*

⌒

HENRY JAMES
MALVERN, MARCH 29TH 1870

TO WILLIAM JAMES
*And so Minny went on, sleeping less & less, waking wider & wider, until
she awaked absolutely! I had a dream of telling her of England and of her
immensely enjoying my stories, But instead of my discoursing to her, I
shall have her forever talking to me, Amen Amen, to all she may say. The
more I think of her the more perfectly satisfied I am to have her translated from this changing realm of fact to the steady realm of thought.*

SEVEN

LATER I WOULD RECALL THE SHADOWS OF THE TREES LYING across Quincy Street, how sharp and definite they were, as if drawn with a ruler. I would remember a brief flash of well-being, the last I would have for a while. Then Mother was telling me that William had gone to the Somerville Asylum, and I was not to discuss this with anyone outside the family.

Somerville! Was it that bad?

"What is supposed to be wrong with him?"

Mother was vague. Hypochondria, melancholia, and unwholesome habits were cited along with William's need for rest. "You know how he will always burn the candle at both ends. I suppose he will need a different climate soon."

I felt a surge of rage toward her. Somerville! Where so many Bostonians went and never came out.

"Climate has nothing to do with Will's troubles, dear," Father called from the verandah. "His problem is that he has been poisoned by empirical doctrines."

What he meant, I believe, was that William was an unbeliever. When I'd queried William about his philosophy recently, his answers had been cryptic. "When the world seems to me base and evil, my will is palsied." I asked if he still planned to go into science, and he said, "I am about as little fitted by nature to be a worker in science of any sort as anyone can be. Yet my only ideal of life is the scientific life."

We were forbidden to visit or write to him; family influences were considered baleful at this juncture, apparently. Aunt Kate was in Italy with a Van Buren cousin. Harry was still feasting on England. Wilky and Bob were in Milwaukee trying to get a start in the railroad business. The hush that fell over the house was like death, and if I did not distract myself, my deepest fear slipped through the cracks: My parents dead, my brothers gone, claimed by marriage and families, and myself alone, a sad wandering shade. There seemed to be an inevitability about it, like an oncoming train.

I took to spending mornings in William's room. His window afforded a view of the slender elms and the red brick of Harvard Yard, the young men jostling each other on the diagonal footpaths. You could set your clock by President Eliot leaving his house at one o'clock and returning at three-forty-five. From one side, in profile, you'd never guess that a large port-wine birthmark covered most of the other cheek. It was as if there were two President Eliots, one with the birthmark, the other without.

I was hungry for any trace of William. A hint of pipe smoke on a velvet dressing gown. A list, in his small, neat hand, in the pocket of his Norfolk jacket. A pillow that retained the shape of his head. I unearthed his extensive "physiognomic collection" from a drawer, and noted the addition of two Germans with monocles and a delicately pretty young lady with an aigrette in her hair. (William, who dabbled in phrenology, prevailed on everyone he knew to send him cabinet photographs, even of strangers. He had over a hundred.) On his dresser, next to his silver comb and brush set, sat a framed photograph of Minny, at age fourteen, with her hair brutally chopped off. She'd done it herself, evidently with sheep shears. She said she wanted to feel the wind in her hair, but I suspected she'd had lice.

Sitting cross-legged on William's disheveled bed, I scrutinized the books stacked on his nightstand. Herbert Spencer's *Principles of Psychology, Vol. 1* defeated me at once with a passage so long and dull I could not continue, and Thomas H. Huxley's *The Scientific Aspects of Positivism* was not much livelier. Two books were left. *Divine Love and Wisdom* by Emanuel Swedenborg and *Christianity The Logic of Creation* by Henry James, Sr. It seemed that William had been reading Father and Swedenborg just before going mad. This was a little odd in view of his oft-stated opinion of the paternal prose, neatly summed up by the frontispiece he designed for Father's books—a man flogging a dead horse. But recently, it appeared, he'd been actually trying to *understand* Father's Ideas. How had he become a stranger whose thoughts I could only guess at?

There must be a clue here somewhere, I thought. William's library was as vast as it was eclectic. My mind swam trying to read the titles. Tomes of philosophy, French volumes on ether and obstetrics, German texts on physiology. My eyes fell on a maroon volume, *The Physiology and Pathology of the Mind*, by Henry Maudsley. Shortly before William went "away," I recalled Mother remarking, "I see him hanging his head over a large maroon volume, and then he goes around with a peculiar *stricken* look." Was this the offending book? I flipped through the pages, and came to an underscored passage:

> *Multitudes of human beings come into the world weighted with a destiny against which they have neither the will nor the power to contend; they are the step-children of nature, and groan under the worst of all tyrannies—the tyranny of a bad organization.*

This must have been meaningful to William, for the margins bristled with arrows and exclamation marks. I flipped to another chapter and landed on a doubly underlined passage.

> *The ordinary hysterical symptoms may pass by degrees into chronic insanity. Loss of power of will is a characteristic of hysteria in all its Protean forms, and with the perverted sensations and disordered movements there is always some degree of moral perversion.*

A dying fly buzzed in the window casement. I slammed the horrid book shut and stuffed it back on the shelf between an obstetrics textbook and a volume entitled *Psychologie Morbide*.

The next day, the room had a sour smell, which I traced to a half-eaten apple in the wastebasket. Like a cat burglar, I rifled through each of the drawers in his desk, discovering a small, worn leather notebook.

This flipped open to a place where several pages had been torn out, leaving jagged edges. Just before the torn section was a page of notes on a book called *Du Haschish et d'Alienation Mentale* by J. Moreau, some observations about insanity. Right after the ripped-out pages I came upon the saddest lines ever written, in William's hand:

> *I may not study, make or enjoy, but I can will. I can find some real life*
> *in the mere respect for other forms of life. Nature & life have unfitted*
> *me for any affectionate relations with other individuals—it is well to*
> *know the limits of one's individual faculties.*

It tortured me not to know what he'd confided in the missing pages. Something about Minny? A suicide note, which he later tore up? Or something I could not even imagine? Perhaps there was a hard, unknowable core in everyone; perhaps it was ultimately impossible to bridge the gap between people. I was holding the diary in my hand like a hot coal when I heard Mother's steps on the stairs. I quickly stuffed it back into the drawer, and pretended to be scanning the bookshelves.

"Alice?" She peered in anxiously.

"Hello, Mother. I was just looking up a word in William's German dictionary." I held up this thick volume. "Do you know what *Vorstellung* means?" She did not. Neither did I. I'd just read the word in one of William's diary entries.

A few days later, while Mother and the maids were occupied with beating the carpets, I returned to William's diary and found a page with a cross, marked with the initials M and T and the date March 6, 1870. Under it was the following melancholy passage:

> *By the big part of me that's in the tomb with you may I realize and*
> *believe in the immediacy of death! May I feel that every torment suf-*
> *fered here passes and is as a breath of wind—every pleasure too. Minny,*
> *your death makes me feel the nothingness of all our egotistic fury—The*
> *inevitable release is sure . . . tragedy is at the heart of all of us. Go to*
> *meet it instead of dodging it all your days and being run down by it.*
> *Use your death (or your life, it's all one).* tat tvam asi.

Shortly after writing that, William went to Somerville. Strangely, apart from the particulars, I knew how he felt. Perhaps it was part of the James temperament to arrive at these bleak and stony outcrops of existence.

"We expect the rest to do him a great deal of good," Mother told all our friends, as if William were at a health resort and not a madhouse. A memory came back to me: William and I sitting on the verandah drinking lemonade while Mother and Aunt Kate knelt in the fresh loam planting seedlings, in ecstasies over the hollyhocks.

"How do you suppose they remain so cheerful in the face of the pain of existence?" William said.

"It's just the way they are, I suppose."

"It's because they are healthy-minded. Not sick souls . . . like us, Alice."

Along with missing William, I felt remorse for snubbing Minny the last time I saw her. It was too late to make amends, obviously. Not long after her death, Elly and Kitty came to stay a few nights in Cambridge, both limp from days of weeping. Having yoked herself in marriage to a much older Emmett cousin, Kitty was expecting a baby, who would inevitably bear the imprint of all this grief, poor thing. And Elly was about to wed another Emmett greybeard. There was an infinite supply of them evidently.

"Isn't it awful?" I said to Mother. "To sell yourself for life!"

"It's nothing to do with selling, Alice. They have no choice, poor girls; they must settle. They have nothing to live on."

Still, that *was* selling yourself.

In Balzac's *La Fille aux Yeux d'Or* there was a character who

came from a country where women are not beings, but things— chattels, with which one does as one wills, which one buys, sells, and slays; in short, which one uses for one's caprices as you, here, use a piece of furniture.

I thanked my lucky stars that I was not from such a country. But was there such a great difference between being "bought and sold" and marrying a man you don't love because you have no money and no means of getting any?

"I'm sure the girls will make a go of it," Mother said. "Love grows over time."

I was not disposed to believe this. Only Minny seemed to be holding out for something better, and where had that got her? If she had lived, she would have become a spinster adjunct to one of her sisters' households. In the stories I read in *Godey's*, young women of noble character were rescued from a cruel fate at the last moment, but that had not happened to the Temples, and I did not think it would happen to me. On the whole, it seemed that noble character was rarely rewarded.

Two months later, William returned from Somerville fatter, healthier, and quite cheerful. He never spoke of what happened there, and the superintendent told our parents not to broach the subject. "He must put it behind him and never speak of it again," Mother said.

It was a relief to see him taking an interest in life again, going to parties in high spirits, hosting meetings of the Metaphysical Club, setting off for the new laboratory he shared with his medical school friends Jim Putnam and Henry Bowditch, to work on physiological experiments that he suddenly thought would be quite significant. Around this time, he discovered a French philosopher whom he would credit with his salvation. A Monsieur Renouvier, who believed that a person was not *completely* at the mercy of Nature; that even in a largely mechanical world, there was a small space for an independent will. Just a spark was enough for William. Standing on that ground, he could reclaim his life. I marveled that something as dry as philosophy could affect someone so personally, but that was William.

In the late spring of 1870 the Nortons returned to Cambridge, laden with several new Tintorettos, a Veronese, a Tiepolo, an uncomfortable Louis Quinze loveseat and matching chairs, several precious quartos and first editions, in addition to a great many Italian and French phrases and tales of Ruskin and Carlyle, Leslie Stephen, Elizabeth Gaskell, and William Morris. Grace Norton flaunted her new Paris fashions, and even the children were prattling in Italian and French.

"Isn't it monstrous?" Sara laughed. "They are like little wind-up toys. Have you ever met an affected six-year-old?"

"Not that I recall."

"Well, have a little chat with Sally one of these days."

"Can't you influence them, as their aunt?"

"Oh, I don't wield much influence in that household. Those children have too many old-maid aunts as it is."

"There will never be a shortage of maiden aunts in Boston, I suppose."

Our reunion was so affectionate I felt guilty for having previously struck Sara dead in my mind. I didn't mind hearing her say that she'd missed me "excruciatingly" and couldn't wait to tell me all about the Nortons' European inanities.

A few days later, walking along the tow-path of the Charles, Sara said she wanted to discuss our Emerald Hours. I wondered whether any other pair in human history had ever uttered the sentence, *I want to discuss our Emerald Hours.* But it did not seem the right time to say this to Sara, who seemed nervous and brittle. Her eyes were fixed on the ground in front of her and she was speaking haltingly, as if from a memorized text, telling me she'd read in "an authoritative medical book" that a woman who became "too attached" to her own sex would coarsen her nature, endanger her future as a mother, and possibly develop facial hair and become masculine in appearance.

Forgive me, but I burst out laughing.

"What?" Sara looked hurt.

"Sorry. I was just picturing you with a handle-bar mustache."

This elicited a tight little smile. "Please don't make light of this, Alice."

Seeing how fragile she looked, I saw how hard it was for Sara to have this conversation and how nervous she was about my reaction.

"Don't worry, Sara. It is fine with me. To put all that behind us."

Actually, it was a relief.

— EIGHT ~

I MUST POINT OUT, IN MY DEFENSE, THAT OVER THE YEARS MY
mind did its best to suppress my body, with its howling rages, sicken-
ing dreads, and ravening desires. It declared martial law and policed
the insanities arising from my thighs, my hands, the pit of my stomach.
It held me hostage at times with sudden, incomprehensible faints and
savage blasts of rage or terror.

"What does it feel like?" William asked.

"Like the feeling you have before you sneeze, only some kink in
your organization prevents you from sneezing and you are left with a
ghastly pressure in each and every cell of your body."

"Hmm," he said, after a pensive pause. "Like an unscratchable itch?"

"Yes, but worse." There was a volcano erupting inside me at times.
Everyone knew you could not control a volcano.

But there had been a time *before*; I was fairly certain of that. Hard
as I might try, this lost Eden gleamed and glittered just out of reach.
For all I knew, everyone was homesick for a native land that may never
have actually existed. But my friends were uncomprehending when I
alluded to this.

Only William seemed to recognize the thing I described. "I know
exactly what you mean, Alice. The lost paradise."

"So what *is* it exactly, William?"

"Father would say it is Divine Nature. Elusiveness seems to be its
essential characteristic."

Maybe this nameless homesickness was what drove William to
fanatically embrace philosophy and metaphysics, Harry to worship

at the shrine of art, Bob to drink immoderately and experience frequent religious conversions, and me to—well, what *did* I do? That
was the question.

In the spring of 1872 my family decided I would profit from a Grand
Tour of Europe with Harry and Aunt Kate. I was, at this time, considered delicate but *much* improved since my darkest days, and it
was hoped that the softer European air would complete my cure. We
crossed the Atlantic on a fast Cunard screw steamer, the *Algeria*. As the
ship skirted the shores of Fire Island and headed out into the Atlantic, I
felt something new, auspicious, and boundless well up inside me. I was
ready to take the plunge.

For the first month we "did" England. Devonshire, Exeter, the
ancient town of Chester. Visiting the Royal Leamington Spa, I felt no
shiver of foreboding, though perhaps I should have. After Oxford and
the Cotswolds and four perfect days in Lytton, we pushed on toward
London, stopping in Wells and Salisbury, "doing" Salisbury Cathedral
and Stonehenge. At Wilton House, I spent a memorable forty-eight
hours in communion with that glorious object, the Van Dyck portrait
of the Pembroke family. I can't tell you what a relief it was to discover
that I was not numb to great art, as I'd feared (based on my tepid reaction to the Norton pictures and aesthetic commentary). I may have
been ignorant, but a picture *did* speak to me, after all.

While Aunt Kate went off to gather parasols, shawls, guidebooks,
and digestive biscuits, I scanned her half-completed letter to 20 Quincy
Street. (Yes, I was in the habit of reading any letter left lying around. In
my defense I cite the lifelong necessity of compensating for being the
youngest and most ignorant member of the family, as well as the fact
that the others did it, too.)

An account of Harry's virtues consumed two paragraphs:

If you were to see him invariably folding in the most precise manner the
shawls and rugs which are brought in from our drives and smoothing
them down in some quiet corner, with the parasols and umbrellas—

and more along those lines. Of me (like most people, I was principally interested in reading about that most fascinating of beings, myself) Aunt Kate observed,

She takes it all very calmly and is never at any time unduly excited, which of course enables her to bear her pleasures in a more lastingly beneficial way.

My absence of excitement—emulating the patient barnacle—was my cardinal virtue now.

In London we stayed at the Charing Cross Hotel, and the noise, filthy air, and teeming multitudes were oppressive. Could there really be so many poor, everyone filthy and ragged like people out of Dickens? As far as I could tell, their greatest, perhaps their sole, amusement was to watch the rich in their finery dismount from their carriages outside the grand houses. I soon wearied Aunt Kate and Harry with my diatribes, so after racing through the standard tourist sites, we made our way speedily to Paris, where letters from Quincy Street awaited us. In his letter to me, Father confided that as soon as I sailed, he settled into my empty room every afternoon to do his reading, feeling *alone with my darling, whom we love consumedly as usual and rejoice in every letter that comes as a love letter.* The letter went on in that vein, a love letter itself, for Father was incapable of expressing himself any other way.

To live in Paris had been Harry's goal since he was a boy of twelve. He'd arranged to stay on after Aunt Kate and I were to sail home in the autumn, and I wondered if he would ever come back. His hunger for the Parisian life was written all over his face, which sometimes wore an expression verging on the predatory.

Harry's first passion, in fact, was the French theater. During our childhood years in Paris he could often be found in a mild trance near a playbill stuck to a post. At the age of twelve, he was already an obsessed fan, conversant with the names of all the great actresses and the dramatic monologues for which they were famous. (William used to tease him about his *préciosité*, advising him to kick a ball around once in a while and get his clothes dirty. Harry smiled and paid no attention.)

For obvious reasons, Aunt Kate and I left the choice of plays to him, and we went twice to the Comédie Française, seeing a performance of Molière's *Mariage Forcé* one day and two days later, Alfred de Musset's *Il Ne Faut Jurer de Rien.*

Afterwards, we strolled along the rue de Richelieu at twilight, past jewelers, expensive restaurants, and chic cafés where people drank aperitifs at marble-topped tables and talked with their hands in the air. Harry was in a sublime mood, remarking that after Molière's tremendous farce, *Il Ne Faut Jurer* was "like a fine sherry after a long ale."

The subject of refreshments made me wonder if you could get absinthe in France nowadays. Aunt Kate was audibly searching her memory for the address of a jeweler on the rue de Richelieu where she'd purchased a brooch years ago. I linked arms with Harry, who was minutely analyzing the play we'd seen. Did we notice how, in the drawing-room scene, the eccentric baroness sits with her tapestry, making distracted small talk with the *abbé* as she counts her stitches? While on the other side of the room her daughter, in white muslin and blue ribbons, is taking a dancing lesson from a dancing teacher in a red wig and tights.

"Yes, what about it, Harry?" Aunt Kate said.

"Well, what an art to preserve the tone of accidental conversation! That is quite foreign to British invention."

"I thought the girl's dancing was rather good," said Aunt Kate.

But Harry had not finished. Did we catch how, in a later scene, "the young girl, listening in the park to the passionate whisperings of the hero, drops her arms half awkwardly to her sides in fascinated self-surrender. That gesture spoke volumes. Unhappily for us as actors, we are not a gesticulating people."

The phrase "fascinated self-surrender" set off something inside me. I asked Harry whom did he mean exactly when he said 'we'?

"I mean the Anglo-Saxon race in general."

He had a point. The vibrant and animated French did make Anglo-Saxons seem dull and wooden. Maybe we needed to drink stronger coffee. Or absinthe. Furthermore, it was clear that females of the Anglo-Saxon race did not have the first notion of how to tie a scarf, drape a shawl, dress a bonnet, or affix an orchid to one's bosom or one's hat.

"If you gesticulate too much in real life," Aunt Kate joked, "you run the risk of knocking the glasses off a waiter's tray."

Harry had contracted to write a series of travel essays for the *Nation* aimed at the new market of Americans on the Grand Tour. We were running into hordes of them at every tourist attraction, clutching their Baedeckers or their Thomas Cooks, their American voices, loud, nasal, and flat, floating through the air. (Like the rest of my family, especially William, I was very sensitive to voices and easily irked by bad-voiced people, though I knew they probably could not help it.) Harry frequently solicited my opinions of and reactions to various sights, and I felt flattered until I began to suspect that I was his ideal reader in the sense that I embodied the eager but uninformed American Abroad.

"Harry, when you write your pieces for the *Nation* do you practice on me?"

"What do you mean?"

"I mean, plumb the depths of my ignorance so you know what to tell your readers?"

Harry just laughed. Aunt Kate said, "Don't be absurd, dear."

We were staying at the Hotel Rastadt off the rue de la Paix, and in the second week we took the horse-omnibus to the Louvre every day. Harry remarked that the last time he'd visited the Louvre it was with Charles Norton "and it was heavy work, as he takes art too seriously."

"Well, you needn't worry about us, Harry. We are barbarians."

"Speak for yourself, Alice," Aunt Kate said, laughing.

We agreed to take the museum in sections every morning for at least a week, no more than two hours at a time. Harry believed that two hours was the limit for appreciating art; after that you could absorb no more. One day we admired the Venetians, then it was ancient Greek and Hellenistic amphoras, then a room full of Watteaus. Day by day, we became intimate with Dutch and Flemish interiors, English landscapes, the painters of the court of Louis XIV, mannerists, portraitists, still lifes, Napoleonic battle scenes, madonnas thin and dour, rosy and smiling, stiff, animated, maternal, virginal; whole rooms devoted to classical or neo-classical Dianas, Floras, and Neptunes. What a treat to be in a country that *had* art museums.

Lacking Harry's specialized aesthetic vocabulary, I was unable to articulate my experience of the sublime, but I felt it in every pore. Some pictures affected me corporeally, like a beautiful *crise de nerfs*. Others made me feel that I was opening my eyes on my first day on earth. Contemplating the scenes of ordinary Flemish and Dutch people, captured in the act of drinking, smoking or playing cards, I felt as if I were seeing them through the eyes of God, and was moved to tears.

"What is wrong, dear?" asked Aunt Kate, who always seemed to be right on my heels. "Are you feeling ill?"

"No, Aunt Kate, a gnat flew into my eye. I believe I've removed it with my handkerchief."

"Well, don't overdo, my girl. Be sure to say when you've had enough of museums."

Sometimes I'd hover near the copyists at their easels. Most were women, many quite young. Harry said they were low on the social ladder, barely middle class, and most likely did not have enough of a *dot* to marry. Marriage in France had nothing to do with love; it was a financial arrangement between families, he said. (Harry had mysterious ways of picking up this sort of information from the air.)

"And then you commit adultery as often as possible!" I said.

Harry was taking copious notes in his black notebook every day. Respectful of his genius, Aunt Kate took care not to disturb him, and whenever she had a yen to talk sidled over to me. "I've never really understood Titian," she'd say. Or, "I've seen quite enough crucifixions for today; how about you?" If only Aunt Kate would vanish for an hour or two, so I could be alone with my God. Not the church God to whom people directed their tiresome, self-centered prayers. My God (and I use the term loosely) was speaking to me through beauty, revealing every inch of His creation. He dwelled in the secret heart of things, I saw clearly now, but I wouldn't try to explain this to anyone else.

One day in the Louvre I caught a glimpse of a band of schoolgirls, lined up in pairs, each pair holding hands. They were being herded briskly through the halls by two elderly sisters in butterfly wimples, past pagan nudes and debauches toward pietàs, crucifixions, and annunciations. The girls wore identical frocks and pinafores and appeared well-behaved, modest, and obedient, except for a pair near the rear. One of the girls leaned into her partner to whisper into her ear, eliciting a saucy smile. That smile! It flickered for an instant and was gone, mysterious and fleeting. You could almost feel the girl's hot breath on your ear.

Leaving the Louvre, we tried to stroll through the Tuileries, but stroll was the wrong word, for the fresh wounds of the Franco-Prussian war here were shocking to behold. The Palace was a blackened shell and in the ruined gardens starved crones sat on cracked stone benches mumbling to pigeons and sometimes competing with them for crusts of bread. Not far away were the *hôtels particuliers*, with their private inner courts, the carriages of the rich with their coats of arms, beautifully dressed women with costly jewelry hanging from their alabaster necks.

Thanks to Baron Haussmann's tear-downs, wide modern boulevards led in the most rational fashion from civic monument to civic monument. Under the surface, though, I could feel the pulse of the old Paris, the Paris of our childhood, quainter, darker, hidden, with crooked buildings and twisting cobbled streets. It tugged at me like a tide. What had been left behind back there, at the age of seven or eight or nine, that felt so precious?

Eight different governesses came and went during our family's time abroad, between 1855 and 1860, and heaven only knows how many tutors. The reason they stayed for such short intervals and left suddenly, sometimes in tears, had something to do with Father, which remained mysterious.

"He has such soaring hopes," Mother confided to Aunt Kate, "but he always ends up disillusioned. He tells the tutors he does not want the boys 'oppressed' by too systematic instruction and then he finds fault with the lack of system. And it is for the boys' education principally that we came to Europe."

Was that true? Being quiet and easily overlooked, I had an unfortunate tendency to overhear mystifying adult conversations. I *thought* we were in Europe because it had Art and History and Cathedrals and Concierges and Soldiers, et cetera, and so that Father could meet European men of letters and discuss his Ideas. There seemed to be so much I didn't know.

In those days Father's Ideas seemed no more or less true than fairy tales about wicked queens, trolls, and fairy spells. In the little amateur theatricals William wrote for us to perform there was often a bearded figure, limping about, speaking glorious religious gibberish, and Father would laugh louder than anyone. (He was prone to laughing or weeping immoderately—like a great river that periodically overflowed its banks.)

For all I knew, all fathers limped on one leg, thought the world was a dream, wrote books that no one read, gave lectures no one understood, and traveled to Europe with their entire library packed into trunks. (Father's books were the first thing unpacked whenever we arrived anywhere.)

It was years before I found out that no other family was like ours.

The old Paris was partially eclipsed now by Baron Haussmann's modern Paris. Smart restaurants hid behind vaulted Pompeiian-style colonnades or surprised you with a stained-glass cupola over the dining room. You might also come across a procession of new communicants in white dresses, like barley-sugar angels with expressive little faces, walking into a cathedral that had been in use for almost a thousand years.

There was no denying it: Paris was worldliness, layer upon layer of it. The priests looked like old *roués*, the mother superiors like mandarins. The full moon, the color of old gold, seemed to say, "I've seen it all." Why had Father brought us here as children if he so despised "the world." Did he fail to see the worldliness, or did he secretly embrace it? And was the world really the opposite of the divine, or were they two faces of a single mystery?

My mind fell into silence, but it was not empty.

My "improvement" was duly noted in Harry's weekly letter home, which I read over his shoulder in a bistro. This assessment, half obscured by his forearm, was accurate as far as it went. Something that had long been dormant inside me *was* coming to life. What it was exactly I could not say.

While Harry left to spend a day wandering about some artistic quarters that interested him, Aunt Kate and I plunged into one of the *grands magasins*—the modern "shopping paradises for women," as the newspapers called them. In a happy daze I tried on gloves, hats, scarves, shawls, and jewelry, and the looking glasses, flatteringly lit, seemed to reveal a more glamorous potential me. "We may have to buy another trunk for our loot," said Aunt Kate, as transfixed as I by the fashion utopia around us. Its *luxe et volupté*, if not the *calme*, was so far beyond what Boston or even New York offered it might have been an absinthe vision.

It should be noted that Aunt Kate's medications alone took up a sizable portion of a trunk. On the marble-topped dresser in our shared hotel room I'd taken an inventory. Paregoric, Tincture of Arnica, Pepsin tablets, Dr. Baker's Blood Builder, The Famous Swiss Sleeping Draught, a hot water bottle. To this cache would be added her new purchases: fig laxative, *Eau de la Jeunesse* complexion cream, French Arsenic Complexion Wafers, Dr. Pasteur's Microbe Destroyer, and a "ladies syringe" that I suspected was for Female Problems.

Every day it was becoming harder for me to tolerate Aunt Kate, whose voice and predictable comments grated on my ears. She was clearly incapable of understanding the miracle that was unfolding within me, the way Paris was inundating my senses and healing my brokenness. She also had a baleful genius for landing by instinct on the very subject I most wished to avoid. In the hansom on the way back from one of the shopping paradises, she badgered me for twenty minutes with questions about Sara. "Have you heard from Sara lately, dear? I imagine Charles is grateful for her help with the children." I did not want to think about Sara just now. Her sister Susan had died in childbirth several months ago, and Sara and Theodora were swept up in the care of their six motherless nieces and nephews. There were ominous signs that Charles was becoming swept up in Sara, as well, a situation too heart-sickening to contemplate and one I definitely wished to avoid with my aunt, who was like a dog with a bone when she got the scent of something.

"I'm sure she is terribly busy, Aunt Kate."

To be honest, it was a challenge to share Aunt Kate's room and be privy to her thoughts, her ointments, her snores, not to mention the actual air she breathed (for when you share a room with a person, are you not breathing in the air she has just breathed out, which has been in her *lungs*?). At night I'd fling open every window, inadvertently beckoning a cloud of moths to come in and immolate themselves in our candles. Fortunately, Aunt Kate dropped off quickly, and I would go sit with Harry on his balcony in the warm, dense, humming night, with the gas-lamps strung like pearls along the avenues.

"Are you going to scribble your travel notes tonight, Harry?" I asked him in our third week.

"No, I may go out later, walk around a bit." He shifted uncomfortably in his chair.

"Where?"

"I-I haven't decided yet."

We sat in silence, listening to the French voices floating on the soft air.

"Do you remember that grand *hôtel particulier* we lived in, with the enormous chandeliers and lots of gilt and ormolu—the one that overlooked the Champs-Élysées? You boys had your lessons inside the parapets, and I envied you. Or did I just dream that?"

"No. That was the era of Monsieur Claudel, the tutor who had written an essay that was mentioned favorably by Sainte-Beuve."

"Mentioned favorably by Sainte-Beuve! Well, that might explain how you got so literary, Harry. I remember sitting on the balcony watching ladies having fittings in a dressmaking establishment across the street. And in another window I saw young ballerinas practicing *pliés*. I thought they were princesses, like the ones in my storybooks. I was heartbroken when Mother told me I could not become a ballerina. She did not say why. Oh, Harry, remember Mademoiselle Danse?"

"*There* was a woman with a history, as they say."

"I remember when she told me of Madame de Staël, who wrote *Considérations sur la Révolution Française*, the most important book of the century on the subject. Madame de Staël stood up to Napoleon, she said, and was exiled to St. Petersburg. I'd never *dreamed* my sex could do anything important enough to be remembered after death. It made a rather strong impression."

I saw Harry smile fondly at the memory of the most sophisticated and Parisian of our governesses. He and William often came along on our babyish outings to the Punch and Judy shows when Mademoiselle Danse was in charge.

"Take me with you, Harry," I blurted now. "Please! I want to see Paris at midnight."

Although this was clearly not what he had in mind, I saw him struggle to be reasonable. "Father gave me particular instructions to take good care of you. I wouldn't want to expose you to anything—"

"Oh, for heaven's sake, Harry! I didn't come to Europe to avoid *seeing* things! I am over twenty-one, and Father has no right to hand me over to you like a set of crockery."

Harry turned quiet, apparently chewing this over. You could never accuse him of being insufficiently thoughtful. I pushed my advantage, steepling my hands and making a funny beseeching face. "*Please*, Harry. It's my only chance; don't you see? Anyhow, didn't Mademoiselle Danse explain *everything* to us when we were young?"

"That she did," he chuckled. "I remember her saying that Victor Hugo was man, woman, poet, the king, the people. He was *everything*; he had *seen* all, *done* all, *felt* all. And Robbie asked, 'Is he the same as God, then?' To which Mademoiselle said, 'My dear boy, God is not a member of the Académie Française!'"

Something I'd forgotten came back to me then. Mademoiselle Danse taking me aside one day after our lessons to say, "You are a very clever girl, Alice. Cleverer than your brothers." (She meant Wilky and Robbie, who were in the schoolroom with me, while William and Harry were under the tutelage of M. Claudel.) "Unfortunately, because you are a *jeune fille*, your mind will be considered secondary to your manners and your bonnets. I will tell your parents that you deserve to be rigorously educated, but I can't guarantee they will listen." Although I was flattered, I rather dreaded this "rigorous" education, which, in any case, never came to pass.

"If you *don't* take me out, Harry, I shall be obliged to go on my own, disguised in one of your best London suits— *à la* George Sand. That is something you ought to try to prevent."

A long pause. "All right, Alice. Where would you like to go?"

"Well, I'd like to see Paris spread out at my feet in a blaze of light. Where is the highest point in the city?"

"That would be Montmartre, but I don't—"

"Yes! Take me there!"

At this outburst, Harry retreated into one of his long, pregnant silences. Then he said, "We may run into—improprieties."

"Oh Harry, do you have any idea how a woman yearns to see an impropriety? Why do you think George Sand wandered about the city at night in trousers? She wanted to see things *as they are!*"

"How I'd love to meet that woman!" (Five years later he would.) Perhaps George Sand's name—or the memory of Mademoiselle Danse—worked on his mind like an incantation, reminding him that writers, regardless of gender, needed to see something of the world, because he somewhat reluctantly agreed to be my guide.

The night was misty, the cobblestones slick; the air smelled of the river. We hailed a cab on the corner of the rue de la Paix, and eventually found ourselves ascending the slopes of Montmartre. When we reached the place where the road ended, Harry asked the driver to wait, and he and I stepped down into a dark lane smelling of earth and manure and recent rain. From the highest point we could reach, we gazed out upon a sea of mist in which rows of gaslights gleamed murkily.

When we returned to where we'd left the cab, it was gone. We had no choice but to walk downhill, a situation that pleased me and made Henry palpably nervous.

"I can't believe he abandoned us, Harry, after subjecting us to the whole story of his mother's rheumatism. I suppose the poor woman *has* been a martyr to it, but still."

"Give us an arm, Alice. It's steep." It was; I had to grip his arm, teetering in my silly shoes. "Can you manage?"

"It's these *shoes*, Harry. The heels are specially designed to catch in every crack. Yet another plot to hobble our sex."

While I was transported by Montmartre's exoticism, it did not escape my notice that Harry was uneasy, striding fast as I struggled to keep up. We passed an ivy-covered cottage with a thatched roof. Several largish farm animals could be heard shuffling about in the dark yard. Perhaps to calm his nerves, my brother assumed the role of tour guide. "Until last year, this was still the countryside. Since *l'année terrible* Montmartre and Belleville have been absorbed within the city limits, but, as you see, it is still quite rural."

It was. We passed a stable on the left and then the slope began to level off. The mist was growing denser, but there were lights ahead. Passing a brasserie whose patrons were obviously drunk and riotous, we kept going, past a cistern and a small orchard. A white cat regarded us regally from the top of a wall. Another brasserie appeared.

My shoes pinched more and more painfully and I tugged on Harry's sleeve, pleading piteously, "Could we *please* stop here and have something to drink?" His pause was full of reluctance. I couldn't believe he was being so stodgy and unadventurous. Why was he set against this neighborhood, which, though admittedly poor, was lovely in its way?

Years later I would realize that the surviving *Communards* had taken refuge in these alleys only months before our visit, with guns and cannons, and the streets had run with blood. Harry was no doubt recalling this, and had not failed to notice that the brasserie I was pointing to, with its discreet exterior, low ceilings and red interior walls, looked like a *brasserie de femmes*, where men came in search of prostitutes. He would have been poised to leave quickly if this turned out to be the case. But I was ignorant of *brasseries de femmes* and the reddish glow made me think of firelight on the walls of a cave.

When we walked in, a few people were sitting at a zinc-topped bar, others at tables, drinking or playing cards, or talking softly, or kissing. (In Boston no one ever kissed—*really* kissed—in public.) Everyone's faces were murkily reflected in the mirrored walls. A violin was playing a beautiful and melancholy tune, which Harry identified as Brahms's *Hungarian Dance*.

A maître d' in a swallowtail dinner jacket strode briskly toward us, unsmiling, and said abruptly, "*Oui*, m'dame, m'sieur?"

At that moment we both absorbed the fact that "he" was a woman, with her hair cropped short like a man's. She did not carry menus, look around for a table to lead us to, or behave in any welcoming way.

"Perhaps you are at the wrong address, m'sieur? You are no doubt seeking another establishment?" With her hands on her hips, she aimed an arctic stare at Harry, who began to stammer. I think he'd just noticed that the couple dancing not far from us was a pair of women, both wearing bonnets. I had seen this already, and, I will confess, my heart soared. This was how the world should be, everybody leading the life they wanted and chose. How normal the women looked, like women you might run across shopping on Tremont Street. The one whose face I could see wore a dreamy expression, as the violin pursued its haunting melody.

The café was an island of women! Apart from Harry, not a single male in the establishment, unless the violinists were. (It was hard to tell.) We had stumbled onto a passage to a secret demimonde, which had always existed perhaps in the underbelly of Paris. An old memory surfaced of Mademoiselle Danse pointing out places where "men went with men" and "women went with women." Perhaps Mademoiselle herself had loved women. Was that why she was dismissed? With Father, there could be any number of reasons.

Harry's manner had turned stiff and cold and he told the maître d' (or maîtresse d'?) in impeccable French that we had indeed made a mistake and would be leaving at once.

Out on the street, he said, "I think we'd best find a cab quickly and return to the hotel." He seemed so edgy I didn't dare oppose him, although I should have liked to wander about some more.

An elegant young man in gloves of puce passed us, then turned around and walked backwards, favoring Harry with a long, smoldering glance, which he studiously ignored.

"This is a strange *quartier,* isn't it, Harry? Like walking into someone else's dream."

He did not reply. A nearly opaque white mist hovered near the ground now, slurring the edges of things. Walking through it was like walking through a cloud—moist, briny, vaporous. At one point my body seemed to dissolve into mist, too, and this sense of being bodiless was as beautiful as casting off heavy armor. The real life inside me was calling to me in the song of my blood; I had only to let go of something. What was it?

Glancing over at Harry, I saw his mouth set in a grim line. How nervous he was. What a fate to be responsible for me. What a fate to *be* someone like me for whom others felt responsible. Difficult to say which was worse. While Harry cast about for a carriage, I kept my eyes open wide, drinking in every detail as if it had to last me for the rest of my life.

"If we can only find a cab now."

"Relax, Harry. My virtue has not been sullied. I'm having the most delightful adventure. It is so seldom that a girl has a proper adventure." My words helped not at all. Harry was looking about in mounting desperation for a hansom. A few minutes later, a pair of men, one with implausibly yellow hair and a jaunty carved walking stick, descended from a cab, and walked off down the street, their arms twined around each other's waists, murmuring *doucement*. Harry quickly took possession of their cab.

On the way back he didn't speak of the café nor did I. It was an untouchable topic; there were no words to broach it. As the city slid past, the streetlamps haloed in mist, I imagined that the women I'd seen dancing were wives and mothers during the day, supervising the lessons of their children, ordering viands, giving teas. Married off at the age of fifteen or sixteen to unsuitable men, their only solace was the one evening each month they met at the brasserie. They would give themselves up passionately to each other, for it would have to last through the next thirty days and nights.

Or they were copyists, spending their days copying Van Dyck or Rubens in the Louvre, each secretly working on a portrait of the other. After their deaths, the portraits would be unveiled and declared to be masterpieces, and both artists would be admitted to the Académie. But when I realized I could not name a single woman who had painted a masterpiece or been admitted to the Académie, my spirits sank a little. Why was it that women's lives were always secondary and somehow fruitless?

***

The thought of living in Paris was forming itself in my mind. I made fabulous plans. I would visit the Louvre often, perhaps learn to paint myself. I would attend the Comédie Française regularly and see all the great actresses in the classic roles of Racine, Corneille, and Molière. To be lifted out of sorrow into beauty! Through the incomprehensible workings of fate, I would live here and become a writer, writing under a *nom de plume* so as not to embarrass my family. But what would I write *about*? Everything that mattered could not be said. Well, I'd sort that out later.

Every night now I was having immense dreams, from which I woke with a sense of having travelled very far. It required no effort at all; it was all unfolding from the bliss of pure existence. Over the next few days, Harry, Aunt Kate, and I visited Notre Dame and Île de la Cité, the Palais Royal, the Bois de Boulogne, and the Luxembourg gardens. We took the train out to Chartres and to Versailles. One evening, as we sauntered along the boulevard after a late dinner, bolstered by a few glasses of champagne, I was singing softly to myself verses from the opera we'd seen earlier in the day. *Ô nuit enchanteresse, Ô souvenir charmant!* I sang to myself. *Doux rêve! folle ivresse! Divin ravissement!* Under the spell of this "divine ravishment" my aunt's disapproval glanced off me harmlessly as a dying fly. In Paris I was a free woman. Every cell in my body vibrated with possibility.

Passing an illuminated fountain, feeling the fine mist on my skin, I sat down on the ledge of the pool and removed my shoes and stockings. Then, without a sidelong glance at my aunt and brother, I waded into the water with its reflected lights. It was surprisingly easy to erase Harry and Aunt Kate from my mind. Standing near the spray, I adopted the poses of various statues and pictures we'd seen. Diana Surprised by Actaeon. Flora, Goddess of Flowers. Venus at her Bath. How effortless it was to be a goddess in a Parisian fountain.

French people smiled genially as they passed. "*Quelle belle statue,*" said a man with a spade-shaped beard, as Aunt Kate and Harry looked on in horror. (Yes, I glanced at them before turning quickly away.) In Paris I might live as I *was* instead of exhausting myself trying to be what I was not. I was done with all that. What Aunt Kate or Harry would do about it I didn't know; I cared only about being *real*. I stepped out of the water and sat on the edge of the pool, lifting my bare feet in the air and shaking the water off them. Then I pulled my stockings on over my damp feet.

The next morning at breakfast I appeared in a butter-colored sunfrock announcing that it was too hot to wear a corset and I was sick to death of feeling my sweat collect about my middle. Aunt Kate cast a dark look in my direction. "My dear girl! You can't go out like that!"

"Why not? It is just—natural, Aunt Kate."

"You don't have to see yourself but *we* have to look at you." She was aiming for a jocular tone but no one was fooled. I dug in my heels.

"Are you saying you can't bear the sight of me as God made me? Do you really think the Creator intended women to be encased in steel?"

Harry looked on in astonishment as we bickered like jackdaws until I agreed, rather sullenly, to wear an Egyptian cotton shawl over my shoulders that day. At intervals during the day I remarked on how marvelous it felt to breathe and move without whalebone; I felt like the wind.

The next morning after breakfast, Aunt Kate went round the corner to buy a newspaper, and Harry seized the moment to speak to me about my "manners" toward our aunt.

"She suffers, Alice, when you treat her so high-handedly. She is completely devoted to your happiness on this trip."

"I'm not *trying* to be rude, Harry. I am simply trying to carve out a little space for myself. When she talks all the time, I can't hear myself think. I can't explain it properly. . . . When she breaks into my thoughts, I might as well be on Boylston Street." I felt near tears; I saw that even Harry didn't really understand my feelings. No one did.

Harry asked me to try a little harder, and I said I would, though the truth was I was sick and tired of being good.

⟨ornament⟩

Henry James, Jr.
Hotel Rastadt. Rue Nue. St. Augustin, Paris
June 10th

To Mr. and Mrs. Henry James, Sr.
Alice is like a person coming at last into the possession of the faculty of pleasure and movement. In Paris she is a rejuvenated creature, display-ing more gaiety, more elasticity, more genuine youthful animal spirits than I have ever seen in her. She and AK find plenty of occupation with milliners and dressmakers. I think she will find that her mind is richly stocked in delightful memories.

⟨ornament⟩

Mrs. Henry James
20 Quincy Street
Cambridge
June 17th

To Alice James
My daughter a child of France! What has become of that high moral nature on which I have always based such hopes for you in this world and the next? That you should so soon have succumbed to this assault upon your senses, so easily have been carried captive by the mere delights of eating and drinking and seeing and dressing I should not have believed and indeed I see it all now, to be merely the effect of a little cerebral derangement produced by the supernatural effort you made in crossing the Channel.

HENRY JAMES, SR.
CAMBRIDGE, MASS.
JUNE 23, 1872

TO ALICE JAMES
I have lain awake most of the night thinking of my darling daughter so far away in body, so near in soul because so full of Divine desire, et cetera. Harry's letter frightens me by an account of what he calls your 'exploits.' Please remember, my darling, to slow down and take things in a leisurely way. I console myself by remembering that you have always had such power to control imprudence, et cetera, and I count on that now.

～ NINE ～

THE DAY AFTER I ABANDONED MY CORSET, THE BOOTTS ARRIVED from Bellosguardo. They'd been anxious to escape the heat of Tuscany, little suspecting that Paris was baking under its own heat wave. Francis Boott, who prided himself on his impeccable taste in all things, suggested we all dine at Le Grand Véfour, on the rue Saint-Honoré.

"It will be too rich for our blood," Aunt Kate grumbled as she fastened her heavy jade earrings to her sagging earlobes. "We shall have to economize in Switzerland and Italy." Harry gave one of his Gallic shrugs, as if to say, The Bootts are the Bootts; *que voulez-vous*? I, submerged in my Parisian dream, made polite noises in the general direction of my aunt without actually listening to her.

Catching sight of the Bootts sitting forlornly at their table, I was struck by how alone in the world the pair was, how hard they had to struggle to amuse themselves. I had never seen this so clearly before. Francis Boott, though intelligent and often charming, was a difficult man—vain, moody, prone to sulks and injured feelings. He would undoubtedly have preferred a son, but when his wife died, leaving him with an infant daughter, he vowed to make her the intellectual equal of anyone. Lizzy was his revenge on the world, which failed to appreciate his talent as a composer (he'd set Longfellow's verses to music) or his opinions as an art critic. Independently wealthy, he moved from Boston to Europe, rented a wing of a castle in Bellosguardo, and arranged for a rigorous education by private tutors. Lizzy was the result, her father's masterpiece. She knew four or five languages and most of the arts and sciences, painted with a high degree of mastery, and played the piano beautifully. In addition, she was lovely to look at.

Le Grand Véfour looked expensive. I noticed Aunt Kate's eyes narrow to slits at the sight of the pink satin banquettes and the naked *putti* scooting across the cerulean sky of the rococo ceiling. It was like being inside a jewelry box.

After a flurry of kissing, hugging, and exclamations about the heat, we took our seats and pondered the wine list. When the talk turned to Switzerland, I begged the Bootts to consider joining our party. I was thinking how nice it would be to have a friend my age to lighten the burden of Aunt Kate—and even, I had to admit, of dear over-cautious Harry. Lizzy and her father brightened at the prospect. Francis Boott, predictably, knew all the best Swiss hotels.

The next morning, over *cafés crèmes* and croissants, Aunt Kate informed me that she and Harry had decided, in view of the heat wave and the discomforts of Paris, to travel to Switzerland earlier than planned and seek out the alpine air. We would rent a carriage at the end of the week. I could not but hear this as a great betrayal. Not to be consulted, to be treated like a child! Only by mentally counting the crumbs on the tablecloth and pricking the meaty part of my palm with my fork did I avoid exploding. All I managed to blurt out was, "But I'm just beginning to feel at home here!"

"We've had a bounteous helping of Paris, dear. We've done the *grands magasins,* had our hair dressed in the finest salons, been to the theatre, seen all the museums"—and she went on in this vein, itemizing every place we'd been—"and won't it be a relief to escape the heat and the rude concierges! And *you,* dear, haven't been sleeping!"

True enough, but I didn't *need* much sleep. I was living on beauty now. With my brain and body perfectly synchronized, life had no hard edges; it did not wear me down. I was beginning to glimpse the person I *could* be. But my aunt could not understand this; even Harry did not. Their minds were fixed on Switzerland.

Perhaps the sudden change in plans had something to do with recent letters from Quincy Street. After the gravity of my breakdowns, I expected my parents to be pleased by any sign of gaiety in me, but, instead, they were alarmed. Father advised me soberly to control my imprudence. After my thrilled accounts of Paris fashions and cuisine, my mother wrote me a letter that began, in shock, "My daughter a child of France!" I visualized their phrases engraved on my tombstone.

Alice James 1848–??
Captive of the Mere Delights of
Eating, Drinking, Seeing, and Dressing

From over the ocean, they were putting out long tentacles and gathering me in, infecting me with their anxieties, and I was powerless to defend myself. Was it because they had known me since birth and could easily reduce me to infancy in their minds? As the old self-doubt pressed down upon my spirit, I felt my thoughts take on the coloration of 20 Quincy Street again. I began to obsessively question the hairdo I'd acquired at a celebrated Parisian salon. What if I was wrong? Wrong about everything?

I resigned myself to Switzerland.

The next day, Harry received a *petit bleu* from Clover and Henry Adams. "We are sick of smoldering ruins and insubstantial Frenchmen and *hungering* for the sight of a few solid Bostonians," Clover wrote. Having married a few months earlier, she and Henry were on a year-long wedding journey. And thus, on the eve of our departure for Switzerland, we had a Boston evening with the Bootts and Adamses at a restaurant on the rue Vivienne, which Henry Adams recommended for the perfection of its *foie gras* and black truffles. Aunt Kate scowled about the prices, whispering dramatically to me that this was what happened when you dined with people in a different income bracket.

Clover and Henry were already there when we arrived, waving to us from what was obviously one of the best tables. They'd just spent two months in England, where the Adams connections were potent, Henry's father having been ambassador to Britain during the Civil War years. More recently, they'd "done" Germany. As his eyes swept down the wine list, Henry Adams, scion of two American Presidents, announced, "We have seen many Sleeping Beauty castles, lost twelve thalers at whist, and visited the cathedral at Cologne, which Clover thought ugly."

"It was, Henry! I much preferred that old church where eleven thousand virgins were killed, and their bones stuck all over the walls. Their skulls decorated every nook and cranny." She turned to Mr. Boott and me. "Only the Germans would commit such an atrocity. Look at what the Prussians have done here!"

"What hotel was this?" said Aunt Kate, who had a habit of not paying attention to what someone was saying until a word caught her interest, whereupon she would pounce on it with vigor.

"A church in Germany, Aunt Kate," Harry whispered.

A sallow pockmarked waiter took our orders, bowing obsequiously and complimenting us on our fluent French, which he seemed to find extraordinary in people of our national origin.

"We are in the most appalling hotel," Henry Adams said, as the wine was poured. "Our room was bombed by the Commune and still bears the scars. The chambermaid told Clover, 'They wanted to kill us and Madame knows that is not agreeable.'"

"And the Tuileries palace is a burnt-out shell, just like the Hotel de Ville," Clover added. "And now the French have to *pay* the Prussians for wrecking their capital."

"We have been hearing the most ghastly stories of what people ate during the siege," Aunt Kate said.

"Yes," I said, warming to the topic, "after they ran out of horses, a man told us, the restaurants served a rat paté that was surprisingly tasty. Another delicacy was *épagniel*—spaniel. After that it was tigers and zebras from the zoological gardens. Hardly a creature in Paris left untasted, apparently."

"Please, dear, we are about to dine," Aunt Kate said. "And surely that can't be true about the zoo animals."

I raised my eyes heavenward. I was tired of being corrected continually. Cutlery clattered near the door to the kitchen; voices were raised. A waiter darted to our table with our soups on a tray.

I looked across the table at Clover, whose wit and charm made you forget she was not especially pretty. In the blink of an eye she'd become a new creature, Mrs. Henry Adams, with stationery and call-ing cards printed in that name, her old identity as Miss Marion Hooper extinguished. The birth of the Wife was the death of the Maiden, I thought. I recalled an evening years back when Harry returned from the Nortons' looking transported. He'd been sitting out on the piazza with a party that included Clover Hooper, about whom he exulted, "She is Voltaire in petticoats!"

William said, "Why are you telling *me*, Harry? *I* discovered Clover Hooper."

William and Harry were always "discovering" women—as if they had not existed before!

Compared with the Adamses' year-long wedding journey, which would include the Nile, my little expedition, with Aunt Kate in charge and calling the shots, seemed tame and predictable. My mind simply could not encompass a year-long honeymoon—a whole *year* with a man you'd known previously only at dinner parties on Marlborough Street suddenly stuck to you like a burr day and night!

Clover was saying, "Have you noticed that the cab drivers are all from the country and don't know their way around? We had one the other day who couldn't find the place. I said to him, 'I advise you to study a map of Paris; you'll find it interesting.' Do you know what he said? 'Madame, one cannot know everything.' How sad and bedimmed Paris seems after its defeat. And yet Mr. Worth does a brisk business."

Fashionable gowns by the great couturier Worth adorned the *crème de la crème* of womanhood not just in Europe but in Boston and other major American cities. I wondered if I could carry off a Worth gown or if I would come out resembling an upholstered sofa.

"Is it true that Mr. Worth makes you wait for hours?" Lizzy asked. "They say that even princesses have to wait for the great man."

"Oh, Mr. Worth!" Clover waved a hand dismissively. "He is just a little English haberdasher, originally. He took me immediately and I have as much style as the concierge at our hotel. He fusses over Americans just to rub the duchesses the wrong way. You ought to have a costume made just to experience his atelier."

I chuckled at the thought.

"Really! He has about a hundred beautiful *modistes*, whom he holds under some sort of fairy spell, and he snaps his fingers, causing fabrics of all sorts to materialize. He folds and wraps things around you. It is very like an opium dream by De Quincy."

Then, with her disarming manner of absorbed attention, she leaned in toward me. "Alice, I am *famished* for Boston news! My father writes to me, but being a man he leaves out the most interesting things. I know nothing gets past you. How are the dear *Nortons*? Has Charles expurgated anyone lately?"

She smiled slyly. Charles Norton was celebrated for authoring the Lives and Letters of great literary figures, who could die assured that not a single note of questionable taste—or hint of life—would survive the process. Clover was quite familiar with my views on "Nortonism."

"Well, Charlemagne has been distinguishing himself lately by telling people that Venice in its glory was the highest form of civilization conceivable to the human mind. He went on to say it was such a pity that men at the present time should not wear swords and go about keeping them bright! Imagine Don Carlos himself with a sword!"

Clover laughed gaily. Then, apparently recalling the recent death of young Mrs. Norton, she gathered her features into a sober mien. "How will poor old Charles raise all those children on his own? Aren't there an awful lot of them?"

"Six, counting the one that killed its mother. Everyone seems to think they'll be raised by their aunts, with the assistance of nursemaids and governesses. Charles won't have much to do with 'em before the age of twelve, I shouldn't think."

"Just so you know, Alice—" Clover flashed me a conspiratorial smile—"I'm submitting to Worth's *only* because I have been bullied into it. My mother-in-law doesn't care for the way I dress."

It dawned on me that the incomparable Clover might actually care what I thought of her, which surprised me very much.

Her husband said, "No, dear, what she doesn't like is that you don't waltz."

"I told her it was not in my line! Alice, I wish you could have seen how she *glowered* at me in London!"

Both Clover and Henry apparently found this memory amusing. Plates were cleared, other plates arrived. Clover confided, "I just bought a sad painting resembling Boston Common on a dreary November afternoon, with a row of leafless trees. The artist lost his mind and is now in a *maison de santé* in Bonn. He must have painted this while he was breaking down."

Henry Adams mentioned that he intended to take photographs—his new hobby—when they sailed up the Nile, and hoped his equipment would hold up to the heat. "By the way, Clover and I dined the other night with Mr. Emerson, who had just been up the Nile with Ellen. He apparently found the journey a 'perpetual humiliation.' Wasn't that what he said, dear?"

"I believe he said the antiquities mocked him."

"That's right! 'The people despise us,' he said, 'because we are helpless babes who cannot speak or understand a word they say.' He went on to say that the obelisks, temples, and sphinxes 'defy us with their histories which we cannot spell.' Or something of the sort. It was a very odd reaction."

"It made you shiver, rather," Clover said.

"He had no interest whatsoever in the antiquities," Henry said. "How true it is that the mind sees only what it has the means of seeing."

After a silence, Clover burst out suddenly, "Traveling would be quite perfect if only one could go *home* at night!" She looked forlorn for a moment, and I guessed she was homesick. Maybe that was why she'd been drawn to the melancholy painting that reminded her of Boston. Then we all parted, promising to meet again in Italy—but this would not happen because the Adamses would be laid low with the Roman Fever by the time we got there.

In the hansom Harry said, "Egypt had best look out. The Adamses drive a hard bargain. They will come back to America with a boatload of priceless antiquities, you can depend on it."

⸺ TEN ⸺

THE FOLLOWING DAY, A SWELTERING TUESDAY, HARRY, AUNT Kate, and I piled into a hired coach and headed for the Swiss border. "I am praying for a mere *soupçon* of a breeze," Aunt Kate said, fanning her flushed face. "So far the air is entirely hot and stagnant."

"All the more reason to eschew a corset, Aunt Kate."

"Gracious, Alice, what is this mania about corsets? I wouldn't *dream* of going without one."

"It's up to you. If you die of heatstroke we can bury you in it."

"Alice!" But she allowed herself a small smile.

"They seem extremely fond of each other, don't they?" Harry offered. "The Adamses. When I first heard of their engagement I worried that Clover's gaiety might be extinguished by the Adams gloom."

"It is not hard to see how Monsieur Adams might extinguish someone," I said.

"Oh, Henry is all right. It's just the Adams manner. They put such stock in affecting not to care about anything."

"Of *course* Clover will be happy. Her sister is *very* happy," Aunt Kate tilted her heat-flushed face in Harry's direction. "Everyone says Ellen and Whitman Gurney are the happiest couple in Cambridge. When they are obliged to be apart even for an afternoon they act as if they'd lost each other forever."

"Perhaps there is such a thing as being too happy," Harry said.

"How absurd, Harry! How can anyone be *too* happy?" said Aunt Kate, fanning her face with a copy of *Le Figaro* while expelling air through pursed lips. She looked near collapse. "I keep sticking my head out hoping for a breeze. So *unseasonable*. You'd think we were in Naples. Next thing you know, we'll run into malaria or typhoid."

"Well, if we succumb, at least we will have done Paris," I said. Aunt Kate laughed, not realizing that I was perfectly serious.

Crossing the border at Saint-Gingolph, near one end of Lake Geneva, we made our way toward Geneva, and with every mile I felt paradise recede and the heaviness of existence press down on me again. Why? We were in a picturesque country, about to pay a sentimental visit to a city we'd lived in as children, in the house belonging to the Russian invalid with the mushroom hat. Perhaps it was just a passing irritation due to the heat and dust; once we reached the hotel, I would probably revive.

Geneva was pleasant enough. We paid a visit to our old house and to the boarding school Harry had attended with William and Wilky. He confessed that he'd been miserable at the school, which was all science, dead creatures, rocks, phials of smelly chemicals. And mathematics too! While William adored it, Harry yearned desperately for the *longueurs* of home. He said he preferred the summer he had malaria.

By now Aunt Kate's voice and incessant platitudes were grating on my nerves, and I failed to be as moved by the scenery as I'd hoped. After ten days of visiting picturesque towns, we moved on to Villeneuve, where the Bootts had planned to rendezvous with us. Their absence was another disappointment. The heat remained oppressive, and after a few days, we made our way to Bern and Interlaken and then settled in Grindelwald, a quaint alpine town 3,400 feet in elevation, at a resort favored by English mountain climbers.

"Just smell this air, Alice," Aunt Kate said. "Crystalline! The best air on earth for invalids! That is why there are so many resorts for consumptives here. It should do you a world of good, my pet."

"I am not consumptive *yet*, Aunt Kate."

"Of course not, but the climate is excellent for nerves, too."

Nerves, nerves, nerves—that wearisome topic. Why did God give people nerves if they were going to cause so much trouble? So far the famous Swiss charm was quite lost on me.

Five days later, the Bootts arrived, preceded by a flurry of telegrams. Lizzy and I fell into each other's arms. We had both sorely missed the company of friends our age, and had topics to discuss and things to laugh about. But the euphoria was short-lived. Traveling with the Bootts, I learned to my dismay, was like walking down a beautiful boulevard with a pebble in your shoe. You could go nowhere without being lectured by Mr. Boott about Palladian columns or the pre-Raphaelites, with the impeccably educated Lizzy chiming in and making you (well, me) feel like a crude lump.

I'd briefly considered asking Mr. Boott for advice on how I might live in Paris, but I saw now that he'd inevitably say something to Harry or Aunt Kate, who would then explain to me why I could not live abroad, why it would be selfish of me to want to, and where did I think the money was going to come from? I had an unfortunate habit of harboring secret wishes, one of which, right then, was to set up housekeeping with Harry in a Paris flat after Aunt Kate sailed home. This was not utterly insane; brother–sister households were not uncommon. But my thoughts had plunged back to earth since leaving Paris, and I could not ignore the sense that Harry, loving brother though he was, had no great desire to be burdened with a "delicate" sister. Indeed, I suspected he was fleeing to Paris in part to *escape* family. If he heard about my silly flat-sharing fantasy and recoiled, it would break my heart.

Our hotel was awash in mountaineering Englishmen and their hearty families. In the dining room and common rooms, English people would wait for the Jameses and Bootts to start the conversation. Harry said their reticence was a form of politeness; they were counting on others to make overtures, not wanting to presume. Aunt Kate, however, could not be diverted from her entrenched theory that an American should *never* open a conversation with an English person, as that left the American vulnerable to being snubbed. Thus several meals passed in near silence, with Aunt Kate studiously pretending the English were invisible.

Harry appeared to be studying Lizzy closely, as if she were an Old Master. Perhaps he meant to put her in a story. Maybe he was falling in love with her. He began to speak of Lizzy in her learned aspect as

"produced," by which he meant brought to a level beyond "finished."
Her manner as well as her intellect were "produced," he observed; she
was precisely what a young woman ought to be according to European
standards, a *jeune fille bien elevée*, learned and accomplished yet modest, sweet, and possessed of that indefinable quality of "repose" that
American women so conspicuously lacked (according to Harry). She
never put herself forward, and performed only when her father gently
pulled the strings.

On our second day, we lunched together at the hotel restaurant
alongside rosy English climbing families. The Bootts were immersed in
three weeks' worth of mail, and didn't say much, Aunt Kate seemed to
be gearing up to discuss a book review in *La Revue des Deux Mondes*.
Harry had just slit open an envelope from William, from Mount Desert
Island. Too antsy to wait for him to read the whole letter in his slow and
thoughtful way, I tugged at his sleeve and said, "C'mon, Harry. You
can't hog it all to yourself. What does he say?"

"Well, he is taking many sea baths. Kicking over the traces of civilization. Wishes he might never return to the 'aetiolated life' of Boston."

"No surprise there. What else?"

"He takes me sternly to task for using too many foreign phrases in
my *Nation* letters; says I must be more plainspoken if I am not to alien-
ate Americans. By which, he seems to mean commercial travelers on
trains—there is quite a long digression about them. Oh, and he detects
'something cold, thin-blooded & priggish' in my stories."

I laughed, as did Harry.

"Oh, but how unkind," Lizzy said, looking concerned and laying a
sympathetic hand on Harry's arm.

"Oh no, not at all!" Harry explained. "In our family we have a long
tradition of abusive literary criticism—don't we, Alice? William's violent denigrations of my work are often quite useful."

Lizzy seemed mystified. She didn't have siblings; what did
she know?

When she went off to paint a view that afternoon, Harry tagged
along, carrying her easel as if he were her squire. And the next day,
and the one after that. Every morning they would politely invite me to

accompany them, and I'd say, "No, thank you; think I'll rest today." As far as I was concerned, once you've seen one glacier you've seen them all, and the sight of an alpine meadow abloom with wildflowers did not set my heart afire, either. And I certainly lacked the energy to compete with Lizzy's erudition.

Maybe there *was* something wrong with me. Recent letters from Quincy Street dwelled obsessively on the dire possibility that our party would descend into Italy before the heat was over and "compromise Alice's strength." I reverted to practicing my principal hobbies, resting and saving my strength, and everyone seemed to approve.

Staying behind at the hotel, however, left me within range of Aunt Kate, who seemed liable to unburden herself at any moment. I'd noted with creeping horror that she was flaunting her new costumes from the Paris shopping paradises, which were too dressy for the Alps. She was also spending an undue amount of time in front of looking glasses, pinning on brooches, studying earrings, experimenting with crimps in her hair. I recognized these as ominous signs that she'd taken a fancy to Francis Boott. There was a doomed romance if there ever was one!

Didn't she know that Francis Boott did not traffic in the tender affections? I eluded her by insisting that my sick headaches required complete solitude, and there was some truth to this. From time to time I felt as if all the oxygen had been sucked from the air.

To William, I wrote a letter with my latest impressions of Frankie (as we referred to Mr. Boott in our family):

> *He keeps one in a continued state of irritation either of pleasure of or displeasure, you hardly know which. Then he'll be so nice and handsome and honest that you can't but forgive him all his absurdities— until he provokes you again. On the whole, he is the most delightful but uncomfortable infant of sixty conceivable.*

This was true. He would throw a tantrum like an infant of six; the provocation could be as slight as an inadequate wine list or a chateau of which some feature spoiled the period detail. He would go into a sulk, at times even seemed on the verge of tears.

"What do you and Lizzy talk about?" I asked Harry one evening.

"Oh, you know—art and the landscape and whatnot. She is exceedingly well-informed on things Italian."

"Does she actually know *everything*?"

"I have yet to find a subject of which she is ignorant."

It struck me one day that none of us really wanted to be here. Harry preferred cities, as did Aunt Kate. Mr. Boott spent most of his time talking about things in Venice and Rome and paid scant attention to nature, and a gouty toe kept him from walking much. Who knew what Lizzy wanted? Her painting, of a high alpine meadow with a craggy peak in the background, developed day by day, and was technically excellent but somehow did not move the heart (in my humble opinion).

We had come to the Alps primarily for my sake, after my "slight overexcitement" in Paris. But I soon exhausted the views and identified all the wildflowers in the inn's botany book and was reduced to reading *Daniel Deronda* and *The Eustace Diamonds* in my room or on the terrace while trying to avoid a heart-to-heart with Aunt Kate. (While I was not unsympathetic to unrequited love, the nakedness of her feelings alarmed me.) My thoughts were slipping into monotonous grooves, and an unpleasant episode with the snakes in my stomach kept me on edge most of the night. My aunt remarked at breakfast that I was looking "peaky" and urged me to avail myself of lots of cream.

It was all too plain that Aunt Kate's campaign for Mr. Boott's heart was stalled. It would be hard to say whether he even noticed the changes in her toilette, the addition of a glittering hair ornament, the fake roses in her cheeks. One morning, whilst slipping past the Bootts, who were in the library, I overheard Mr. Boott say to Lizzy, "If we linger much longer, I fear things may become rather awkward."

Not long afterward, the Bootts made their farewell and went off toward some *Schloss*, I forget which. Fortunately, even when brutally thwarted, Aunt Kate was rarely found in the depths of gloom for long: her affective life was pitched more toward the moderate range than the hysterical, and she succeeded in righting her ship and was herself again by the time we took the Gotthard railway to Italy.

Surveying the peaks as they slipped past, Harry remarked, "There are limits to the satisfaction you can get from staring at a mountain which you have neither ascended nor are likely to ascend." I wondered if we would read this *aperçu* in the *Nation* soon. Did your own words surprise you when you saw them in print?

My family had been praising my letters to the skies, assuring me they'd been read aloud at several gatherings and passed along to "the boys." Brother Bob wrote that "Alice is turning out to be the genius of the family," and William compared me not unfavorably to Madame de Sévigné. While my parents urged me to be prudent and rein in my impulses, William's letters counseled me to "let your mind go to sleep and lead a mere life of the senses." Aunt Kate advised me to consume more milk and red meat. I was the sort of girl other people were always trying to fix.

But if I'd been Madame de Sévigné reincarnated, I would still have to sail home in October, while Harry remained in Paris.

It took half an hour for our train to pass through the modern wonder that was the Mt. Cenis tunnel and soon we were whizzing past a sign that read COL DU MONT CENIS, 2083 M. and on into Italy.

We chatted about the Bootts: Lizzy's painting, Mr. Boott's music, Lizzy's peerless education. "It goes to show what a European education can accomplish in a girl," Aunt Kate said. "Such an education would be impossible in America."

"That's quite true," Harry said.

"How good is her painting?" I asked him.

"Very proficient. Considerable mastery. But, in the end, feminine painting is only an accomplishment."

"*Always*, Harry? Invariably?" This irritated me, although it was a relief that he didn't consider Lizzy a great artist.

"Well, how many great female artists can you name?"

The answer was zero.

We went silent, watching the snow-capped peaks slip by. I asked, "Harry, does Lizzy ever strike you as a little—hmm—lifeless?"

"What *can* you mean, Alice?" said Aunt Kate. "She is a lovely girl in every respect. And such a nice, neat figure, too."

Harry became thoughtful, staring out at the blue enamel sky and the boulder-strewn moraines. A landscape for giants, inhuman in scale. At length, he said, "You're right, Alice. There is a deadly languor about Lizzy at times, as if under all her accomplishments there is no one there."

"Well, think about it, Harry. All her life she has tried to be what her father wants and thus has no idea who she is."

"Poor dear girl, growing up without a mother. But daughters generally adore their fathers, don't they?"

"Yes, Aunt Kate. Remember Iphigenia. She went willingly, I suppose."

"Was she the one who killed her father?"

"No, her father killed *her* to appease the god of winds. Her brother later killed the mother, after the mother killed the father for killing Iphigenia. It was a very high-strung family."

"Oh, dear child, you need another shawl—you're shivering. Find the heavy tartan one if you can, Harry."

Then we passed into Italy, to drink in antiquity, olive groves, the Duomo, the Medicis and the Sforzas, Roman aqueducts, the canals of Venice, Tintoretto et al, all the popes and heretics and saints and martyrs, the Sistine Chapel, the Colosseum and its blood-soaked stones. In Venice a plague of mosquitoes disturbed our sleep. In Torcello we ate innumerable figs and had ices every night. As we sat eating grapes on a bench in the gardens of the Villa Borghese, I said, "The chief difference between Europe and America seems to be that people here sit on benches all day staring at you as if you were a picture." The next day Harry wrote in his journal:

> The great difference between public places in America and Europe is in the number of unoccupied people of every age and condition sitting about on benches and staring at you, from your hat to your boots, as you pass. Europe is certainly the continent of the practised stare.

He had, as usual, expressed it so much better than I.

Why was I unable to absorb Italy deeply, as I had Paris? Owing to some defect in my nature, my life had a peculiar tendency to burst into bloom briefly, only to turn flat, stale, and unprofitable a short while later.

To make a long story short, our sailing date came, and Harry accompanied us all the way to Liverpool and showed us into our stateroom (which I hoped would not soon be adorned with our vomit). I made a mental list of things I would have to do without: Gothic stained glass, gardens with ingenious topiary, old masters, chic cafés, centuries of history, art museums, copyists, chateaux, ancient gargoyles, brasseries catering to women who loved women, *les grands magasins*. Until the whistle blew, I harbored the absurd hope that Harry would ask me to stay on in Paris with him. I had pictured it so vividly, down to the faces of the gargoyles on the building I'd selected as our future address. But Harry said good-bye, and Aunt Kate and I sailed toward America.

Back home, I tried to prolong the aftertaste of Europe by having a French breakfast of chocolate and a roll, but by late November I told Mother that it no longer agreed with me. One day Mother and I were on Newbury Street doing the marketing and stopped to look at the bonnets displayed in a milliner's window, none of which looked remotely fashionable to a person recently returned from Paris. Dead leaves scuttled along the sides of the road; most people wore sour expressions.

On the horse-cars back to Cambridge I looked across the frozen river at the backs of the brownstones of Beacon Street. Gelid laundry hung stiffly on a line, a pair of crows pecked at something down by the riverbank. No wonder Harry didn't want to come home. In his letters he complained of the early nightfall and claimed to be nostalgic for Quincy Street, but he was probably just trying to spare our feelings.

As our eyes fastened on the frozen mudflats of Charlestown, Mother asked if I knew how bereft Father had been while I was abroad. "With tears in his eyes he would say, How I wish Alice were here to read the *Advertiser* aloud to me, to cheer us up with her jokes." She had not wanted to worry me while I was abroad, but Father's health *did* suffer during my absence. He came down with a bad grippe, which triggered a painful eruption of his eczema, and other things along those lines. She honestly did not see how I could go abroad again in Father's lifetime.

A lump formed in my throat. "But, Mother, Harry is abroad. William spent almost two years in Germany. The boys are in Wisconsin. Why is Father not bereft without them?"

"Young men must make their way in the world, dear. A daughter is a special comfort." Although her tone was matter-of-fact, her eyes were sorrowful. Perhaps she did understand how I felt and was sorry, but not enough to commute my sentence. I saw that I would never "make my way in the world," and any gifts I possessed would wither inside me.

"I have never understood why you children are so enamored of the French," Mother added, warming to one of her favorite themes. "So many are indecent, their houses are freezing in winter, their servants are dirty, their writers write filth, the tradesmen cheat you at every turn. I always say, I don't know what God will *do* about the French on Judgment Day."

"Fortunately, Mother, it won't be up to you."

Was it possible for a person to be born in the wrong country, like a cuckoo's egg slipped into a warbler's nest? As winter ground down on us in earnest, life in Boston became emptier. One night I overheard Mother say to Father, "I do worry that after such overstimulation, it may not be possible to reduce her to the ordinary domestic scene." But I *must* be reduced to it; I should not be indulged in too much frivolity, which in the long run could spoil my character.

Alice is busy trying to idle, Mother wrote to Harry, *and it is always very hard depressing work, but I think it will tell in the end.*

Paris seemed by then infinitely distant. If Harry did not send us letters bearing that postmark, I might have thought I'd dreamed it.

One morning I found myself in the library with Father, who was fond of saying he liked to "have a daughter by my side to help me with my rhetoric." A fire roared in the grate. I was reading *A Slight Misunderstanding* by Mérimée when suddenly something came roaring out of some circle of hell and enveloped me in a fever, a rage. My book slid to the floor, and I glanced over at Father dipping his pen in the inkwell, writing his next unreadable book. How rosy and innocent he appeared. Without warning I felt my hands curling into talons to rake the side of his face. I saw it in my mind as if it had already happened: the parallel gashes in his cheek, the scarlet drops on the carpet, Father's shock and sorrow, my remorse.

But *why*, when his fatherly feelings were so pronounced he would weep at the sight of his children's dear faces? (As William was fond of saying, the philoprogenitive faculty was exceptionally well developed in him.) I was a monster. I sat on my hands, trembling and grinding my molars until the impulse subsided. To steady my mind, I dug my fingernails into my palm and recited the planets in the solar system, the names of the seven seas, the Seven Wonders of the World, until the pressure eased.

Naturally my family had no idea of the storms raging inside me and I was in no hurry to tell them.

WILLIAM JAMES
THE VILLA ONOFRE, ROME
OCTOBER 3RD 1873

TO ALICE JAMES
Thou seemest to me so beautiful from here, so intelligent, so affectionate, so in all respects the thing that a brother should most desire that I don't see how when I get home I can do any thing else than sit with my arm round thy waist appealing to thee for confirmation of everything I say, for approbation of everything I do, and admiration for everything I am, and never, never for a moment being disappointed.

ELEVEN

1874

"I REALLY THINK YOUR BROTHER MAKES HIMSELF ILL BY THINK-ing about himself so much," Mother was saying as we prepared the front parlor for my Bee. We'd polished the silver candelabra, folded the linen napkins, removed crumbs from the carpet and straightened the portrait of Grandmother Walsh (garbed, thanks to the painter's artifice, in a style I liked to call *"Après Moi, le Déluge"*). Mother meant William, of course. Whenever Harry mentioned any trace of ill health in his letters from Europe, she worried and sent him pages of sympathy and suggestions about rest and good climates.

"But William is much *improved*, Mother. He says he has trained his eyes to read for a certain number of hours a day."

"I suppose," she said dubiously. She paused to count out the dessert plates. "But *why* must he express every fluctuation of feeling and every unfavorable symptom? Never thinking of the effect on those around him!"

For the second year, William was teaching Comparative Anatomy at Harvard, where he was a rising star. There was little trace of the gaunt and tormented young man who had gone to the Somerville asylum four years before, although, being William, he still claimed to suffer from periodic waves of insomnia, skin erup-tions, mood-swings, melancholy, overwhelming fatigue, and a host of other symptoms that he was prone to over-analyze and treat with dubious folk remedies. He was always recommending his "tinctures" to everyone and, as far as I could tell, none of them ever worked. Certainly not on me. But wasn't this William's way of trying to make sense of things? While Mother complained about his morbidness privately, I noticed she passed up no opportunity to boast about his Harvard appointment to our friends.

She was saying now, "Do you think we ought to use the big or the medium-sized damask, dear?"

I shrugged, not caring enough to have an opinion.

While we were unfolding the tablecloth, footsteps shook the porch and the door flew open. Dropping his leather case on the floor, William flopped down heavily on the horsehair sofa, propping his boots on the armrest. "My students are infants!" he groaned. "How about a nice, cool lemonade, Alice?"

"I'm very much occupied at the moment, William, as you can plainly see."

"For heaven's sake, Will, get those muddy boots off the sofa," said Mother.

"My boys need an immense amount of looking after. You can't imagine. Today they were supposed to be dissecting pigeons to study the muscles—"

"I thought you cut up frogs."

"Oh, we cut up fish, *fleisch*, fowl, whatever you like. Anyhow, one young man had scraped the breastbone clean and said he found no muscles. I asked what that heap of stuff was which he had removed. He said it was 'meat' which he had taken off to get at the muscles!"

"The Bee is arriving in fifteen minutes, William," Mother said. "We don't have time to dilly-dally and discuss pigeons."

"Oh, the *Bee*! Then I am right on time." He extracted his watch from his vest pocket and sat up eagerly. "I always love seeing all the girls. And, by the way, Mother, there is not a trace of mud on my boots. A leaf or two, perhaps." Propping one foot on his knee, he dug out two frayed brown leaves that were stuck to the sole and placed them on an end table. Mother grimaced.

"You are not *at all* welcome at the Bee, William," I told him, with my hands on my hips for emphasis. "Pray find some way to distract yourself."

"How cold and cruel you are, Alice. At least let me eavesdrop. You don't know how I dream of penetrating the ultimate mystery—what women talk about when no men are present."

"We talk only about men. How could we possibly have other interests?"

Mother called from the dining room. "Alice, do you want to use Grandma Walsh's tea set or the Wedgwood?"

"Whatever you think, Mother."

"Is that true?" said William.

"What?"

"*Do* the girls talk about men? Do they—perchance—mention *me*? Will the beautiful Levering sisters be present this afternoon?"

"When I am permitted to attend Harvard and take your Comparative Whatever course, you can spy on my Bee. As long as we women remain in bondage, the answer is no."

"Bondage!" Mother scoffed. "Who has been filling your mind with this stuff and nonsense, Alice?"

"Comparative *Anatomy and Physiology*, Alice. That is the title of my course. It grieves me that my only sister should forget. It shows how little you care. And you didn't answer my question about the Levering girls."

"They don't belong to our Bee, and they are said to be quite stupid."

"Very beautiful, however."

"*Please*, William, go upstairs before the girls come! If they see you, there will be a logjam at the front door and we'll never get started." People hung around William like bees around clover. He didn't need to learn mesmerism to entrance people, but he learned it anyway.

Nine girls arrived in quick succession. There would have been eleven if Nanny Ashburner were not in England and Susy Dixwell had not been laid low with a grippe. Marny Storer arrived with Lizzy Sparks, Carrie Thayer a few minutes later, breathless and red-faced, followed by Sara and Fanny. The married Bees included Mabel Lowell, Fanny Dixwell Holmes, Ellen Gurney, and Clover Adams, but Mabel and Fanny were absent today. Of the new members, Lillian Horsfeld was quite nice once you recovered from the orgy of hugging and gushing she put you through. I was still making up my mind about Julia Marcou.

Marny Storer was in an expansive mood, possibly due to recent developments in her "secret" romance with Roger Warner, which everyone knew about and which was being conducted in the Bostonian manner, over tomes of constitutional law. She asked what everyone thought of Mr. Eliot's engagement. I said, "Well, I think it throws an eerie light on the nature of men and their capacity to renew their existence."

"What do you mean, Alice?" asked Ellen Gurney, smiling. She was the former Ellen Hooper, sister of Clover, and within our Bee was the authority on matters relating to President Eliot, as her husband was Dean of Harvard and the president's right-hand man. They were on a crusade to modernize and expand Harvard with a modern curriculum and graduate schools modeled on Germany's. Most of the Overseers dragged their feet and opposed every change.

"Surely he has greatly lost in dignity by it," I explained, apropos of Mr. Eliot's love life. "Not that he shouldn't marry again, poor man, if he wants to, but that he should have fallen in love again *so completely* and chosen someone so unsuitable. He is as much excited and transported as if he were a man of twenty, my father says."

"It only shows that he is truly in love, Alice," said Carrie Thayer, who seemed to derive her opinions from women's magazines. "Old people can fall in love, too."

Mother came in and poured, as was customary. Everyone praised the pineapple upside-down cake, then returned to knitting, crocheting, needlework, and gossip. Marny Storer mentioned that one of the Lowell women had suffered a breakdown and was said to be resting in Somerville. To which Clover Adams said, "Believe me, if you've seen Somerville, rest is the last word that applies." Clover and Ellen (as well as their brother Ned) were presumed to have considerable expertise about insanity in general and the Somerville asylum in particular, as their father, Dr. Hooper, volunteered his services there. As children they had played croquet on the lawn with some of the milder lunatics and had amusing stories. (That their aunt, Susan Sturgis Bigelow, suffered a breakdown and killed herself went unmentioned, although everyone in Boston knew about it.)

"Of course," Clover said, between sips of tea, "the insane asylum is the goal of every good and conscientious Bostonian. Mrs. X has a baby. She becomes insane and goes to Somerville. Baby grows up and promptly retires there. The great circle of life!"

My wool was soft as a cloud and my needles clicked as I churned out squares of yellow and white in alternate rows of knit and purl. I was trying to form a mental picture of my newborn nephew as either a tiny replica of Wilky with some features of Carrie thrown in, or vice versa. It was provoking that Wilky's letters contained no specifics about what the infant looked like, which was what we most wanted to know.

I did not fail to note that over half the Bee were sewing things for their own hope chests, and no one said a thing, although our avowed purpose was to sew for the hospital and the poor down on the marsh. I should have seen it coming, I suppose: the way men would invade the world of women and ruin it. How they'd pick off the women one by one, like predators. It seemed to start with Mabel Lowell, who married a man no one had heard of and returned transformed into a dull matron. Did no one else perceive the deadly glaze that came over these new brides?

Why this mania for engagements? To be bound forever by the heaviest chains of matrimony to a stranger who might keep repeating the same jokes—or worse! Of course, I'd be the first to admit that my suitors were few and easily discouraged. "My only prey are widowers," I'd written to Nanny Ashburner last week. "I'd like to try my hand with bachelors first."

"Isn't it an unjust world?" I remarked to Lizzy Boott the day after the Bee. It was hot and muggy, and we were lying about like limp lettuce on the Bootts' verandah, gossiping and reading the *Revue des Deux Mondes* and the *Nation*. (The Bootts had moved back to Boston last year.) "The male sex gets to shop around for as long as they choose, and we have to take the first offer lest we wither on the vine!" Lizzy readily agreed and five minutes later was speculating tediously about the status of Freddy Mason's affections for her. Even worse, Freddy himself turned up, interrupting our conversation, and then had nothing to say—just sat there like a tidy parcel done up at Metcalf's.

Still, if asked how I was that summer, I would have had no hesitation in saying that I was very well, so well, in fact, that to be better would be superfluous. I'd taken several trips, to Quebec and Niagara with Aunt Kate, to New York by myself. The travel cheered me up immensely, and I vowed that in the future I would travel by myself a good deal, at least to New York. My parents and Aunt Kate were convinced that all my troubles lay behind me; in their letters to Harry and "the boys," they noted the vigor of my excursions and pronounced me "perfectly well."

William and I were the only "children" at 20 Quincy Street now. Bob and Wilky would go on living in the Midwest with their brides and babies for the foreseeable future. Harry was still abroad, having become enamored of Italy. His recent letters home told of riding horseback every morning through the *campagna* outside Rome, in the shadow of ancient aqueducts. Five women had invited themselves to ride with him, he reported. Mother wondered who these women were and if they were very forward. Father said, "Don't worry so much, dear. The Angel"—as Harry was known in our family due to his angelic disposition—"has a good, solid character and it sounds as if he's in good hands."

"That unhealthy climate, though!" Mother exclaimed over Sunday dinner, restlessly smoothing the tablecloth with her hand. "I don't know *why* Harry insists that Italy is the place where he feels most himself. Why can't he feel like himself in Boston?"

For Mother, reality was a canvas that could be reshaped almost indefinitely. Even the past could be altered, if necessary, through the force of her disapproval. William should *never* have gone to Germany. I should *not* have put my health in jeopardy by going ice skating when the temperature hovered around ten degrees. Bob and Wilky should *certainly not* have bought that derelict plantation in Florida and tried to farm it with a band of freed slaves. (Both "the boys" had been officers in the two Negro regiments from Massachusetts, and had the highest esteem for their soldiers. They'd tried to do something noble for the freedmen, but, having no head for business, had quickly gone bankrupt.) All of this should *never* have happened.

Father said now, "Harry must go *somewhere* for inspiration, dear! I don't see how he could have written 'The Madonna of the Future' in Boston."

"*Hmmf,*" she said.

Whenever Harry described a great pleasure in his letters, he would write, "Forgive me!" and reassure us that the outing he'd just described had palled in the end or that the American colony in Rome was "a very poor affair." I did not believe him.

"Harry has reached a fork in the road," William said, reaching for the water pitcher, "and must either return soon, or remain in Europe forever. I've told him he can't write about Europe for Europeans. Naturally, America will be hard for him at first."

"Why should it be hard for him? It's his *home,*" Mother said, looking tearful. No one took this up.

"Do you think Harry is very much changed?" I asked William.

"When I visited him last fall his Italian was very fluent. When speaking to Italians, he'd address them with arrogant manners and theatrical gestures. I asked him why his whole manner changed in Italian. He said, what did I mean?"

"If Boston people and Boston things are good enough for Mr. Howells, why shouldn't they be for Harry? You'd think he'd wish to be closer to the *Atlantic Monthly.*"

"Yes, Mother," I said, scrutinizing the advertisements in the *Transcript,* "and he could write novellas about the Famous Vegetable Cure for Female Weakness. They claim here it cures ALL female disorders including feelings of languor, sparkles before the eyes, a dragging sensation in the groin . . . "

"Really? Let me see that, Alice!" William rudely snatched the newspaper out of my hand and held it beyond my reach while he scanned it. "By George, you're right. Here it is, right next to a lady in a bustle. Languor, sparkles before the eyes; sounds like neurasthenia to me."

"I don't care for this new bustle style," said Father. "In our day women would never be mistaken for sofas. They dressed simply and elegantly; isn't that right, dear?"

Mother was tapping her water glass with her fingernail. When others strayed from the topic, she would become uneasy until she managed to steer the conversation back to, in this case, Harry's health and the Italian climate. "Remember, Will, when you and Harry were so ill with the Roman Fever? And so far from home! I don't understand why Harry has chosen to put his health in peril again."

Citing poor health, William had taken a leave of absence from teaching the previous autumn to join Harry in Rome for several months. Almost immediately, the two of them were stricken with the Roman Fever, and for weeks William was desperately homesick and, in that febrile, melancholy state, penned letters home bemoaning the shortcomings of Italian civilization. Whenever a letter arrived from abroad, Father would bring it to the next Shady Hill dinner party to read aloud, and one night he arrived with two letters. When he announced he had letters from William in Rome, all the Nortons from old Mrs. Norton down to young Sally brightened visibly.

Sara whispered into my ear, "For heaven's sake don't mention Italy to *Charles*. It's just like rolling a stone downhill." Her breath was warm, and our eyes met, just for a moment, and there it was again. Like striking a match.

"Wait and see, Sara. The Nortons are in for a shock."

I knew Father and I could see the fiendish glow behind his spectacles as, feigning innocence, he read that William felt his mind

being opened to the past like an unwilling oyster, and that with all this dead civilization crowding in upon my consciousness, I feel like one still obliged to eat more & more grapes and pears, and pineapples, when the state of the system imperiously demands a fat Irish stew.

On and on it went, his jeremiad against "moribund latinity." Italy, he lamented, couldn't *help injuring all one's active powers, for the weight of the past here is fatal.* Father's voice became especially sonorous when he read: *Even art comes before one here more as a problem. I think that that end is better served by the stray photographs which enter our homes.*

Charlemagne's countenance appeared to darken at this passage in particular.

"My goodness," old Mrs. Norton said later, as I was saying good-bye. "And Harry loving Italy so! How on earth do your two brothers get along there, dear?"

From Italy, in his wretched, homesick state, William had written me the tenderest, most fraternal letters, of which I could recall whole passages by heart. *Thou seemest to me so beautiful from here, so intelligent, etc.* But no sooner did he return home than he started scheming to get back to Europe. Wherever he was, it was his nature to long for where he was not. He wrote to Harry warning him that if he came home, he would have to "eat his bread in sorrow" for some time (I managed to sneak a look at the first paragraph when William left it on a table), which must mean that William felt that he was eating *his* bread in sorrow. If my brothers only knew what it was like to be a female, stuck in Cambridge in perpetuity, eating your bread in sorrow year after year, and no one wants to hear a peep out of *you*.

Now William was saying, "I recall Harry turning the most ghastly hue. Later I realized it was the exact color of many of the Roman buildings. Yellow ochre, I believe. Roman Fever, by the way, Mother, is only malaria by another name."

"Well, why not call it that?"

"How was Mrs. Sargent's 'aesthetic tea' yesterday, William?" Father asked. "What was aesthetic about it?"

"Oh, it meant that certain individuals read poetry while others sat and longed for them to stop so that they might start talking again. Afterwards I had a long and drastic dose of Miss Putnam, relieved, happily, by the incoming of Miss Bessie Green."

"Well, poetry might at least relieve the awkward silences that characterize so many Cambridge teas," I said while inwardly steaming over the mention of Bessie Green, a loud, silly, and man-crazed girl with whom I hoped William was not too smitten.

My own European tour was two years behind me and it was pathetic how often I consoled myself with the memories, like polished gemstones I took out to fondle secretly. When Harry's letters were read aloud, I burned with longing and envy and feared that my emotions must be visible to others. No one seemed to notice, however.

"I wish at *least* that Harry would go on to Switzerland or someplace like that," Mother was saying. "A cool, bracing climate, not a stagnant one, is what he requires now. Don't you think so, Will?"

"You could be right, Mother. The effect of climate on health has never been explained to my satisfaction."

I snatched the newspaper back from William and held it out of his reach while I flipped to the back pages and scanned them. "Oh, look! It's there again! An obviously fraudulent company is attempting to lure the maidens of Boston into purchasing and raising silkworms. Someone should expose them, don't you think so?" I passed it to William.

"And look what they're charging!"

"It would be a source of income for poor women, I suppose," Mother said, "and it would not take them out of the home."

"Mother, it is an obvious fraud. I feel moved to write a churlish letter to the editor."

"You won't sign your name, will you, pet?"

"I *shall* use my name, Father, and I shall say that I am the daughter of one Henry James and the sister of another, and better than both."

In early September, Mrs. Tappan gave a ball for her daughter Ellen and her fiancé, a Mr. Dixey, at her Beacon Street mansion, which had a real ballroom on the third floor. Young, unmarried women were obliged to go to these Back Bay balls, just as young men must go to war. That night I hovered near the punch bowl, trying to blend in so that it would not be too apparent I was a wallflower. The gown that had seemed so pretty at home was eclipsed now by dozens of creations in taffeta, velvet, and satin. My slippers rubbed painfully against my heels; I would have to put a poultice on them when I got home.

Meanwhile, I strove for a blithe and bubbly demeanor, which was what was generally prized in a young woman, as far I could tell. I would be the first to admit I lacked the talent and inclination for flirting, which seemed daft to me when I saw other girls doing it. Why did they make themselves seem so insipid? Something I read in *Godey's* came back to me: "How to Converse with Young Men." It advised one to talk about what the young man was interested in and "draw him out." Although I'd attempted this a few times, it always proved monotonous in the end. Why did most people have to be so *boring?*

While hugging the shores of the punch bowl at the Tappans', I subjected myself to a frank self-assessment. I was still young. My hair shone brightly after it was washed, my eyes were "intelligent" (or so I'd been told), my figure was not bad. My complexion was unblemished, if not "bright." That my gown was unbecoming was perhaps not fatal. I was considered witty. This, however, might not be an asset.

Sometimes a young man would appear to be walking toward me, and then do an about-face, as if suddenly recalling urgent business at the other end of the ballroom. "If you only smiled, dear, you'd be radiant." Mother's oft-repeated advice. Remembering it now, I fake-smiled, but I could not sustain it; the muscles in my cheeks ached and then twitched and, really, what was there to smile about?

"Hello, Miss James!" Oh, not Ned Codman! He'd caught my fake smile and apparently believed it was directed at him. Now he was stuck to me like a burr. On the other hand, he'd rescued me from being a wallflower, and one had to be slightly grateful for that. How abject was a woman's fate, when all was said and done!

"Hello," I said. "Are you still working at—at—?"

"Yes, I am, Miss James! National Union Bank," he said brightly. I could imagine no fate more deadly than working at a bank, but I kept this to myself. "Mrs. Tappan has pulled out all the stops tonight, hasn't she?"

Ned was a beanpole, tall and gawky, with jug-ears that stuck out. The light coming through them turned them a rosy pink; their translucency reminded me of something— tropical fish? His Adam's apple bobbed up and down when he talked.

On those rare occasions when I imagined having a suitor, it was never one of these gauche Boston boys (except for the beautiful Charley Jackson, whom I'd marry in an instant, but he was unlikely to ask me). Otherwise, my ideal lover was a mysterious stranger, perhaps someone from abroad, who could perceive the depths of my soul. If I wound up with Ned or someone like him, I'd spend the remainder of my natural life staring at his Adam's apple until I eventually went insane and attacked it with a fish knife.

"It does help that Mrs. Tappan is immensely rich," I observed. "The Sturgis treasure is well nigh inexhaustible, so they say."

Ned looked uneasy. You were not supposed to talk about money, although everyone in Boston was secretly preoccupied with it. Ned asked if he could fetch me a sandwich and I said, "Oh, yes, that would be nice," and he left and returned a short while later bearing a small, dry triangular sandwich. It did not go down easily. We were standing near the tall windows then and I discreetly set the sandwich remnants on the windowsill behind me as Ned ponderously considered the prospects of the Harvard crew that fall. Smiling my best fake smile, I mentally composed a paragraph to Nanny describing Ned Codman's ears and plodding conversation, Mrs. Tappan in her imperial aspect, Ellen Tappan gazing adoringly at her fiancé, the suave gold digger.

Behind me, I could hear Fanny Morse chatting with Charley Jackson, who was her cousin. Through Fanny, I *might* have an inside track with Charley, if only Fanny Appleton would leave the picture. Three-quarters of an hour ago, Charley and I had just begun talking when Richard Dana came along and held forth tediously on the subject of his sister's wedding, derailing our conversation. If only I could shake Ned off now and sidle over to Fanny, insert myself into the conversation, and work my charms (if I had any) on Charley. Although he was said to be secretly engaged to Miss Appleton, he always brightened when he saw me and laughed at my jokes, which lesser men failed to appreciate. There was room for hope. Faint hope but still.

At present, however, here was Mr. Codman and his Adam's apple. When he'd concluded his meandering tale, I asked, "Have you met the prospective bridegroom?"

"Oh yes. He seems a good fellow. I understand he is a keen sailor, which is always a plus, Miss James." He smiled, rather nervously.

"Really? He struck me as quite shallow. As the engagement is to be a long one, I hope he will not become weary of Ellen before the wedding."

"Oh!" Poor Ned looked stunned. His ears turned crimson. "Don't you think they are in love?"

Just then my mother, stiff and fortresslike in her gown, was giving me an encouraging smile from the matrons' chairs. Why? Oh yes, a boy was talking to me. I forced myself to focus on Ned and said, "If Ellen gets out from under her mother's tyranny she may come out all right, I suppose. But why is it that love affairs in real life appeal so much less to one's sympathy than they do in the silliest novel?"

I had to suppress a yawn; poor Ned was having a deadly soporific effect upon me. I thought yearningly of my bed and the novel I was reading, while he applied himself to consuming a piece of cake, his Adam's apple bobbing like mad. With his mouth half full, he said, "Well, I happen to think Boston engagements are a fine thing—and capital for the Race, too!"

"Oh, the *Race*," I said wearily.

Now Ned was visibly searching for an escape, and who could blame him? He finally found an exit line—he had to tell his cousin they should leave separately, or was it together?—and scurried across the room. I leaned back against the long windows, savoring the feel of the cool glass against my bare back, reminding myself that attending balls was like visiting the dentist. You just had to grit your teeth and get through it.

Regrettably, the beautiful Charley Jackson was now on the other side of the room talking to a young woman I didn't recognize. Lilla Cabot and Sargy Perry strolled past me, arm and arm, in the direction of the refreshment table, lost in their mutual self-regard. Their engagement was a joke; they had nothing to live on, Sargy was very immature, and Lilla was, well, Lilla. It was hard to forget overhearing her say, "Alice James is a hard woman to please. I pity the man who tries." While wondering gloomily why I was so misunderstood, I saw Sara waltz by in the arms of a dark-haired man I did not know. I studied her expression to see if she was falling in love. It would happen one day.

Dante could not have devised a more hellish torture than the "German" at the end of a Back Bay ball. With the inane repetitiveness of a children's game, a couple dances, then each seeks a new partner, presenting her/him with a favor (a nosegay, a hair ornament, a handkerchief), and those couples dance in turn and then seek other partners, bestowing more favors, and so on until everyone is waltzing. Until you have spent an eternity on a Louis Quinze tuffet, your gloved hands in your lap and a martyr's smile on your lips, whilst the chairs around you empty like trees in winter, you have no idea of humiliation. Fortunately, it ends eventually.

Two days later, on a warm September day, Sara, Fanny, and I were sunning ourselves on the steps of the Harvard greenhouse, leaning back like passengers on the deck of an ocean liner. Fanny was describing her visit to an immigrant family on the bad side of Beacon Hill; she'd found three small children prostrated by the heat; the youngest could not be revived. "You cannot convince them that fresh air is good for them."

Then Lizzy Boott came scampering across the lawn to meet us, as arranged, after her daily two-hour piano practice. Fanny had her impoverished families to occupy her, Sara had the Norton children, Lizzy her music and painting and languages. What did I have?

When the conversation turned to the ball, I observed a horrid metamorphosis taking place in my friends.

"Isn't Mr. Dixey awfully good looking?" Lizzy said.

Sara and Fanny agreed that he was and proceeded to minutely analyze Ellen's dress, the flowers in her hair, the ices, the flutes of champagne. Then they moved on to who danced with whom, who said what to whom, what the favors were in the German. What had *happened* to them that their minds could be captured by trivial things, like monkeys bewitched by shiny objects? The mention of the German made me grind my teeth. Why call it a German when it was a French invention? The French called it a Cotillion.

"I was very disappointed in Mr. Dixey's flimsiness," I remarked. "Isn't he simply the flimsiest of beings?"

"Why do you say that, Alice?" Fanny asked.

I attempted to explain what was plain as day to me. "It's perfectly obvious he's just a little society type. And that he should have preyed on Ellen Tappan, of all people!"

A secret glance passed between Sara and Fanny. It lasted less than a second but in that interval I registered the fact that my closest friends considered me queer in certain respects and no doubt discussed my queerness when I was absent. It struck a chill through my bones. I looked down at the daisy in my hand and saw that I had stripped it of its petals. I dropped it on the ground.

Why did the hand of fate weigh on me so heavily, while my friends were eager for what life would bring? I believed that love should shake a person to the depths of her being, like the people in the Bible who stood near Jesus and were changed in the twinkling of an eye. Most people, however, refused to rise above the ordinary. While hovering near the punch bowl, I'd had a chance to scrutinize the betrothed couple. Ellen looked flushed and happy, but that probably had more to do with the party, her gown, and being the center of attention. The rest of her life would inevitably be a letdown.

"By the way," I said, "I talked for far too long with Richard Dana. The personal appearance of the Dana family, even irradiated by the most intense joy, could never be called impressive, don't you agree?" My friends stared at me. I continued my little harangue. "Owing to Mr. Dana's gushing, I had only a word or two with the beautiful Charles Jackson." Lizzy and Fanny smiled tolerantly. Sara looked squirmy and irritable, probably due to the heat. "I am forced to admit that Miss Appleton is not bad looking," I added. "I had to refrain from looking in the glass for some time after I came home."

I expected *some* amusement from my friends. Fanny and Lizzy chuckled a little but Sara was still staring quizzically at me.

"Don't you see, Alice, that you frighten people?"

"How absurd, Sara. Who'd be afraid of me? Don't tell me *you* are."

Sara's hair was coming undone and she twisted the escaped strands into a knot and secured it again with combs and pins.

"I mean people who don't know you, Alice. Men principally. Some poor man offers to fetch you a Roman punch and you say something arch and obscure about elective affinities. Poor Frank Loring thought you were making fun of him!"

This was so unfair! Was it my fault if a person did not know his

Goethe? As the midday sun glared down from the zenith, the sweat stung my scalp under my plaited chignon. Why was Sara attacking me? Why were my friends drifting away? I searched my mind for some way to restore harmony.

"Oh! I must tell you all about the idiotic conversation I had with Jane Norton at the Godkins' the other night. She said she thought all the young women of Boston, instead of devoting ourselves to painting, clubs, societies and such, ought to stay at home in a constant state of matrimonial expectation. She implied that we are all so happy together that men say to themselves, 'Oh, they're so happy we won't marry them!'"

Lizzy and Fanny laughed. Lizzy said, "I can't help noticing that Miss Norton has avoided the wedded state herself. Maybe she attended too many painting classes."

"And then," I continued, "she went on a tirade against waterproofs, and her own gown as she was speaking was of so hideous a description that it cried out to be covered by a waterproof."

Sara's face had taken on a crumpled look I knew well, and when she spoke it was in her most strained, I-am-more-sensitive-than-you-can-possibly-imagine voice. "Alice, if you could only hear yourself. You are so *hard*." I recalled Father saying much the same thing to me once, urging communion with Divine Nature. But hard was the last thing I was. Sara, of all people, should know this.

Everything had changed since Susan died, leaving the six small Nortons. This situation brought Sara and Theodora into the daily orbit of the Nortons, including Charles. Soon there were ominous signs that he was wooing Sara—about which subject I'd wasted much ink speculating in letters to Nanny. At one point Sara fled to New York suddenly and mysteriously and stayed away several months.

"Most likely he has proposed and she has refused him," I wrote to Nanny during that period. "No one says so but I gather from something Theodora said that Sara plans to stay away until he gets over it." Ellen Gurney and I had discussed the situation at length. Ellen's view was that Sara was a rare, exquisite creature, much too good for Charles, but that he would wear her down with sheer persistence. I hoped she was wrong. I wrote to Sara during the time she was in New York, *If you don't come home soon I shall in desperation elope with the handsome butcher's boy,* but her letters were vague and evasive and said little about missing me.

When she returned to Cambridge, her lips were sealed on the subject of her brother-in-law. The danger had subsided, it seemed, and Charles was transferring his affections to Theodora. But a metamorphosis had taken place in Sara, which I did not understand. After her troubles, she assumed the air of a woman of experience and treated me as if I were a naïve girl. She declined to confide in me at all about her Norton problems, and this was unutterably painful to me.

Now she said, "If you only knew how Jane cares for those dear children—and Grace, too—you might have a little Christian charity, Alice, or at least refrain from mocking what you don't understand."

I stared off in the direction of the Charles River and its diamond sparkles. No one knew what to say.

"Just think!" I said after a long silence. "Mr. Dixey has leased Ellen for life! Isn't it awful, horrible, and incomprehensible?"

⁓ T W E L V E ⁓

1875

FOR OVER A MONTH MOTHER HAD BEEN PREDICTING THAT Harry would come home soon, and this time her maternal antennae did not fail her. In early October a steamer docked and out walked an older, confident, handsome, sun-bronzed Harry.

I was content just to gaze upon my second brother and take in his stories while Mother and Aunt Kate fluttered around, ordering the cook to make his favorite dishes, going through his clothes and sewing on buttons, asking concerned questions about his health and the quality of the air in his room. He was a stranger now—almost. Formerly shy and tongue-tied, he was displaying a new talent as a raconteur, his youthful stammer concealed behind thoughtful measured pauses. He was invited to no end of teas and dinners, at which people listened reverently to his tales of life at the Palazzo Barberini, where William Wetmore Storey, a sculptor from Boston, was installed, along with his wife and a band of bohemian artists. To hear Harry tell it, it was an Old World paradise of liveried servants, cavernous fifteenth-century halls, every alcove bristling with neoclassical Venuses and Pans.

"Is he still doing sibyls?" Clover Adams asked. "When we were there, there were sibyls on all sides. Sibyls sitting, sibyls standing, sibyls with legs crossed, with legs uncrossed. You've never seen so many sibyls in your life!" Harry admitted that there were probably more sibyls than the world required. Now that Europe had polished and finished him, the Adamses craved his society more than ever and persisted in trying to persuade him to "come home" for good. Father took Harry as his guest to the Saturday Club, and although he was polite, he did not seem genuinely enthusiastic about the Boston cognoscenti. Mother confided to me, "I trust he will feel more and more that it is much better to live near his family and with his own countrymen, than to lead the recluse life he led abroad."

Recluse life? Was she daft? What about the glamorous *palazzo*, the liveried servants, the expatriate artists, the beautiful and idle women who went riding with Harry in the Roman *campagna*? After a month and a half, you could see that Cambridge society was already wearing thin for him. Though he tried to mask his feelings, I noted a number of dismissive remarks about the "flimsiness" of American vegetation, the "aridity" of Yankee social life, and the strangeness of a country where men talked only of business and women ruled over the arts. And American hostesses had no respect for one's work, according to him. To be in Harry's company was to be made excruciatingly aware of everything America lacked: great art, an established leisure class, stately homes, proper piazzas with proper fountains, well-trained servants, literary salons, ladies with repose, civilized clubs for gentlemen.

At Shady Hill he was apt to fall into arcane Ruskinian discussions with the Nortons, peppered with words like *campanile* and *loggia*. One evening, I overheard him telling Grace that he felt it was his duty to "attempt to live at home before I grow older"—as if it were a penance. Later he murmured over his after-dinner brandy, "Europe is fading away into a pleasant dream. I mean to keep a firm grip on the Old World in some way or other." He now seemed more comfortable at Shady Hill than anywhere else.

He was becoming as mysterious as Father, who had the habit, shared by none of the other fathers we knew, of going off on mysterious trips and coming back a week or two later. William had inherited this proclivity for sudden impulsive journeys to change the weather in his head, and it occurred to me now that Harry resembled Father in the way he parceled himself out. Many people had a piece of him, I thought, but no one, including me, had the whole story.

"We are a disappointment to him, I think," I whispered to Sara one warm evening on the piazza at Shady Hill. "We don't even speak Italian." Sara had been making comic faces at me behind her hand every time the word *Ruskin* issued from Charles's mouth. He was in full didactic mode ("It is always to be remembered that . . . " "It will be found on observation that. . . ") and Father was looking quite dyspeptic. It was asserted by someone that Ruskin was the first to interpret the decline of art and taste as the sign of a general cultural crisis. Harry noted that people's ideas of sky were derived from pictures more than reality. Grace said that the relationship of art, morality, and social justice formed a "holy trinity." What on earth did she mean?

"Speaking of matters Italian, Alice," Sara whispered into my ear. Her breath smelled pleasantly of wine. "I *wish* you could have seen old Grace batting her eyes at the Italian professor the other night. Oh, the stories I could tell." Sara had by now passed out of the phase of being charitable about her out-laws.

"Please do describe *all* her dissolute pruderies to me."

"Later. Old Mrs. Norton is giving us the evil eye. Oh, look at poor Theo, trying to get on her good side." I glanced over at Theodora Sedgwick, picking at her food in a nervous, rabbity manner, a smile frozen on her face, nodding compulsively at Mrs. Norton.

"It won't do any good," Sara continued. "Mrs. Norton has ordered Charles not to take on a new wife, at least until all the children are grown, and he would never dream of disobeying her. This is strictly *entre nous*, of course."

She moved her chair closer to mine and, gazing levelly into my eyes, caught a stray strand of my hair and tucked it tenderly behind my ear. In the guise of hair maintenance, she managed to stroke my cheek and neck briefly with her fingertips. Then she rested her bare arm on the back of my chair, brushing against my bare shoulders. What was this? Just being chums?

After dark at the Nortons, we younger women habitually kicked off our evening slippers under the table and put these instruments of torture back on only as we were leaving. Now, as Grace launched into a pointless anecdote about dining in London with Elizabeth Gaskell (for whom young Lily—Elizabeth Gaskell Norton—was named), I felt Sara's stockinged foot on mine, first as the lightest of caresses, like moth wings against the skin. A faint smile played at the corners of her lips. Inching her toes slowly down toward mine, she massaged my foot in a way that made me catch my breath, and then she was working her way slowly back up to my ankle. You had to hand it to her; Sara could do more with her toes than most people with their fingers. In every cell of my body I felt myself open helplessly to her touch, and knew at that moment I would have sold out my own mother for an hour in Sara's arms.

But we had put that behind us. I stared down at my hands gripping my sherry glass, trying not to smile.

Despite his Italian inclinations, Harry evidently took to heart his professed goal of seeking his literary material in America. By December he'd decided to *try* living in New York, where he could be near his editors, mingle with other men of letters, and support himself with reviews and journalism.

"Do you think you'll be happy there, Harry?" I asked him. I'd recently made a couple of trips to New York City myself, but to actually live in New York, as Harry was about to, was a pipe-dream for me.

"I have no plans of liking or disliking, of being happy or the reverse," he said. "I shall take what comes, make the best of it, and dream inveterately."

Who was this new stoical Harry who behaved as if there was something he must renounce in order to live in America? The week before, at a dinner party at the Howells, I'd found him surrounded by a crowd of girls. One girl, flirting aggressively, kept trying to pin him down on whether he would attend her tea next Thursday. When he said he must write that day, she teased him, saying she'd heard he was a "woman hater"—was it true? I saw Harry recoil, becoming frosty and remote. This was someone I was meeting for the first time.

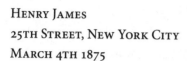

HENRY JAMES
25TH STREET, NEW YORK CITY
MARCH 4TH 1875

To WILLIAM JAMES

I am sorry to report that life here is dull and unrelenting. Mornings I work on Roderick Hudson. What a treadmill to be serialized in the Atlantic! I am subject to nightmares in which the magazine comes out with blank pages where RH should be, covering me with shame. The monthly payments are not enough to live on here, so my afternoons are devoted to writing reviews and critical notes on books which are uniformly bad & which I skim. Journalism—bah!

You were right all along. I probably am ruined for America but I shall keep trying. Don't breathe a word of this to M & F—or A.

HENRY JAMES
25TH ST., NYC,
APRIL 1ST, '75

To MISS GRACE NORTON

Before I came here. I didn't realize how wedded I was to life in Italy, and what I wouldn't give now for the sight of a proper piazza with a proper fountain! Instead, there is the el spewing coal and live embers onto the street, the hideous brown-stones with their lumpen balustrades, the ceaseless ugly grind of commerce. For literary material there are only two sources here: (1) the brash world of high finance (where I have no entrée even were I inclined to write about stockbrokers) & (2) the hot-house social circuit of the hostesses in their Fifth Avenue mansions. That milieu I could penetrate if I felt the urge, but I don't somehow. Culture is entirely in the hands of women here. The men are all too busy making

*money. I'm told they work like dogs, all the time; there is no leisure class
here apparently. I sometimes meet your brother-in-law Arthur Sedgwick
at a little bohemian chop-house near the Nation's offices in Beekman
Place. He seems to be getting on well as a journalist.*

JOURNAL OF HENRY JAMES—NYC, APRIL 15, 1875

*I've told no one here it is my birthday. It is late & I ought to try to sleep
on my lumpy bed, but the air is like the steam from a cauldron & I must
set down my impressions of tonight. (This journal entry will go directly on
the pyre when I am on my deathbed.) Despite my better judgment I met
Arthur S. after work at our usual chop-house; as soon as I arrived I saw
that he was already drunk. He had no idea it was my birthday. He wanted
to discuss Boston. There was nothing I wanted to discuss less; in large part
I moved to New York to avoid talking or thinking about Boston.*

*"I don't miss Cambridge much, do you? Or Boston," he said, exhaling twin streams of smoke through his nostrils. "By the way, Harry, how
is that very serious sister of yours?"*

*"Quite well, although I don't know that I'd call Alice serious. We
think of her as rather the wit of the family."*

*"Well, she always looks so serious." He poured himself another glass
of port and tossed back a few swallows while I wondered what he was
getting at. Then he drawled, "Harry, would you say our sisters are old
maids? At what age does one cross that threshold? I ask because you
write so much about women. You seem to read their minds. What do
you think?"*

*I sensed that he was being disingenuous and said, "Oh, I believe
Alice, Sara, and Theodora are still relatively young maids."*

*"You know, a couple of years ago I thought Charles would become
my brother-in-law for a second time. At that time it was Sara he wanted."*

"I vaguely recall hearing something of the sort. Evidently it didn't happen."

"No, but poor Sara had a terrible time. Whenever she was hanging laundry on the line she'd feel him watching her broodingly from the

piazza. When he talked to her, his eyes would stray to her bosom. One day she was on the floor playing jacks with the children, and Charles sat down next to her, feigning interest in the game. At one point she leaned forward from her knees to gather up the jacks and felt his hand graze her bottom, so lightly it was almost deniable. After that, she fled to New York, leaving the field to the more receptive Theodora. Haven't you seen Theo going around with her secret little grin, quoting Charles's opinions every-where? When you run across them in the woods, she is always buttoning her blouse, Charles fumbling with his trousers. It is quite comical, really."

I sat there stone-faced, hoping that Arthur's confiding mood would pass. Clamping my forearm with his hand, he began to whisper urgently, "I have never told anyone this, Harry, but you are a man of the world. Some years ago, I came back to Kirkland Street late at night. It was dur-ing a heat wave and I happened to glance out at the back garden, and, by Jove, there were Sara and Alice without a stitch on. They were standing in the moonlight with their arms around each other and their hair falling down, like nymphs on a Grecian amphora."

He was still clutching my forearm, bringing his face so close that I could make out a sliver of meat caught between two incisors.

"Oh, well, women are affectionate with one another. It signifies nothing," I said, hoping to staunch the flow. By now, I was yearning for my forlorn apartment on 25th St. and the dreadful novels I was supposed to review. I hoped (and thought it probable) that Arthur would recall nothing of this conversation tomorrow morning.

"I suppose"—Arthur was speaking thickly now—"there are old maids and then there are old maids." His face brightened and he wagged his index finger playfully at me. "Now that's what you should write about, Harry-boy—the Boston Marriage."

"Perhaps you should do it," I said in my coldest tone as I counted out the change in my palm.

Curiously, however much I was revolted by Arthur's indelicate harangue, there was a brief spark in my brain that told me that someday I may in fact "do" the Boston Marriage.

ALICE JAMES
20 QUINCY ST., CAMBRIDGE
MAY 23RD, 1876

To MISS NANNY ASHBURNER
I am with Miss Katherine Loring & have charge of the historical young women. I think I shall enjoy it & I know it will do me lots of good. Don't you want to become one of my students? I will write you the wisest of letters about any period of the world you choose. You can laugh and think me as much of a humbug as you choose, you can't do so more than I have myself . . .

P.S. We who have had all our lives, more books than we know what do with can't conceive of the feeling that people have for them who have been shut out from them always. They look upon them as something sacred apparently & some of the letters I get are most touching.

⌐ THIRTEEN ⌐

As Fanny Morse was explaining the project, I was half-listening to her and half-listening to the ice-coated twigs tinkling like fairy chimes in the wind. Last night's freezing rain had hung a splendid fringe of icicles on Mr. Eliot's eaves that looked sharp as swords. I'd formed a vivid mental picture of a passing Harvard student being killed instantly by an icicle piercing his hat and brain, and was mentally composing the headline in the *Boston Evening Transcript—Harvard student skewered by icicle*, or should it be *transfixed*?—when Fanny said something about nervous invalidism, that wearisome topic.

She was talking about Miss Anna Ticknor, who was so broken-down nervously a year ago that she spent six months at Dr. Weir Mitchell's rest-cure farm in Pennsylvania, without success. The copious rich food forced upon her there inspired a lifelong distaste for food and the proscription against reading made her an even more fanatical reader. In the end, she returned to her house on Chestnut Street, hired a companion/nurse, and accepted invalidism as her lot.

I knew where this was going, of course. Fanny was using Miss Ticknor's nerves—which she obviously equated more or less with mine—to lure me into Miss Ticknor's Society to Encourage Studies at Home. I had nothing against societies, but I assumed this one would turn out to be as old-maidish and earnest as so many others. The Rights of Women were powerfully magnetizing the social atmosphere of Boston during this period, and everyone was abuzz about it. Still, the choices for Woman remained few: Wife and mother, on the one hand; social reformer on the other. Both unpaid. What else was there? Editress of a magazine for ladies, schoolmistress at a girls' school or a dame school for infants, composer of soporific rhymes and/or moralistic stories to run next to pie recipes in women's magazines. Nurse? Clara Barton aside, nursing was a plebeian occupation, and I had no wish to handle sick bodies; dealing with my own was onerous enough. There were a handful of dry, bespectacled medical doctoresses in Boston who delivered babies, but I did not care for the sight of blood, which, come to think of it, would rule out nursing as well. People were always saying in those days how far Woman had risen, serving on the Boston school board, attending the new women's colleges and the land-grant coeducational colleges of the west, even, in the case of some extreme bluestockings, graduate school. But my friends and I had missed the chance to go to college, having been born a decade too soon.

"Fanny, do you ever wish for a nor'easter or something—just to liven things up?"

"Not really." I watched her worried eyebrows bunch up. "Anyhow, during one period in bed, Miss Ticknor began to feel oppressed by the number of volumes in her library, which was her father's, as you know, and is considered the finest private library in Boston."

"That may be, but I don't think Miss Ticknor can rest on her laurels, library-wise. William may well overtake her at some point."

Plowing past my irrelevancies, Fanny went on to relate that Miss Ticknor, seized by a desire to share her books with women who had none, did what any self-respecting Boston bluestocking would do—gathered the intellectual women of Boston and Cambridge around her and founded a society, the Society to Encourage Studies at Home.

"Do bear in mind, Fanny, that I am the misguided product of Father's pedagogical experiments. I have a very shaky intellectual foundation. I'm not sure I ever learned fractions. No Latin at all, of course."

Fanny, I am obliged to admit, was a model of forbearance. "No one's asking you to teach Latin, Alice. Anyhow, we're not teachers; we are called Managers. Our students are sent books and we correspond with them about their reading. It would be easy for someone as well-read as you."

She showed me a pamphlet describing the Society that was given out to students. I flipped to the end, where there were a few paragraphs cautioning female students against "overdoing," culminating in a burst of feminine poetry. I read these lines aloud:

> *Lose not thyself nor give thy humors way,*
> *God gave them to thee under lock and key!*

"What does *that* mean, Fanny? That God locks us up but supplies us with a key? Or are the humors—whatever they are—meant to be locked up? It is not at all clear."

"Don't worry about it, Alice. Health is a sort of fixation with Miss Ticknor, because she was such a terrible invalid."

"I hope at least she is not the fussbudget type of invalid."

Fanny looked weary, and I thought I could read her mind. My bouts of invalidism were my way of withdrawing from life, and would no doubt continue until I became completely housebound and set in my ways, like Miss Ticknor *before* she started the Society to Encourage Studies at Home. (Not that she was entirely normal now. Fanny did mention that meetings with her were "like being swept up in the tail of a comet.")

In Boston, it should be noted, the habit of introspection (or "thinking about yourself too much"), especially when combined with the condition of "having too much time on your hands," was deemed morbid, leading inevitably to queer behavior if not to the asylum. Fanny was trying to rescue me from this fate by getting me interested in "something outside of myself." That I was naturally inclined toward the inner world more than the outer was something I could not explain to her.

But, reading the disappointment on her face, I did feel contrite for being such a hard nut to crack. "Oh, but pay no attention to my silliness, Fanny. I *shall* think about joining your Society. It is very kind of you to invite me." She did not look like she believed me.

Over the next two months, she threw herself into the Society and became less available to her friends, prompting Sara to grumble about "Fanny's prairie ladies." One day I was drifting through the dining room looking for the *Advertiser*, standing near the dumbwaiter. Through the shaft I could hear Mother and Aunt Kate talking down in the kitchen as they inventoried the dry goods. Aunt Kate was saying, "What she needs, poor girl, is a constant change of air for a year or more. Her Cambridge life seems *blighting* to her." I drew in my breath. I thought I'd convinced everyone I was fine.

"I don't know *why*," I heard Mother say. "Other girls manage to flourish in Cambridge." As they drifted off toward the pantry, I waited. When they moved in my direction again, I heard Mother say, "Her health does seem to improve when she has something to do other than contemplate her own uselessness." I almost dropped the cup and saucer I was holding. All these years, had Aunt Kate been my secret ally, pleading my case with Mother, while I went about like an unfinished sentence? Blighted!

And so to curtail further contemplation of my uselessness, I invited Fanny to tell me more about the Society. Delighted, she took me through all the printed materials, the reading lists, the charter, the lists of Managers and the students who paid two dollars to sign up. The charter emphasized the founders' desire to stay out of the newspapers and to educate Woman without taking her out of her proper Sphere, compromising her domestic duties, or overtaxing her sensitive Nervous System.

"Most of our students have no books and no libraries," she explained. "They are *starved* for the written word! We send them books, and they write essays and we reply by mail. It's like an extended intellectual conversation!" The Society had compiled a lending library, she explained, organizing itself into six departments, English, History, Art, French, German, and Natural Science. The Manager in charge of each discipline compiled a reading list.

When I told William about the Society, I expected him to joke about hen parties, but he took it very seriously.

"You *must* do it, Alice. The women of the world need you as a professoress."

"But I have had no coherent education, having been torn up by the roots repeatedly as a child, due to Father's Ideas."

"No more do I. Mr. Eliot seemed to have this idea I could teach and I couldn't bear to disappoint the poor man. It has given me a reason to get up in the morning. That may sound like a trivial thing but—"

"It's not."

"No." A moment passed in which we silently understood each other.

And so I said yes.

Fanny actually clapped her hands together in her exuberance. "Next week we'll meet with Miss Loring, who is in charge of the historical young women."

"I fear the learned Miss Loring will be dismayed by my unsystematic scholarship."

"Oh, come, Alice. Everyone knows you're the brightest star in our constellation."

"I am?" This was a genuine surprise to me.

In a departure from my usual *modus operandi*, I made a major decision without consulting my parents or Aunt Kate. I could not face their anxious hovering and I had already made up my mind.

Miss Katherine Peabody Loring was a Boston female powerhouse two years my junior, who was involved in numberless intellectual and charitable causes and spoke up frequently for the Rights of Woman. I'd met her first at a North Shore luncheon given by Fanny on December 27, 1873 (a date that would later be memorialized as our anniversary, though of course we did not know this yet). She was the type of woman of whom people said, "Such a pity she is not a man! If she were a man, she'd be running a great company." In her presence I feared being unmasked as a useless dilettante and was quiet and subdued at the first meetings of the History department, which consisted only of Miss Loring, Fanny Jackson née Appleton, and me. (I was quickly able to forgive Fanny for marrying the beautiful Charley Jackson and discovered I liked her very much.)

The History Department was so popular that Miss Loring had fifteen students to supervise, Fanny sixteen, and I fourteen. Over the next months, I came to know my students through their letters and essays on the French Revolution, the Napoleonic wars, and the British Empire. As I read their letters, I marveled at these lives, seemingly so bleak and so remote from mine. Often, contemplating a pioneer woman's struggles to educate herself despite every conceivable hardship, I dissolved in tears. Other students were more comfortably settled in places like Illinois, yet even they were condemned to what I considered a cultural wasteland, without public libraries, lecture series, Browning societies, Dante circles, visits from Mr. Charles Dickens, or any of Boston's considerable intellectual amenities. Most of my students were intelligent and intellectually curious but had, until now, no access to the world of ideas.

Sara's references to our "rusticated scholars" and "sages of the sagebrush" became more frequent and caustic.

"Why don't *you* join, Sara?" Fanny said.

"Please! I have no time for feminine crusades. I am much too occupied with the children." Meaning the young Nortons.

In my letters to Nanny I treated the subject in a jocular manner—in case she thought the Society was silly and because I still felt a fraud as a teacher—but in the PS I admitted to being deeply moved by the sacredness of books in my students' eyes.

In late August, Harry returned from New York. I had been attentively reading his *Transatlantic Sketches*, among which I recognized some of the places we'd visited with him. But how changed they were in his account, in which Harry wandered lonely as a cloud, having insights. He'd also published a first collection of stories, *A Passionate Pilgrim*, which Mr. Howells reviewed in the *Atlantic Monthly* in a gushing way. (*We may compare him with the greatest, and find none greater than he.*) Other critics were less flattering, for apparently Harry's artistic interests, tailored English suits, and sharp tongue did not endear him to every American. I hoped he wasn't too hurt by the snide reviews.

But the *Transatlantic Sketches* received favorable reviews, sold a thousand copies, and seemed destined for a long life in the bookshops. More and more Americans were swarming over Europe now, apparently, needing to know what to appreciate.

His time in New York had shown him that he would be obliged to work like a dog as a journalist, mass-producing reviews and notices, just to stay afloat. In the months he'd lived there he churned out 39 reviews and notices for the *Atlantic Monthly,* the *Nation*, and *Galaxy*, which were artistically unsatisfying and barely covered his rent, leaving no time for his fiction. The robust sales of *Transatlantic Sketches* encouraged him to think he might try Paris.

He was explaining all this to me in his thorough, painstaking way as we circled Fresh Pond on a muggy August afternoon, serenaded by bullfrogs. I'd had no idea he felt that way about New York; he certainly hadn't told me. Maybe he only confided in the Nortons nowadays. Now he was listing everything that fatigued him about New York—the journalistic rat-race, the summer heat, his lonely apartment, the constant scribbling of reviews, the elevated train that spewed flecks of coal and live embers onto the street. (Through his eyes I could see it as if it were a painting.) The city lacked conveniences and social atmosphere, he said; the scenery did not speak to him, and neither did the world of trade, the real life of the city.

I had been hoping for months to visit him in New York, but he never invited me, no doubt because he was working so hard. Now I was trying to absorb what he'd just told me. "But Boston, Harry. Why can't you live in Boston?"

That was when he confessed that he'd written to the New York *Tribune* offering to replace their Paris correspondent, and the editor had hired him. He'd also persuaded the *Atlantic Monthly* to advance him four hundred dollars and now thought he could afford Paris better than New York. He already had a ticket and a sailing date.

Harry the schemer! Clearly he'd always meant to go back, had only pretended to "try" New York. I'd overheard Father telling Mr. Howells last week that Harry had "no power to push himself into notice, but must await the spontaneous recognition of the world around him." He was dead wrong. Harry's ambition was grandiose!

If only he'd leave quickly and get it over with. These good-byes took so much out of one. I felt the air becoming thin, as if I were floating out in lifeless space. Words were spilling out of me in a torrent. I heard myself complain that the Norton children were not real children at all but more like rare hybrids grown in a hothouse. I'd seen little Lily having a fit over a blueberry stain on her pinafore. "She kept saying, Oh dear! Oh dear! Papa will be angry, won't he? Auntie will be displeased. Over and over again. It was frightful, Harry."

I'd been wounded to discover that Harry had written Grace Norton several long, thoughtful letters from New York and none to me. The Nortons stood for everything that was luring him away—art, refinement, old cultures, private parks, aesthetic theories. Wherever he went, he'd be buoyed by their letters of introduction. (They knew everyone, naturally.) I had a bleak presentiment of life after he sailed. Dining with the Nortons in the room with the Tintorettos, the children displayed like Infantas, Grace gushing, "I have just had the most *delicious* letter from Harry."

Harry was staring fixedly at his boots, the furrow between his eyebrows deepening.

"Strange things occur in the woods, I hear," I said, pounding my walking stick into the ground with unusual ferocity. "Don Carlo and Theodora appear suddenly from behind bushes and trees, or skirting the edge of the horizon. For a widower of fifty with six children at his back it is almost immoral; don't you think so, Harry?"

He made no reply. The subject clearly embarrassed him, and this made me more adamant. I wanted to get a rise out of him—something passionate, not evasive.

"They say old Mrs. Norton has put her foot down about Charles bringing a new wife into the family. Apparently, they will have to wait for her to expire."

"It may be some time. Mrs. Norton is very spry." Harry passed his hand over his face, slippery with sweat.

I knew I was growing strident, but could not seem to stop. There is something about a rant that is strangely satisfying. "It might be a good plan, when Charlemagne marries his young wife and starts a fresh brood, to dispose of some half dozen of his children to their various aunts. Wouldn't you agree, Harry?"

I had gone too far and I knew it. The corners of Harry's mouth turned down. He was too indebted to the Nortons to see them as characters in a farce. We walked in silence for a few minutes, our boots squelching through the muddy patches. My throat felt parched. Whatever my brothers might do, I was doomed to remain behind. Father would go on winding the clocks at night, Mother would keep the household accounts and carp about the Sullen Laundress and the price of coal. Father would go off to the Saturday Club and come back with anecdotes. The *Advertiser* would be read in the morning, the *Transcript* in the evening, and there would be discussions of who had died and who had produced an infant.

After a pregnant pause, Harry promised me that he would think of me whenever he had a new and startling sensation, that he would describe everything to me so I could feel it too. I felt absurdly grateful.

He sailed a month later on a slow Cunarder bound for Liverpool. The crossing was rough, with gale winds. Anthony Trollope was a fellow passenger and Harry talked to him daily, finding him one of the dullest Britons he had met. "I take possession of the Old World," he wrote us. "I inhale it—I appropriate it! I shall immortalize myself; *vous allez voir!*"

He was right about that.

In Cambridge the trees were losing their leaves. I watched them drift slowly past the windows to turn brown on the ground. Late autumn was the saddest season. How wrenching to watch everything in the natural world die in its turn and to foresee what lay ahead— black ice, short daylight, influenza, blizzards, Father losing his balance on icy sidewalks.

From Paris Harry reported that he was living in a third-floor apartment at 29 rue de Luxembourg and writing a new serial called *The American*. He told us that the waiters in restaurants were his chief society, and Mother worried that he was lonely and hoped he would get Paris out of his system soon. I knew this would never happen. (Some months later, we would read that Christopher Newman, of *The American*, imagines that the worst punishment for an American in Paris is "to be carried home in irons and compelled to live in Boston.")

Not long afterward, Harry met Ivan Turgenev, who took him under his wing and introduced him to Flaubert and George Sand.

Within a few months he was attending Flaubert's literary *cénacles* at the high end of the Faubourg Saint-Honoré. To me he confessed that he was seeing much of *the little rabble of Flaubert's satellites*, including Guy de Maupassant, Edmond de Goncourt, Emile Zola, and Alphonse Daudet. Most of the Frenchmen were immoral and insular, in his opinion. Each of these letters, postmarked Paris, made me feel that I was living a kind of exile.

Harry did not forget his promise, and wrote me,

Whenever I see anything very stunning, I long for the presence of my lovely sister, & in default of it promise myself to make the object present to her eyes by means of the most graphic and spirituelle descriptions.

⌒ FOURTEEN ⌒

1876

IT WAS STRANGE TO SEE MYSELF THROUGH MY STUDENTS' EYES, as the learned Miss James, dwelling in an earthly paradise of books, libraries, lectures, and civilization. (Only one of my students guessed that I was also the sister of an Author.) I ought to have been grateful for my good fortune, but it sometimes struck me that, despite the brutal realities of life on the Plains and the monotony and absence of libraries on the Prairie, my students were happier than I. Certainly, the few books they received in the mail from the Society were more precious to them than all of Boston's culture to me.

But I enjoyed being a professoress more than I'd expected. I would venture to say I felt useful for the first time in my life. Corresponding with my students, reading the books along with them, commenting on their essays, even correcting their grammar and spelling felt like a sort of calling. Imagine: something I was good at—other than neurasthenic vapors! Suddenly people were commenting on how well I looked, on my "brightness" and "animal spirits," from which I inferred how wan and woebegone I'd been before. I began to understand what a profession offered a man.

Fascinated by my students, William peppered me with questions, and insisted on reading all their letters. One student, from California, wrote that she enjoyed the lesson plan and the essay topics Miss James suggested, which were so different from the brain-numbing tedium of the school she'd attended.

In my school days we had to write essays on such subjects as "Mother, Home and Heaven." And "We are Here but How long will it last?" Your topics, Miss James, have some meat to them.

"I am in love with her already," William said. "Does she say if she is married?"

"I believe she is."

"Then I am too late. Alas."

His favorite student was Bessie Klemperer, in the Dakota Territory, who wrote that the only books in her home were a German-English dictionary and a Bible. She confided in her fourth letter that she'd been a mail-order bride, sent west by her impoverished Pennsylvania family; the bride-price bought a much-needed plow. Mrs. Klemperer was obliged to hide her Society books in the root cellar so that her husband would not sell or burn them during one of his drunken fits. Fearing she would be *nothing but a cipher in the world's history*, she read whenever she had a spare moment, hardly sleeping or eating. *I craved so much and there seemed no access possible to anything I wanted.*

"What a woman, Alice! She has the spirit of a Crusader."

"A mail-order bride, William. Sent out like a bolt of calico. Imagine your first glimpse of the grizzled codger who will own you, body and soul." I shuddered.

"Perhaps I ought to take a train out there and rescue this Mrs. Klemperer. But we don't know what she looks like, do we?"

"It is very disappointing, William, to think you would be influenced by something as superficial as looks."

"Men are barbarians, Alice. We can't help it."

"I hope, Alice," Mother said at dinner, "you are not ruining your eyes by writing long letters to your Western women. Especially do not write too much by candlelight, which Dr. Beach says can cause severe eyestrain."

"Alice's professorship is an immense thing for her, Mother," William said. "She is an excellent professoress. Let her be."

"I suppose Miss Loring must be very intellectual. Is she, dear?"

"Well, she is rather a fiend for history."

"Would you say she is a bluestocking? Isn't she one of the women behind the Harvard Annex?"

"Yes, to the second question. From what I could glimpse of her stockings, they are grey." I was in no hurry to reveal to them how fatally I was falling under Katherine Loring's spell.

Father said, "They say that Mrs. Hemenway and other extreme feminists are *hounding* Eliot to let women into Harvard and like a sensible man he won't."

"And did you hear, dear? Julia Ward Howe *preached* Sunday in Dr. E.H. Clarke's church!"

Before I had time to reflect, I blurted, "I *wish* I had been there to hear what Mrs. Howe said. I'm sure it was more interesting that the usual fare."

Father had mischief in his eyes. "Well, Alice, you know what Dr. Johnson said about women preaching. It is like a dog walking on its hind legs. It is not done well but you are surprised that it is done at all." He guffawed merrily.

For a moment I felt that my head would explode. What came out of my mouth next took me by surprise. "I should like to know why is it that *men* are always telling women what we are like and how we *ought* to be. Why should we permit the other sex to define us?"

I saw that William, across from me, was watching me with keen interest.

"That's all very well, darling," Father said, "but don't forget it was Eve who listened to the serpent."

"The Adam and Eve story was written by some *man*, Father, and haven't you said the Bible is metaphorical? I'm quite sure Yahweh himself did not descend from a thundercloud to accuse woman of taking marching orders from snakes!"

How weary I was of being good! How I should respect myself if I could burst out and make everyone wretched for twenty-four hours. Like the gilded Latin words discharged by medieval saints in pictures, words spilled from me without forethought. "You might make the case, Father, that the history of womankind is a series of absurd pronouncements by men. How would you feel if every book you picked up told you, 'Men are overly muscled, hairy creatures, of whom little can be expected on account of their inadequate brains. They are occasionally useful for war and moving heavy furniture and not much else, but because wars are sometimes necessary, women must appear to support them in the delusion that they are the superior sex.'"

The seas had parted and I waited to see what would happen next. My senses felt keenly alive, as if I were a wild animal in the forest. William set down his fork and gazed at me as if I'd just swung through the room on a trapeze. Father looked briefly like an ox stunned by a blow, but quickly recovered. Mother's lips were pressed together in displeasure and she was nervously picking at nonexistent crumbs on the tablecloth. "How absurd, Alice," she said. "I mean, does Miss Loring agitate for the suffrage and say that we should go about in Amelia Bloomers, freeing ourselves from the 'tyranny of men'?"

Father chortled at this.

William said, "If Miss Loring supports the female suffrage, Mother, I salute her!"

"Oh, not you too, William," Father said.

"Yes, Father. In *The Subjection of Women*, John Stuart Mill points out that the present swallowing up of the woman in the man grows out of men's egotism. All the fine phrases about women's 'higher' function, their mission to 'refine,' et cetera, amount to insincere flattery and ill atone for the loss of opportunity for moral growth that results from open, independent mingling in the business of the world."

I was startled to hear him define the dilemma of womankind so accurately. I'd no idea he'd given the matter any thought.

The higher mission to refine was, of course, central to Father's concept of Woman. Hadn't we just heard him, talking before the Women's Club of Boston, describe with unmingled disgust his horror of any woman who "forsakes the sanctity and privacy of her home to battle and unsex herself in the hot and dusty arena of the world"? I would venture to say he was more insistent on this principle than most men of his generation. Naturally, he was roused to battle by William's words, as William intended. "Meddling in the business of the world! I suppose you think that is desirable, William." And *you,* my girl"—aiming one of his penetrating looks at me—"are you swallowing these toxic modern doctrines? I have always had such high hopes for you!"

I did not answer and became absorbed in buttering my roll, savoring the oddly sweet afterglow of having stood up to Father. Such was the potency of Katherine Peabody Loring, my new friend.

"Mingling, Father," William said. "Not meddling."

To Father "the world" stood for everything that was not divine; it was a fallen world, unredeemed. Still he enjoyed himself in it; wasn't that inconsistent? At this point Mother tried to change the subject by saying brightly that Bob's infant daughter, Mary, was large for a girl and had a prodigious appetite.

"It is so nice to have a girl in the family finally," I said, "but I do wish they'd tell us what she *looks* like."

"This shows you to be a hypocrite, Alice," said William, waving his knife in my direction. "After Edward was born you said, and I quote, I am glad he is a boy and not another miserable girl."

"I merely wished for the poor babe to be one of the oppressors rather than one of the oppressed."

Father leaned forward in his chair and nailed me with a look that made me feel like a butterfly on a pin. In his wrathful aspect, Father could be powerful and tempestuous, like Zeus with his thunderbolts. He said, "Do you consider yourself *oppressed*, dear girl?"

In fact, I'd never pondered the subject of female oppression with any seriousness. It was true that I did not have to scurry around with coal scuttles and chamber pots at first light. I was a pampered member of the capitalist class and therefore an oppressor of others. Yet, compared with my brothers, who had an infinity of choices (with which all of them struggled mightily, I am the first to admit), only one sort of life was available to me. My fate had been prearranged by biology.

"You know what these agitating ladies are saying now? Now that we've freed the slaves, the next step is to *free women!*" Father said, breaking into a great belly laugh. This prompted me to recall something Katherine said about men using ridicule as a weapon against women.

"Will, dear," Mother said, "didn't you write a notice of John Stuart Mill's book in which you *disagreed* with his thesis? I seem to remember that you sided with the other fellow."

"So I did, Mother, in sixty-nine. Which does not prevent me from seeing it from the other point of view now."

"Who would have guessed that these pioneer women would be so fond of books!" Mother said, shaking her head, and rang the bell for the maid.

⌒ FIFTEEN ⌒

1877

TOWARD THE END OF JUNE, I ASKED WILLIAM IF KATHERINE and I might spend a few weeks at his "Shanty" in the Adirondacks.

William was always recommending the Shanty to everyone as the panacea for all earthly ills, but few people took him up on it. With Jim Putnam and Henry Bowditch, he'd started coming to the Keene Valley when they were all in medical school. Pooling their funds, they bought an abandoned cabin they called the Shanty, which expanded over the years into a collection of weathered wooden shacks clustered in the tall grass behind the local inn, Beede's. Cold water was available for washing; bathing was done in an icy brook; everything was as rustic as possible.

"By all means, Alice!" He looked rather taken aback, mindful of my well-known skepticism about discomfort, black flies, poison ivy, and other aspects of raw nature. Then he said, "Does this have anything to do with the marvelous Miss Loring's proficiency with the ax, the tent pole, and the open fire?" I admitted this was so, and he said, "Well, if she can get my lazy, shiftless sister off the sofa and all the way to the Adirondacks, she is a miracle-worker indeed."

We left in late July, hoping to miss the black fly season. If there was a single biting fly, I threatened to flee instantly to a hotel. It was a long journey. From New York City, we headed north to Saratoga Springs. After the sun set, the window became a dark mirror in which my reflection rode beside me like a more adventurous identical twin. After a night in a local inn, we took a single-track line through wild, almost primeval forest. As lakes, waterfalls, beaver dams, evergreens, and brief glimpses of magnificent peaks flew past, Katherine and I knitted and talked and read aloud to each other from Harry's new novel, *Roderick Hudson*. We both thought it was a marvel (or if Katherine felt differently she knew better than to say so to me). As the forest outside became increasingly primeval, I began to wonder what I'd gotten myself into and rued the day I solicited holiday advice from William of all people. But here we were at Lake Placid station. From here it was a dusty, jolting carriage ride to Beede's. The inn, of unpainted clapboard, looked bare and unwelcoming, but it was a four-star hotel compared with the Shanty, which did its best to live up to its name.

"This *is* rustic." It was all I could do, frankly, not to burst into tears, for I was suddenly overcome by fatigue and a lost forsaken sense of being parted from everything comforting and familiar. This vacation, I suddenly felt, was a great mistake.

"Isn't it *grand*?" Katherine said, thereby demonstrating that in this respect at least she was my polar opposite.

While I thought wistfully of civilized inns I'd known, Katherine sprang into action, locating lanterns, candles, fire tools, blackened cooking pots and utensils, and an assortment of bedding. In one of the cupboards, reeking of mildew, we found wooden puzzle pieces in disarray, and determined that they came from three different puzzles and that more than half the pieces were missing. Then we stood together before a tattered map tacked to a wall.

I was beginning to feel less panicked standing next to Katherine, who could obviously cope with anything.

"What are all these queer little symbols?" Katherine asked.

"It looks like a record of past mountaineering feats by William and his friends. This thing here"—a comic figure with its hair standing on end in terror—"must be a symbol for a trail they consider hair-raising."

"It's very well executed!"

"William was an artist first. When we lived in Newport he studied under William Morris Hunt and was said to have a 'future.' Father made him go into science instead and that backfired as far as Father was concerned, because it turned Will into an atheist."

"Your family is so . . . dramatic."

"You could say that. After going into science, he never touched a paintbrush again. Seems a shame, because he was very talented, but that's William for you."

"Well, let's avoid the hair-raising trails." I knew that Katherine was equal to any trail but was thinking of my limitations. How kind she was.

Over the next few days we did a lot of rambling. We rambled over the easy trails and a few "moderate" ones, identifying cones and conifers, picking wild raspberries and admiring the peaks as they changed color with the time of day. We went botanizing and pressed wildflowers between the pages of a book. Katherine, whose uncle was the great Harvard botanist Asa Gray, knew all the trees and flowers and their Latin names. (The Shanty had a mildewed copy of Gray's botany guide next to the candleholders.) She could read the woods like a book and knew which plants were edible and which poisonous, how to build a shelter and survive in a storm, how to tell which animals had passed from their tracks and scat.

"How *did* you acquire all this forest lore, Kath? You could go off tomorrow and live in the woods like a hermit."

"Yes, I really could." She shrugged in an eloquent way that I was already coming to love.

We were sitting before the fire, wrapped in moth-eaten woolen blankets, eating the meal we'd managed to cook on the hearth. Under interrogation, Katherine was cajoled into admitting that as a girl she could run like the wind, climb the tallest trees, and whittle anything you liked out of wood. "But none of this was worth a wooden nickel if you were a girl."

"Oh, Katherine! Did your brothers tease you?"

"No. They treated me like another brother. We were the best of companions."

"Lucky you. I have a sad recollection of being in the woods in Newport with Robbie and Wilky. They asked if I wanted to play cowboys and Indians, and, being gullible, I said yes. That time they tied me to a tree with a clothesline and told me I was a captive and shouldn't expect to get out of it alive. Then they went off and forgot about me. I died a hundred deaths in the next hour."

"That's terrible, Alice! Did you ever get free?"

"I suppose I must have. Strangely, I don't remember how."

"Being the youngest in the family must have been hard for someone as sensitive as you." She spoke so sympathetically, with such a tender expression, that tears welled in my eyes.

In the late afternoon, after a little hiking and looking at views, we peeled off all our clothes and bathed in a frigid pool fed by an icy brook. Out of the corner of my eye, I covertly admired the lines of Katherine's body. Unlike most people, she was more beautiful undressed than dressed; her clothes just muddled the impression. I liked the fact that her beauty was a veiled, secret thing, not divined at first glance, overlooked by most. When she took off her spectacles her near-sighted blue eyes were very beautiful and so were her lashes. In order not to gawk, I lifted my eyes to the sky and studied a pair of hawks riding the thermals far above us. "I wonder what those hawks are so interested in. Hope it's not us."

"We'd be rather a mouthful, I think."

"Was your childhood happy, Katherine? I can never figure out if mine was happy or tragic." I laughed to show I'd meant this light-heartedly.

"Yes, it was—until I saw the unfairness. I wondered why the world of men was outdoors, interesting and filled with adventure, and the world of women was indoors, narrow and boring. My mother, poor dear, was always trying to form me into a charming young lady—unsuccessfully, as you can see." She laughed. "As a result I became a bit lonely, I suppose."

"Then you must tell me everything about yourself and become less lonely."

The glance Katherine gave me made me giddy for a moment.

Over the next few days, we did campy things like gather wildflowers, look at interesting birds and other wildlife through binoculars, cook primitive meals on the hearth and consume them while watching the sun sink behind the saw-toothed ridgeline in a blaze of amber or tangerine. We made an unsuccessful attempt at one of the wooden puzzles. At night we lit candles and lanterns and made a fire with the logs that Katherine had split with an ax earlier in the day.

I'd watched her chopping wood just before sunset, admiring her grace and strength, recognizing in a flash that she carried in her person all the masculine virtues as well as the feminine ones (for she was devoting her life to helping the less fortunate, as good women did). Pregnant with this illumination, I sat in awed silence, gazing at the peaks around me, the bright fingernail paring of moon between the cedars, the whole world astonishingly aglow and alive.

Later I would tell Katherine that this was the moment I saw into her soul and *knew* that we were intended for each other. Katherine said she knew it the day I came to volunteer in the History Department. "I was just waiting for you to find out!"

That night as we lay bundled in blankets, feeling the hard wooden floor beneath our bones but not minding because we were together, there came a scuffling noise outside.

"What kind of animal is *that*?" I asked. If anyone would know, it would be Katherine.

"A large one, from the sound of it. Bigger than a porcupine or a skunk, I'd say. Maybe a large, clumsy raccoon."

"A bear?"

"Possibly."

I saw that Katherine was unafraid and this made me unafraid, too.

A few minutes later the "animal" revealed itself to be Dr. Charley Putnam, brother of William's great friend Jim Putnam, and also a physician. He was puttering around the camp in the dark, not realizing that anyone else was there. Running into us, he became flustered, blushing and apologizing and asking if we needed anything.

"You know, Charley, I think we're running out of oil for the hurricane lamp," Katherine said.

"There is some at Beede's. I'll bring it by tomorrow if you like. Will that be soon enough, or do you need some right now?"

"No, we're fine for tonight. Thank you!"

"I suppose this makes us the foolish virgins, not the wise ones," I ventured.

Charley lapsed into silence. "Ah. Well, good night, then."

After he stole off to his lair, we could not stop laughing.

"He didn't pick up on the Bible reference, did he?" I said.

"I rather think not." Katherine chuckled heartily.

"Did you see his carpet slippers? I suppose that behind those slippers and maiden-aunt ways there might lurk a certain virile charm."

"Think of the irony, Alice. Two maidens alone in the primeval forest—menaced by Charley Putnam of Marlborough Street."

"It's safe to say that nothing dangerous could *ever* come from Marlborough Street."

Charley's gawky intrusion, the mood of hilarity, the moon, the crystalline air, and our perfect understanding of each other's jokes led to what came next, which marked the beginning of our life together.

We stayed up most of the night talking in each other's arms. I told Katherine about Aunt Kate's disastrous marriage to the unsuitable Captain, Mother's inability to gain the respect of our French servants, Father's impenetrable mysticism, our years in Europe and the governesses who came and went mysteriously. I told her of my love for my brothers, my horror of the German at the end of a Back Bay ball, my perplexity about my future. I said that although the idea of marriage was anathema to me, I would like to collect at least one marriage proposal.

"Why?"

"Well, I suppose, to hang on the wall like a diploma, so to speak."

Katherine hooted with laughter, and this made me laugh, too.

"Tell me about your childhood, Katherine. I want to know *everything* about you."

"Well, every Christmas, I'd ask my parents for a coonskin cap, a bowie knife, or a bow and arrow, and on Christmas morning I'd find a dollhouse or a tea set. No one seemed to notice that only Louisa played with these things. She'd chatter away at her dolls for hours, dressing and undressing them. I thought she was daft."

"What an extraordinary child you must have been, Katherine," I said, stroking her hair.

"I don't know about that. As I was falling asleep, I would fantasize about running away to sea. I learned celestial navigation from a book, and my father gave me a sextant. I think he sympathized secretly, but he had no choice but to leave me to Mother to mold into a proper female. And she did try very hard, poor woman."

I laughed and kissed her on the mouth. "I think you've turned out very nicely, but I daresay your mother had little to do with it."

"I had a plan, an insane one, admittedly. When I turned thirteen I planned to stow away on one of the merchant ships docked at Long Wharf. If I mastered all the necessary skills I believed I'd be taken on as a seaman. Apparently, one could be hired when one was thirteen. Of course, one also had to be a boy. I didn't discover that part until I was eleven, and it was a terribly bitter pill to swallow all at once: That I was only a girl and would always be a girl, bad luck on ships, fated to stay home, spending the rest of my natural life marching around Boston with Mother and Louisa making calls. Did you have to do that?"

Lying on my side, I was tracing the lines of Katherine's face with my fingertips. "Oh, yes, calling on elderly forlornities. The great female pastime," I sighed. "They should have seen your greatness, Katherine, and worshipped it."

She blushed. "Don't be absurd, Alice."

"But you are so *good*, Katherine. And you always know exactly what to do. I want to know how you *got* that way. When I met you at Fanny Morse's luncheon—do you remember?"

"How could I forget meeting *you*?"

I'd never seen myself as the sort of person who makes an unforgettable impression. It was lovely to think I had. "You'd just contrived to send food and supplies into Paris by balloon when the city was under siege by the Prussians. I thought, If she can do that, there is nothing she cannot accomplish."

"Someday I'll have to tell you what I thought of you," Katherine said with a mischievous smile.

The next morning, I sat outside at a splintered wooden table in a pool of white sunshine, writing letters. I wrote to my parents, Fanny Morse, Nanny Ashburner, and Sara. *The shanty lacks nothing in the way of discomfort and is no doubt after camping the worst thing*, I wrote to Sara.

We stumbled gratefully over the stones in the brook and bathed therein, but one tub in the hand is worth fifty brooks in the bush. I refrained from praising Katherine to Sara, who shortly before we left said irritably, "This Miss Loring is quite the paragon from what you say! Does she have any faults at all?" To Nanny, however, I permitted myself to write, *There is nothing she cannot do from hewing wood & drawing water to driving runaway horses & educating all the women in North America.*

⌐ SIXTEEN ⌐

FIRST CAME THE WILD NOR'EASTER THAT LASHED THE TREES, tore off branches and shingles, and sent them flying through the air. The sky darkened and rain fell so hard the drops bounced off the ground. Hail spattered at the windows like pebbles thrown by unruly children. Streets became gushing streams in minutes.

The next day, the air turned crisp, with the slightly metallic taste of fall. We were eating our Sunday joint. Mother had just asked Aunt Kate to pass the rolls. Father was saying, "I am bewildered and disgusted by the young men, so worldly, so handsome, so impudent, I meet in the cars," when he suddenly fell sideways, rigid as a felled tree, his mouth frozen in an "oh" of surprise. He lost consciousness. Dr. Beach was sent for, listened to his heart, felt his pulse, shone a light in his eyes, and said it was a stroke. He could not say whether he would recover. "He may have one foot in the next world already," he said, which, I thought sorrowfully, meant that poor Father had no feet in this world at all.

With the assistance of our large, muscular cook, we managed to carry him upstairs to his bed, where he regained consciousness after a few hours. For the next month, he lay mute and listless, while Mother, Aunt Kate, and I took turns picking bits of food out of his long beard, setting a bedpan under him, wiping the drool from his chin. His eyes followed us and he was strangely docile, a large, helpless infant. His first utterances were difficult to decipher. As I told Nanny in my letter:

He is entirely unable to write or think & as his whole existence
consisted in the one or the other the days seem very long to him now.
Whatever his philosophy is he certainly practices it in his own life.

Over the next weeks, his speech grew clearer and he was able to sit up, but now he became childishly irritated by a fold in the bedclothes, the light coming through a slit in the blinds. Objects defeated him. He'd stare at a cup as if he'd never seen one before, grasp a spoon upside-down and try to eat his custard with its handle. While Mother and Aunt Kate took everything in stride (how did they do that?) I was tortured by the idea that the person inhabiting Father's body was a self-centered, petulant stranger whom I wasn't sure I could love.

But he continued to improve and steadily, if slowly, regained the power of speech. For a period he was mentally back in his childhood in Albany before his leg was lost, and one day he wept for hours over what his father's cruel Puritan God had done to him. Father's childhood in Albany had always seemed mythic, belonging to an archaic time, an age of giants. The iconically wealthy and pious William James of Albany went through three wives and fathered thirteen children. My brothers and I knew the key elements of the myth by heart: The fire, the amputation, Father's quarrel with his father, his banishment, his marriage to Mother and their early years in a Fourierite commune in France. The great Vastation, followed by the great Illumination. But from a child's perspective, it was a tale of unceasing pain and terror.

By three months after the stroke, Father had recovered most of his faculties. He was able to hobble about with a cane and eat meals in the dining room with the family. Whenever he drank wine, however, he talked as if he had pebbles in his mouth. His fork would go skidding and skittering around his plate, and several times during every meal the utensil would get stuck under the plate's edge, clacking and clattering between plate and table as Father grappled with it like a demon.

"Parietal lobe damage," William whispered to me. "His brain can't tell him where the plate ends and the table begins."

We'd had no dinner guests in months, and turned down all invitations. Seeing Mother's serene public mask, telling everyone that Father was improving steadily, I felt nauseous. Every meal broke my heart and, unable to eat, I shed ten pounds in a month and a half. I could not escape the sense that I'd brought about some irreparable harm to my father. If I'd wished him dead by daydreaming of going back to Europe, I tried to cancel it by vowing to stay home by his side from now on. Since Katherine had exposed the fallacies of Father's Ideas, I even denied myself Katherine's company for a time. But that only made things worse, and I felt as if I were living on a cold planet far removed from the sun.

Father kept improving, however, until by the week before Christmas, there was scant evidence of the stroke.

"It is a Christmas miracle," Mother announced to Dr. Beach, who tried to make out that he'd predicted just such an outcome, when in fact he had predicted the opposite. On Christmas Eve most Bostonians attended church. The Jameses did not. I myself had never set foot in a place of worship except in Europe to gawk at architectural details. William found himself in a church for the first time when he attended Edward Emerson's wedding. Sometimes Mother or Aunt Kate would say wistfully, "Wouldn't it be nice *just once* to hear Phillips Brooks preach? He is said to be very good!" or "It would be lovely to sing Christmas hymns in a church on Christmas Eve!" But Father continued to insist that "professional religion is the devil's subtlest device for keeping the human soul in bondage."

"But, Father, you have not set foot in a church in forty years," William reminded him. "For all you know, things have changed greatly since your Calvinist childhood."

"It is idle to expect any revival of the Church," he said with a dismissive gesture. "The Bible would have to be written over again."

"Well, perhaps you are the man to do it, Father."

Father chuckled at this.

For Christmas I received a beautiful leather-covered desk for my professoress duties; William, a set of precision dissecting tools made in Germany. "Why are you *encouraging* him?" I said to my parents.

William threw a sofa cushion at me from across the room, and I caught it and tossed it back in his face. Sitting in front of the tree (a late concession of Father's; for most of my life, our household had been barren of any such pagan rituals), we read aloud the Christmas letters from Wilky and Bob and tried to visualize each of them celebrating Christmas. It was not hard to picture them in front of Christmas trees in snowy Wisconsin, with wives and small children gathered round; Mother drifted readily into detailed speculations about each grandchild and how he or she might have greeted his or her gift. But Harry's bachelor Christmas in France was harder to fathom.

"I do hope he isn't alone on Christmas Day," Mother said, tearing up. "I will be uneasy about him until he finds a wife to manage the practical details of existence. Especially as he is so far from his family."

"The Angel is very good at getting himself invited to nice places, Mother," William pointed out. "He's probably at a great manor house in Normandy, being waited on hand and foot by liveried servants. I don't feel sorry for him. He is no doubt feeling very sorry for us living in the American wilderness."

At Christmas dinner Father presided in the old way, carving the goose, joking with Mother, reassuring Aunt Kate that not only did the gravy have no lumps, it was possibly the most *homogeneous* gravy he had ever tasted.

Between Christmas and New Year's, Cambridge was buried under a foot and a half of snow, and Fanny, Sara, and I rented a horse and sleigh and flew through the white streets silently, covered in fur, like characters in Tolstoy. Mauve trees stood in the silvered fields. The frosty wind snatched our breath away and bits of ice blew into our faces and reddened our cheeks.

Holding her muff protectively in front of her face, Sara announced she had important news; but we must promise not to be angry with her.

"We can't hear you if you mumble into your muff, Sara," I said.

Removing her muff from her mouth, she imparted her news, which was that she had resolved to apply herself in earnest to the task of finding a husband.

"A husband!" I said. "I hear they are a good deal of trouble most of the time."

Sara laughed and said that we must take into account how fundamentally weak-minded she was. "I am not like you two. Maybe it's because I am an orphan, but I feel as if I'm just dangling, like a loose thread. So I am going to England a month from now—to Yarmouth, to stay with cousins there."

"You're *not!*" said Fanny. "You *can't!*" I said.

It was a blow. Lizzy Boott and her father had recently returned to Europe, too. The ranks of our friends were thinning. If things kept going in this direction, I would be the last spinster in Boston.

"I will miss you both dreadfully, and you must write me so I don't perish of loneliness. But it's now or never. Boston has been a poor fishing ground, I must say. Look at what poor Theodora has caught!"

"Your plan is not a very romantic one, Sara," I said—but I said it gently.

"It's not my fault, Alice. It's that cursed war! The fine flower of Boston manhood buried on the battlefields, and a generation of spinsters withering on the vine. Even the insipid stories in *Godey's* allude to the shortage of men."

"Surely there are *some* nice men still among the living. William, for example?"

William and Sara were always flirting; you could not miss their mutual attraction. But William flirted with many girls.

"You know I *adore* William, but he is so whimsical! He can't provide the ballast I require. I am like dandelion fluff, scattered by every breeze. I need to graft myself to something solid—a large family preferably belonging to the class of landed gentry."

"You're mixing your metaphors, Sara," I pointed out. "What *are* you—dangling thread, dandelion fluff, a boat needing ballast, or a plant in need of staking?"

Sara smiled and shrugged her shoulders helplessly.

"Landed gentry!" Fanny said. "My, my, my!"

"In that case you are wise to go fishing in England," I said. "Better that than some malarial plantation in Georgia. I wish you all success and happiness, Sara." (This was true; I really did.)

"Thank you." Tears welled in her beautiful grey eyes. "We are friends forever, nothing can change that. I hope you two don't despise me for being so—practical."

"How could we despise you?" Fanny and I cried, nearly in unison.

There came a hush during which we listened to the wind soughing in the hemlocks and white pines. Sara took out her handkerchief and dabbed at her tear-stained face, then smiled through her tears. "By the way, Alice, has it escaped your notice that your brother is desperately in love with Alice Gibbens?"

I felt the blood drain from my face. It was a year since Father returned from a meeting of the Radical Club and announced, "William, I have met your future wife." This turned out to be Alice Gibbens, a schoolteacher of twenty-six. An intense, turbulent relationship ensued, with many ruptures, long searching talks, multiple misunderstandings. Anyone familiar with William, his jagged emotions and shifting moods, would not be greatly astonished to learn that his courtship of Miss Gibbens was a *via dolorosa*, strewn with obstacles, secret guilt, elaborate thirty-page confessions. He appeared to be doing his best to convince Miss Gibbens that he was the worst possible choice for a husband. Several months ago, he told me sadly that it was all over. "She does not love me," he said after reading her latest letter from Canada, where she'd fled to escape his moods. "She cares no more for me than for a dead leaf, nor ever will."

"Oh, I believe that is all over now," I told Sara.

I'd met Miss Gibbens and liked her at first. Then, when I began to observe how deviously she was sinking her claws into William, I began to detest her. I confess to being relieved that she was out of the picture.

"I wouldn't be so sure," Sara said.

After I reached home that evening, I stood for a while in the middle of Quincy Street in the midwinter dark without a cloak or bonnet or gloves and let the icy pellets lash my face. Then I wiped my eyes and went inside to take up my life again.

Why, I wondered, was everyone I cared about insisting on living in England all of a sudden?

In early January a letter arrived from Harry reporting that he'd crossed the Channel, disembarked at Folkstone, and made his way to London, his new home. *I have burned my ships behind me—let my apartment. I always meant sooner or later to go to London.* Despite the filthy weather—*dirty fog-paste, like Thames mud in solution*—he pronounced himself as happy as could be.

⌒ SEVENTEEN ⌒

1878

WHEN THE NEWS ARRIVED THE FOLLOWING SPRING OF THE SUC-
cess of Sara's "fishing expedition," I was unsurprised. It was as I'd foreseen (and I consider myself a bit of a seeress in these matters). I knew
Sara to be capable of a steely resolve in pursuit of what she felt her
happiness required, and it took her no more than five months to hook
a rather large fish, namely William Erasmus Darwin, the eldest son of
Mr. Charles Darwin. Harry described him in a letter as *a gentle, kindly,
reasonable, liberal, bald-headed, dull-eyed, British-featured, sandy-
haired insulaire.* He was older than Sara, but perhaps that was what she
needed for ballast.

Harry attended the wedding and sent us a lengthy report.

Six months earlier, Nanny Ashburner had married a Mr. Richards
from Maine, and thus I was doubly bereft (while being required to
act pleased, even overjoyed, about their happiness). Swept up in her
usual maelstrom of noble causes and good works, Katherine was often
unavailable; she was a woman of action and I was a woman of—what?—
indolence, I suppose. It appeared that what I'd dreaded and joked
about for years—being "the last bloom unplucked"—was indeed coming to pass. There was still Fanny, but she had one besotted suitor after
her, and I had never had one apart from the simple, mouth-breathing
stable-boy in Ripton, Vermont, who proposed to everything in a skirt.
But I pulled myself together and managed to sound as thrilled in my
letters as was required of friends of the newly engaged or married.

In the fall Sara brought her new husband to Cambridge, where they were feted at a great many receptions. (Sara was a great favorite in Cambridge-Boston, and the Darwin family had numerous Boston connections.) I found Mr. Darwin exactly as Harry described and liked him very much. The odd thing was that Sara herself did not appear as happy as a newly married woman ought to be. She did not look well either—bone-white and too thin—and seemed to be dragging herself through the events, her manner flat and listless. What had happened to her in England to reduce her to a ghostly simulacrum of herself?

"I cannot forgive her for her lack of enthusiasm for her new husband," I said to Fanny following one reception for the newlyweds. "When you think of the hordes of lovelorn spinsters . . . "

"Oh Alice, don't be too hard on her. Marriage isn't always a bed of roses."

"Well, she shouldn't have taken it on then!"

"When we take something on, do we ever really know what we *are* taking on? Let us wish for Sara's happiness."

After a pause, I said, "You're right, Fanny. You must help me to be more charitable." Though it was irksome that so many of the best young women of Cambridge were being carried off like the Sabine women, I would keep these thoughts to myself. For myself and Katherine, there would be no rites, no well wishes, no receptions, no wedding journeys, no acknowledgment whatsoever of our union.

But that was not the worst. The worst was still to come.

In April 1878, William announced his engagement to Alice Gibbens. I received the news as if it were an electrocution. The first few times Miss Gibbens came to call, I had to slip away quickly up the back stairs, as I simply could not bear to see the loving looks that passed between that Alice (the false Alice, to me) and William. Or, for that matter, my parents' excessive fondness for Miss Gibbens, with her "melting brown eyes." Father was enchanted, having "discovered" this goddess, after all. Mother was charmed by her practicality and thrift and the fact that she had worked as a teacher to help support her family; she would make a good wife for a poor man like William, who had to work for a living. I did not see how I could forgive her for stealing William, my parents, and the name Alice James in the bargain.

The truth burned like lye. Alice Gibbens would come first with William forever. If we were all shipwrecked he would save her first and leave me to drown. I recognized that my thoughts were extreme, but Miss Gibbens's perfections were nails driven into my flesh; I felt my very psychic existence to be in peril and had to save myself somehow. *Sauve qui peut!* When I was obliged to interact with my future sister-in-law, I withdrew into an implacable coldness and revenged myself by talking over her head in the James family code. "Have you heard?" I'd say, "The Children are going to the Shore, and so is Charlemagne. And the Ancient Houri of Kirkland Street has been lecturing lately on the French ladies of the eighteenth century!" Miss Gibbens would smile, vaguely and uncomprehendingly, ignorant of the fact that the Children were the family of Professor Childs, Charlemagne was Charles Norton, and the Ancient Houri of Kirkland Street was Grace Norton. Once, when I'd snubbed Miss Gibbens in this way, I caught a flash of pure hatred on William's face. He would hate me from now on, I supposed. Such things could not be repaired. But no one in the family was much interested in my sufferings. What was I compared to a blissful engaged couple?

"You should see the way she prattles on about books with Father, pretending to be so intellectual," I harped to Katherine the long-suffering. How good and patient she was during my slough of despond.

"Well, isn't she *actually* intellectual?"

"Katherine dear, given our bond, I expect you to dislike her alongside me."

"My loyalty to you is absolute, darling, but in the end you will have to swallow her, you know."

I did not think I could. Almost overnight, I became ill. My mind moved along a narrow groove. It was like dreaming with my eyes open. The dream was unchanging and oppressive; a nightmare in which things became muddled and I lost my way at every step. My parents would shoot me searching glances and ask if I were feeling poorly, and I would say I was perfectly fine. The others did not understand because they were healthy-minded. William was not by nature perhaps, but evidently Alice Gibbens had made him so.

Healthy-minded people couldn't grasp that just getting out of bed could be as exhausting as laying track for the railroad. To dress myself or dress my hair was beyond my powers. Paralyzed by my image in the mirror, I'd break out in a cold sweat and watch my shaking hand set the hairbrush down on the dresser scarf. Someone would find me later, with one side of my hair pinned and the other side hanging loose, staring at my face in the glass as if wondering whose it was.

My stomach was pierced with sharp pains; presently I was having fits almost every night. Sometimes it was Mother or Aunt Kate, but usually it was Father who comforted me. I saw during my lucid intervals that I provided something for him—a congregation of one. We would talk softly for hours, or rather Father would talk and I would listen. He would talk about whatever came into his mind—Wilky's war wounds, the failure of the boys' Florida plantation, the evils of slavery, the horrors of the class system in Europe, Mother's perfections, the "pusillanimous clergy," Father's troubled relations with his old Transcendentalist friends. He told me one night that his trouble was that he'd always been "exploding with love." I recognized that I was hearing a conversation he was always having with himself. I tried to tell him that I, too, was exploding with love. Although I might appear to be a cold, thin-blooded person, inside my heart I was a geyser. Chagrined by feeling so much, I'd perfected a way of veiling myself. I told Father that I wished there were a bromide I could take to relieve me of feeling everything so intensely, so I could be normal. He said not to wish for that; it was a fine thing to feel deeply, but I must channel it into Divine Nature.

I began saying I'd be better off dead.

"Darling girl, the ennui and disgust of life which lead so many suffering souls every year to suicide—these are an avowal that we are nothing and all vanity, that we are absolutely without help in ourselves."

I heard the words but they could not reach me. My thoughts came at me thick and deep and swirling like snow in a heavy fog. Through the long nights, Father stroked my fevered brow and urged me to hold fast to my "inner being" and "give no thought to the illusory phenomenal form." Then why must I have clothes made for the phenomenal form? And how to simply "give no thought" to something that was devouring your very soul? I'd have to find my own way out of the maze.

"Perhaps I don't have an inner being, Father. Or I did and it got lost." Tears were coursing down my cheeks.

"Of course you have, darling."

He said, "Your long sickness, and Harry's, and Willy's, have been an immense discipline for me, in gradually teaching me to universalize my sympathies."

"What do you mean, Father?"

"When some terrible thing strikes one of my children, the thought comes to me that if it happened to a stranger's child I would be unmoved. And so I ask God to let me feel as much for any other creature as I do for my own children."

"I see." I absorbed Father's nightly sermons the way a baby takes in the words of a lullaby. Sometimes he'd laugh and say he'd "never been guilty of a stroke of business" and that his main objective in life was "to do justice to my children." Then he was back to the two trees in the garden, a metaphor I'd never really grasped. But his loving voice was a dike that held back the dark raging sea. He told me of his childhood in Albany, describing his parents and brothers and sisters—not neglecting sister Janet, whose insanity took the form of intense religiosity and was at first mistaken for saintliness.

"Like Kitty Prince?"

"Kitty is a queer one, isn't she?" he chuckled.

I did not want to become another Aunt Janet or Cousin Kitty; I'd sooner cut off my legs!

Perhaps to escape the madhouse, William suddenly voiced an inclination to marry quickly and quietly, and he and Miss Gibbens were wed on July 10, 1878 at Alice's grandmother's house, across from Boston Common. A friend of the family, Rufus Ellis, read the vows. Present were the bride's mother and her two sisters, Margaret and Mary, and Mother and Father, but none of William's siblings. The others had good excuses; my absence was an admission of the gravity of my illness. Afterwards the new Mr. and Mrs. William James took the train to New

York City; the next day they caught a train as far as Saratoga Springs, and from there a local to the Adirondacks and the Shanty.

I saw it all in my mind's eye. The dining car with its starched white tablecloths and swinging lamps, the smell of pine needles, creosote, and sun-warmed dust at the Shanty, the crystalline pool in which the newlyweds would bathe together naked, under a vault of stars. That Katherine and I, too, had "honeymooned" under the same stars and fallen in love among the same cedars and hemlocks and white pines was unmentionable, like a mad relative in Somerville. I knew my family well enough to intuit the vague things that were being said about me when anyone inquired—that I was indisposed, a bit under the weather, getting my strength back, and all of that. I myself did not think I would make it.

Twelve years later, in Leamington, England, I would write of this period: *This was the time when I went down to the dark sea, its dark waters closed over me, and I knew neither hope nor peace.* Every night I went under, drowning. I was shown many things during the night that evaporated in the morning. The black sadness washed over me again and again. Some nights I would throw myself sobbing into the arms of whichever parent was at my bedside. *What will become of me? When you are gone—what will become of me?* I had seen my stroke-broken father, my mother without her teeth; they were old and would not last forever.

You will always have your brothers, dear.

"Will I? Harry, in London, cherishes his privacy. Bob and Wilky I hardly know anymore and they live in Wisconsin. William will be cohabiting with a pack of Gibbenses—they *surely* won't want a deranged in-law in the spare room. Particularly after I spoiled their wedding."

You were ill, darling; I am sure William understands.

I was not at all certain of that.

"I shouldn't have done it, should I? Spoiled William's wedding! I should have stuffed myself into that ghastly canary-yellow frock and made an appearance. An apparition, I should say. Oh, I am beyond forgiving!" Weeping copiously and unable to stop, I was aware that this was not my finest hour.

It will be all right, dear. Don't worry about the future. You will be well provided for. You will be able to buy your own house one day! Perhaps at the Shore?

That was not the point. It was not a house I needed but a home.

In the morning a slice of bright white daylight entered through the space where the curtains didn't meet and moved across the floor toward me like a knife. Through the open window I overheard Father talking to Aunt Kate on the verandah. "Alice," I heard him say, "is most days on the verge of insanity and suicide." (Toward suicide Father held an ancient Greek attitude; he did not consider it a sin but urged me solemnly not to take my life in a "distressing manner.") I became fixated on the idea that my parents no longer loved me; that I had become a mad stranger who lived in their house. Mother's mask of resignation and the weariness in Father's eyes accused me silently.

It was my worst breakdown. The only person who seemed to understand was four thousand miles away. Harry wrote me, "It is inconsiderate of William to have chosen such a moment for making merry."

By late autumn, there was no escaping the conjugal bliss of Mr. and Mrs. William James. They were living right around the corner now, in rented rooms on Harvard Street, which meant that "Mrs. Alice" called on Mother and Father every day, spinning her bright webs around them. In addition to possessing melting brown eyes ("listening eyes," William called them, and she would have to do a lot of listening, married to William), she was charming, intelligent, and well-read, and, on top of all these marvels, *enceinte* with the next James grandchild.

It was obvious that the new Alice could not be driven away by snubbing. She was William's for life, and he hers. Nothing could undo that. There was nothing for it but to eat the entire indigestible meal of William's marriage. No one would ever know how hard it was, the parts of myself I had to conquer and subdue.

I started by forcing myself to be polite to my new sister-in-law. Gritting my teeth, I'd smile and lend her books and ask her if she had felt the baby move and whether she thought it was a boy or a girl. I started knitting things for the baby and told everyone how excited I was to become an aunt again. My letters to friends were full of praise for my sister-in-law. *She is a truly lovely being, so sweet and gentle & with so much intelligence besides.*

By the time the baby—Henry James III—entered the world on May 18, 1879, I had more or less come to terms with the marriage. When baby Harry was three weeks old, Alice asked if I wished to hold him. I didn't: He was at the small and floppy stage, and babies were apt to take a dim view of me in any case. He would almost certainly wail upon finding himself in my non-nurturing arms, and I would be mortified. But how could I refuse? When he was placed in my arms, he didn't cry, to my relief, just gazed at me solemnly as if we knew each other already, as if we'd known each other for a thousand years. Then his tiny features seized up and he sneezed. It was probably his first sneeze and sounded like a baby rabbit sneezing and the astonishment on his tiny face stole my heart. Here was a baby I could truly love.

PART THREE

⌒ ONE ⌒

1889

So I FINALLY CRACKED UNDER THE WEIGHT OF DUTY AND NICE manners. (At least that is one story I tell myself.) Perhaps I had to go a little crazy to quit being a dutiful daughter and sister. Something inside me was ravenous, you see, and becoming a nervous wreck was the only way forward for a person like me. Not that I *chose* invalidism, but when it chose me, I suppose I took it up with a certain zeal. Henry might understand. How he makes his characters suffer! How much they are required to renounce! Poor Isabel Archer, stuck forever in loveless matrimony to a pedantic man with a marked resemblance to Francis Boott. Renunciation remains sorrow, though sorrow nobly born. And I should know.

For more than two years, I have been stranded, Robinson Crusoe-like, on the island of myself, my castaway condition having begun the day Katherine sailed back to America. That was two years ago. Some days I could fling myself against the walls of my rooms like a wasp in a jam jar. It came to me not long after Katherine left that I shall never recover. I shall simply keep living as I have lived for years, getting a little better and a little worse—more worse than better, on the whole.

My existence is somewhat restricted intellectually, confined as it is to Nurse and Miss Clarke. For one who grew up amidst the hilarity of Father and William, it wasn't easy, but I did eventually adapt to the Saharan expanses of my solitude. My callers have dwindled to a trickle: Miss Wilcutt, an old maid with a brain tumor, young Miss

Leppington who suffers from seizures and a religious conscience, Miss Percy, a cheerful, literal-minded aristocrat who comes by with her pug and expects me to fawn over it. Of course, there is my landlady, Miss Clarke, and the usual pack of Mind Cure ladies.

Although Henry remains the best of brothers, he has made himself scarce lately, for the Season is upon him. The London Season lasts from April until August, when everyone goes off to the country to shoot at poor defenseless animals. Henry claims to despise the Season, says it is like trying to move around in a too crowded room, but he always goes, and apparently people fight like rabid dogs to be seated near him. I think they hope he will write about them, and it never seems to occur to them that their portraits might not be entirely flattering.

My period has come round again like a bad joke. Since I am never to have children, it seems a lot of bother for nothing, like having a closet full of clothes all the wrong size. I must say, the fertility of the poor here is an overwhelming force like the Connaught floods, every creature helpless before it. How God must love little children; he rains more of them down every day, on the poor above all.

Nurse is resolute in her approval of infants whether or not they have food, clothing, or shelter. I see from her sly expression this morning that she has brought back a sizeable conversational nugget from her descent into the streets and shops of Leamington. "Fancy, Miss, on my way to the bakery I ran into the Brooks children near the pump-house, four of them—"

"Oh, Nurse!" I see the smile she is trying to suppress and have guessed the dénouement.

"And Becky Brooks says to me, 'Mama was very bad last night and then the lady came and brought her a baby.'"

"One more tiny voice to swell the vast human wail, Nurse!"

Nurse's face clouds over. "Certainly you can be happy about a new baby, Miss."

"You can hardly regard this infant as a lucky stroke, Nurse. Poor pinched-faced Becky Brooks, eight years old, already goes around with the two-year-old stuck to her like—like an *excrescence*. What is that child's name?"

"Eliza."

"Why is she not walking yet, Nurse? And only says 'la la.' Two years old! I suppose now we'll be seeing that sad little Charlotte dragging the new baby around like a sack of potatoes. Didn't you say she was simple?"

"Yes, but a good girl, Miss."

"That's hardly the point. She is only five and shouldn't be burdened with a baby."

Nurse retreats briefly into one of her sulks. It is very enervating that she insists on thinking charitably and optimistically about everyone and refuses to see how the poor are daily betrayed by God and England. I feel that it is my responsibility to make her face the facts.

"They do their best, Miss. God will provide."

"Tell me, Nurse. If God ever lifted a finger for *les misérables*, do you think the Bachellers would have to stay in bed until noon because they get less hungry that way?"

"I am very sorry I ever told you that, Miss, since it bothers you so much."

"You know I don't wish to be spared any detail."

"Well, if you are determined to dwell on upsetting things . . . " Sucking in her cheeks, she bustles around straightening cushions that are already straight.

"Perhaps you are right, Nurse," I say to mollify her. "Tell me, do you think it is unnatural in a woman not to want children?" I can't help wringing my hands over these poor worn-out creatures, tied down like Gulliver by countless small mouths and stomachs. I am thinking principally of the mothers.

"I reckon most want them, Miss." She has picked up her knitting and settled into the armchair near the window.

"Would you say it is natural to have fifteen children? Twenty? Mrs. Eberly—the plump lady with gout, remember?—told me of a family in Birmingham with twenty-five children. They are sent out in groups of eight in different directions. I wonder if the parents are hoping one or two will get lost along the way. One of the groups must have nine in it, come to think of it."

Nurse sinks deeper into her sullen mood. Is it my imagination or do her knitting needles click more rapidly?

"Twenty-five infants! Think of it, Nurse. How feeble and diluted the parental instinct must be, trickling down through twenty-five. Imagine being personally responsible for the cutting of eight hundred teeth!"

"Oh, I believe the teeth come in all on their own, Miss."

⌐ T W O ⌐

JUST NOW, THE TICKING OF THE CLOCK IS OPPRESSIVE. MY VISI-
tor is due at four, but at twenty past has not arrived. The waiting makes
me jittery and heartsick and I can feel the "snakes" in my stomach
start to writhe. Sometimes I wish that no one would visit me, or would
arrive without announcing it beforehand; it would save my nerves a
great deal of wear and tear.

All morning Nurse has been unable to suppress her curiosity,
owing to all the misinformation she has been fed by her church Guild.
"So she is the daughter of Mr. Darwin, Miss?"

"Daughter-in-*law*, Nurse. Before her marriage she was Sara
Sedgwick, a good friend of mine in America. I have told you about her.
In 1877 she married Mr. Darwin's eldest son and moved to England."

"Oh yes. Is the son very like the father?" Translation: Does the
whole family have cloven hooves?

"I never met Mr. Charles Darwin. All I can tell you is that this Mr.
Darwin has been rather bald since he was a young man." Young*ish*. He
was pushing forty when he married Sara.

Sara arrives at half past four with a dozen roses for me. She always
brings flowers, either to save the trouble of finding something more
original or because she views me as a hopeless invalid confined to a
sickroom, needing a profusion of flowers.

"Well, Sara, you find me, as always, at my lifelong occupation
of 'improving.' I'm afraid all the physicians of England have washed
their hands of me."

She smiles thinly, as if a real laugh would require a vitality beyond her powers, then spends about twenty minutes complaining of the difficulties of getting here. She looks unwell and I watch the familiar deadly "gone" look steal over her face minute by minute. It is like watching an eclipse of the sun, and an enormous lump wells up in my throat and I feel as if I might weep. But I must not. Nanny Ashburner Richards thinks Sara is a hypochondriac, but I think anyone who looks so ill must really be.

Nurse hovers nearby with a dust cloth, trying to mask her curiosity. The blue dusk deepens and the lamps are lit with a hiss. Sara has been complaining about her servants, how they over-starch the linens and her housekeeper pretends not to understand her English. I attempt to steer the conversation to national differences in hopes of injecting a little life into it. "Henry says the main desire in the British bosom is not to be left last with the host and hostess after an entertainment of any kind, so at a given moment there is a regular stampede."

"Oh, Alice, I don't think that is the rule at all."

"He also says Englishwomen look entirely differently in Paris to what they do in London, not handsome at all, but big and clumsy."

"I think Henry is a little inclined to overgeneralize national characteristics. I suppose it sells books, doesn't it?"

Searching for something to ignite a real conversation, I try another gambit. "Can you imagine anything so inconceivably dreary as the existence led by royalty? How they must long to see a *back*." At this the old Sara unexpectedly comes to life. She bursts out laughing and the light comes back to her eyes. I am reminded of the way she used to laugh in the old days, clutching her sides and pleading, "Please, Alice, *promise* not to say anything funny for the next five minutes."

"Oh Alice!" she says now. "No one ever made me laugh like you. I'll never forget your dramatic recitation of 'The Angel in the House.' That was possibly your finest hour, though there were so many it would be hard to say."

"I'd nearly forgotten that." It comes back to me now: A *tableau vivant* we did based on the saccharine painting hanging in the Misses Ashburners' back parlor. Somewhere in most homes in those years there was a painting of "The Angel in the House," playing the piano or darning socks while her little angels play companionably on the carpet and her lord and master smokes his pipe and reads the newspaper. For the *tableau* I'd garbed myself as the sainted woman in the painting while Bob played the part of my husband and, departing from the usual rules governing *tableaux vivants*, I recited a few lines of the cloying poem.

Lifting my eyes heavenward, I recite now, "Man must be pleased; but *him* to please is woman's pleasure."

Sara's eyes tear up, and she dabs at the corners with her handkerchief. Unable to recall what comes next, I recite the only other lines I remember: *She loves with love that cannot tire;/and when, ah woe, she loves alone,/Through passionate duty love springs higher,/As grass grows taller round a stone.*

"I have never quite fathomed how love compares to grass growing up around a stone," I say. "The whole poem is daft, isn't it?"

Sara is gazing at me with infinite tenderness. "Very daft," she says. "And the absurd notion that love springs from duty and that Home is so holy to our sex that we should never wish to set a foot outside the door. Oh, but Alice, I didn't mean—" She blushes, evidently recalling that I never go out.

I brush this aside. "It's all right, Sara. But what do you think the poet means by *when she loves alone?* Can it be that the husband has become *weary* of the poor drudge?"

Sara laughs merrily, and it is like the sun emerging from behind a cloud. "Ah well, who could blame him? Imagine living with a martyr like that; you'd almost *have* to be very wicked to balance things out." As she says this, her upper lip curls in a way familiar to me from the days when she mocked the pieties of our youth. I am surprised by a memory of her hand up my skirt at Shady Hill as Charles Norton droned on about the ancient Greeks, the hint of a smile at the corners of her mouth. If we could fly back there, to reckless love, to youth and hopefulness, just for an hour. But no one can, of course.

The sun ducks back behind a cloudbank. Before long, Sara has launched into a tale about a luncheon with the Prince of Wales and some Princesses Royal, which she describes in some detail before becoming gloomily preoccupied with her horticultural problems. She mentions a book I haven't read and tells me that Grace Norton is in England with Sally and Lily, who are young ladies now.

"I expect their father wants them to acquire English accents," I say.

Sara shrugs. "I don't see anything wrong with that." I can't help noting that a few English inflections have rubbed off on Sara herself, but I suppose she has a right to them, being English on her mother's side.

Grace never calls on me, of course. Visits Henry often, sympathizing with him about the loathsome burden of an invalid sister. *We are all so concerned, by all means don't let your work suffer,* et cetera. I must have some of Mrs. Piper's occult powers because I can read Grace like a book, even from afar.

As for Sara, what happened to the young girl who dreamed of running away to live with the Bedouins, who drank absinthe, quoted Baudelaire, and sneered at all conformity? I was a fairly conventional young girl (though subversive in my mind) until Sara showed me other possibilities.

Something I had forgotten floats into my mind, something Sara said years ago, when she was visiting America with her new husband. Someone was asking about her honeymoon in Italy. She was speaking into her teacup and so faintly that you wondered if you'd misheard. I recall the word "disappointing." Or maybe it was "discouraging." I believed she was referring to the lack of amenities at their hotel, but now I wonder. Was the marriage unconsummated? Or consummated too brutally, as sometimes happens (I am told)? We only see the surfaces of people, even those closest to us; the rest is unspeakable mystery.

⌐ THREE ⌐

THE FIRST THING PEOPLE WONDER ABOUT INVALIDS IS HOW WE occupy our time. First of all, pain consumes a good deal of our attention. It comes in so many dizzying varieties: pounding, grinding, drilling, whacking, constant, floating, intermittent, sharp, dull, radiating; tooth pain, head pain, joint pain, stomach pain, bone pain—I've known them all. (I could teach the physicians a thing or two, but they don't listen, not to a woman anyhow.)

When the pain is very bad, I have Nurse give me morphia, and then, although I still feel the pain, it seems to have nothing to do with me.

When callers ask how I pass the hours, I say I read a good deal and leave it at that, but, in fact, there are a thousand small ways to amuse oneself without leaving one's bed. I really ought to print up a pamphlet on the subject.

Trying to recall things, for example.

You think up categories and make lists: All the hats I've worn, the rivers I've crossed, the twelve labors of Hercules, the hotels I've stayed in from Paris to Quebec, the names, in alphabetical order, of the girls in my class at Mrs. Agassiz's school. The word for nightgown in French (*chemise de nuit*), the first lines of a Victor Hugo poem (*Est-ce ma faute à moi si vous n'êtes pas grands? Vous aimez les hiboux, les fouines, les tyrans,/Le mistral, le simoun, l'écueil, la lune rousse*), the names of the Sapphic ladies in Balzac's *La Fille Aux Yeux d'Or*.

You'd be astonished at how absorbed you can become in a railway timetable; with it as your magic carpet you can travel from the Gare Saint-Lazare in Paris to Boulogne-sur-Mer, watching the countryside rush backwards in your memory. It is fantastic what the mind retains in its hidden pockets. Woods and fields, stone houses, apple orchards, storks nesting in chimneys, village squares with their band shells and their *mairies*, young women in kerchiefs whispering together on a bench. Yesterday I spent most of the morning recalling the ball-gowns of my youth. My first grown-up formal gown had a hoop-skirt. A hoop-skirt was a death trap; it could launch a woman off a cliff in a stiff wind or, if her skirt caught fire, trap her inside the metal cage to burn to death, as happened to poor Mrs. Longfellow of Brattle Street.

The hoop-skirt, and the petticoats undergirding it, eventually shrank to the sleek silhouette of the polonaise; then, unfortunately, for reasons known only to a handful of Parisian couturiers, the polonaise commenced gradually to gather into a puffball over the buttocks, ultimately becoming the bustle. For several years women resembled swaybacked horses, with shelves jutting out from their hindquarters on which you could have rested a wine bottle and glasses. (What a strange notion of female anatomy our young men must have had!) Need I add that these costumes were weighed down by numberless tassels, flounces, braids, beads, jewels, bangles, and other furbelows? To be a woman is to be weighed down.

In the days when I was *not* yet weighed down, when I was a child running free in a short skirt, a powerful reverie would steal over me and it was as natural as breathing or feeling the sun on my skin. Then, inexplicably, when I was about thirteen, a door slammed shut and my secret world, my luminous inner world, became inaccessible to me. Does this happen to everyone? Did I notice it more because of our family's social isolation? Soon I could scarcely remember the past at all; it all became very remote, like teething rings or baby teeth.

But a year or two ago, the past began coming back. Now everything I recall or imagine feels realer than real: the stones are cold and damp to the touch, the colors jewel-like in the stained-glass windows, the scent of vinegar and earth pungent on the stone steps of the cellar.

Well, let me take you there.

The sisters make us kneel on the flagstones to pray; the discomfort is supposed to pull our thoughts away from worldly things and back to God. But whenever I try to think of God I see only ugly Sister Augustine and am filled with a great repugnance. I open one eye a slit, glimpse the girl next to me in the pew. Her eyes are closed, her hands steepled in prayer, but there is the hint of a saucy smile at the corners of her mouth.

I shut my eyes, open them again. The mysterious smile is still there. Are these the schoolgirls I glimpsed in the Louvre sixteen years ago? Or have I somehow entered the Paris convent where George Sand was educated? I can't say, but here, as in George Sand's convent, the pupils have sorted themselves into three groups, *les sages* (the good), *les bêtes* (the stupid), and *les diables* (the devils). No question about it, Vivienne (for that is the girl's name) is a *diable*. So am I. "Don't open your eyes," I whisper. "Pretend you are praying, but talk to me."

"*D'accord.*" The dimple in her cheek deepens as she tries to suppress a smile.

"If you could wish for one person here to die, who would it be?" How easy it is to whisper out of the side of your mouth while scarcely moving your lips. One of the many useful talents fostered in a convent school.

"Would I go to hell for wishing it?"

"No, you'd get a free pass. You'd be off the hook."

"Well, Sister Augustine then. *Je la déteste.*" Vivienne snaps her fingers soundlessly, holding her hand just below the prayer rail. A wide smile breaks out behind her steepled hands. "Is she gone? *Elle est disparue?*"

"Yes, the only trace of her is a little pile of bones and her crucifix on its heavy chain. Now listen carefully, Vivienne. Tonight we will meet in the small chapel with the baptismal font, the one near the staircase that leads down to the cellar. As soon as Sister Boniface starts to snore, we'll sneak down."

We have just discovered that in the cellar there are dank stone steps, smelling of earth, mice, and rot, leading to the underground catacombs. These catacombs go on forever, we have heard, beneath the streets of Paris. Who could resist such an adventure? Yet we tremble to think what monstrosities might lurk in those subterranean tunnels.

That night, as it happens, Vivienne falls asleep before Sister Boniface does, and I don't have the heart to wake her. It is so cold in the dormitory that little cloud-puffs rise from the girls' mouths. There are delicate frost flowers etched on the lower half of most of the windows. I lie awake most of the night, hearing the bells toll the hours, thinking of Vivienne's smile, my rosary, my evensong.

A knock on the door jars me out of this daydream. It is Miss Percy, one of my most faithful callers, in an apple-green walking dress with a rose-colored polonaise. She is accompanied by an elderly lady I've never seen before.

"The door downstairs was on the latch so I just walked up. I hope you don't mind, Miss James."

Miss Percy is an Englishwoman of the useful information sort, a type Henry says is more common among the men here.

"Oh, yes, Miss Clarke has taken to leaving the front door unlatched, as the newlywed couple upstairs cannot seem to hold on to their key. I hear them in the corridor—'You had it, Darling.'

'No, Ducks, I am sure I saw you put it in your vest pocket this morning.'"

The newlywed husband bounds downstairs at half past eight every weekday morning, a series of fast thuds, a pause for the landing, another series of thuds. I know them by heart. Count to three and he bounces into view striding across the crossroads, where ragged children sweep the dirt and straw back and forth. He takes his hat off with his left hand, runs his right hand through his hair, puts the hat on again, and disappears. At half past five he bounds up the stairs again like a half-grown puppy. His wife meets him in the hall, and there are kisses and murmured endearments. The rhythms of this young couple, like the five daily mail deliveries and Nurse's venturings out, punctuate the monotony of my days. There is always something to look forward to.

"In the beginning marriage must feel like playing house," I remark to my visitors. "Until it gets to be a chore."

"Yes, I expect so," Miss Percy says, and introduces me to Mrs. Arnold, an elderly lady with skin tags on her eyelids resembling barnacles on a log. Apart from this, she is rather elegant and has a beautiful smile. She suffers from malaria, she informs me cheerfully. It is incurable and waxes and wanes, "but when you've had it as long as I have, it simply becomes part of your life. It is curious how one becomes accustomed to things, isn't it, Miss James? I am not sure I would be willing to give up my malaria now that it has become part of my character."

Miss Percy, sipping the tea that Nurse has brought in, appears deeply puzzled. After doing her customary 360-degree scan of the room, she asks, "How do you occupy yourself all day, Miss James? If I were stuck in a room all day, I should go barking mad, I think."

This is a tactless thing to say to an invalid, but Miss Percy is a good egg and means well. "Oh, I read, write letters, stare out the window. I have become a connoisseur of skies and clouds. Also, I am capable of an immense amount of wool-gathering."

I am thinking, *Oh my dear, if you only knew!*

I ask Mrs. Arnold where she contracted her disease, and she tells me India. She is the widow of a civil engineer and spent thirty years on the subcontinent, living on in Lucknow for several years after her husband's death. I steel myself for the usual condescension toward the duskier races, but Mrs. Arnold is not one of those. If she hadn't fallen ill, she never would have returned, she tells me. "My heart is in India. Unfortunately, this body requires a northern climate." (I like the way she says *this body*, as if it were an object only loosely connected with herself. I have a feeling Mrs. Arnold and I may become friends.)

Miss Percy chooses this moment to interrogate me about where we got the buns I am serving and to reflect on their resemblance to a pastry baked by a friend's cook. It is some time before we manage to get out of this rut and back to India. Mrs. Arnold describes several things that interest me greatly: a temple in Calcutta where monkeys are worshipped as gods, weddings where six-year-old brides, weighed down with gold jewelry, weep for their mothers, a city on the Ganges where the sickly flock to die because it is considered auspicious to die there.

"The Hindoos do not hide death. They put a dead relative on an open pyre and everyone sits around and watches it burn; you see the skin blacken and the fat crackle and the arms fall off. If you take a boat down the Ganges at night, you pass dozens of bodies burning on the ghats like candles in the night. After that it is impossible not to see the body as a temporary abode."

She smiles and so do I. Miss Percy arches an eyebrow. I suppose I will get an earful on the subject of pagan idolatry another day.

Leamington, Mrs. Arnold adds, reminds her of Benares, the city on the Ganges where it is considered auspicious to die. Both are waiting rooms for eternity, but here there is a great gulf between heaven and earth, she says, while in India the next world feels very near, separated by the subtlest of screens. I am finding Mrs. Arnold very interesting and hope she will visit again.

HENRY JAMES
DE VERE GARDENS, KENSINGTON
JANUARY 1889

To WILLIAM JAMES
Alice is not unhappy, but she is homesick. I don't think she likes England or the English very much—the people, their mind, their tone, their hypocrisy. This is partly owing to the confined life she leads and to the passive, fragmentary way she sees people. Also to her being such a tremendously convinced Home Ruler.

WILLIAM JAMES
FEBRUARY 11TH, CAMBRIDGE

To MISS ALICE JAMES
I ask everyone, Alice, who has seen you whether you are homesick, and can't make out how it is, either from their replies or yr. letters. You being caught over there is the strangest fate. Mary Watson was in the

cars last evening and told me of her visit to you last summer, praising (like everyone else) yr charm, brilliancy and beauty. Why don't you have yr photog. sold as a professional? There would also be an American market. . . . Wendell Holmes is going to vote for Harrison, God knows why, except to show the shady side of himself.

⌒ FOUR ⌒

IT BEGAN AS A COMMONPLACE BOOK. YOU KNOW THE SORT OF thing, for aren't they all the same? Favorite poems (on Love, Motherhood, God) copied out next to keepsakes from balls, steamship ticket stubs, inspirational passages from literature, sympathy cards from friends. My book was far from inspirational, however, being almost exclusively devoted to newspaper clippings documenting my obsessions. What can I say? I am a shut-in.

I believe I've mentioned that when I am too ill to read, Nurse reads aloud to me from the *Standard,* the *Times,* the *Telegraph,* or the *Pall Mall Gazette* in her high clear voice. On the Irish Question, Parliamentary debates and so on, she wraps herself in my opinions a hundred percent. I have heard her say, "Of course I know nothing about it myself, but I know someone who says so-and-so. My patient Miss James and *she* must know."

Sadly, however, I can't seem to cure her of that dismal "sense of one's betters" that poisons everything here. Yesterday she and I were reading a newspaper story about a visit two of the princesses paid to a hospital. I said, "When, Nurse, have you seen a dying child recover because a princess has passed through a ward?" She kept insisting that it was terribly kind of the royals to visit the sick. She won't hear a word against them. (Miss Clarke is even more devoted; the Queen's Jubilee is memorialized on her tea towels, a tea cozy, an apron, and a serving plate.)

"Well, they ought to do *something* to justify the cost of keeping 'em," I said, at which Nurse went silent as a clam and began to knit strenuously. I told her that I couldn't stop thinking about young Georgie Cross, about whom she'd told me. After the girl's mother died of cancer, she was placed with a "lydy" and put in charge of six children at one shilling per week and one change of underwear. Imagine getting by with a single change of underwear per week and never having a bath, whilst having to dress and undress countless pampered children all day long! I casually remarked that if the royal household had one fewer horse, a hundred Georgies could have a whole week's worth of underwear. Unfortunately, during my harangue I made reference to the "tinsel monarchy" and Nurse reacted as if I'd slapped her. I must watch my tongue and avoid attacking her sacred cows, however absurd they may strike me.

In the newspapers Nurse and I have been reading about Mr. Balfour, about Henry Morton Stanley plowing through darkest Africa, shooting at everything that moves. About Robert Browning, dead. (A pity he didn't die before he made such a spectacle of himself with Edward Fitzgerald.) Every day the great men go on shouting in Parliament, starting wars, massacring Arabs, Indians, and Africans, acquiring medals and titles. To me they are like children, knowing nothing of real life.

After a while I began to cut out and save the stories that tore at my heart:

> *The lad who opened the door said his mother was in the Banstead Lunatic Asylum, suffering from melancholia brought on through starvation . . .*

> *The comments, which appeared in our columns on Monday last on the case of the man Mark Henry Vaile, who fell dead through starvation has excited considerable interest.*

> *On Wednesday afternoon a parish officer called for the first time and desired to take all the children to the workhouse . . .*

As my clippings collected in unsightly drifts on the end-tables, poor Nurse was growing quite distraught. "Miss," she said, "if you insist on saving these nasty things, perhaps you ought to paste them into a proper album." I saw from her expression that she was prepared for a fight and was surprised when I capitulated immediately. "You are quite right, Nurse. It is best to be systematic about a hobby if one undertakes one."

The next morning she ventured out in a bone-chilling rain under the cheerless skies of Leamington (I, of course, live untouched by weather, as one does in dreams or the afterlife) and returned with a nice scrapbook from the stationer's.

This introduced a fresh dilemma, for now I was obliged to mull over various organizational schemes and categories. Victims of Poverty, Absurd Parliamentary Debates, the Parnell Case, Moral Blindness, Royal Blunders, Heartless Tories, Irish Home Rule, Despicable British Institutions, Injustices to Women, Stanley in Africa, Incidents of Casual Cruelty toward the Natives of the Empire. I saw that this could lead to an endlessly ramifying scheme that wearied my brain just to think about. Finally I decided just to file them by date.

At some point something surprising happened. Gradually I found myself penning whole paragraphs of commentary, which soon overshadowed the clippings. I began to entertain the occasional fantasy that my clippings and commentary would be published after my death, exposing the numberless ways the poor and defenseless have been wronged on this damp island. (Of course, it is more likely that some future relative, stumbling on this collection of yellowing clippings about events and people long forgotten, will think, "Great-Aunt Alice was a regular magpie, wasn't she? Surely we can throw out her rubbish now.")

After pasting clippings into my book religiously for several months, I woke up one morning with a premonition so keen it was as if I'd been shown my entry in the Book of Fate. I would start a diary, a secret one. I knew suddenly that I'd always been meant to do this, though I did wonder why anyone would be fascinated by the ruminations of a shut-in. Still, it was obvious that I must be my own Boswell.

*I think that if I get into the habit of writing a bit about what happens,
or rather what doesn't happen, I may lose a little of the sense of loneliness and desolation which abides with me.*

Such was my tentative first entry. At first I was haunted by a vision
of my heirs finding an empty book, as if I'd never really lived or had any
significance, even for myself. I'd imagine Charles Norton enthroned in
his little empyrean in Cambridge, with Mrs. Isabella Stewart Gardner
(of the legendary beautiful arms) on his right, and Mr. Howells on his
left, and who knows who else drinking in his golden phrases. I would
wonder why he was considered such a great man and taken so seriously
while I remained a nonentity.

As time went on, I was throwing myself into my diary with the
zeal of a prisoner in solitary confinement scratching his tale on his
cell walls.

*My circumstances allowing for nothing but the ejaculation of one-syl-
labled reflections, a written monologue by that most interesting being,
myself, may have its consolations. I shall at least have it all my own way.*

True, no adoring crowds hung on my every word (except for
faithful Nurse, who can always be counted on for praise, like a faithful
retainer in a play by Racine), yet somehow my solitude was becoming
green and fertile and my life sweet to my sight.

My past has begun to dribble back to me, luminous and laden
with import. So far I have refrained from revealing the existence of the
diary to anyone but Nurse, to whom I dictate my words when I am too
ill to write. She is as awed in the performance of this task as if she were
amanuensis to Mr. Gladstone himself.

⮜ FIVE ⮞

Such is my life—micro-events punctuated by deadly sameness—yet at the same time an indescribable sea change is taking place within me. Why this is I cannot say.

A note from Venice yesterday reports that Henry has suffered a light attack of jaundice, but this morning's note reports that he is sitting up and eating a mutton chop. Apparently he has an excellent doctor *and* an impassioned gondolier taking care of him. The she-novelist fidgets in the background evidently.

Will Constance Fenimore Woolson take advantage of Henry's weakness to put a love philter in his food? I am obliged to confess that for several years now I have resented the time Henry spends with her, though she is slightly older, unbeautiful, and deaf as a post. When she invited Katherine to stay with her in Oxford two years ago—when K was conducting her research on the higher education of the female—it began to seem that the mild-mannered Miss Woolson might be my Nemesis. (K assured me I had bats in my belfry.)

Now I have begun to think I have been all wrong about Miss Woolson. Her letters to me have been very sympathetic and gracious. Well, we shall see.

My headache has a drilling quality today, and there appear to be gnats crawling over my eyeballs; I must blink to push aside a sort of veil of them in order to read. For the past week my feet have been two blocks of ice, then this morning a surge of heat shot from my toes all the way up to my midsection. I won't try your patience by detailing all my afflictions; I only wish to remind you that during the events recounted here I have never been a well woman, not even for a day. I am, if anything, less ambulatory than a year ago. My headaches and stomachaches are Olympian in intensity and my "going off" at midday is as predictable as the church bells that ring on Sunday mornings.

All around me people are rushing about *doing* things and strenuously believing they are happy. They work so hard at it, your heart goes out to them. I do nothing and a new kind of joy wells up inside me. Whence does it come, this beauty not of this world, which arises from nowhere and dissolves into nothing? I could not tell you what it is, yet it is my purest pleasure.

While Nurse is out and about, I find my way back to the convent school in Paris. The chill is growing more penetrating. It is dark now when we rise in the morning, and we are obliged to break a thin crust of ice in the basins to wash our faces. My hands and feet stay numb all morning. Perhaps they are training us to be penitents. Will hairshirts be next? A short while ago I passed through a girlish mystical phase during which I heard dead saints offering me spiritual advice and briefly aspired to die a virgin martyr so that my relics would acquire supernatural powers. This did not last long, as it quickly became obvious that even a small discomfort like cold feet broke my spirit. Also, I began to see the barbarities buried under the surface of religion and when I read a smuggled copy of Voltaire, *Écrasez l'infame* became my motto.

I complain at every turn, but you never do; you are the brave one, Vivienne.

Do you remember when the note I passed to you in the schoolroom was found and turned over to Mother Superior? As it depicted her in unflattering terms, she was not pleased, and I was on bread and water for three weeks. My thoughts verged on delirium. Hunger exacerbated the cold and I wondered if I should die of it, would I get to be a martyr? What would my symbol be, a *potage* with an X across it? The other pupils were told that I had suffered a cerebral derangement from bad vapors and overexcitement, and no one was allowed to speak to me. I would see you in chapel casting longing looks in my direction, communicating with the subtlest of signals—a raised eyebrow, a wink, the flash of a sad downturned clown mouth. Our love grew in silence, like a vine that finds its way around every obstacle.

One night at vespers, I knelt on the flagstones, next to you, aware that half of me was miserable (kneeling on cold flagstones, shivering, hungry) while the other half was swooning with pleasure. I blew softly on your neck, your face, your hands. Remember when we wrote to each other on the fogged windowpanes, love notes in our special disappearing code? Can you feel a small warm breeze brushing your skin—like the touch of a butterfly's wings?

Oh, but here is Nurse, returned from her marketing. She strides briskly over to a window and begins hoisting it. Without a word to me. Am I an inanimate object?

"What are you *doing*, Nurse?"

"Getting you some fresh air, Miss. It is very mild today."

"Let me be the judge of that. Your mild may not be my mild."

When the sash sticks at half an inch open, I breathe a sigh of relief. But Nurse keeps at it and finally succeeds in raising it, whereupon the world whooshes into my room. I'd actually forgotten what outdoors smells and sounds like: the odor of dung and straw, the calls of the match-girl and the chair-mender, the wailing children, the barking dogs, people shouting on the street. My poor senses, bereft all winter, hardly know what to make of it all.

"It is probably too chilly," I say, though it does occur to me that a little fresh air might dispel the miasma of sour sweat left over from the parlor maid's recent dusting foray. Poor things. They can't help it, having no means of bathing.

"It really is quite warm, Miss. It would be a pity to keep the window shut."

I can't deny this. The air is not as chilly as I'd feared. Oh, and there is the postman in his red tunic with gold epaulettes bringing round the second post. I am reluctant, however, to capitulate so easily to Nurse's schemes. When you are dependent on people for your survival, you must maintain your millimeter of selfhood however you can.

I allow her to keep the window open while she gives me the latest news on the Bachellers. Two weeks ago I gave Mrs. B an old night-gown of mine (to *wear*, I thought) and she thinks it is so fine that she has set it aside for her "boorial." If I were in her shoes (or her car-pet slippers, for she cannot wear shoes on her ruined feet), I suppose I'd be looking forward to boorial, too. And she was proudly wearing around her neck a blue ribbon that came with my pincushion. My heart goes out to these poor souls, gathering scraps like nesting birds. To them "Miss James" is a semi-mythic creature, inconceivably rich and exotically American.

Then Nurse reads to me from the *Telegraph*, from which we learn that the troops of Her *Christian* Majesty have been engaged in killing three thousand dervishes in Iraq by depriving them of water. I am out-raged and long very much to rant, but Nurse is too smooth a surface on which to hang a rant, so I will do it later in the pages of my secret diary.

My harangues have had *some* effect on her, though. She is begin-ning to grasp that the privileged classes enjoy their pleasures *at the expense of* the poor, and are entirely unapologetic about it. Last week she returned quite downcast from the funeral of old Mrs. Bond. She described how the daughter and grandchildren stood by the grave a long time, waiting. Finally, a parson came, pulled a book out of his pocket, read over the service, turned and walked away. He never spoke to the family or even looked at them.

The next morning Nurse assumes her drill-sergeant aspect and insists I must go out and breathe some fresh air. Even thinking about going out in the bath chair makes me feel exposed, a snail without a shell. But Nurse insists, and I surrender in the end. At first the world is utterly overwhelming, and I wish I could stop up my ears as well as my nose. After we've gone two or three blocks, a bird sings a piercingly sweet three-note song and my heart cracks open. Near the pump house we run into the Brooks children pulling a dog along by a rope round its neck. "The woman as wants to lose it gave it to us and we's 'ad it all afternoon," Becky Brooks informs us. About ten minutes later, we meet Alice Edwards with the new baby of that family appended and inquire after its health. "He would be better if Mother hadn't let him fall out of bed last night. She didn't find it out until twelve o'clock," the girl says.

Yet the baby is smiling up at a sky the French would call *moutonné*, azure with many fluffy little clouds resembling herds of sheep.

Although Nurse is too slight to manage the bath chair easily, she gamely pushes me through orchards and gooseberry bushes to the garden in front of the Hawkes farmhouse. It is so beautiful I am in tears. An old weathered farmer with only two yellow teeth in his head smiles at us. On the way back we pass a one-eyed boy of twelve, very poor and rough, tenderly carrying a tiny baby. I feel as if I were meeting characters from a favorite book I have been reading for years, and I pass the rest of the day in a sort of ecstatic trance.

During the night something wakes me, and I am in dense darkness, sensing some menace in the room. It is not a dream. Something *is* happening and presently it solidifies into the form of a man sprawled in my armchair. My mind freezes, a panicked rabbit, and then, unbelievably, a *second* creature is lumbering toward me. I feel the hairs at the back of my neck stand erect. And then the creature sprawls onto my bed, shaking the mattress like a dinghy in a gale, while fumes of liquor assail my nostrils.

"Hullo, what's this? Roger, I didn't know you'd engaged us a lady of the evening. Bit long in the tooth but it'll do."

My heart races. The apparition clears some rattling phlegm from its throat, and the mattress heaves again as he lunges toward me. His heavy head comes to rest on my chest, and I am pinned in place while he nuzzles at the front of my nightdress like a truffle pig. Hideous! Something about this is eerily familiar—being helpless, my limbs pinned down by a brute. Am I reliving something I dreamt or something that happened before?

My eyes squeeze shut. No use fighting. It will happen now, whatever it will be.

Against my shuttered lids, a pinkish glow, like dawn. My eyes open to a lamp floating across the room. Attached to it is Nurse, in nightdress and cap. My angel of deliverance. The man whose head rests on my chest emits a rattling snore. The one in the armchair groans. I lose track of what happens next. Nurse says something sensible and scolding, and the inebriated cleric and his companion—for they are my apparitions—slink away.

The next day Nurse confers with Miss Clarke and establishes that the two drunken young men blundered into my apartment by mistake. Apologies are proffered but Miss Clarke understands that the cleric must leave. This does not happen all at once, and in the meantime he scuttles around furtively, pointedly avoiding Nurse on the street and the landing.

Now I must have Nurse sitting by my bedside knitting until I fall asleep.

"You understand that I cannot feel safe, Nurse, as long as the parson is here."

"Miss Clarke will have him out by month's end. Do not worry so much, Miss. It was just a mistake. It won't happen again."

"You of all people, Nurse, should know how my mind cramps around things."

"Ah, Miss, I know it. I told Father, Miss James is the most sensitive lady I ever nursed!"

I am struck by the heavy-handedness of fate. In my utter seclusion, to be invaded by two drunken men in the middle of the night! I think of it now and my hair stands on end!

⌐ S I X ⌐

Arriving on my doorstep in mid-May just as the Misses Lawrence are preparing to depart, Henry is as stunned as I was the first time to meet this pair of identical twins of fifty, dressed identically. Today they wear gowns of pea green and bonnets with scarlet flowers, and one of them remarks, upon being introduced to H., "I'm sorry that we must wend our way home. We have such a headache today."

"Do they always dress identically?" he asks after they disappear round the corner.

"Yes, and they suffer from the same diseases. Water on the knee and enlarged hearts, I believe."

"Did one of them really say, *We* have a headache?"

"Yes, and they are also apt to say, 'Oh, that always disagrees with us.' Pleasure and pain are shared equally, it seems."

"When they share a headache, do you suppose it is a half-strength headache for each of them?"

"We'll never know. But to see one Miss Lawrence gazing fondly at the other is almost an obscenity, Henry, like catching someone smiling lovingly at her own reflection in a looking glass. The *real* mystery is why Nature went to the trouble of creating two Misses Lawrence, when one might have sufficed."

Henry settles himself in the armchair and stretches out his legs, stiff from his train journey. Nurse brings us tea and muffins, all aflutter. (She worships the famous Mr. James and flits around him like a besotted moth round a candle.) Finally, she excuses herself and goes out to call on friends.

Having missed my brother sorely, I can only gaze at him fondly while he conveys his gossip. He informs me that Wendell Holmes is in London now, being wined and dined and winning every Briton's admiration.

"I wonder what they *see* in him. Don't you?"

"Well, Alice, he *is* very intelligent and a great success at the law."

"But don't we always see people as they were when we first knew them? I always thought Wendell had the air of a shady man performing a card trick. Do you remember how he used to flirt with every pretty girl by telling them his war stories, how heroically he swam across the river with the ball in his foot, how the soldiers looked with their heads shot off? I had to hear the whole story three times, as I happened each time to be sitting near a young woman Wendell wished to impress. One of the Temple girls, usually."

Henry barely laughs. He seems edgy; I wonder why.

"Why, what *is* eating you, Henry? You are all fidgety."

He tells me gently that Aunt Kate is gravely ill in New York City.

"But I was writing to her this very morning!" Irrationally, I am about to produce my letter as proof that Aunt Kate is all right.

She is being cared for by our Walsh and Wyckoff relations, he tells me, and William writes that they say she cannot last long. As a warm rain falls outside, and the muslin curtains billow, Harry and I reminisce about our aunt, who was a third parent to us, whose passing will be the end of that generation. We recall her wide-brimmed gardening hat; her coterie of trusted doctors; her constant presence during the years we spent in Europe as children; how, unlike Mother, she adored all things French.

"Do you remember, Harry, how once a week the Empress Eugénie would pass along the Champs-Élysées in her polished black coach with the footmen in the imperial uniform? People along the avenue would *bow* to her as she passed. It was just as if one of my fairy tales had come to life. I expected elves and pots of gold next. 'Is an empress as good as a queen?' I asked Aunt Kate. 'Does she live in a palace?' She said, '*That* empress and her husband are nothing but well-dressed ruffians.' Father made a shushing gesture to warn her not to display her republican sentiments (which he shared, of course) so immoderately, especially in front of the servants."

"Yes," Henry smiles at the memory. "He always said there were spies everywhere, which was quite true. How Louis Napoleon and his beastly Empire made Father's gorge rise!"

My brother takes the night train back to London in the evening. I think he plans to go off to the country but has not told me yet, fearing that his departure on top of the news about Aunt Kate might shatter what little sanity remains to me.

Later I have a long teary talk with Nurse, who by now is almost as well-acquainted with the members of my family as I am. "I hate to think of poor Aunt Kate left to the mercy of those Wyckoffs, Nurse. They are a shady branch of the family. Cousin Howard Wyckoff, after poisoning himself with drink and becoming a lifelong burden on Cousin Helen, left all his money to some worthless cousins and not a dime to Aunt Kate, who had done so much for them. Albert Wyckoff is even more ghastly, and his wife spends all her days betting at the horse-races."

"How dreadful!" Nurse says, obviously titillated by the disclosure of such debauched James relatives.

"Yes. I do wish my aunt could be cared for by William and Alice, but there is no question of her traveling now, unfortunately."

"Miss, is she a believer?'

"Oh, Nurse, who knows? We have such peculiar ways of believing in our family. She has lived her life for others."

"Well, then, it will be all right." She means that Aunt Kate *probably* won't go to hell.

HENRY JAMES
DE VERE GARDENS, KENSINGTON
MARCH 20, 1889

TO WILLIAM JAMES
Seeing Alice last week confirmed my impression that her meager tabby

cat little society there is too poor to be "kept up" and for all practical purposes she is wholly alone. Not that she admits for a moment that she suffers from it. Her interest in politics & in the Irish question &c almost constitutes a roomful for her.

⎯ SEVEN ⎯

WHAT A PITY THE YOUNG ARE UNGRATEFUL AND HEEDLESS OF the aged, believing them to have been born faded and incapable of vivid emotions. I wish I'd been kinder to poor Aunt Kate. If her life had a theme, it was her intense longing to absorb herself in a few individuals, in the members of our family primarily. After the deaths of my parents, I am afraid I let her down very badly.

After Mother's sudden death from asthma in January 1882, Father and I moved our household to Mt. Vernon Street, on Beacon Hill, where I was thrown abruptly into the role of lady of the house, in charge of the account book, the servants, and the care and feeding of Father. I did not find it easy and began to suffer from a constant apprehension that something needed doing and I did not know what it was. So much to do! Ovens needed black leading, ashes needed raking, flues needed cleaning, menus needed devising, linens needed washing, mending, starching, ironing. Oh, you have no idea!

I caught the smirks on the servants' faces and knew that they were prepared to laugh behind my back, ignore my orders, and allow the tradesmen to cheat me. I was in an agony of anxiety that I would fail Father. Then, one morning, I woke up knowing exactly what to do; perhaps I had dreamt the solution. I went to Mother's wardrobe, put on her grey worsted cloak with the fox fur collar, and walked down the hill. I felt my body assume her carriage, her manner of walking, even her thoughts. Carrying her marketing basket, I went from shop to shop, listening for her voice in my head to tell me how much to spend for a roast, that the laundresses should be engaged for Thursday and

Friday, that the clothes-horse needed mending. I found myself effort-lessly using Mother's phrasing when I went over menus with Cook or gave orders to the butcher's boy.

Every so often Father would address me as "Mary darling" and I treasured that as a sign of his trust. The streets of Beacon Hill were steep, cobbled, slippery in wet or icy weather, and thus impossible for a man with a cork leg, but Father's interest in life was over. After a few months, Aunt Kate came up from New York to help out, and we took turns in the sickroom, plumping Father's pillows, giving him sponge baths, applying wet cloths to his parched lips. I read to him from the *Transcript* and from the poems of Matthew Arnold and Tennyson. We started in on *War and Peace*.

"Don't read me any more Russians," he said irritably when we'd reached the end of the second chapter. "I can't keep track of their names." A month earlier he'd been wild about Tolstoy.

We tried Wilkie Collins and he complained of the melodrama, and after that he wearied of *The Mill on the Floss*. "Too womanly! She goes on and on! She should have been ruthlessly edited!" I didn't entirely disagree. We embarked next on a sentimental novel by Mr. Howells, and Father said, "Who *cares* if the boy loves the girl or the girl loves the boy or whether they get married? None of it matters—don't you see?" Finally he wished only to hear passages from his books and smiled dotingly at his own prose. I suppose in time your life becomes a story you tell yourself.

I saw that my aunt was watching me closely to see if I would fall apart, something for which I'd shown a decided aptitude in the past. When Father's health went into a steep decline, Harry crossed the ocean and called in Dr. Beach, who diagnosed "softening of the brain" and said Father might live for some time if he took some nourishment. But he turned his head away whenever food was offered.

It was slow suicide, and I recalled ruefully the long days and lon-ger nights that Father spent talking *me* out of suicide during my *annus horribilis* of 1878. It was clear I could not talk *him* out of it, and I did not try. He knew what he wanted. Before long, his parchment skin was stretched tightly over the bones of his face. His mouth was a lipless cavity. From week to week he shriveled and shrank like a human raisin, and there was a smell about him, like rotting fruit. None of which bothered *him* in the least.

"You see how it is with me, darling," he'd say cheerfully, demonstrating a twiglike arm, the sparrow bones of his clavicle.

One day, while Aunt Kate and I were going over the next day's menu and ordering the roast that Father would not touch, she broached the subject we'd avoided so far. "Dr. Beach says your father cannot last more than a month or so. Have you given any thought to where and how you will live? Afterwards." I pointed out that Dr. Beach did not have the best record for medical accuracy and mumbled something about possibly going to live in my house in Manchester-by-the-Sea, the one I had built for Father and me but in which Father would never set foot.

"You wouldn't mind the damp?"

"I don't know, Aunt Kate." That is when it hit me how unprepared I was to be mistress of an empty house. In my anguish I blocked out poor Aunt Kate's prattle briefly and when my attention returned, she was rambling on about Twelfth Street and Fourteenth Street and Murray Hill. "You've always liked New York City, haven't you, Alice? I remember your saying how much you liked the fashions and the theater."

Oh no! Aunt Kate seemed to assume that she and I would *live* together! Picture the despair that fell over me, imagining our tame spinster rituals, little trips to Newport or Southampton, sherries by the fire, I lending an ear to Aunt Kate's opinions on the book reviews in the *Nation* and the fashions in *Godey's*. Not to mention the poisonous effect she would have on my relations with Katherine, of whom she did not approve. Maybe that was why she wanted us to live together—to save me from the evil Katherine.

It was unthinkable. Perhaps you would need to have lived with Aunt Kate and absorbed her through the bone to understand why I could not consent, but I did not know how to explain this.

I asked Father one day where he wished to be buried and what his epitaph should say. He said, "Here lies a man who has thought all his life that the ceremonies attending birth, marriage, and death were all damned nonsense. Don't put a word more."

I was waiting. For what? For Father to say that I'd meant something to him, that it grieved him to leave me, I suppose. Had he not said he could not bear to be parted from me, even for a few months? No, that was what Mother *told* me he said; perhaps Father himself had never actually said that I was the "sun of his existence" and thus it was unthinkable that I should go abroad again in his lifetime. Certainly he was prepared to leave me now without a backward glance. His letters to me over the years had been scarcely distinguishable from love letters; he was that kind of man, larger than life. But now, apart from his oft-expressed desire to "leave this disgusting world," he did not speak of his feelings at all. He fixed his gaze on the window, becoming obsessed with some sparrows perched on the ledge. I couldn't help but notice that he was far more interested in those sparrows than me.

In his last weeks he seemed literally not to see me. As he lay dying, I was becoming a ghost to him. If he registered my presence at all, he'd say, "Shouldn't you be mending the linens?" The only person he wanted near him now was Aunt Kate. Whenever I passed his bedroom I'd see her rubbing his stump with oil, murmuring to him. He was a happy infant again. Perhaps his dying brain mistook Aunt Kate for his Mary; perhaps the second sister finally enjoyed the happiness denied her fifty years earlier.

And then Father's last words. The morning of the day he died he was heard to say, "Such good boys, I have such good boys." Later his face brightened and he exclaimed in a hoarse whisper, "There is my Mary!" Before the sun set, he was dead, reunited with his Mary, and I left behind like a stray dog.

For several weeks I'd been suffering ghastly attacks of indigestion and nervous fits, lying in my bedroom most of the time with the curtains drawn. Even a slit of light was torture to my eyes. Katherine moved in to care for me, giving me opium for the blinding pain in my head. I have a bleary recollection of Aunt Kate coming into the bedroom one day as I was weeping, and saying, "For goodness' sake, Alice, you'd think you were the only one in this family with any feelings! Can't you think of anyone else for once?"

Arguments could unquestionably be brought forth to support this view of me, I suppose, but I blurted, "Who *are* you? I thought you were my aunt but now I wonder if you are a vampire." I did not know if I'd said that or merely thought it. Aunt Kate dissolved at some point (things appear and disappear mysteriously when you are on opium) and Katherine said, "That was rather rough, Alice."

"What?"

"Calling your aunt a vampire." But she was wearing a faint smile.

"Did I? Well, no one ought to pay attention to the ravings of an opium drunkard."

Sometime later I reportedly announced (again I have no memory of this), "Aunt Kate *is* a psychic vampire, Katherine. Don't you see how she feeds on the lives and emotions of others? She is an intimacy thief!" I was shocked when Katherine told me later what I'd said, but isn't it the things you *can't* say aloud that sicken you slowly over time?

William was on sabbatical in Europe the whole time Father was dying, staying in Harry's flat in London while Harry was in Boston. The brothers had switched places! Feeling *awfully blue and homesick* amidst the distant politeness of Londoners, William confided in a letter to us, *I feel as if I might die tonight and London not feel it.* William's Alice and Harry were launching telegrams and letters almost daily urging him *not* to cut short his sabbatical and come home, as everyone knew that under the circumstances impractical, moody William would be more hindrance than help.

In the befogged days after Father's death, "Mrs. Alice" came over to the house to go through cupboards and attend to various practical matters, and, finding herself in the dining room one evening with Katherine, she began to question her sternly about the opium she was giving me. Didn't she know it could turn me into an addict? Had she consulted Harry, who as my brother and current head of household, should properly be managing his sister's affairs? (All this was what Katherine told me later.)

Katherine said, "Are you questioning my position with regard to Alice? Or Alice's medical care, about which you are completely uninformed?"

That made my sister-in-law back down.

"If you had any idea how she suffers, you would not question it," Katherine went on. "She is very ill, and when have you ever put out a helping hand? When have you invited her to a meal at your house or treated her like a sister?"

Mrs. Alice turned crimson, Katherine said. She said she'd been terribly tied down with the babies and the housework and William's being abroad and her father-in-law's illness. And, yes, poor Alice, being the daughter, was more bereaved than anyone. She knew that. She twisted her gloves in her hands, and seemed at a loss for words.

Her glance fell over the table, set for two, strayed into the dark bedroom Katherine and I were sharing, and returned to Katherine's face. "We do appreciate, Miss Loring, the devoted care you take of Alice," she said, pulling on her long woolen gloves. "I assume that yours is more than an ordinary friendship. That you are . . . friends for life?"

"You assume correctly."

"That is how it is, then."

EIGHT

A SPIDER HAS BEEN BUSY SPINNING A WEB IN THE WINDOW CASE-
ment since shortly after dawn. On top of its beauty, the web is a death
trap, and as I lie there watching it, a small white moth flies straight
into it. Its struggles are unbearable to watch, so I free it, tearing several
sticky strands and making a mess of that part of the web, so painstak-
ingly constructed this very morning. The moth flies off to the sanctu-
ary of a cream-colored curtain, to dream of eating holes in my woolens.
Did I do the right thing? After all, I have cheated the spider of a well-
earned meal. It is not easy being a god.

Afterwards, I close my eyes and drift off.

"Do you remember where we left off? We were as usual on our
knees in the tomblike chill of the chapel, with its stained glass depicting past Christian atrocities. I had just breathed on your neck, Vivienne.
Do you feel a warm breeze smelling of tropical flowers and the sea?"

Hiding your smile behind your hands, you whisper out of the side
of your mouth. "Isn't that odd, *chère* Aurore, since we are in a drafty
stone chapel in Paris in wintertime!"

"*Attends, chérie!* We must train our minds in difficult austeri-
ties"—the sisters have helpfully provided instructive pamphlets on this
subject—"until we can transport ourselves at will to a distant tropical
land. India, perhaps?"

"Yes!" Your eyes shine. The luminosity of your eyes is one of the
seven wonders of my world. "Are we going there to baptize pagan babies?"

A fit of giggles seizes us. We have to hear about these accursed
pagan babies *ad nauseam* here. The sisters consider it vital to baptize

them so that they will not spend eternity in limbo, but if you ask me, limbo doesn't sound so bad.

We wait for nighttime. Then I see your feet flying over the cold flagstones, and you slip, shivering, into my bed and pull the covers up over our heads. I feel your breath like a hot spring flowing into a cool pool. Soon we are far away. You press your ear to my chest as if to listen to my heart. I feel the goose-bumps on your arms and start to kiss them away.

"Be careful, Aurore! Sister will hear."

"You forget that tonight we have Sister Dominique, who is stone deaf."

"It would be helpful if she were blind as well," you say, and we muffle our laughter with the pillow.

Our kisses become more fervent. "Have you seen any pagan babies around?" I ask, breathless from kissing.

"*Mais bien sûr,*" you say, with some pretty French gestures. "But, you know, here in India everyone goes up on the roof to sleep in the hot season. The cry of the lovesick peacocks in the courtyard drives one mad with desire."

I am tracing the line of your cheek and jaw with my index and middle fingers, and you stretch and purr like a cat. Then you seize the front of my gown hungrily, and, trembling, unbutton the innumerable tiny cloth-covered buttons. I like the way you savor each bit of flesh uncovered. You whisper breathily in my ear, "We are supposed to tell the Hindoos about Jesus but I think they are bored to death with the subject."

I giggle helplessly. "There is so much more to life than Jesus, Jesus, Jesus." Lying on my back I draw you down to me. I tug the straps of your nightgown down off your shoulders and your breasts tumble out, round as mangoes. You kiss me firmly on the mouth. Your mouth tastes fruity from the candies you hoard and eat under the covers. "So, then," you say, with a look of lovely *volupté*, "we let the beautiful Indian ladies with their long blue-black hair tell us about *their* gods. Much more interesting than ours, *n'est-ce pas?*"

"Yes, and so many of them, too." I can scarcely speak for the waves of pleasure crashing through me. "They've got one for everything—a goddess of childbirth, a god of the monsoon, even a goddess of small-pox. *Ah, comme tu es diabolique!*"

A loud snore erupts from sleeping Sister Dominque, causing us both to jump a foot. I am struck with helpless hilarity at the thought that she can't hear herself snore. When I mention this to you, you laugh so hard the tears stream down your cheeks. Now the air feels like the steam rising from a laundry tub. Well, of course—we're in India! We sneak out of bed, and, holding hands, patter out of the room in our bare feet and ascend a rude wooden ladder, trembling in our night-dresses. From the roof, the moon is huge and full and looks so close to earth that it seems to brush against the branches of the neem tree. Or do I mean the banyan tree?

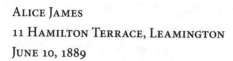

ALICE JAMES
11 HAMILTON TERRACE, LEAMINGTON
JUNE 10, 1889

To WILLIAM JAMES
A life-interest in a shawl, with reversion to the male heir, is so extraordinary & ludicrous a bequest that I can hardly think it could have been very seriously meant. My desire would, naturally, be to renounce my passing claim to that also, as I can hardly conceive of myself, under any conditions, as so abject as to grasp at a life-interest in a shawl!

P.S. If the shawl were left to me outright, I should leave it to you, William, on condition that you wrap it about you while you perform that unaeasthetic duty, which will one day fall to you, of passing my skin and bones through the Custom House.

HENRY JAMES
11 HAMILTON TERRACE, LEAMINGTON
MAY 24, 1889

To WILLIAM JAMES
Alice told me she didn't remember definitely how she had written to you, but that her letter proceeded really from a sense that she had been snubbed in her innermost, and later, on receipt of your letter, that she had been still more snubbed. Your mistake was, I take it, that you wrote to her too much as a well woman.

She cried to me about the cruelty or at least infelicity of AK's taking from her, in her miserably limited little helpless life, the luxury of devising for herself the disposal of the objects in question. She has had a bad time of it ever since Aunt Kate began seriously to fail. She only gets on so long as nothing happens.

⁓ NINE ⁓

I AM SORRY TO SAY THAT AUNT KATE DID NOT PASS LIGHTLY through the mists and veils of eternity. This is what happens when your kin are in thrall to soothsayers. My brother Bob (now residing in Concord) and William's Alice were having one of their frequent "sittings" with Mrs. Piper, in Boston. (I have never wavered in my opinion of Mrs. P. I'd sooner walk naked in Piccadilly than allow that seeress to gaze upon the mysteries of my soul!) Aunt Kate was known to be gravely ill, and Alice asked after her health. "She is poorly," Mrs. P. replied and went on to blurt, a few minutes later, "Why, Aunt Kate's here! All around me I hear voices saying, 'Aunt Kate's come!'" (All this is recounted in the *Proceedings of the Society for Psychical Research*, if you care to look it up.) When Alice and Bob pressed her for details, they were informed that Aunt Kate had died early that morning.

Galvanized by this message, Bob bolted from the room and flew to the office of the American Society for Psychical Research, where William happened to be. An official statement was extracted from Bob, noting the date and time. A few hours later, William, at home, received a telegram from Cousin Lilla Walsh, notifying him that Aunt Kate had died that very morning. But since Aunt Kate's illness was known to all parties, how difficult would it have been for the pythoness to guess that she'd "passed over"?

I don't think Aunt Kate can be blamed for this sorry manifestation.

For the past few weeks I've been contemplating her life, and it occurs to me that she never sensed how much we resisted her. My failing her, after Father's death, must have seemed a great and ungrateful betrayal; my inability to explain myself, and hers to understand the situation, made it all the sadder and more ugly.

A week later, Henry is back with me again, *bon comme le pain.* I ask him if he knows what the Captain did to Aunt Kate exactly. He doesn't, but recalls Father saying that the Captain "banished smiles and tears, laughter and all human sympathies to the opposite hemisphere." Poor Aunt Kate: her one romance ending so disastrously, her only souvenir the "Mrs." that afterward was appended to her maiden name. Mrs. Walsh.

"It is rather a mystery, Henry. Don't you wish you could travel back in time?"

"Maybe some of it is in a letter somewhere. Though probably not."

"Oh, Henry, didn't I *tell* you? Right after Father died, when I was so ill, Aunt Kate took the family letters from Father's chest of drawers and began tossing them into the fire. Katherine caught her red-handed and protested, 'But those are James family papers!' Aunt Kate said it was better that 'the children' not read them. Doesn't it *grieve* you that our past is gone, wiped clean? Surely it was not Aunt Kate's place to censor *our* family letters! What do you think she was trying to prevent our knowing? Maybe she was trying to eliminate every unflattering glimpse of herself."

After a long, uncomfortable pause, Henry says, "Aunt Kate did the proper thing."

Oh! Why didn't I see it before? Henry burns many of the letters he receives. I've seen him at work by the fireplace, pruning his legacy. After an awkward silence, he adds, "It was not Katherine's place—well, never mind." With an uneasy glance at me, he falls silent.

"How can you *say* that, Henry?"

"You know what vultures the press and the public can be, Alice."

"But Aunt Kate is of no possible interest to either."

Clearing his throat, my brother shifts uneasily in his chair, and then the scales fall from my eyes. He is nervous about *his* public and *his* reputation and *his* posthumous life. And evidently agrees with Aunt Kate that Katherine is an interloper in our family, despite having kept me alive by sheer willpower for months at a time. But some things cannot be spoken. Being so much at odds with William, I can hardly afford to quarrel with Henry, too; a person has only so much spleen at hand at any given time. I am glad at any rate that I have not told him of my diary. He would view it as part of *his* "remains," not as *mes beaux restes*. Perhaps I *shall* leave instructions to have it published.

A heavy silence weighs upon us.

Over the next weeks, further postmortem effects transpire through Aunt Kate's last will and testament. To start with, she had a much larger estate than any of us suspected. After leaving $10,000 each to William and to Wilky's widow, she left the bulk of her estate to some obscure Walsh cousins in Connecticut and some Cochrane relatives in Minnesota of whom we'd scarcely heard before. She left nothing to Bob. Henry was given a choice of some heirlooms. I received a bit of family silver and a "life-interest" in a valuable shawl, which, according to the will, must revert to a male heir upon my demise.

"Why has my aunt, who was a second mother to me, treated me like a distant relation of no account?" I sob to Nurse. "I don't mind her leaving her money to those who need it more, but this shawl business is a slap in the face." (I am pleased to say that Nurse feels very injured on my account.) A day or two later, enlightenment dawns. Aunt Kate was determined to keep the shawl from passing on to Katherine's evil shoulders after my demise. How unspeakably it pains me to think of this.

When I try to communicate my feelings to William (by letter, of course) he regards me as a mad Fury, or so I discover later. Aunt Kate's gift of the bulk of her fortune to the mysterious far-flung Cochranes instead of to our family, with whom she lived for years at a time, is a great enigma, the other being that William is the only member of our family to receive a sizable sum. With his large brood, he needs money more than I do, but poor Henry is feeling the pinch these days and I'd always thought he was our aunt's favorite. Maybe, at the end, her affections flowed to the fertile branches of the family tree instead of the fallow ones; perhaps she yearned to perpetuate herself through the generations.

Anyway, I make the mistake of writing William a long epistle in which the following passage appears: *Your ease in your position as*

exceptional nephew, etc. showed an artless healthy-mindedness sugges-
tive of primitive man. Perhaps I did go a bit far, but I was provoked.
Anyhow, it was a joke!

William's next letter blasts me to kingdom come, taking me to
task for taking Aunt Kate's bequest "so hard" and pointing out, as if I
were simple-minded, that other relatives are more in need of cash than
I. As is William himself, evidently. His letter runs on for pages about
the expense of the maintenance of two houses, property taxes, servants' salaries, Harry's school tuition, the expense of traveling abroad
to replenish himself every time he breaks down. As if I were trying to
steal the bread out of his children's mouths!

As I read the letter, the teacup shakes in my hand and slops tea
into the saucer. I consider breaking off relations with William. When
I mention this to Henry the next time he visits, he says, "I understand
how you feel, Alice, but you must know our bonds can never, ever be
severed." But I wonder how William and I will manage to go on from
here, and this thought pains me more than I can say. It has not escaped
Nurse's notice that I fell ill shortly after William's letters darkened our
threshold, and she took the unprecedented step of writing William
to inform him that his letters were making me ill. Henry also wrote
to him explaining that there was nothing materialistic in my feelings
about the will. William eventually apologized, after a fashion, probably
mostly to placate Harry.

⌁ TEN ⌁

FROM MY INVALID-COUCH I WATCH A BOWLEGGED OLD WOMAN in a shabby grey dress lumber along Hamilton Terrace, rocking from hip to hip, every gust inflating her skirts like a sail. I *feel* the rocking gait, the heaviness of limbs, the cold fingers of the wind up my skirt. I feel the hunger gnawing at the ragged children's bellies and the sharp flesh-craving of the crows that dive repeatedly into the road. I don't know why this has started happening, this wandering out of my skin; I certainly don't intend to mention it to Nurse or Henry. Still, it's oddly enjoyable.

The honeymooning couple who were always misplacing their key are dead, of scarlet fever. Poor young things, married for less than forty days. At least they went to eternity madly in love and didn't have to witness the toll time would have exacted. The Bachellers, Brookses, and Edwardses have added a total of five unfortunate infants to their broods in the past two years, burdening the older children with more small siblings to tote around. Since his nocturnal invasion of my rooms, the parson has vanished from sight.

I've begun to wonder lately if life is a sort of dream. It is true that the physical world *seems* real and solid enough: fire burns, water reliably boils at 212 degrees Fahrenheit, if you fall from a great height you break your bones. It appears that you and I inhabit the same world, with the same planets and constellations and laws of momentum, gravity, and whatnot, but I have thought long and hard, and however I try to think my way around it, it seems inescapable that the world I know comes to me through my senses. Without the senses there would *be* no world at all. All of it might be the dream of a solitary dreamer dreaming a world into existence, including millions of other people who appear to live alongside one. Can we ever *know* there is anything out there?

This is what I am meditating on when my bell rings, announcing a visit from Mrs. Arnold. I am overjoyed to see her again, especially without Miss Percy attached. She reports that she is much improved after taking a course of the waters at the Royal Leamington Spa, attributing her revival particularly to "Swiss showers" and certain mineral waters. She does look less weary and definitely less sallow than before.

I tell her that I have been told in the strictest terms by doctors that I must await some miracle of nature that will render me capable of taking the waters and so far this has failed to transpire. "And," I add, "these doctors tell you that you will either die or recover. But you *don't* die. And you *don't* recover. I have been at these alternations since I was nineteen and I am neither dead nor recovered." Mrs. Arnold smiles knowingly. We chronic invalids understand one another; we live in a different universe than the healthy.

We chat a little about the neighborhood, and its residents, and I mutter something about the parsons in this town having that wearying quality that oozes from attenuated piety.

She beams at this. "I am so relieved to hear you say so, Miss James. I feel the same way about the clergymen here. The way they are always thrusting their tracts at you! One of them nearly knocked me to the pavement last week."

"It never seems to occur to them that you might have your own relations with God already," I say. "And the emphasis on sin! Prostrating themselves and saying fifty times a day that they are miserable sinners. If they are sinners, why don't they stop, and if not, why lie about it, above all to God? I've a good mind to print up some tracts of my own to oppress the parsons with."

Mrs. Arnold laughs, triggering a coughing fit. When she has recovered, she tucks her handkerchief into her pocket and says she imagines that she and I might have a thing or two to teach the parsons. She looks me over appraisingly. "Am I wrong in thinking you have the mystic temperament, Miss James?"

This takes me by surprise. I've never seen myself as a mystic, but then I've never met one apart from my father. I give her a brief synopsis of Father's Vastation and conversion and beliefs and the effect of all this mysticism on our family. "Although I have never been able to 'take on' Swedenborg," I tell her, "I've never been able to take this world at face value either. I am stuck betwixt and between, it appears."

Then something occurs to me. "As you lived many years in India, perhaps you can explain something to me. My brother William was fond of quoting certain Hindoo writings. There was a holy book he was quite enthusiastic about, involving a charioteer who was a god in disguise. What god would that have been?"

After a long, thoughtful pause, Mrs. Arnold says, "I almost never speak of this, but since you ask, Miss James. . . . When I lived in India I would occasionally visit Hindoo temples to see the art, as one does, you know. Inside a temple there is generally a statue of a god, which the priest of the temple dresses and drapes with jewelry as if it were a very beloved doll. People make pilgrimages, leave food and flowers. You must imagine clouds of smoke and incense, Sanskrit chants no one understands (including the Indians), sweets left to rot on the altar. I looked on it as pagan idolatry at first, being a typical boring Anglican memsahib like everyone else in our little colony." She smiles, somewhat wistfully.

"Then my son died of a fever, and I lost all interest in life. The world became barren and empty, and not just for a few months. It went on for years. It was, I suppose, what your father would have called a Vastation. One day I visited a certain temple dedicated to Krishna. Do you know him?" She asks this as if he were a person with whom I might be acquainted. I say no.

"He is the god you mentioned who is disguised as a charioteer in the *Bhagavad Gita*, which is the text your brother must have been reading. In one of his aspects, he is fatally attractive to women; he has midnight blue skin and beautiful eyes. There were milkmaids, called *gopis*, who danced with him in the forest at night, losing themselves in the ecstasy."

"I'm very surprised that the women would have been permitted to wander off to the forest like that. In India!"

"Exactly. You are very perceptive, Miss James. Every religion contains an element that is the antithesis of all the rest. Imagine good Hindoo wives and mothers—who in India are *completely* defined as wives and mothers, scarcely people in their own right—stealing out at night, abandoning husbands and children to dance with the God of Love. It is the forbidden, the unthinkable. In Indian society, more than ours, your identity rests *entirely* on your social role, and, of course, this is especially true of females. Yet there it is, Miss James."

"I have often dreamed of that sort of encounter," I say. Then I wonder what on earth I mean. "I mean, it makes perfect sense to me."

Mrs. Arnold gives me a radiant smile.

"Each *gopi* is made to feel she is the god's only beloved, and in her experience this is true. After her immersion in the sublime, her life as a dutiful wife and mother is over, or rather it ceases to be her real life. A direct experience of the divine is always disruptive, you see, Miss James."

"Well, that would explain a lot about Father," I say, and ponder this while masticating the seedcake Nurse brought us.

Then I ask, "By any chance, do you know what this means?" In the margin of the *Evening Standard*, I write *tat tvam asi*—the strange words William wrote in his diary shortly before he went to Somerville. At the time I took it for some sort of fairy spell, but now it occurs to me that the words might be Hindustani or something of that sort.

It takes Mrs. Arnold only a second to decode. "It's Sanskrit. It means, 'That thou art.'"

Depend on William to know Sanskrit phrases. I ask her what *that* refers to.

"Excellent question. Call it God. Or, better yet, the infinite. Is your brother a mystic?"

"I suppose he is in his way—as well as a great many other things. He is nothing if not multifaceted."

Her eyes search mine, as if trying to determine if I am the sort of person to be trusted with a secret. Then she confides that she had "a sort of vision" one day in a temple dedicated to Krishna. It was indescribable, she says; she was galvanized as if lightning had passed through her. She could never tell her husband or friends about it; they'd think she'd gone native. "How do you describe an experience that lifts you out of your life, your personal history, your culture, everything, and gives you new life?"

After she leaves, I think about that for a long time.

⁓ ELEVEN ⁓

AT FIRST I THINK IT IS A HORRIFIC DREAM FROM WHICH I HAVE
just awakened, petrified and breathless. Then I grasp that it is actually
happening, in the flat above mine. I make out the screams and groans
of a woman apparently being tortured, the angry growls of a man, and
a second woman (I think) ranting like a fishwife. My good little Nurse
wakes up, throws on her flannel dressing gown, and flies upstairs.

I hear her running footsteps on the stairs, the creak of a door
opening, then a man bellowing. Hyena howls from a woman. Nurse's
words are indistinct. A door bangs open and the screaming spills out
onto the landing. The fishwife woman screeches some more, the man
roars at high volume. "If you bother us again, I swear I'll fillet you like
a fish, and that finicky old lady you work for, too."

Not having made the acquaintance of my new neighbors, I am
surprised they are aware of my existence. Nurse returns, pale and
tremulous, and describes the squalid scene unfolding up there. An
unmarried couple, "very drunk and coarse, Miss," are in the process
of bringing an infant into the world with the assistance of an equally
inebriated nurse. When Nurse offered medical assistance, the people
hurled profanities at her and threatened her (and me) with violence.

And then the ghastly birth goes on *all night* right over my head,
noisily, agonizingly, until I wish the woman would just die and no one
else would ever have to bring an infant into the world.

The next morning the "parents" and their nurse are still drunk.
The infant is dead. The mother, Miss Clarke tells us, did not want
to see "the brat," a beautiful infant boy who lived for three hours.

They had not brought a rag to wrap the poor child in, which certainly seems suspicious to me. When told "it" was dead, the mother was glad and worried about whether the doctor could bring her waist into shape. She had laced herself as tight as possible to conceal the pregnancy. And then she asked, "Oh, where is my sealskin jacket?" I assume the police will investigate and that murder charges will perhaps be filed. But nothing happens.

I implore Nurse not to leave my side the next night. I cannot stop shaking and my heart is in great distress.

"Beating irregular again, Miss?"

"Strange jumps and hideous sinkings. It has never been this bad before."

Nurse strokes my fevered brow and says, "Let me get you a bromide and we'll see about fetching a doctor. If only Mr. James or Miss Loring was here!" Bringing me a glass of water, she mixes in a mustard-colored powder, and helps me to sit up and drink it. From her anxiety I deduce that I must appear one step from the grave.

"No, Nurse! I can't face another doctor."

"Then, I shall cable Mr. James in Italy and he will know what to do."

"Oh, how do you *bear* it?"

"What, Miss?"

"The suffering, the wretched lives people lead."

"Oh, it is well enough for me. I am very sorry for your headaches and other pains, Miss." She really is. What a dear person she is.

"Did you ever hear such howls? Like the hounds of hell. I can still hear them! Oh, the lot of women is hard, Nurse."

"Well, Miss, since you ask, I have heard and seen worse."

"I wish you had not told me that. My mind has already gone into such a cramp about it."

"It is a blessing the poor little thing only lived a few hours. Such a life it would have led."

"I suspect deeds of darkness, Nurse. Even in the best case, a human soul was surely left to die. Are they—those people—?"

"Constable made them leave. The good lord only knows where they will go."

And there the tale ends. Apparently no one is interested in inquiring further into the death of an innocent infant.

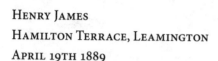

HENRY JAMES
HAMILTON TERRACE, LEAMINGTON
APRIL 19TH 1889

To WILLIAM JAMES

I found myself the subject of a telegraphic call and rushed to Alice's side to learn that she had had a very bad attack of the heart—it threatened to be fatal for some hours. . . . The violence of the heart was brought on by nervous agitation about the miserable accouchement that took place in the flat above hers. (It is always dread and fear with her.) She was thrown into such a state of nervous terror I had to remain with her for a week.

It is odd how, in her extreme seclusion, she is liable to assaults of chance from the outside. For the present, she has taken the rest of the house for herself.

WILLIAM JAMES
CAMBRIDGE, MASS
APRIL 30TH, 1889

To HENRY JAMES

The Physiological Congress in Paris begins Aug. 5. I can't help feeling in my bones that I ought to go, so I probably shall. If so, I shall be on the Cephalonia, sailing June 22. I shall disembark at Queenstown, as I am more than curious to see the Emerald Isle. Then I shall come to you. How good it will be to see poor Alice again and to hear your discourse.

HENRY JAMES
DE VERE GARDENS, LONDON
MAY 25TH, 1889

TO WILLIAM JAMES
It is much better I shouldn't tell Alice anything of your approach till you are here, as you are quite right in supposing that every form of expectation and waiting &c is a bad element for her . . . The whole business of AK's will was a particularly bad time for her—for she shared in the disconcerted feeling I had (and tried to hide from her) that AK's large estimate of the needs of the Stamford Walshes (as well as the faraway Minnesota Cochranes) as compared with her sense of ours, with whom her life had been passed, seems a slap in the face.

⟶ TWELVE ⟵

Summoned by Nurse's telegram, Henry arrives at my door very peaked, and I deduce from his anxious expression that I do not appear in the pink of health. (I have more or less avoided looking glasses lately.) Ignoring my protests, he engages a new doctor, a Dr. Wilmot, a fox-hunter with a delicate *parfum* of dog, turf, and wet leather about him. As the doctor shines his light into my eyes and ears and listens to my heart, I attempt to explain how my nerves have been affected by the grim drama overhead—the "snakes" in my stomach, the suffocating fear, the racing heart, the "going off," and all the rest. One of these days I shall have all my symptoms printed in a pamphlet to avoid repeating them to each new doctor.

I conclude my sorry tale by saying, "My mind has simply cramped upon it, Doctor! Have you ever heard of such a thing?" I cannot stop shaking. I must be a sorry spectacle, yet the good doctor does not comment on this or reply to my question. More proof of Henry's observation that while Americans feel compelled to respond to anything that is said, the English understand that it is unnecessary. The doctor and his penlight search my face as if looking for contraband, his small eyes blinking behind his wire spectacles.

"Have your eyes always been so *protuberant*, Miss James?"

"I wasn't aware they were. What does that signify?"

"Oh, nothing at all, most of the time."

"By cramp," I try again, "I mean a sort of muscular contraction of the mind. It will seize a thought and hang on like a terrier. And then my sleep goes to pieces, which throws my pneumo-gastric nerve into distress . . ." My Boston doctor and the first doctor I saw in London were emphatic about the role of the pneumo-gastric nerve in my illness, which they diagnosed as suppressed gout, but Dr. Wilmot does not appear to have heard of this sort of gout or of the pneumo-gastric nerve.

"I see, Miss James." He pauses for an interval that could pass for thoughtfulness. "It is salutary in such cases to rest the organism as much as possible, particularly after meals. A short walk as long as it is not on hard pavement can be salubrious. Lots of fresh air. That is my recommendation."

"But I have been unable to walk for some time, Doctor! I live chained to a couch, four pillows, and three shawls."

"Ah yes, quite." He whips out a pad and writes an order for a tincture of belladonna for my "neurasthenic headache" and a different bromide for sleep and another for nerves.

"In two years' time, Miss James, you may try a hydropathic treatment, but it would be very dangerous now."

"It is very strange, Doctor. Living in a spa town, I am like an atheist at a holy shrine."

"Perhaps eighteen months, Miss James, we shall see." He smiles, pats my knee, and passes from view. Henry escorts him down the stairs to his shiny brougham, and then returns to spend the day with me, having booked a room at his favorite inn. He is so appalled by my weakness that he will remain a week by my side. I am reclined as usual on the daybed near the window, he sits in the chair next to me, and we watch the facades of the buildings opposite turn rosy with the sunset, each window aglow with a little orange flame. In the distance gas flares blaze in the encroaching dark.

"Mental cramps are not his specialty, evidently," I say.

"No, he knows there is no cure for it at the chemist."

My arms suddenly make a flapping motion like a seagull, a movement that happens without my intending it. My gracious brother behaves as if it is perfectly normal for one's sister to flap her wings. I tell him, "The most striking thing, Henry, is that he was incapable of a single theory or generalization. Did you no-no-notice?" I am shivering now and my lips behave as if I'd just come in from a dip in a cold ocean.

"I'm not sure what you mean."

"His mind seemed entirely particulate. As if he has me-memorized all the parts but has no sense of the whole!!"

"He came highly recommended."

Poor Henry; he sounds miffed. My breakdown has snatched him away from his work and social life and he must feel like a clam pried from its shell. Habits and customs are important and necessary to his peace of mind. It is unusual to meet a creature with so strong an artistic inclination *and* an almost physical repulsion from all personal disorder. Yet here he is, by my side.

I must admit, it is lovely to have him all to myself for a little while.

Several days later, when I no longer seem likely to expire in the next moment, he delivers some news he'd withheld before. Edmund Gurney, of the Society for Psychical Research, has died. He is—*was*—a good friend of William's and used to attend my "salon" in London.

"What? The beautiful, poetical Mr. Gurney? He was so young!"

"The cause was chloroform, self-administered."

"Suicide?"

"There is to be an inquest."

"Oh, poor Mr. Gurney. I can't say I am surprised, though. They say his ghosts in Brighton turned out to be frauds and he had already put them in his book. I also think it was to escape his tactless and inconceivably literal-minded wife."

"But she is very beautiful."

"Yes, but the story I heard of the marriage was this, Henry. Some half dozen young men were on a search for 'beings.' One of them found a 'being' in a Pimlico lodging-house, the daughter of a solicitor who had died, leaving a large family in poverty. Mr. Fred Myers, who seems an even greater idiot than ever, persuaded Mr. Gurney to marry her. Apparently, Mr. Gurney wrote to all his friends saying that he was going to marry a young woman much beneath him, who as his wife would have finer opportunities. But I do admire him now for terminating himself so unapologetically."

"We don't know yet. It might not be suicide."

"Oh, it *is*, Henry. It is."

Poor, dear Henry is looking more drawn and worn-out by the day. 'Tis a sad fate that he should have me wrapped around him like the old woman of the sea. In an attempt to atone for this, I tell him a little anecdote about Miss Clarke, using some of her phrasing. "You might as well use the pearls that drop from my lips, Henry, so they stay in the family."

"Perhaps *you* should write, Alice," he says.

"Oh no, my scope is so narrow. I don't go into society, as you know. Besides, it is vulgar in a woman—or so Father used to say." I wait to hear what Henry will say.

"I don't believe that."

"Oh, by the way, on Katherine's recommendation, I have been reading your Miss Woolson. I think her 'Miss Grief' is a very fine and tragic story. Don't you agree?" "Miss Grief" is about a woman named Aarona Moncreif, a writer and a genius but poor, shabby and unattractive, who is rejected by the male-dominated publishing world. The author who rejects her bears a slight resemblance to my brother. I might add that there is a whiff of Sapphism around Aarona, about whose writing the term "perversity" is frequently employed. Katherine told me after spending a few days with Miss Woolson in Cambridge that she thought she belonged to the tribe of women who love women.

"Oh yes, she is a most meticulous writer," Henry says.

Faint praise, I think.

"Miss Woolson sees into the depths of a woman's heart, doesn't she?" I say, feeling the impulse to defend her. A barely perceptible irritation flits across Henry's face, which he masks with a practiced smile. Less and less do I suspect Miss Woolson of scheming to steal Henry's heart. The relationship between them is more complicated but nonetheless intense. I confine myself to saying that her work deserves more attention, and Henry agrees.

However much he may care for his Miss Woolson, he obviously does not consider her his literary equal. I wonder if he has ever stolen any pearls from *her* lips and used them in his stories?

"Oh, that reminds me, Henry." I shuffle through a pile of clippings on my tea tray and pass one to him. "This is from the *Pall Mall*

Gazette. A letter to the editor written by a man who was bitten by a mosquito at Henley."

He looks perplexed.

"One of my *documents humains*, Henry! Didn't you say that everyone in England cultivates an all-consuming hobby, the queerer the better? This is mine. I can't very well cultivate obscure varieties of roses in my present state of health." So far Henry is aware only that I have a notebook in which I paste odd clippings, and knows nothing of the secret diary.

He reads the clipping thoughtfully and says, "Hmm."

"And *these* are all the letters written in response." I pass him a stack of related clippings. "The discussion was about whether mosquitoes could survive a British winter. Most people thought not. One letter was from a Fellow of the Royal Entomological Society!"

"It is an extraordinarily microscopic focus!"

"Isn't it?! I have always said that this is the ideal country for an invalid. Tell me something, Henry, did you ever think of *not* writing?"

A long Henryesque pause, and finally he says, "Without art my life would be a howling desert."

The phrase sticks to my mind long after he leaves.

Eventually, I think, you must come to the end of yourself—and then what? I sometimes feel that I am in a sort of afterlife now, a nonphysical realm of recollection and reflection, in which I must work out the solution to an important riddle before I can progress. But what is the riddle?

Three weeks later, on a day when the sky resembles yellow custard and a warm drizzle blurs the view from my windows, Henry appears unexpectedly at midday, just after I have reached the end of volume three of George Eliot's collected letters.

"What an abject coward she seems to have been about physical pain, Henry, jotting down every headache as if it were the end of the world! She has greatly fallen in my estimation."

"She was still a great writer!"

"Yes, of course—but such whining!"

I notice then my brother is staring down at his shoes as if they were causing him a secret anguish. I wonder who has died this time and am on tenterhooks while Nurse pours our tea. Then he grasps both my hands, and says gravely, "Alice, I have something to tell you."

"Oh! You're *not* getting married?"

If he were stolen from me, I don't know if I'd be able to bear it. And what a chore it will be to pretend to be happy, as I did, perhaps none too convincingly, when William married Alice Gibbens.

"Certainly not," he says, with a smile. "It is that William is here."

I turn white as a sheet (I actually feel the blood draining from my face) and the teaspoon trembles in my hand. I stare at my brother. "*Here?*"

"He is waiting now in the Holly Walk for the news to be broken to you, and if you survive the shock, I am to tie my handkerchief to the balcony. May I tell him he may come up?"

"Of course," I say just before passing out.

— THIRTEEN —

IT WAS A SMALL SWOON, CONSIDERING THE MAGNITUDE OF THE shock. Shocks pleasant and unpleasant undo me equally, and when my body stops trembling and my tears stop flowing—at the sight of that dear face after six years!—I assure William that he is the good sort of shock. He is in tears, too, I should note, and the first thing he gasped was rather odd. "Why, Alice, you've become so beautiful. Your suffering has refined you."

"Well, thank you, William. You're not so bad yourself." Though wearing the haggard look of sleeplessness, he nevertheless manages to look young and vital. While Henry has grown portly over the years, William has gone in the opposite direction and is lean as a greyhound.

I explain that my *nerves* are prone to these fits and that my mind has nothing to say about it. "I remember describing my nerves to you once in the old days, William, and you said, 'Oh, yes, like bottled lightning.' It was as if you'd read my mind!"

"It was a description of a woman in a novel I read."

"I think I remember that novel," Henry says.

"Oh, I can't believe I'm not dreaming. You, William, in Leamington, next to Miss Clarke's wallpaper. Can you *believe* it, Henry?"

"It *is* rather an appalling pattern!" William says.

"Isn't it? Clarkey is immensely proud of it. It is called Marie Antoinette, don't ask me why. Miss Clarke is a dear, though. She is sure to catch you on the stairs as you attempt to leave. I believe she has a scrapbook devoted to both my famous brothers."

William laughs. "Pompeiian Red is all the rage in Boston this season. I believe Alice is considering it for the dining room of our new house. If she insists on a frieze of erupting volcanoes, I shall have to put my foot down!"

"Oh but, William, isn't it the most extraordinary luck that I fell ill in the only land in which lodging houses exist! But now you must tell me about your Psychological Congress."

"Physiological Congress. It has been timed to coincide with the *Exposition Universelle*, of course."

"How wonderful. M. Eiffel's tower is being called an 'abomination' and an 'eyesore' in the papers. You must go see it, William." At this point Nurse comes in with tea, rolls, and gooseberry jam on a tray, and I watch William struggle to maintain a straight face when she curtsies to him. I'd almost forgotten that Americans don't curtsy and are unaccustomed to slavish manners on the part of their domestics.

After she goes out to visit her family, William says, "Your little nurse, Emily, seems a jewel. And what a beautiful face!"

"Oh, she *is*, to endure all my snubs and my, to her, unknowable mysteries. Speaking of mysteries, William, they say there is little doubt that your friend, poor chloroformed Mr. Gurney, committed suicide. What a pity to hide it! Every educated person who kills himself does something toward lessening the superstition, I think."

"It is terribly sad."

"His wife, Kate, would call on me and pour out her troubles. She said he worked on his psychical research day and night, never took her anywhere and went around telling everyone he'd married beneath him!"

"Oh, I don't believe it was *that* bad," Henry says.

I say, "Wait and see, Henry. That is one widow who will toss out her weeds at the first opportunity. I am surprised, by the way, that the women here seem to do constantly what so rarely happens at home, namely marry again. You'd think that the wife part of you would have been sufficiently developed in one experiment, or that you might like to contemplate the situation from the *bereft* point of view for a while."

"Gurney's death is a great loss to me," William says. "It seems one of death's stupidest strokes, for I know of no one whose life task was begun on a more far-reaching scale."

"Oh, I am *very* sorry, William. It *was* heroic of him to suppress his vanity to the extent of confessing that the game is too hard."

We are quiet for a few minutes, listening to the ticking of the clock on the mantel. "Now," I say, "you must tell me all about your children. I want to hear every detail. I am their aunt. Don't leave anything out."

He begins to describe them, beginning with solid, reliable, intellectually precocious Harry, "who, fortunate child, has inherited his mother's temperament. He can always be counted on to take what falls to him with equanimity. When Bill does not get what he wants, he fills the welkin with lamentation. I think he is much as Father must have been as a child."

"And little Peggy of the soulful dark eyes?"

"She has a mouthful of teeth and runs about with a cracker always clutched in her fist. Her grandmother thinks she has an unusually vivid inner life. We like to think she shows promise of becoming another Sister Alice—except that she is a chatterbox and you were a quiet child."

"Who could get a word in edgewise, in *our* family? In another family, I might have been the Demosthenes of my sex." William tosses his head back and laughs. He has one of the world's best laughs.

"Please, William, do promise me that you will *educate* your children. Leave Europe for later, when they are old enough to have a Grand Emotion. Do not tear them up by the roots every few months, as we were."

William gazes at me as if he is trying either to memorize my features or to correlate them with my self of six years ago. It has been that long.

"We were hotel children, weren't we?" Henry says.

"Do you remember the school in Boulogne where there were only English boys?" William asks. "They were astonished to find we spoke English, not 'American.' How like Father to place us in a French school in which no French was spoken!"

"Fortunately, the schools never lasted long," Henry says.

"I *liked* the schools. I liked playing with other boys. The school in Geneva, where we boarded with Wilky, was a rollicking good time."

Henry proceeds to recite from memory the names of all of our tutors and mademoiselles.

I say, "I simply worshipped Mademoiselle Guyot, who passed out those red candies that turned our tongues red. Didn't Father denounce her at the dinner table for teaching us Papist idolatries?"

"I remember it well," William says. "He pounded his fist and shouted, 'Prayers are haggling and God does not haggle!' Poor Mademoiselle was gone the next day."

"Oh, my heart was broken, you know. For weeks I kept praying to her *bon dieu*, who seemed so nice. I didn't trust Father's inscrutable deity to listen to my prayers or keep track of my good and bad deeds."

"The one I remember best was the worldly Mademoiselle Danse," Henry says.

"She disappeared suddenly, didn't she?" William says.

"Didn't they all?" Henry says. "Father said something about her being an 'adventuress' but never explained."

"Yes!" I say, remembering now. "Do you know what I thought that meant? I thought she was an explorer and I pictured her floating down a muddy river in the part of our map of Africa labeled 'Unexplored Regions.' Oh, William, are you as *appalled* by this Stanley character as Henry and I are? Gouging a path through Africa, slaughtering everything in his path."

After discussing Stanley's horrors, we move on to Ireland and Home Rule and Parnell and the Unionists. Well, I do—and William listens politely. "The thought of the Irish flinging themselves against the dense wall of British brutality for seven centuries—well, you know my feelings, William. I got so worked up over the Parnell trial that I went off whenever I read anything on the subject."

I want to seize the opportunity to carp about the British a bit more while my brothers are here, as I can't do this with most of my callers, who *are* British. Although William in some moods is prone to despise the entire island and its inhabitants, he does love his London tailor and British gentlemen's clubs and is very fond of his British Psychical friends. (I like the Sidgwicks, but Fred Myers is a horror and poor Mr. Gurney was quite deluded and is now terribly dead.) I tell him, "I can't *fathom* the English. They pass special legislation about a dog's broken leg but celebrate foxes being torn to shreds. And it is simply inconceivable the lives the poor lead here."

"Surely we have our poor at home."

"Yes, but the poor here are *different*, William. So many centuries have gone into the making of 'em." Turning to Henry, I say, "What do fashionable people *make* of the army of ragged, grimy, coughing people they see everywhere? I suppose after a while they just don't see them. The poor must bother them no more than a cloud of gnats."

Henry makes a gesture of muted assent, or perhaps neutrality.

I broach the subject of the recent dockers' strike, and then say to William, "Did you see that two hundred trades in London have gained a ten percent increase in wages as a consequence, the masters caving in to keep the men from going on strike?" William looks blank. Doesn't he read the newspapers? Or do American newspapers ignore Europe? I am just warming up to a rantlet about imperial actions from Baghdad to Delhi, when I stop and laugh at myself. "Imagine the millions of the Empire being pigeon-holed by a creature whose field of vision is populated by a landlady, a nurse, and two chair-men, one perpetually drunk. It is all very funny. So, William, do tell us what your Congress is about."

He explains that it will bring together researchers from England, Germany, Austria, Italy, France, and the United States for the first time and he expresses his admiration for some French researchers who have been studying hysterics. "They spend hours with a single patient, hypnotizing her (or him) and assembling a psychic biography."

"But why should the patient *wish* to be hypnotized?"

"Sometimes when there is a great shock, such as a railway crash, the trauma is forgotten, but not entirely. The memory goes underground. The process is called dissociation. Pierre Janet will hypnotize a patient and uncover the fixed ideas dwelling in the depths of her mind, ideas of which she is unaware but which are making her ill."

Henry volunteers that *idées fixes* are a part of the French character, Balzac's characters being a case in point.

"For example," William says, "there was a girl who left home in what is called a fugue state."

"Fugue?" I say. "That sounds lovely."

"No, it means—well, never mind. Janet hypnotized her and put a pencil in her hand and she wrote, 'I left home because *maman* accuses me of having a lover and it is not true. I sold my jewels to pay my railroad fare. I took such and such a train.'"

"Maybe she was lying, William. In French novels it's nothing but adultery, adultery, adultery."

"She wasn't. Under hypnosis, the girl related everything that happened with precision, while continuing to insist she remembered nothing about it. She was not lying, Alice. She had a secondary personality. It had split off from the rest of her mind because of some great disturbance."

"But, William: when this man hypnotizes the lunatics, what good does this do *them*?"

"Well, once he has excavated their harmful memories, as it were, he erases or changes them by means of suggestion. He gives the patient a new set of memories."

"What do you mean, suggestion?"

"Hypnotic suggestion."

"Oh, hypnotism! There is such interest in the Mind Cure here, William. I wish you could meet Mrs. Lucian Carr. *Hundreds* of her friends have been cured and she cures herself whenever the necessity arises, having listened to a course of twelve lectures by her prophetess. The funny thing is, when I asked Mrs. Carr what attitude of mind one must assume, she could make no articulate sound, notwithstanding her thirty hours of instruction. She finally said it was 'to lose oneself in the Infinite!' Imagine!"

William looks—well, chagrined, I suppose. I must have inadvertently struck at one of his sacred cows. Then I see that there is more to it. I believe William aspires to cure *me* with this mesmerism mumbo-jumbo. While it is sweet of him to want to see me well, his view of me as a spineless *malade imaginaire* is unflattering. However, he loves me and means well, so I let it pass.

"How restless Father was!" I say. "Remember how he'd start to pace around the house, and we'd know that soon he'd go somewhere on a train and come back a week later. Where did he *go*?"

None of us has an answer. "We had no idea of ordinary life at all! I was shunned at Mrs. Agassiz's school, you know. For two years I hardly dared open my mouth."

"I thought you liked it there," William says.

"Eventually, but in the beginning I was a traveler without a map. I simply had no idea what the Assemblies were, or the North Shore, or someone's Cousin Frank or Aunt Harriet. You know how all Bostonians are related to everyone else in a tangled web of kinship that you are expected somehow to grasp?"

In the presence of my two brothers, I suddenly have the strangest feeling that I have one leg in 1889 and the other in 1860; that our parents are simultaneously alive and dead; that William, Henry, and I are not just our current ages but all the ages we have been. Whatever our age, it seems, we feel the same inside. I enjoy this pleasantly disembodied feeling, and wish time would stop and this moment with my brothers would last forever.

"Are you going to read a paper at the Congress, William?" I ask.

"I have been asked to give the Opening Remarks. I had no idea anyone had heard of me. Being susceptible to flattery, I said yes."

"That's *wonderful*! What will you say?"

"Oh, I'll write something on the ferry or at my hotel in Boulogne. I can generally count on salt air and sea breezes to revive my brain."

"Oh, William, you are going to *Boulogne*! Please do go to all our old places. I *so* loved the medieval ramparts with the English stone cannonballs stuck in them. Oh, remember the dread episode of the bonnet?"

Even Henry's memory fails on this. "What bonnet?"

"It was Mademoiselle Cusin's Christmas present from us—remember? For some reason I was the one delegated to give the instructions for making it. It was the first important mission I'd ever been entrusted with and I was very anxious to succeed. The shop was on the rue Victor Hugo. You took me there, William."

"I did?"

"Yes, and then you *deserted* me!"

He obviously hasn't the faintest idea what I am talking about, whereas for me the event was so disturbing it is permanently etched on my brain.

I describe my ordeal, how the milliners kept bringing out different materials while speaking rapidly and incomprehensibly in French. They stood behind the counter, impatient, as I stood mute and paralyzed. In my panic, I fixed my eyes on a piece of pink material laid out next to a strip of blue on the tall counter I had to stand on tiptoes to see, and mumbled, *Oui, comme ça.*

"On Christmas day Mademoiselle unwrapped the present, which I saw immediately was atrocious. The pink made you think of a bad sunburn, the blue was dead and lifeless, the design hideous. She made a display of joy but wore it only once, on a visit to the *campagne,* where we met only peasants. The bonnet was a stain on my character, a great failure. I foresaw that my whole life would probably be an unmitigated mistake. Why did you *leave* me, William?"

"I recall vaguely going to an art store with the intention of buying watercolors and buying, instead, some naughty *cartes de visite.* Egyptian Dancing Girls, they were called. It was amazing what you could get in France, even in those days. I didn't think I'd be needed, being completely ignorant of millinery matters."

"I was *seven,* William!"

He is quiet, taking this in. For an instant he looks as if he might weep. Finally, he says, "I was and am a dull clod, Alice. It grieves me that I abandoned you. I hope you can forgive me."

"Well, I'm not sure you would have managed a better-looking bonnet."

"Certainly not. I cannot be trusted to pick out a button."

He mentions that his English friends from the Society for Psychical Research will be coming to the Congress and presenting papers. The Sidgwicks will be trying to drum up support for their international Census of Hallucinations.

"Oh, yes, they told me about their Census. The Sidgwicks have been charming to me, William, and still come all the way to Leamington to call on me. They are the last remnant of my London *salon,* faithful to the end, while the others have melted away. Nora Sidgwick is the most delightful embodiment of the modern bluestocking, don't you think? How *is* Mrs. Piper, by the way? Bob seems to be spending all his time with her. That can't be good for him."

"Poor Bob," says Henry.

"Oh *don't* let's talk about Bob," William says. "He just stayed a week at our house and exhausted poor Alice by pouring out his miseries until the wee hours. He threw our household into turmoil as usual, and the children kept asking, 'When is he *going?*'"

"It is so sad about Aunt Kate, isn't it?"

"Yes. Lilla Walsh said she was incapable of conversation toward the end. She'd try to say something and then lapse into resignation, saying, 'I can't talk it.'"

We carefully avoid the minefield of our aunt's will. That has been disposed of in letters and shall nevermore be spoken of—by me, anyway. "Poor Aunt Kate, who so loved stating her opinions," I say. "I suppose we shall all end like that."

As the light drains from the sky, the three of us sit in wistful silence, recalling the years when we lived like a small tribe isolated on an island, with our own peculiar language and customs—the good and bad of it known only to us and to Bob now.

"Life is so odd, isn't it?" I tell William I can still picture everything in Cambridge, as clearly as if I were standing there—Harvard Square, the horse-cars, the mansions on "Tory Row," Mr. Eliot and his port-wine birthmark. "Who is Charlemagne expurgating now?"

"I'm not sure. He hosts Dante evenings these days. The smart set goes. Howells says his spoken Italian is actually quite poor."

"Oh, Charles is far too self-conscious to have a gift for languages. And how is Grace? You know about her wedding gift to Mabel Quincy, I assume?"

"What is that?"

"I am *shocked* you don't know, William, since it was Alice who wrote me of it. It was Grace's own inept and graceless translation of Montaigne. Before wrapping the book to give to Mabel, she *glued* the naughty pages together. Even strained through Grace's polysyllabic fog, the passages were apparently unsuitable for a bride-to-be, although Grace herself did not shy from contemplating them, depraved spinster that she is."

William laughs lustily at this, and then the talk turns to William's new house, currently under construction on the former Shady Hill property. "They've put in three new streets—mine is Irving Street. I am hoping to move in when I return." He fumbles in his satchel and finds the blueprints. Spreading them out on my lap, he explains all the rooms and their features.

After that, we move on to Cambridge friends. "Winnie Howells"—daughter of the novelist—"is sicker than ever," William says. "Nerves, apparently. Weir Mitchell, the rest-cure man, has her now, so I suppose she will gain."

"Oh, William! That dreadful man."

As the little clock on the mantel chimes the hour, I draw my shawl around me. "You don't know what it means to have a few laughs, William. I never go out, you know. I have no idea of life at large. I see mostly women, when I see anyone, and British women—well, the minds of even the most intelligent are simply cul-de-sacs, more or less long. The dead wall you always come to in time."

Several minutes of deep silence pass.

"Nurse thinks I am a godless savage because I have no outward ritual, little realizing that I am wholly devoted to the Unknowable Mystery Behind Phenomena!" William smiles at this, knowing what I mean. "Anyhow, William, I hope you are coming back here afterwards on your way to Liverpool?"

"I shall return, bearing tales of the Exposition. But first I am making a side trip to Geneva to gaze upon our old house. Remember it, Alice?"

"Yes. I loved the garden. Remember our Russian landlady, who was a terrible invalid, and sat reading under a lime tree, in her mushroom hat, always so happy?"

~~~⌒~~~

Ongoing letter from William James to Mrs William James
Hotel Rastadt, Paris. August 3rd, 1889.

After I had paced the street for 3/4 of an hour and begun to give up all hope, suddenly Harry's portly form appeared on the balcony cheering me on. I rushed up—A. was on her bed, in a fainting, panting condition, white as a sheet, with outstretched arms into which I threw myself. She kept gasping out, "You understand, don't you, it's all my body, it's all physical, I can't help it."

Alice in person is elegant and graceful, and talked and laughed in a charming way, making me feel ashamed of my dull and ponderous way with her these last years. The tone of invective and sarcasm that sounded shrill in her letters is uttered in a soft, laughing way, and gives an entirely different impression. I'm afraid I am a dull clod, unfit to deal with airy creations like Alice. But I think she has forgiven me.

As I kissed her good-bye, she gazed at me with moist eyes and, clasping both my hands in hers, said, "It is sad, William, to think of you, with your love of kith and kin, left alone in Cambridge with the family melted like snow from about you. Our dead— les morts qui sont toujours vivants." I live in the bosom of a large family and Alice has only Henry, but to her, "family" means the original family circle. A helpless invalid, she feels sorry for me. (I must admit I suffered a twinge of jealousy seeing H and A's intimacy, their private jokes and references.)

On our way out H & I ran into A's landlady, Miss Clarke, a friendly garrulous woman of early middle age with massive red arms. She told me, "Miss James is a perfect angel and means so much to us. I don't know how we'd get along without her." This statement was clarified when Harry explained that A. is obsessed with the poor families of the neighborhood, knows every detail of their wretched lives, and keeps them afloat with gifts of money and clothes.

As for Harry, he'd warned me in a letter, "I am as broad as I am long, as fat as a butter tub & as red as a British materfamilias." When he met me at the station, I almost didn't recognize him. He seemed a thorough Englishman, having covered himself with strange, heavy, alien manners and customs, like a marine crustacean with barnacles. After a few hours in his company, however, he became once more the same dear good innocent Harry of his youth. I am sorry to say that he is saving not a cent, so my vision of him paralyzed in our spare room, is stronger than ever. He seems quite helpless in that regard.

WILLIAM JAMES
PARIS, AUGUST 6TH, 1889

To MRS. WILLIAM JAMES
My darling—Haven't managed to mail this yet, as new things keep happening. Tonight I found three quills poking out of the mattress cording! My sleep has gone to pieces—Took two chloral hydrate last night, and got two hours of what might technically be called sleep but was not refreshing in the least. Also: heat, drain smells, cries of inebriates and putains on the street. I long for you (and home) more desperately than I thought possible and begin to wonder if I shall go to Switzerland after all.

Today the Congress was dominated by Pierre Janet. He has the most unruly eyebrows ever seen on a Frenchman and told stories of his hysterics that would make Zola blush. If only Sister Alice could see him, but great French doctors don't make house calls in England (or even possibly in France) and how could Alice cross the Channel if seasickness almost killed her two and a half years ago? She and H are as ignorant of science as the beasts of the field. I must tread carefully.

Tell our Harry I almost mistook the man from the telegraph office for one of his lead soldiers. Tell Bill to stay away from Mrs. Waring's roses, and give Peggy a hug and kiss from her devoted Papa—

DARLING (AUGUST 7TH) . . .

This letter goes on and on. I must tell you about the strange man I met at dinner tonight. He is a Dr. Freud, a Viennese neurologist. As I sat down he was carefully excising the center of a slice of bread in a manner that hinted at surgical training. But for such a methodical man he was subject to such flights of fancy! He had heard of me, and confided that he'd read several of my papers. I am quite amazed that I am known to anyone here.

Dr. Freud clearly dislikes Dr. Janet—and couldn't explain why. And he is peculiarly fascinated with dreams, recommended strongly that I study mine, warning that "the interpretation is heavy work." I thought only gypsies paid heed to dreams! He had little interest in the Exposition, and seemed to prefer the Buffalo Bill Cody show in Neuilly, where he was absolutely riveted (and horrified) by Annie Oakley! Seems to suspect Americans of all kinds of barbarities.

Can't fall asleep—it is 2:15 am in this stifling hotel room. Perhaps Dr. Freud has had a strange druglike effect on me. He told me at dinner about the hysterical patients he is treating with hypnotism—all women, some American. He said he prefers women patients because their minds are open, less "barricaded." Would you agree, darling?

We men are such heavy, blundering, obtuse creatures; we require taming by our womenfolk. Even at the age of not yet two, don't you think Peggy is having a civilizing influence on the boys? I am getting more homesick by the minute; I don't think I can bear to go to Switzerland now, I would only envy the men I see going home to wives and children, with parcels under their arms.

JOURNAL OF WJ 8/9/89

While Herr Doktor Freud & I were talking, I described Sister Alice— her hysterically paralyzed legs and general broken-downness—identifying her as a "female relation of mine." I immediately felt like a mouse that has attracted the attention of a cat. He peppered me with prying

*questions, which made me feel it would be unnerving to be his patient. I
mentioned that the young woman had been too ill to attend her brother's
wedding, whereupon, he said, "Ach, a wedding, you say? Weddings give
rise to all kinds of complexes. Is it possible that the young woman was in
love with—who was it?—the brother?"*

"Surely not," I said. "They are brother and sister."

*"It happens, Dr. James," he said in an irritating manner, "even in
the most respectable families. Say that in the girl's mind the brother is
her suitor, her sweetheart, her husband even. Perhaps the brother has led
her on unconsciously by flirting with her at an impressionable age. The
girl becomes over-stimulated. Naturally, the desire for sexual intercourse
with the brother is too charged for her to acknowledge and becomes submerged in her unconscious, giving rise to symptoms."*

*I suppressed the urge to fling my wine into Dr. Freud's face. Is
brother/sister incest really so common in Austrian families? How can he
presume to know all about a person he has never met? Also, I don't like
this word unconscious. This region of our being is not unconscious, like a
person in a coma; it is subliminal. All the gods as well as the devils come
to us through the subliminal door.*

*I didn't flirt with my sister, not intentionally, anyhow, but I sup-
pose Dr. Freud might see it differently. I can't make up my mind if he is a
grand halluciné or a genius—perhaps a bit of both. When I brought up
Pierre Janet, he went silent, then said, "If I may speak frankly, Professor
James, I don't trust Janet, although he is Charcot's protégé and there is no
one I admire more than Charcot. There is something unheimlich about
Janet, don't you find?"*

I don't know what he meant. It was all in all quite a queer evening.

～～

JOURNAL OF WJ CONT.
8/10, 1 AM

*I forgot to mention Freud's queer confession last night. He told me, within
a half hour of meeting, that he suffered from a fear of travel (Reisefieber).*

This was due apparently to an experience of seeing his mother's nude body in a sleeping car when he was two years old. Can anyone really remember being two years old? Why should the mother's body inspire such shock in an infant?

As my brain whirred and sleep eluded me, I thought more about Sister Alice and my possible guilt in that regard. I was revisited by the memory of her anguished face when Minny came to visit and we stayed up all night talking in front of the fire. Fresh snow covering roofs, streets, and fields like a white duvet, Alice sat there with us for over an hour, sensing that we wanted to speak privately and determined to prevent this; she has never really cared for any of the Temples. At last she left, favoring us with one of her most disdainful glances on the way out. Remembering what happened afterward, I almost wish she had stayed. But I will try to fall asleep now.

~~~~~

JOURNAL OF WJ, CONT 2:30 AM
NO LUCK WITH SLEEP . . .

After Alice left the room, Minny felt free to unburden herself about Elly's engagement to Temple Emmet, three decades her senior. "She does it out of duty. But if they are not appalled at what they do, why should I worry? My future brother-in-law has invited me to travel to California with them, and as the doctors seem to think it will be good for my lungs, I will go, I think."

I wondered if she meant to leave forever and could not bring myself to ask. "If you strike gold, please write to me and I will come out by the next train and help you run the mine. I have nothing else to do now."

"I certainly will, Willy." She smiled wistfully. "But aren't you a doctor now?"

"Only technically." I explained that my oral examination, by Dr. Holmes, lasted all of fifteen minutes. "I shall confine myself to prescribing medicines for friends and family, hoping they don't die."

Shouldn't have mentioned dying. Did not know the status of Minny's health. V. thin and pale. Staying in Pelham, New York, with Kitty and her husband (another elderly Emmet), forbidden by her doctors to return to the damp of Newport.

She asked me if I knew a cure for sleeplessness.

"How many hours are you sleeping at night?"

"Oh, I don't sleep. I have given it up." She laughed at herself, and I promised to send her a few tablets of the new wonder drug Chloral. Another bond between us—sleeplessness.

The next part is painful to recall. We stayed up all night & I deluged her with all my philosophical distress—the full catastrophe that was WJ. Horrible recital.

She drew her crocheted shawl around her, her face tinged pink in the reflected firelight. Her irises were the color of the Atlantic on a clear, cold day in January. If she were not my cousin, I knew without a doubt that I would be in love with her. In fact, I was in love with her. I decided to tell her that night.

About Elly's marriage of convenience she said, "It is the irretrievableness of the step that is so overwhelming to my mind. I have told no one else of my feelings—only you, Willy." Said she was certain now she would never marry. She'd renounced everything, even God, and found a wild, pagan happiness in the simplest things—the sky, the play of light on a wall, the hush of falling snow. "I do not understand Uncle Henry's view of Creation. When he says it was not a single event in time but is continually occurring through some process, what does he mean? It truly makes no sense to me."

Forgot to mention the terrible row at dinner. Never saw Father so irate as when Minny challenged his beliefs, trembling but unflinching. No woman had ever stood up to him like that, and I was quite sure she won the debate. Am fading now, will attempt sleep.

～

JOURNAL OF WJ, CONT 3:15 AM

No, instead of trying to sleep I'll continue writing for as long as it takes. Altho' my memory is usually execrable, I remember everything about that long night twenty years ago.

Minny told me that she'd concluded that she was a natural stoic, an "unrepentant pagan."

"That is brave," I said.

"Not at all, Willy. While lying awake at night, I have done an immense amount of thinking. Hour after hour I pondered the doctrine of vicarious atonement, which your father subscribes to. Has Jesus taken on all our sins and released us? I took it in deeply for over a month. I thought so much about Jesus in my sleeplessness that I began to feel very close to him, as if I lived inside his mind. I can't describe it properly. It probably sounds mad."

"It doesn't." What an extraordinary being my cousin was. My own struggles seemed small and distant in her presence, as if they were trinkets. If we could only be together, I might become the man I was meant to be. Or such was my deluded idea.

"Finally, William, I found I could not accept it. I gave it up. And now I am a happy pagan child."

Just before dawn, I blurted it out—asked Minny to marry me. She looked startled. I explained I meant a "white marriage"—we'd go to Europe, living together like brother and sister. I would take her to the best spas of Europe & she would be cured of her consumption, I of my hypochondria, &c. What a self-centered and unbalanced young man was I! What a blessing that we outgrow our youth! To convince M. that a real marriage between us would be a crime against nature, I subjected her to an incoherent rant about my degeneracy and my vices, the suicidal urges crashing through me, &c, &c. I cringe to recall it. Was there ever a more self-defeating marriage proposal?

Poor M. sat there silently, hands folded in her lap, regarding me levelly. She said gently that she would consider my offer and write to me of her decision.

Her letter arrived two weeks later. She'd had two "very bad" hemorrhages and her doctor told her, "My dear young lady, your right lung is diseased!" and she replied, "Well, Doctor, even if my right lung is all gone I should make a stand with my left." Then another doctor said her lungs were not so bad after all and so she thought she would go to California. She was turning me down.

Only now, with Minny twenty years dead, can I allow myself to notice that underneath my hurt and disappointment lurked another emotion. Relief. Less than 2 months later came the horrible news from Pelham that she was dead. Elly & Kitty said she'd fought desperately, agonizingly, to live. How it tortured me to picture my remarkable cousin as a poor, suffering creature, all her gifts reduced to the struggle for breath. If it all comes to this, what is life worth?

JOURNAL OF WJ, CONT 5 AM

Still not a wink of sleep.

There is more, I'm afraid. A breakdown after M's death, the Somerville Asylum. A room of green and white tiles. Shivering inside a wet sheet, teeth clacking like dominos. A painting of a girl in a white muslin dress standing on a bluff overlooking the sea, meant to drive me mad. Or madder. The doctors are all in on it. "Don't jump, Minny!" But my words can't reach her and she tumbles, her white dress billowing around her like a spinnaker. Hypodermic needle in left arm. "For your own good." Helpless.

All color drains from world, then a dead field, the color of grey volcanic ash, endless. All around me the bodies of dead soldiers, grey-skinned, in heaps. All the fine dead Boston boys! I am sent here to this asylum because I am a shirker. A brief, panicked, doomed struggle. Grey turns to black. No more WJ, end of story.

In the greyness a pinpoint of light, like a very bright star rising in the east. Impossible to look away. I and this orb more brilliant than a thousand suns are one, made of the same substance. It contains the seeds of everything and floods me with bliss. A voice says, "Thou hast overcome the world."

My body no more to me than a pile of dirty laundry. Oh! the shock of going back into it, like diving into an icy pond. Muscles ache, eyeballs like peeled tomatoes, throat parched, hands lashed to the bedstead with rubber cords. Then I remember. I chose to go back. Why? Minny went and did not return. I made the wrong choice and must live with it. I weep behind the mask they have put over my eyes.

Written on my intake form (I read very well upside-down): Hypochondria, Melancholia, Chronic Masturbation. Not until my honeymoon did I realize there was nothing wrong with me. Something tugging at the fringes of my mind, tho'. What Freud said at dinner about a railway sleeping carriage when he was two.

I was 2 in 1844, the year of Father's Vastation. Living in Windsor, England. No memory of it. No, something. Making faces at baby Harry. I'd growl like a bear and Harry would bounce up and down, laughing and waving his arms. If I growled louder, Harry's mouth would turn down at the corners and he'd burst into tears. Every time. I kept crossing that boundary between laughter and tears, making Harry laugh, then cry, then laugh again. Other things I remember: Hail beating on the roof, snails leaving glistening slime trails on the flagstones, a steep staircase, floral wallpaper in my parents' bedroom. And this: Father with his head in Mother's lap blubbering like infant, Aunt Kate standing by the washstand, her lips pressed together in a grim line.

Chest tight, face hot. Run outside. Grass high, higher than my head. Pick a dandelion and blow, watch the wind tear it apart. Sky stretches blue, away and away. World so big, Willy little. Where mama, papa, aunty, nanny, brudder, everyone? Gone. Tears burn in my eyes. Desolation rips at my heart. Did not know it was possible to be so alone.

⌒ FOURTEEN ⌒

"HAVE YOU EVER KNOWN A PERSON TO CHANGE HIS MIND SO OFTEN, Henry? He is just like a blob of mercury; you can't put a finger on him."

Naturally, we are speaking of William, who just left us for Liverpool to catch his steamer home. In a spasm of homesickness in his Paris hotel, he cancelled his plans for Switzerland and booked passage on an earlier ship, but while sitting here by my bedside yesterday, his mind had already shifted to a plan for bringing the whole family back to Europe next time.

"He is so like Father, isn't he?" I say. "Do you suppose he is ever content where he *is*?"

"I think that when he first arrives home he will describe his homecoming in terms Odysseus might have used about Ithaca. Then the petty annoyances of life will grate on him and he'll read the shipping news and start dreaming of foreign ports. In a year or two he'll come back to Europe, which he will love at first but which will inevitably disappoint him, each country in its turn, and on it will go."

"Probably everyone is like that, but William is *more* so. He is more of everything than most people, wouldn't you say?"

While he was here, he told us about his Congress, which I could not entirely absorb due to my ignorance of physiology, et cetera, but there was apparently a great deal of hysteria and mesmerism in it. "As in a dream," he told us, "I heard speaker after speaker refer to the published work of Monsieur Weelyam James. One Frenchman described 'Le Sentiment de l'Effort' as 'the greatest work in psychology ever written.' I had no idea anyone had heard of me."

"The greatest *ever written*, William!" I said. "You and Henry can divide the spoils between you—Henry taking Britain and you the continent. What did you say in your talk, by the way?"

"I've already forgotten; insomnia has torn my mind to pieces. All I can tell you is that Nora Sidgwick rushed up to me afterwards and said, 'We are so happy you are *as* you are.'"

"What did she mean by that?"

"I don't know."

"Oh, your European fame will bring *such* joy to Miss Clarke, you have no idea. Now tell us about the Exposition. Was it ablaze with electric light, and what was that like?"

"Much brighter. Altogether different from gaslight. Some elderly ladies complained that it exposed all their wrinkles."

"Did you go to the top of Mr. Eiffel's 'abomination'?" Henry asked.

"Yes, I stepped into a large box with about sixty other people and we ascended through the air. It lurched a little. You feel it in your stomach."

I shuddered, thinking of my snakes.

"Some people groaned and obviously regretted getting in, but I loved the sensation of leaving the earth. After a few minutes, the box stops with a loud clunk, and the uniformed man calls out 'All change here!' You cross a narrow bridge to another box. It is called an Otis Elevator, and it takes you up to the top. Or near enough."

"Why two boxes instead of one?" Henry asked.

"I don't know. I wondered myself."

"Wait, William," I said. "Let me close my eyes. Now please describe in detail the view from up there."

"The walls are glass on two sides, and you can see down to the Exhibition gardens, two hundred seventy-five meters below. I remember the figure from the newspaper."

The scene bloomed in my mind as William described it. How touchingly small the things of earth, mere toys, seen from the air. I saw the silver ribbon of the Seine, the small puffs of black smoke hanging over the railway line. A view heretofore known only to birds and a few balloonists.

"What about the *habitats humains*? The newspaper said there are all sorts of dwellings recreated in meticulous detail."

"Yes. A Lapland house, next to a palatial Persian dwelling. A wooden Germanic house on stilts, a circular Gallic hut, and many others. Then you must imagine, Alice, *people* from everywhere—that is the principal thing—people of every color and race and in every costume. Egyptian donkey boys, African kings, witch doctors, Japanese geishas, Arab carpet merchants—well, I could go on and on. It was all like an opium dream and made me wish to spend the rest of my life as a *flâneur.*"

"You walk too fast to be a *flâneur*, William. They stroll languidly, lost in their reveries."

"Lord Houghton said the rue de Caire is the most impresssive of the exhibits," Henry said.

"I agree. It consists of several blocks of a Cairo souk recreated in Paris. It even has fifty or sixty Egyptian donkeys, cared for by the same number of donkey boys."

"One boy per donkey?" I asked.

"Well, I like to think so. My attention was drawn to a tent where beautiful ladies straight out of *The Arabian Nights* did a wiggling dance with their stomachs bared."

"Who wants to see a bare stomach?"

"I might have said that before, but these ladies changed my mind. After that I rambled around, drinking Russian tea from a samovar and, later, Turkish coffee from tiny cups."

"How did you ever sleep after that?"

"Oh, I didn't. I am going home now principally to sleep."

"What else did you do?"

"Well, from a trio of Canadian Indians I bought two tiny canoes made of birch-bark for Harry and Billy, then I began to wonder what to get for Peggy. Oh, Alice, I almost forgot! I brought you a little something."

After rummaging through his suitcase, he brought out a beautiful pair of jet earrings and a necklace of ivory and jet. I almost burst into tears. They seemed far too precious for the likes of me, and I couldn't think where I'd wear them. But I recovered and thanked him profusely and then closed my eyes again as William resumed his tale.

"I saw many other wondrous sights, Alice. You must picture a magnificently robed and turbaned African king feasting on exotic delicacies of some sort."

"How was this king attired?"

"In patterned swaths of yellow, black, and saffron, a turban of the same material, and any number of necklaces and bracelets. Enormous ivory earrings dragged his earlobes practically to his knees. He was a singularly beautiful man and looked as if he could put you in a trance in five seconds flat. Then, let's see, I saw two Siamese Buddhist monks hobnobbing with a Greek Orthodox priest. Don't you wonder what they were talking about, and in what language?"

"Yes, but one thing puzzles me, William. Are the people in the habitats actually who they are supposed to be, or are they actors? Is the African king really a king? Are the carpet merchants really carpet merchants? Where does everyone sleep at night—in the habitats, or in a hotel? And will they be content to go back to Darkest Africa after they've seen Paris?"

"All excellent questions, Alice, to which, sadly, I don't have the answer."

"I'm going in October, and will try to find out for you, Alice."

"Thank you, Henry. Did you see those big machines, William? In that place—what is it called?"

"The Galerie des Machines. Yes. I felt like a man in a myth who is taken, awed and terrified, into the abode of the gods."

"What sort of machines?" Henry asked.

"Oh, pumps, dynamos, transformers, hydraulic elevators. Edison's 'Big Lamps.' I'd seen a few of the things before, at the Exposition in Philadelphia in seventy-six, but they've grown larger and more complex now. Of course I don't understand them at all. The most remarkable machine was this new invention of Mr. Edison's, called a 'phonograph.' It played two 'records.'"

"Records?"

"That is what they call them. The sound is etched into disks somehow, in grooves. I don't understand it, but one played the 'Marseillaise' and 'America,' and on the other record male voices could be heard shouting, *Vive Carnot! Vive La France! Vive la République!*"

"Is the sound clear?"

"No. More like spirits speaking to you drunkenly from another world. I hope the mediums of Boston don't get wind of it."

"What makes the moving walkway move, William?"

"Oh, gears I suppose," he said vaguely. "You are a very exacting interviewer, Alice. Maybe you should take up journalism."

"Sadly, William, the inside of a sickroom is not considered picturesque in our age."

"Well, you glide effortlessly in one direction as other people glide past in the opposite. And such people, as I've said, from all over the world!" He took a pencil and a piece of notepaper and made a little sketch, in which Japanese women in kimonos glide by, and in the opposite direction, a turbaned man with a little boy.

He continued sketching furiously. "Here is something I actually saw. The maharajah, as you can see, is in front holding his small son's hand, while the maharani and the small daughters—whose noses and ears are pierced by blood-red rubies, by the way—trail behind."

I closed my eyes and saw them in my mind, their skin the hue of cinnamon or caramel, clothes the color of persimmons, peonies, French scarlet poppies. Something about this was familiar—what was it? Telling my stories to William, who was writing them down and illustrating them. I was about four, watching the drawings come to life. His drawing of an owl *was* the owl; the little girl, who wins a staring contest with the owl and is crowned Queen of the Night, *was* a real little girl. When William named her Alice, she *was* me—a transformed me.

"As you may know, Alice, the Oriental insists on having his females walk behind him and does not permit them to run amok founding charities, hounding college presidents, and running the world."

"And practicing unscrupulous journalism," Henry added.

"Don't forget that we 'Occidental females' are considered too irrational to vote and are barred from most occupations. According to your friend Francis Parkman, Henry—"

"He's hardly a *friend*, Alice."

"Well, I seem to recall he wrote you a *very* unctuous letter about *The Bostonians.* Wasn't he the model for your Basil Ransom?"

"Among others." Did I detect a faint blush on my brother's cheek? Perhaps he is a little embarrassed about *The Bostonians,* with its lampoons of feminists, psychics, and revered Boston figures like Miss Elizabeth Peabody. Bostonians have not quite forgiven him for this.

"Katherine and I had the misfortune to attend Mr. Parkman's Lowell lecture on The Rights of Women. A more accurate title might have been, Why Women Should Be Merely Ornamental. If females could vote, he said, we'd constitute a large noncombatant class and overwhelm the nation with our emotionalism. He seemed to feel that women could not be trusted to wage war with any regularity."

"Good grief," William sighed, then proceeded to describe other personages, such as Negroes in elegant suits, a Turkish pasha, a flock of Belgian nuns wearing wimples who seemed poised to take flight.

After he departed for the station in late afternoon, Harry and I spent the rest of the day analyzing him. "Didn't you want to laugh," I said, "when he described his new house in New Hampshire? Fourteen doors all opening to the outside! It could be a description of William's mind. He is simply himself, isn't he? A native of the James family and of no other land."

The next day Henry, too, sank below my little horizon, plunging me back into solitude. I think it will take me some time to assimilate the enormous fact of seeing William again after so many years. It is like a reunion with parts of myself that had been wandering in circles, lost, for years.

PART FOUR

～ ONE ～

1890

TODAY IS ONE OF THOSE RARE DAYS WHEN SOMETHING HAPPENS: A large packing crate arrives. Four brawny lads carry it upstairs and break apart the wooden slats, and there it is: the desk with the leather top I was given for Christmas 1877 for my "professoress" duties. I'd asked William and Alice to send it when they dismantled my Manchester house, but I'd forgotten and now it appears in my rooms like a dream object.

If only I could have saved the musty air exhaled by its drawers; once opened, of course, the past was immediately contaminated. How strange to come across your own flotsam and jetsam, your own "remains"! A rusty key to my old steamer trunk, a key to a jewelry box I no longer possess, an envelope, labeled *Alice 1849*, containing a lock of fine baby hair. (I must make sure Mrs. Piper doesn't get her paws on *that* after I "pass over.") In other drawers: bottles of ink, pen-wipers, engraved calling cards of Boston ladies, clippings from *Godey's* (saved as a joke for Sara), a skein of violet yarn, a hatpin, a few outdated American postage stamps, a half-written letter to one of my students from the Society to Encourage Studies at Home (I suppose it is too late to mail it now), cabinet photographs of various friends. And in the two lowest drawers on the right: a cache of family letters.

I can't decide whether Alice and William put them in there on purpose or if they just happened to be there. A quick glance at the envelopes reveals that mingled with Mother's and Father's letters are masses of letters to and from everyone in the family: a nearly random collection of Jamesiana.

I wait several days before tackling them; I am not sure why. Finally, one day after breakfast, I ask Nurse to bring me one of the bundles.

"Which one, Miss?"

"Oh, whatever is on top. Surprise me." This turns out to be a bundle of Mother's letters bound with a blue satin ribbon. Tears spring to my eyes at the sight of her dear handwriting, particularly my name written in her hand. To think that her living hand touched this paper, addressed the envelope, poured out these thoughts through her pen. I feel for some minutes as if a current of electricity had passed through me.

"Are you all right, Miss?"

"*Perfectly* well, Nurse." How unpleasant to have someone watch you as if you were a chimpanzee in the zoo. There are times when I wish Nurse would disappear for a little while. But she does her best, poor girl. It can't be easy catering to my eccentricities.

The first letter I unfold is from Mother to Father.

> *I saw how Alice's spirits sunk last evening in hearing of the recital of all your troubles—and she sighed a deep sigh, and said oh how I wish Father was here. My heart melts with tenderness toward you my precious one.*

The letter is undated and contains no clue to where Father was. Next I come to a pile of Mother's letters to me while I was in the clutches of the Brothers Taylor in New York.

> *I hear such fine accounts of your blooming appearance that I shall expect to hear from the doctor that the great work of restoration is almost completed.*

My blooming appearance! My great restoration! What an optimist she was.

In a letter to William, Father is depicted as being *comforted by Alice's lovely and loving companionship, which he enjoys more than ever because it is not marred by his old anxiety about her.* This was written in 1873 or '74, when I was holding my own nervously, or was believed to be.

It is clear from these letters that our mother was the glue that held our family together; every page is perfumed with her love. Here she is writing to Harry while he was abroad in 1868.

> *What are you living on dear Harry? It seems to me you are living as the lilies and fed like the sparrows. But I know too that you toil and spin, and must conclude that you receive in some mysterious way the fruits of your labour.*

To William in Dresden in 1867: *Beware dear Willy of the fascinations of Fraulein Clara Schmidt or any other such. You know your extreme susceptibility, or rather I know it, so I say beware.* I skim through many loving letters to Wilky and Bob and their wives, reporting on the Boston weather and news and anxious for details about their babies.

Here is something. In December 1872, not long after my return from my Grand Tour of Europe, Mother writes to Harry (in Paris):

> *Alice has found after six weeks' experience at home that the delicious breakfast of chocolate & roll in the morning does not agree with her as it did abroad. There is doubtless a stimulus in it which she could bear there but cannot bear here. She has given it up and is all right again.*

Yes, for a brief period my "French breakfast" could summon an aftertaste of Paris. When it stopped "agreeing" with me, it meant that Europe had entirely faded away. I was not exactly "all right again."

Not long afterwards, when weekly letters began arriving from Harry in Paris, reporting luminous conversations with George Sand, Turgenev, Zola, and Flaubert, my writing hand began to revolt. Given a pencil, it would scribble hateful, spiteful things, things I wasn't aware of thinking. Although I did my utmost to conceal this part of myself, as if it were a claw-hand, my family sensed that I was not as well as might be wished. In a letter to Harry, Mother laments,

Poor child. Why is it that she has gone back so? Can there be anything
in this climate to account for it? She has been trying to write to you for
some time past, but always finds her strength too little for the good long
letter and I dissuade her from it. Do not dwell much on what I have
told you, in your letters, only recognize it as a reason for her not writing.

In 1878, the year of William's marriage, when Father was talking
me out of suicide daily, Mother was calmly telling my brothers that
Alice is not so strong as we might wish or that *Alice has had a little set-*
back. No mention of my being on the brink of insanity.

Oh dear, here is Nurse *again,* come to see if I have fainted and
require revival. She subscribes to the common prejudice that thinking
too much, especially about oneself, is an unhealthy activity. "It's all
right, Nurse," I tell her. "These letters are nectar and ambrosia to me."

"If you say so, Miss."

Having noticed the tear tracks on my cheeks, she loiters nearby,
looking for something to straighten so she can monitor my condition. This is *very* wearisome. "Please, Nurse, don't distress yourself. I
am fine, really." I am thinking, *Don't you have some praying to do?*
Intercessionary prayers for my benighted soul or something? Finally she
leaves, and I pick up another stack of Mother's letters, which turn out
to be commingled with many of Aunt Kate's. (They were as similar in
penmanship as they were in physiognomy.)

Here is Aunt Kate writing to Harry in 1873:

Your mother writes that you learned to love Paris before you left it and
I am so glad that you stayed long enough to do so. I wish so much that
Alice could have had a good long quiet draught of it.

How interesting. While Mother sought answers to my poor health
in the vagaries of climate, Aunt Kate understood perfectly where the
trouble lay. Perhaps I underestimated her.

As church bells in Leamington toll the hour, my mind is back in
Cambridge in the days of our youth. Sitting stiffly in the formal parlor at Quincy Street meeting Wilky's new bride. The letters bring it all

back: how appalled we were by Carrie, a shallow girl flaunting expensive jewelry, and hoped Wilky wouldn't notice our lack of enthusiasm. (He didn't.) After Carrie, Bob's Mary was a breath of fresh air. Mother appreciated her sound practical nature and I adopted her as my little pet and we went around with our arms entwined like a pair of devoted sisters. Having no intellectual side, however, Mary wore thin soon enough, and it was a relief to see her go—to see them both go, I should say, for a euphoric Bob was nearly as exhausting as Bob in a morose state.

I see myself sucking in my breath while Mother pulled on my stays as I don a new costume for Father's lecture on "The Woman Thou Gavest Me." Noting the perplexity on the Bostonian faces, it hits me how bewildering Father's philosophy is to others. Then I see Aunt Kate going off to Dr. Munro for manipulations and coming back smiling mysteriously. Time winds backwards and I am in Newport driving my pony phaeton along the Ocean Drive, looking out on a dark blue ocean frosted with whitecaps. Later I am swatting at flies while Wilky lies delirious in our parlor, the wounds in his ankle and his side refusing to heal. The smell was unforgettable.

After four days' absorption in the letters—it has been like a long trance, to be honest—I feel the chills of a grippe coming on. Perhaps it is the Russian influenza, which, according to the *Telegraph*, is sweeping through Britain, killing scores of people. Having longed for years for some more palpable disease, I begin to pin my hopes on this Slavic 'flu.

"For all we know," I tell Nurse, "the microbes might be cruising through my bloodstream even now." But why bother to discuss this with Nurse, who rejects the Germ Theory and insists that diseases are brought about by drafts and vapors? What a sweet caretaker she is, though. It calms and comforts me to watch her arrange my bedroom for the night, setting out the medicine bottles, filling the pitcher on the washstand, smoothing my covers, bringing me an extra blanket. The blanket feels heavy, almost suffocating, but when I cast it off, my teeth chatter as icy waves sweep through me.

I believe these are symptoms of the Russian influenza.

⁓ T W O ⁓

THE NEXT DAY, THE CHILLS ARE GONE, LEAVING ONLY A HEAVI-
ness in my head and a sense that something inside me is trying to claw
its way out, like a raccoon trapped in a gardening shed. My hopes for
the Russian 'flu are dwindling. Nurse folds me into my violet dressing gown and helps me to sit up, then brings me tea and a soft-boiled
egg on a tray. I can eat only half the egg, and she casts a disapproving
glance at my plate as she clears it.

"I don't seem to have much appetite, Nurse, but at least I have
recovered from the Russian microbes."

"I am glad to hear it, but if I may say so, Miss, I believe what's making you ill are those old family letters of yours."

"They bring back my childhood and youth, Nurse. My parents
come back to life in them, and Aunt Kate and my brother Wilky, almost
as if I had them in the room with me. It is such an exquisite sensation,
you've no idea." She looks dubious, but I am the boss. Rather impa-
tiently, she fetches the next bundle, and I fancy I hear the door shut a
bit emphatically on her way out.

In the beginning was the Word, and the Word was with Father. In
the next bunch of letters, he pops into view, delectably describing meetings of the Saturday Club in the 1860s. Mr. Hawthorne's *divine rusticity*,
Charles Norton's *spectral smiles*, the latest pedantry of Bronson Alcott,
father of the authoress Louisa May.

My heart broke for Hawthorne as that attenuated Charles Norton
kept putting forth his long antennae toward him, stroking his face, and

trying whether his eyes were shut; it was heavenly to see him persist in
ignoring Charles Norton, eating his dinner & doing absolutely nothing
but that.

What fun Father had rolling out his thundering superlatives! Of Mr. Emerson he writes, *He has no sympathy with nature but is a sort of police-spy upon it, chasing it into its hiding-places, and noting its subtlest features, for the purpose of reporting them to the public.* But there had been a time, not long before, when Mr. Emerson had been a god to him. Almost everyone Father put on a pedestal disappointed him in the end.

Speaking of gods, I have just come across a letter in which Father writes that William is the only one of his children with any intellectual gifts. I can't wait to inform William of this confirmation of his genius. Of me Father writes, *Poor dear child! Her brothers are her pride and joy!* True enough, I suppose.

In the next letter I come to, he writes to Mother:

I have often told you when I come thundering down into the dovecote
scattering your and the children's innocent projects of pleasure that I
have no doubt they will all get along much better without me than with
me: and I have made the same admission to the juveniles.

If I was aware of Father's telling us children that we'd be better off without him, I've forgotten it. I do remember him swooping down upon us at our games, covering us with kisses, tears coursing down his cheeks. I wondered why we made him cry. Father looked, at midlife, like a rosy little grocer and was celebrated for his eloquence, wit, and optimism. I never read his books or articles until I was fifteen. After hearing *The Secret of Swedenborg* mocked by my classmates in the school cloakroom, I tried to read a few paragraphs of it and found it too dense to follow, so I picked up *Substance and Shadow* instead and ran smack into this sentence: *The natural inheritance of everyone who is capable of spiritual life, is an unsubdued forest where the wolf howls and every obscene bird of night chatters.* That was when I knew. That unsubdued forest with its obscene bird of night was in the James blood; in mine, in Father's, in Bob's and William's too.

Suddenly an absurd picture pops into my mind: my father holding a rake, wielding a hammer. This is like a magic lantern show projecting an impossible world, for Father had no practical side and was never at any time observed with a tool in his hands. But his *presence*—how to convey that? I am young again, sitting near him, feeling the irresistible pull of his personality. I try to comprehend how Mother, feet planted firmly on the ground, should have fallen into the orbit of this man who spoke in the tongue of angels. For me my father's inner being was a mesmerizing pressure in which one was helplessly caught up, like a riptide. There seemed to be an overwhelming need in him, forever unsatisfied. At the same time it seemed as if he, not Mother, had given me life.

"It is time to take your bromide, Miss, if you are to sleep."

My body practically jumps off the bed at the sound of her voice. "Oh Nurse, I had quite forgotten your existence! I have been traveling back so far!"

"Let me fetch you another candle."

"Oh, don't bother, Nurse. I am just thinking now."

"I don't know how you think so much, Miss, and never run out of things to think about. Have you memorized any poems or great speeches? My father says that is a good thing to do, just in case."

"In case of what?"

"I suppose going to prison, or falling ill. I memorized a few bits of 'The Angel in the House.'"

I refrain from giving my opinion of her poetical tastes. "Somehow I don't see you in prison, Nurse."

Nurse worships her father and quotes him on numerous subjects. Daughters are fated to absorb their fathers' theologies, I suppose. While she packs up my letters, I close my eyes and fall softly through the space inside my head, dates and years running backwards until, just on the border between sleep and waking, I am back at the age when all stories are true.

We are living in Paris, in the grand *hotel particulier* full of gilt and ormolu, and an elderly lady calls on us one evening. For more than thirty years I haven't thought of her, but here she is now, risen from the dead, swathed in black taffeta, her upper arms jiggling like jelly as she cuts her meat at supper. I am riveted by that as well as by her old-fashioned lace cap, the small grey curls pasted like commas on her forehead, and the way the flesh clumps around her elbows in fat little dumplings. *Who is she?* I ask Aunt Kate.

"Why, Alice, she is the lady your papa met in England years ago, before you were born. He went to a spa, very broken down, and she told him about Sweden Borg. He said she saved his life." Indeed, at dinner, the lady and Father are chatting amiably about angels, the New Jerusalem, the Spirits of Mercury, and Dr. Garth Wilkinson, the man for whom Wilky was named, who is also from Sweden Borg. But if this old lady is from Sweden Borg, why does she speak English?

At bedtime, after Mademoiselle Guyot brushes and braids my hair for the night, I press my knees to the cold flagstones and say my little French prayers, and then Mademoiselle snuffs out my candle and is swallowed up by the dark. After a few minutes I remember my doll, Alphonse, left downstairs. I call to Mademoiselle but she is out of earshot. I don't want to go into the darkness, which turns the landing and hallway into the deep dark woods of fairy tales, where ogres and witches and wolves with their eyes shining gold lie in wait for lost children. I have learned from fairy tales to be wary of many things. Wicked kings, spindles that prick, jealous stepmothers, obtuse fathers, surly trolls, bad bargains.

But it is my custom to have Alphonse sleeping by my side, with his head on his own tiny pillow. I don't want to leave him to the mercy of Robbie, who has beheaded or dismembered several of my darlings, resulting in days of weeping and elaborate funerals. I do not understand why he is a kind father to our children when we play house one day and a rampaging madman toward them the next, but there are so many things about boys I don't understand. I get out of bed, shivering, and creep down the wide staircase on tiptoe, the stone floors ice-cold under my bare feet. (I could not find my carpet slippers.)

A small oil lamp burns smokily on a massive low-boy in the hall, its feeble light reflected in a mirror. Above it is a large panoramic painting that frightens me, so I look away. I find Alphonse face-down on the floor next to a majolica urn. As I pick him up and cradle him in my arms, I hear voices. The door to the parlor is ajar. I creep closer and hear the Sweden Borg lady say that the children have lovely manners, and I smile because I like to hear myself praised. I wait to hear more and there comes a prickly feeling in my nose, like the beginning of a sneeze. As I am pinching my nostrils, I hear Father say, "At one time, I said to God in my inmost heart, *Take these dear children away before they know the soil of sin.* I could not bear the thought of these babes forfeiting their innocence and becoming odious to my human heart."

My eyes tear up in the struggle not to sneeze. What is *odious*? What is *forfeiting*? I wait in trepidation, my heart racing like a trapped hummingbird. Since Mademoiselle informed me that you die if your heart stops beating, I have been compulsively checking mine dozens of times a day. It is beating right now, but it could stop at any moment. Dread paralyzes me.

"What dreadful mystery of sin haunted me night and day," Father is saying. "During that time I was on my knees from morning till night. I prayed and God gave me no relief. I fell ill, and would have stayed ill if not for Sweden Borg."

The urge to sneeze has passed, but I must not be seen. I don't want Father to pray for me to return to God. I want a chance to live; I am only seven years old! I fasten my eyes on a worn hanging tapestry depicting a horde of fauns (or something) carrying off a troupe of near-naked women. Where are the fauns taking them, and what will they do to them? And what are fauns anyway, with their horrid faces? (I will ask William, who is the one who told me they were fauns.)

Clutching Alphonse to my chest, I mount the staircase, dwarfed by the high ceilings and vast stony spaces. The ordinary world vanishes. The Giant is nearby; I hear his teeth crunching on someone's bones. There is no escape; everything here belongs to him. A cold dread burrows into my stomach, becoming a sick ache, a nausea. In the Giant's House I am small and powerless, like an ant you step on without even noticing. My heart could stop like a watch at any time; the sight of the Giant would probably do it. I picture myself falling backwards, my hands clutching at my chest, bouncing end over end all the way down the marble stairs. Groping the walls with my hands, I finally reach the top of the stairs and then fumble along the dark, cavernous hall to my bedroom. I tuck Alphonse under the covers, and kneel beside the bed, press my hands together and pray that this cold stone floor that stings my knees will touch God's heart. I pray fervently to *le bon dieu,* in the words Mademoiselle taught me, to cancel out Father's "inmost" prayers about me.

The next morning I wake to songbirds singing sweetly in the watery early-morning light. I hear Aurore's hearty *Bonjour* when she comes to collect the chamber pot and leave off a basin of hot water for washing. And then Mademoiselle comes in and plaits my hair and says I may wear the dotted Swiss muslin today.

"And how were your dreams, dear—pleasant, I hope?"

Because I suffer from frequent nightmares, I am often asked about my dreams. It is believed that when they are bad it is because of something I ate. Last night's dream comes back to me through layers of mist—the old Sweden Borg lady with her dumpling arms, Alphonse missing, half-naked ladies carried off by fauns, Father asking God to take his children back.

"I had a little nightmare but I have forgotten it now."

A month later, Mademoiselle, whom I adore over all other mortals at this time, will mysteriously leave our employ. Father has cast out another governess.

HENRY JAMES SR.
KAY ST., NEWPORT
JUNE 30TH 1861

TO (NAME BLURRED)
Kitty evidently fancies her fiancé, Dr. William Prince, to be the greatest hero that ever lived. She seems to keep up her ardent sympathy for his conjugal bereavement in the old days and is proud to be the ministering handmaid to such stupendous sorrow. I don't think I could conceive of such conscience if I hadn't seen it.

KITTY JAMES
NEWPORT
JULY 2ND 1861

TO JULIUS SEELYE (HER BROTHER-IN-LAW)
I think I never saw such a family. The boys are delightfully companionable, full of intelligence, free from anything that is disagreeable in boys of their age, each one having a strongly marked individuality. I enjoy conversing with Uncle Henry and Aunt Mary too & Alice is a sweet little girl. It is all too nice, most likely a trick of the devil. I will steel myself against the temptation to remain here forever in the bosom of this vivid, amusing family. I have promised myself to Dr. Prince and how could I dream of letting the poor man down?

⟲ THREE ⟳

DOES EVERYONE HAVE A FANTASY OF HOLDING ON TO SOME-thing and keeping it forever? In the end, even letters can't preserve the past; somehow time reaches backwards and alters them when we're not looking. Among Father's letters, I have just stumbled on one in which he chuckles over the peculiarities of our much-older cousin Kitty James. At the time he masked his feelings well, well enough to fool twelve-year-old me, anyway. I thought that Father thought the world of Cousin Kitty.

It was the very beginning of the Civil War, when no one dreamed it would drag on for four bloody years and kill so many. The world was innocent still, and we were living in Newport. From our house on Kay Street, with its Gothic roofs and small tower, I see William strid-ing (with his characteristic long, fast strides) across Bellevue and down Church Street to paint in the atelier of William Morris Hunt. This was also my route to the school I attended for a brief time before Father decided it was unsuitable for some reason.

From my desert isle in Leamington, I take a memory walk down the streets of Newport, lingering over every tree, house, hedge, black-berry bush, widow's walk, balcony, piazza, scraplet of lawn or patch of moss I conjure up. The pets of the neighborhood come vividly to life, sharpening their claws on tree bark or barking at squirrels. I see Elly Temple arching an ironic eyebrow about Aunt Tweedy, whose pink flesh bulges out of her bathing costume, and I hear Minny saying *sotto voce*, "It is very difficult not to think of a pink whale."

Oh! I had nearly forgotten the radiance of early life before habit dulls us and makes everything stale. In this happy state, I fall asleep and wake up an hour later. Nurse brings me tea and a roll and goes out to do the marketing. I am being pulled by a powerful tide back to the summer Kitty James came to visit. 1861. Before the hospital tent with the wounded soldiers, before Wilky and Bob marched off to war, before our family unit was split up, before so many things. The *ancien régime.*

Kitty is in her late twenties and about to be married, and we are in awe of her, at least at first. She is like a fine porcelain figurine and next to her I feel like a crude clay pot. For many years Father and her father, our Uncle William, were not on speaking terms, following a quarrel over religion or a will or both. But fences have been mended now, and the mysterious Kitty being in our midst is proof of that.

Father makes a big show of doting on our cousin, who is pretty, ladylike, intense, and devoutly religious, sharing his scorn for "the world." I am used to being Father's "darling girl" and don't appreciate having my place usurped by a cousin I've never seen before. Kitty's fiancé, Dr. William Prince, is an alienist, in charge of the big lunatic asylum in Northampton, a fact that heightens her allure in Will's eyes. That is another thorn in my flesh. He and Kitty keep disappearing down Bellevue, engrossed in conversation. I don't know where they go, and they don't invite me. Kitty is queenly and aloof, though she pretends to be oh-so-humble. I don't know why Will is so fascinated by lunacy.

"What did Cousin Kitty do to win the heart of her Prince?" I say to the others when she is out of earshot. Ha ha, the fiancé's name is Dr. Prince, get it? But my joke falls flat. When you're the youngest of five, your jokes frequently do.

Now it is Sunday dinner and from the head of the table Father is speaking mysteriously of trees. "Two trees grow in the garden of every man's intelligence, children. One is named the Tree of Life, the other the Tree of Knowledge of Good and Evil." Kitty, on his right, regards him with rapt attention, nodding her head from time to time.

Which trees does Father mean? The tall cypresses that are like stately women, or the fruit trees, good for climbing, bearing pears or cherries or apples? I wonder how a tree can give knowledge of good and evil. "Both trees," he continues, "are indispensable to Man's conscious development, but it is good to eat only of one of them, the tree of life. If we eat of the other or seek to live by it, we inevitably encounter death."

I am mystified. Does this mean not to eat the apples that fall to the ground in the orchards? I certainly don't *want* to eat them, but is that how we encounter death, by eating rotten fruit? William is laughing as usual. He waves his fork in the air and says, "Father, that is just the sort of unintelligible metaphor that doesn't go down well with the reading public."

Oh, a metaphor! I know what that is. Why didn't Father say so?

Kitty smiles like an angel. Her fork trembles. A subtle vibration, rapid as a hummingbird's wings, seems to move through her much of the time. I have never met anyone like her and have to keep reminding myself not to stare.

Father asks her if Dr. Prince is an easy man to get on with, and she says, "Oh, yes, he is." After cataloguing his virtues, she says, "His lips are the thinnest you ever saw, more like a thread than a lip, but I have never seen him excited to resentment now for the nine years and a half that I have known him." I am confused. Nine and a half years? Have they been engaged all this time? And her obsession with her fiancé's lips seems peculiar. But I am only twelve going on thirteen; what do I know?

One overcast afternoon I find myself trapped on the piazza with Kitty and a pitcher of lemonade. Years later, recalling this, I see the condensation on the glasses, hear the carts rattling past, smell the manure from the stable down the road. I am holding a green apple in my left hand and poking a wormhole in it with my finger, feeling the juice collect under my fingernail. Kitty is as usual clothed in white, ready for ascension. In her presence I have the impression of hearing hundreds of tiny needles clicking, like a mechanical loom in the textile factories of Lowell.

Registering my existence, Kitty informs me she *adores* the sea air and the sound of the surf in her ears, and our family is utterly charming; she wishes this happiness could last forever.

"I lie awake these long nights, perfectly quiet, thinking unutterable thoughts!"

"Oh?" I say. "Good ones, I hope?"

"Heavenly, dear!"

We sip our lemonade in silence for a few minutes. I rack my brain for something to say. Then it occurs to me that Kitty probably doesn't care what I think anyhow.

"Do you ever feel, Cousin Alice, that if someone opposes you, you might shatter like glass?"

Although I *do* feel that way at times, I am not about to admit this to Kitty. I shrug and try to avoid meeting her too-intense eyes.

As if guessing my thoughts, she says, "You know the story about the princess who was sent to a water cure because her eyes were too bright—she looked at things and saw too far? That is all my disease is."

Does Cousin Kitty have a disease? I suppose it would be rude to ask what it is.

"I am writing a book for young people," she continues, as if I had asked her to tell me more about herself, "based on my experiences. I plan to have it published, but the girl in it is called Mabel, not Kitty. Even if you are dead it seems dreadful to have everyone know what kind of person you were."

The things that come out of her mouth! Just as I am wondering how to escape without giving offense, she offers to show me the contents of the heart-shaped cloisonné locket she wears around her pretty neck. "All right," I say. She opens it. I lean in close, and make out a lock of reddish-brown hair.

"So Dr. Prince has auburn hair?" I am trying to be polite, although being close to Kitty is making my skin itch. Or maybe it's my mosquito bites.

"Oh dear no, Alice! Dr. Prince's hair has gone completely white from his severe trials!" (As if I should have known this!) "This lock belonged to his late wife." She stares dreamily at the horizon and her beautiful china-blue eyes mist over. "God saw best to take her to Heaven. He saw best to send me to help Dr. Prince get well, and to care for his motherless children, poor little lambs. And so I shall do."

"I see," I say, though I don't at all. Dr. Prince must be an elderly man.

"Dr. Prince's dead wife knows that I have delivered him and Johnnie and Louise and myself from a terrible spell. She loves me very much."

"Who are Johnnie and Louise?"

"Dr. Prince's children. You see, I never wished to be married if I must have children. I dreaded the suffering and the squalling of the first year, but as the doctor already has two, he will not require me to bear him more."

Can a person *choose* whether to have children? Doesn't God just send them as He sees fit? With this thought comes an intimation— a foreboding almost—of a great many other unknowns of which I'd been unaware. The end of childhood is at hand; I feel it in my bones. There is nothing to be done.

"I must stay *always* to be his eldest daughter," Kitty babbles on. "He has a stronger claim on me than my dear father, for he never scolds or misunderstands me. He can never love me as he did his wife, but I never concern myself, Alice. It is certainly as much as I deserve or want." Then she relates more anecdotes illustrative of the doctor's benevolence and his trials and a pile of boring details about the children, while I scan the horizon in desperation, hoping someone will come along and relieve me of Kitty. With her thoughts fixed on the late Mrs. Prince, she tells me in a confiding tone that she is willing to submit to the "martyrdom of the marriage bed." Her eyes, up close, could burn a hole through you.

"You know," she whispers, "it is so beautiful here, and your family is so good and charming, but it cannot last."

"It can't?"

"No, Alice. I am a little like an animal and feel things before they come. I am quietly watching and preparing for the next thundercloud. You had better prepare, too, little cousin."

"Why should *I* prepare?" I am sick of Kitty and her airy-fairy ways and ready for her to go back to Northampton and never return.

"Our Lord is merciful but no thought is secret from Him, Alice."

I quickly review my secret thoughts: (1) I have wished on occasion that Bob would catch a fever and die so I will not be teased so much. (2) When I picture kissing someone, it is usually a girl. (3) I fantasize sometimes about being blown off a cliff in my hoop-skirt (a danger *Godey's* is always warning readers about) and in my imagination it feels lovely, like flying. (4) I am alarmed and frightened by my father's stump. (5) I wish our Temple cousins would stay away from Newport this summer so I can have my brothers to myself. (But there is as much chance of this happening as of Father tiring of Divine Nature.)

I steer clear of Kitty for the rest of the visit, which is not difficult, as she is chiefly interested in William. To my relief, she finally returns to her greybeard and marries him a few months later. After she leaves, while we are doing some sewing on the piazza, Mother casually mentions that Kitty had been a patient in the Northampton Asylum, "suffering from a religious mania, so they say," and met Dr. Prince while in that broken-down state.

"Oh! That would explain how queer she is, Mother! She told me she holds Bible study classes for the inmates. Wouldn't you think they'd resent being preached at by a fellow lunatic?"

"Oh, but she is completely cured, Alice. I believe she looks only to the future now."

No, she is a thorough lunatic; why does no one else see this? But I say nothing and refrain from asking Mother what Kitty might have meant by "the martyrdom of the marriage bed." Some things are best left unknown.

Just *before* Kitty's visit, a shattering thing had happened. Without warning, all my imaginary friends disappeared—the invisible friends who for years kept me company, listened to everything I said, laughed at my jokes, told me their secrets and their stories. I can't explain this. Did I leave them or did they desert me? Anyway, they were gone now, there was no getting them back, and I found myself starkly *alone* for the first time. It was like being orphaned, cast out of a warm, loving world into one that was heartless and alien.

For a long time I blamed Kitty for what happened next, but she was only an omen, like a raven or an owl appearing at your window. In the end there wasn't much to her; it was as if she'd tried to cobble together a personality out of a handful of traits and didn't quite bring it off. Yet her presence seemed to shift things in our family and nothing went right afterward. When I try to peer into that darkness, I lose my way. The Temples are in on it somehow, and the War is coming closer, and soon William will stop painting and go to Harvard to study science. That August I will turn thirteen and a veil will drop over me. By September, all pleasure will be drained from my world: the sailing, the sea-baths, the collections of shells and sea-glass, the romps on the beach—all of it will suddenly leave me cold.

Our Temple cousins do not help matters. By early July, the six of them are, as usual, installed in the house next door with their elderly guardians, Aunt and Uncle Tweedy, and our two households merge into one large, boisterous extended family. Will's attention is captured entirely by the Temple girls, which is irksome. Harry, too, is in thrall to them, as are Wilky and Bob. As soon as the Temples appear I turn into a grey moth in a flock of butterflies.

In a pine grove not far from our house, I come upon William one day kissing Kitty Temple, the eldest of the girls. Her back is pressed against the trunk of a tree, and there is not a millimeter of space between them. Her arms are wrapped around Will's neck, her eyes closed dreamily. I can't see William's face, but for an instant I *feel* what they feel, the tug of intense physical longing. It is a revelation. The air around them quivers with their desire; the trees and tall grasses seem to bend to it. Their kiss rouses feelings and sensations in me I can't name; all I know is that I can't bear to watch them kiss anymore. I call out to them, and they startle and pull apart.

William says it is just for practice, and please don't tell Mother. My eye falls on a column of ants near my foot; I place the toe of my boot in their path and watch the ants swerve around it. You can't help but admire them, marching along in a soldierly column, carrying their immense burdens. I make no answer to William except to scowl. I am not a tattletale; he should know that by now.

William has been working on a portrait of Kitty Temple for weeks. They go off together to Mr. Hunt's studio every day, sometimes with their painter friend John La Farge, and return hours later. I wonder if there *is* a portrait or if they are just going there to kiss some more, with their bodies pressed against each other. At the end of August the painting is unveiled and I feel its power. Your eyes are drawn to Kitty's white neck, her cloud of dark hair, her beautiful hands engaged in some needlework. Despite my fragmentary knowledge of art, I see that William has captured an immortal quality in Kitty; if I'd known the words then, I would have said it was the Eternal Feminine. Was that mysterious quality inside Kitty all along, or did being painted by William make her more beautiful? (William has sketched me numerous times, in caricature style, along with the rest of our family, but I doubt he will ever find me worth an oil painting.)

Was this when I first knew I was set apart from others and could expect nothing from the world? Did it happen all at once, or little by little? Maybe I should have William's Dr. Janet—was that the man's name?—mesmerize me to remember what has slipped through the cracks.

I have a sense of something else that happened that summer which remains just out of reach. I write in my journal,

> I had to peg away pretty hard between twelve and twenty-four, "killing myself"—absorbing into the bone that the better part is to clothe oneself in neutral tints, walk beside still waters, and possess oneself in silence.

But what do I mean by this?

WILLIAM JAMES
95 IRVING STREET, CAMBRIDGE
JUNE 22ND 1890

TO HENRY HOLT (HIS EDITOR)
No one could be more disgusted than I at the sight of the book. No subject is worth being treated in 1,000 pages—it is a loathsome, distended, tumefied, bloated, dropsical mass testifying to but two things: that there is no such thing as a science of psychology, and 2nd that WJ is incapable.

WILLIAM JAMES
95 IRVING ST., CAMBRIDGE
JUNE 19TH 1890

TO MRS. WILLIAM JAMES
TAMWORTH IRON WORKS, NEW HAMPSHIRE
Darling—I just mailed The Principles of Psychology in 5 large boxes. If it burns up at the post office, I don't care for I shan't rewrite it. I miss you dreadfully, but you know that already. I hope you are all well and that black flies aren't feeding on the flesh of our children. We are having a Biblical plague of them here just now, but that is not the worst of my troubles. On the horse-cars on the way home from the PO, a hideous thought burst into my mind. The proofs! I cannot bear to contemplate them. Therefore I intend to leave within the week, before they arrive, and join you in NH. That way, they can't disturb my peace till the end of summer.

    How is the new fraulein working out? I hope she will be tough enough to withstand Billy.

WILLIAM JAMES
95 IRVING STREET, CAMBRIDGE, MASS.
JUNE 26, 1890

TO MRS. WILLIAM JAMES
Darling: You were right. I did not manage to leave. That you know me so well is either reassuring or terrifying, I am not sure which.

You must promise not to laugh or rail against me when I tell you why. Just before I was to leave, I woke up before dawn in a white panic, convinced that the reason Henry Holt hadn't acknowledged receipt of the book was because he loathed it and had not the heart to tell me. For several days I pictured in vivid detail my sorrowful fate as an unpublished professor, pitied and scorned at the Faculty Club, &c. I wrote to Holt that since I hadn't heard from him, I felt no further responsibility whatever about having the thing published.

And the very next day the proofs started arriving, 20 by each of the 4 daily mail deliveries. Thus I am caught & unable to join the rest of you, alas. It is a terrible business, these proofs. I miss you to the point of despair. I see you so clearly in my mind, sitting at your dressing table in your peach-colored gown, the smell of your cold cream, your hair falling down. I weep at the thought of my children's dear faces.

WILLIAM JAMES
95 IRVING ST., CAMBRIDGE.
JULY 6TH 1890

TO HENRY JAMES
Today I went to Somerville to visit poor Kitty Prince and found her thrashing like a demon, pinned down by three nursing matrons and one doctor. She is so shriveled I thought her legs would snap like matchsticks

and watched in horror as the nursing matron pinched her nostrils shut. This forced poor K to open her mouth, into which the red-faced doctor inserted a horrible metal bit and turned a screw that pried her mouth open. All this time she was shaking and quivering from head to toe. When they forced a long brown tube down her throat, the choking sounds were horrific, and, while I gaped in disbelief, the matron inserted a funnel into the end of the tube and poured a pitcher of yellow fluid down Kitty's throat. Raw eggs. Her eyes roved wildly, like a spooked horse.

I asked the doctor why they were torturing her. He said, "She is determined to starve herself to death and we must prevent that. We have orders from the superintendent to force-feed her three times a day." Well, I know the superintendent (Edward Cowles) as a colleague and (I thought) an enlightened scientific man, and I intend to give him a piece of my mind. Why not just let her die if her case is hopeless? (He told me last month that her chances of recovery now are nil.)

TO THE EDITOR OF THE NATION
JULY 4, 1891

Sir: For several years past I have lived in provincial England. Although so far from home, every now and then a transatlantic blast, pure and undefiled, fans to a white heat the fervor of my patriotism.

This morning, most appropriately to the day, a lady from one of our Eastern cities applied to my landlady for apartments. In the process of telling her that she had no rooms for let, the landlady said that there was an invalid in the house, whereupon the lady exclaimed, "In that case perhaps it is just as well that you cannot take us in, for my little girl, who is thirteen, likes to have plenty of liberty and to scream through the house."

Yours very truly,
Invalid

⌒ FOUR ⌒

So I AM PUBLISHED! HOW MUCH MORE DISTINGUISHED ONE'S words look in print; I confess it gives me a little warm glow. I went through almost as many author-processes in composing it as Harry does with one of his novels. He writes that everyone in London has guessed my identity and that I am the talk of the town.

It is a month of miracles. Two weeks later, Katherine arrived *chez moi* after three years' absence! Listed in the shipping news as "Mrs. Peabody," a passenger on the *Cephalonia*, she fortunately succeeded in transforming herself into Miss Katherine Peabody Loring on the train from Liverpool and is with me now.

What bliss it is to huddle in my daybed by the window and dictate my diary entries to K., who, with her self-devised code, takes dictation as quickly as I can talk. She is a wonderful audience; her infectious laughs, wry commentary, and pointed questions spur me on. One thing you should know about Katherine: she is in thrall to words. She once referred to my having "seduced" her with "my language," and occasionally says things like, "I'm not sure how you would put it in your language."

"What do you mean, *my language*? It isn't as if I had my own dialect."

"In my family we think the Jameses talk like Irish bards. I've never heard *anyone* talk like William. At dinner parties most of the table goes silent so they can listen in."

"It was always thus, Katherine. Father had his bardic moments, and William and Henry, even poor Bob. I, on the other hand, express myself entirely normally."

"Not really, dear."

"Give me an example, then."

"All right. When we were discussing your finances yesterday you said, 'My income is a most interesting quantity, with the greatest capacity for diminishing itself and yet still existing.' I made a note of it in my diary."

"I was only stating the facts."

"Most people would have phrased it differently. Anyway, that's only one example."

"Do I figure prominently in your diary, Katherine?" I ask in a teasing tone.

"What do you think?" She flushes a little. In some respects, my beloved is shy, which I find endearing. "I believe I *have* been influenced by your diary a little, Alice. Lately, I've been trying to overcome the Boston tendency to record bare facts. A typical entry in a Loring diary goes like this: *Mild overcast day, temp. 64. 1:30, Dined at Tavern Club with J. Winthrop. Stopped by Doll's afterwards.* You should see my brothers' diaries. Nothing more personal in them than the air temperature."

"Bostonians are unfathomably fascinated with temperature, barometric pressure, and wind speed. Is that because you are a race of sailors?"

Katherine's brothers are men of the law as well as sailors. One is a judge. While judges are necessary, I believe that sitting on the bench may encourage an exalted view of oneself. But as Katherine adores her brothers, I keep this to myself.

"Speaking of brothers," she says, "did I tell you I bumped into William near the post office just before I left? I asked him how he was, and he said, 'Splendid! I have just posted my Index and I can relate to the universe receptively again.' I asked if he meant his Psychology textbook and he said, 'Yes. Nasty little subject! Nothing in it! Everything one wants to know lies *outside*!'"

"That sounds like William. I was afraid he'd go on dragging that manuscript around for the rest of his life. It has been in existence longer than young Harry, who is in long trousers now."

"I did wonder how he manages to teach a subject he despises."

"Oh, he only despises it *sometimes*."

I dictate another paragraph for my diary. Noticing my references to *Inconnu*, Katherine says, "Do you mind my asking, Alice: who is this *Inconnu*?"

"Well, after I 'pass over,' as William's spiritist friends say, *Inconnu* will be the unknown reader who will turn these pages, amazed at the immortal wisdom this finicky old maid harbored under her unprepossessing exterior."

I suppose, in the end, *Inconnu* is an idealized distillation of my surviving family. He/she feels strangely real, linked to me by that peculiar bond of sympathy between author and reader (which I have felt intensely with any author I have loved) and that I feel even now, filling me with quiet radiance.

"Unprepossessing indeed," Katherine chuckles. "Do you want to have your diary published, darling?"

"Oh, I wouldn't dare, Kath. Imagine Father's apoplexy if his only daughter sullied the family name by publishing her hysterical fancies!"

"Your father has departed. Even Aunt Kate is no more. You have as much right as Henry to publish whatever you wish, it seems to me."

"Oh, but you don't *honestly* think . . . this is publishable?"

"I do."

Katherine is monstrously well read. I had not dared to hope that my little diary might possess literary value. I shall have to give this some thought. "I suppose my principal readers will be William and Henry. Maybe Bob if he is in his right mind—or even if he isn't. Later, the odd niece or nephew on a dull, rainy afternoon. William's little Peggy maybe." I don't tell her of my fantasy of a grown-up Peggy reading my diary and thinking, "So this is how Aunt Alice felt. This is how she saw the world! I wish I had known her." It is silly of me; I have never met the child and she is only three years old.

"I saw Peggy with her mother on the cars just before I left. She is a real beauty. And never draws breath, from what I could see."

"I wish I could meet her." I see by K's expression that she regrets having reminded me of the thousands of miles of blustery Atlantic standing between me and home.

"It's quite likely, Kath, that *Inconnu* will think, *Oh, that Aunt Alice! Crazy as a loon!* I'll probably ask you to toss the pages into the fire after I go. Meanwhile, don't breathe a word to anyone, especially Henry. I've told you how he likes to use family letters as kindling."

Sometimes it feels as if someone else inside me is writing, surprising me with thoughts I did not know I had. As if a Book of Alice existed somewhere in a ghostly state, and I have only to discover it and translate it into form.

What wonders abound in Katherine's presence! The crack in the window frame has been sealed against the winter chill, the chimney has been swept, the carpets and portière curtains taken down and flogged, the bow-front clock repaired. The globes of the lamp that hangs from the ceiling have been scrubbed, the mantel of the lamp on the wall has been repaired. The sudden lessening of gloom is like a heavenly vision.

She has been bringing me up to date on her battles on behalf of the Harvard Annex, the women's branch of Harvard. The overseers and many of the faculty have apparently taken a vow to repel, vex, and defeat the female sex at every turn—including, most recently, revoking their library privileges. The dilemma is this: The library is located in Harvard Yard, where women are not permitted to set foot lest they distract the Harvard men from their studies. Yet it is the only Harvard library. So far, the women are banned from it, but there is a proposal afoot to permit female persons to use the library on Sunday afternoons between two and four o'clock.

"I don't see why the sight of a woman should be fatal to scholarship," I say. "I have a good mind to pop off a rantlet to President Eliot myself."

"You may just as well address a brick wall," Katherine says, and stomps off to make a pot of tea. When she comes back with the tea things on a tray, her equanimity seems restored. "I sometimes think it will be a hundred years before women gain basic rights. We probably won't live to see it, Alice. I just have to remind myself that I am only a small link in a very long chain."

One of K's splendid qualities is the way she takes my "going off" in stride and never disapproves, as others are apt to do. Let me try to explain what it is like. First, there is a wooziness, a sinking feeling in your head, followed by a startling *whoosh* as you are drawn downward as if into a funnel. (You may picture the funnel in the pans used for making angel food cake.) Then you go under, and you're gone. All this takes place in a few seconds. It used to frighten me, but when you faint every day, you soon get used to it and it becomes a sort of hobby.

K. claims that just before I go under there is an utter blankness in my eyes. "You just look *gone*. Do you feel as if you've been gone?"

"Yes. Sometimes when I open my eyes, I don't know where or even who I am. The whole story of Alice James has been wiped clean. Do you think death appears to us that way?"

"I suppose we'll find out someday. *If* there is anyone left to find out."

Katherine is agnostic verging on atheist. She calls herself a Unitarian, which can mean anything. Eternity neither awes nor interests her particularly, which is one difference between us. Gathering up her work-reticule and a cushion for her back, she settles down near the window to knit. The sky behind her is cloudless and appears chilly.

"Katherine, does it ever worry you that there might not be enough *room* in heaven for all the people who have lived on earth since the beginning?"

"The good sheep, you mean. The black sheep go elsewhere, so they say." (In reality, neither of us subscribes to the superstition of hell.)

"Imagine the bureaucratic fuss that would be required for accounting for yourself at the Pearly Gates. It'd be like the East India Company. Documents in triplicate and so on. Surely they wouldn't just take your *word* for it! Especially a woman's word. They'd demand documentation, don't you think?"

"It's obvious, darling. The angels must be employed as clerks, scriveners, and bureaucrats."

"I've always said you were a genius, Katherine, and this clinches it."

"You're very perky today. What were you laughing about earlier?"

"Oh, it's this Prussian noblewoman whose memoir I'm reading. Knew every science and language under the sun—like Lizzy Boott, only more so; used to correspond with Descartes, was very handsome. But she had a *bête noire*. Her nose would get red, and she'd shut herself up and see no one. Who among us does not have a red nose at the core of her being which defies all her philosophy?"

I am watching Katherine assemble the components of a lamp, admiring her hands, so familiar to me and so beautiful. Hands that can split wood, soothe runaway horses, do delicate needlepoint, or stroke my fevered brow. (I am rather partial to hands and believe they reveal character.) When she has the lamp up and running, I ask her if she would mind terribly reading to me from the newspapers. "I'd love to close my eyes and take in the world through your lovely voice."

She picks up the *Standard* and scans the front page. "Well, the *Standard* this evening devotes the first paragraph of news to the thrilling fact that the infant daughter of the Duke of Portland was christened in Windsor Castle."

"You don't say!"

"Yes, and only at the foot of the column is there a small mention of the 'impressive gathering' in Hyde Park of the working-men on the eight hours question. The Rothschilds drew their blinds, they say."

"Oh, Katherine, isn't it delicious that these starvelings should make millionaires tremble?"

Then she turns the page and is silent a moment.

"Here is something rather grim. Are you in the mood?" When I nod, she proceeds to read aloud an article about a Hampstead man on trial for subjecting his wretched wife to systematic cruelty. *He had continually threatened to kill her,* K. reads, *either by jumping on her, dashing out her brains, or by inserting a pin or needle behind her ear to penetrate her brain.*

"But can the brain be penetrated so easily?"

"I don't know, but there is more." She reads more of the man's dastardly acts, and suddenly bursts out laughing and can't stop. I am quickly doubled over as well.

"Why are we laughing?" I say. "It is terrible of us."

"We must stop now. We really must." She struggles to regain a serious mien and then, a minute later, glances at me and explodes in laughter again. "Oh dear! What if Emily comes home and finds us cackling like a couple of harpies?"

"Oh, she will be gone for some time. Her Sabbath-day dissipations last from eight-thirty in the morning till five in the afternoon. She visits her family somewhere in the middle of the day, I think."

The article K is reading concludes with the monstrous husband being found guilty and fined ten shillings.

"This must go into my journal, Kath. It so perfectly illustrates man's inhumanity to woman. Does it say whether they are still living together after that?"

"It gives the impression they are. I suppose the poor woman has nowhere to go, and there are probably children."

Thinking of this, our hilarity subsides instantly.

A quarter hour later, Katherine asks me, "Would you like another cup of tea, Alice? Shall I help you get dressed, or is this one of your Marie Antoinette days?" (Referring to that queen's habit of receiving callers in her boudoir.)

"No. I think I *shan't* get dressed today, Katherine. I would much prefer to help *you* get undressed." I smile up at her and tug at her arm so she sits down abruptly next to me. "Nurse will be at her Guild all day, so while the cat's away . . . "

She flashes me a particular intimate smile I love. I begin by unbuttoning her blouse as she fumbles with the buttons of her skirt. So many layers to a woman! Normally, unbuttoning is a trial, but at these times it is a delicious game. I loosen her stays and kiss away the red marks pinched into her shoulders, and when her breasts tumble out I turn my attention to them. Then, she is kissing the inside of my wrist and slowly works her way up my arm and into the hollows of my throat, my eyes mist up with joy. And a great wind comes up and blows away the world and we return to our true selves.

Afterwards, I say, "According to the Bible, Yahweh has strong objections to man lying with man, while about woman lying with woman he is strangely silent. Why do you think that is?"

"Well, as a male God, he fails to see the possibilities. So much for omniscience." She stretches her limbs, graceful as a cat, and smiles tenderly at me.

"I remember William holding forth once on 'inversion,' saying that women, unlike men, could not really be inverts because there was nothing they *could* do."

Katherine bursts into peals of laughter. "Always the expert, your brother." After a long pause, she says. "I can't help noticing, darling. There is a something different about you. Different from *before*, I mean. I can't quite put my finger on it."

"Three years older and that much more shriveled."

She clucks her tongue. "No. What *is* it?" Her eyes travel over me appraisingly.

"I'm sure *I* don't know."

"I see what it is. There is a serenity about you now—underneath your going-off and your headache and leg pains and all of that. Does it have something to do with your diary?"

I smile. How lovely that she can see what others cannot. It is true. There *has* come a great change in me. A congenital faith flows through me now, making all the arid places green—and, well, I can't describe it beyond that.

"It may be because I have given up hope."

"Do you mean, hope that you will get well?"

"Yes. Everyone thinks hope is a good thing, but it is really a sort of disease of the mind. Anyhow, I have *renounced* it and feel so much better. I don't even hope for an answer to the perennial riddle, what is wrong with me? I probably won't ever know, but then there are so many things we don't know, aren't there?"

I watch her take this in. Katherine never, ever tries to talk me out of my feelings. Nor does she urge me to have "positive thoughts," as the Mind Cure ladies do.

"Oh, Katherine, isn't it terrible about poor Winnie Howells? Speaking of undiagnosed illnesses."

"Heartbreaking."

"Sent away to that dreadful Dr. Weir Mitchell's Rest Cure, far from her family. Hounded to eat, eat, eat, and all that time she herself was being eaten by a cancer. The autopsy proved it. I can't get over the injustice. I just received a letter from poor Mr. Howells in response to my condolence letter to him. I think it was the saddest letter ever written."

Our dear girl is gone and we begin to realize it, to yield. But we are helpless. I conjure her back in gleams and glimpses of her old childish self. And he went on to write wistfully of the dear old days when Father and Mother were alive and my brothers and I were young and Winnie was a tiny girl in a scarlet cape. Reading it, I dissolved in a flood of tears.

But now suddenly I am surprised by a memory that makes me laugh out loud.

"What?"

"I was just remembering—you know how short in stature Mr. Howells is?"

"Ye-es."

"Well, one day he and Mrs. Howells were at our house, and he was speaking of a man whom he described as 'about my size.' You must picture Mr. Howells doubled up in a deep armchair, looking smaller if possible than ever. And my mother said, 'Ah, then he must be a very small man?'"

"That does sound like your mother."

"Yes, and poor Mr. Howells was for the next five minutes quite invisible. In fact, Mother was for some time the only person in existence!"

Katherine gives vent to one of her deep laughs, and for a moment I forget that I am a hopeless invalid, that Winnie Howells is dead, and so are my parents and Wilky, and I will never see my native land again.

A week later K. goes off to Cambridge on another fact-finding mission on the higher education of the female. When she returns, she tells me she met an American girl studying there who told her that there is no need to make rules regulating the walking together of male and female students. Almost all the female students are presumed to be future governesses or teachers, and any male student would rather throw himself into the Cam than be guilty of the bad form of walking with any one of them.

WILLIAM JAMES
95 IRVING ST., CAMBRIDGE
SEPTEMBER 18TH 1890

TO HENRY JAMES
My book appeared two days since, and I've ordered the publishers to send a copy to you.

Most of it is unreadable & too long to sell well I'm afraid. Tell Alice I don't burden her with a copy unless she expressly requests it, as I think the sight of it is more fitted to depress her than to cheer her up.

Reviews of The Principles of Psychology

It is literature. It is beautiful, but it is not psychology.
—*Wilhelm Wundt*

. . . . shows that there is no body of doctrines, held by all competent men, that can be set down in a book and called Psychology. . . . [A] work of the imagination.
—*George Santayana*

The author is a veritable storm-bird, fascinated by problems most impossible of solution. . . . [T]he most complete piece of self-evisceration since Marie Bashkertseff.
—*G. Stanley Hall*

. . . materialist to the core . . .
—*Charles Peirce*

"Listen to this, Katherine. Here is a woman who can only see in black and white!" I am reading aloud parts of an essay by William, "The Hidden Self," which has just been published in *Scribner's*. "Imagine! And here's a girl who split into three different people. They come out in the hypnotic trance state, apparently. Lucie One has no awareness of Lucies Two or Three, but Lucie Three does know of Lucies One and Two. It boggles the mind, doesn't it?"

"What do you mean, she *became* three people?"

"Apparently she harbored three separate minds, or personalities, inside her. What do you suppose that would *feel* like?"

"Complicated." A pregnant pause. "If you *believe* it."

"What? You don't?"

"Have *you* ever met anyone like that? In real life?"

"Well, if you mean on *Beacon Street*, Katherine, then no, things of that nature could *never* happen. Certainly not on the water side."

She laughs delightfully. The Lorings live on the water side, the even numbers. When you visit people on the water side of Beacon, they always insist on making you admire the view, no matter how many millions of times you've seen it before. As if the Charles River and the mudflats of Charlestown were the Taj Mahal.

William's essay is a discussion of this Dr. Janet, of the Salpêtrière Hospital in Paris, who uses hypnotism to read the minds of hysterical people (as far as I can make out). After William returned from his Congress, he put off working on his textbook for several months by reading Janet's tome and boiling it down to this essay. Although sending it to me is doubtless part of his diabolical plot to cure me of my "hysteria," I am finding it more interesting than I expected. Katherine takes a dimmer view.

"Kindly suspend your disbelief for a moment, Katherine. The situation with Lucie—that's the girl with three personalities—"

"Do you think that's her real name?"

"Probably not. Anyhow, whenever this Lucie stopped conversing directly with someone, she could no longer see or hear the person. The person to whom she'd been talking simply vanished."

"Some people are like that. Take your Miss Percy. Out of sight, out of mind."

"Not exactly, but you have a point. Monsieur Janet says this sort of thing is proof of—what does he call it?—*the narrowed and contracted nature of the hysterical mind.* Do you find my mind narrow and contracted, Kath?"

"No, quite the opposite. The French are so *odd*, aren't they?"

"They are, and if you want another example: There was a young woman who could feel neither pain nor touch, and when Dr. Janet brought this to her attention, she said, '*C'est tout naturel,* as long as I don't see them; everyone is like that.' Don't you love that, '*C'est tout naturel'*? So French, believing in their rationality, despite all evidence to the contrary."

"Exactly! Like the Parisian cab drivers."

She doesn't need to explain. Katherine's frugalities are legendary, and in Paris her tips to cab men are frequently flung into the road amidst a torrent of French abuse, whereupon K. goes around calmly picking up *centimes* and putting them back into her reticule. This serves to further inflame the driver, and in this manner vivid French curses have been added to her vocabulary. How I wish I could witness this in person. Maybe if I improve through some miracle—oh, stop, Alice! Sometimes hope tries to creep in, but I am determined to weed it out mercilessly. There are such beautiful open spaces beyond hope and fear, and that is where I want to plant my flag.

"How exactly does this Monsieur Janet put people in trance, anyway?"

"It says here he uses 'the orthodox magnetic method of passes made over the face and body.'" I pass my fluttering hand slowly down the length of Katherine's face and torso and intone in a vaguely Slavic accent. "You are becoming v-e-r-y sleepy!'"

Katherine stops to count her stitches, then says, "Fanny Morse tells me that whenever William attends a party, half the guests end up on the carpet, hypnotized."

"Oh, he's been doing that since we were children and saw a stage mesmerist perform in London. William writes here that, when they are in trance, hysterics regain the ability to feel, or see in color, or whatever they were missing—but just for a while. Afterwards, they lapse back into the same old story. And they forget in the waking state what happened to them in trance. I suppose William must think I go into trances all the time."

Another pregnant pause from Katherine. "I wonder, Alice. Do you think it really profits a person to remember *everything*? Perhaps it is better to adopt Emily's attitude toward history and 'let bygones be bygones.'"

One of our pastimes is to plan an imaginary trip to Paris together, a sort of honeymoon. It is unlikely I'd survive a Channel crossing, but that does not stop us from embroidering all sorts of Parisian details: an old hotel with gargoyles and an ancient grumpy concierge who speaks to us without looking up from the smudged register on her desk, café au lait and croissants in bed in the morning. We enjoy brushing imaginary crumbs off our duvet and laughing about our concierge, who persists in believing we are Germans and wishes us *Guten tag* every morning.

And then my bell rings, and sweet, vaporous Miss Leppington comes in with a pair of Mind Cure ladies. One is a lean American widow who was once treated by Mrs. Mary Baker Eddy herself and is stunned to hear that we, being from Boston, have never encountered this great divine. I attempt and fail to elevate the tone of the conversation by quoting from William's article. After some moments of reflection, the American says to the Englishwoman, "You call it hypnotism; *we* call it the Science."

"But," says the Englishwoman, a dowager of the woolen type, "it must be very dangerous to manipulate such a delicate organ as the brain."

"Oh, but they mold the brain so wonderfully now," says the Yankee, resting her chin lightly on her steepled hands. A thin thread of saliva is suspended between an upper tooth and her lower lip. It moves up and down as she talks. I keep waiting for it to break, but it bravely hangs on.

Meanwhile, K. is trying fruitlessly to explain that hypnotism is not the same as massage.

"*How* is it done?" asks the British dowager. "Through the skull, by some marvelous instrument, I suppose? And the weighing of the brain is so wonderful. How do they *do* that?"

Later, Katherine tells me that Miss Leppington whispered to her on the stairs, "I am so glad to see Miss James looking better. There is less going away of her face in weariness and pain."

"*Going away* of my face?"

Katherine shrugs and makes one of her funny faces.

"By the way, did you notice the thread of saliva on the American woman's tooth? Strung between bottom lip and upper incisor, bobbing up and down whenever she talked."

"My, Alice, you are sharp-eyed in your way."

"When that happens, it is all I can think about. I was all but overcome by a desire to reach out and break the thread."

"I'm so glad you refrained."

Several days later, a grievous neuralgia complicated by an infected molar obliges me to assume the horizontal. Katherine stays by my side all day, reading from *Kidnapped*, by Henry's friend Mr. Stevenson. Then she reads aloud from the *Standard*, from which we learn that Henry Morton Stanley is engaged. Who would wed such a creature? And the clericule is *married*! To secure possession of this rare and precious creature, the paper informs us, the bride was obliged to employ five clergymen and four yards of train.

When my toothache blooms into great shivering whacks of pain, Katherine brings in a Mind Curess called Susan, who bids me shut my eyes and say over and over to myself, "I am a child of God and as such pure, perfect, and without flaw." Afterwards she tells me I am too intellectual and "barricaded by my intellectual friends." Two days later, a dentist is summoned to my bower. The pulling of the tooth is curious and interesting like a little lifetime. First the long drawn-out drag, then the twist of the hand and the crack of doom. Afterwards the dentist seizes my face in both his hands, and says, "Bravo, Miss James!"

Having taken a bit of laudanum for the pain, I doze afterwards and have a queer dream. Aunt Kate and I are on the ferry to Dover, crossing the English Channel. The sea is very rough, and the sky ahead is black and ominous. I feel a tremor of foreboding.

"Bad weather ahead," I say.

"Don't give it a thought. The Captain will bring us into port. He is immensely skilled."

My aunt beckons me closer and opens the heart-shaped locket she wears around her neck. Inside is a small cameo of Dr. Munro. "He has been my darling since—well, you know. It will be our secret, dear, like your Sapphic romps. How is Sara, by the way?"

"I didn't realize you knew."

"I have always been able to see *through* you, dear. Just as if you were wearing a sheer muslin dress with no petticoat."

"But aren't you dead, Aunt Kate? Didn't I read about you in the *Proceedings of the Society for Psychical Research*?"

"No one really dies, Alice, so long as others take the trouble to remember us. I'd be grateful if you'd water my grave with your tears from time to time. *Godey's* says it can be helpful to the afterlife."

I wake up to a beatific vision of K. removing streaks of grime from the wallpaper with a speck of India rubber. I love the fact that she is a purely transatlantic and modern personality, cleansed of all the receptive vagueness of the traditional female. (I am obliged to note that while transcribing this little phrase into my diary, she gives vent to a self-deprecating *psshh.)*

Katherine says she loves watching me wake up. For a few minutes, according to her, I have a lost expression, as if I had just arrived from a kingdom over the sea.

"I *am* from a land over the sea."

***

While she is here, I resolve to get my will redone and arrange for my cremation. "It may seem silly, but it will ease my mind to have these details settled. We only die once." I had been discouraged about cremation, having heard from Miss Percy that it was very fussy and expensive. But Katherine makes inquiries and finds that it is only six guineas and one extra for a parson.

"That's very reasonable, is it not?"

"I think so. Would you like to be scattered at sea, darling?"

"Ye gods! Poor sailor that I am! Dry land for me, please."

So it is settled that my ashes are to be placed in some sort of receptacle and sent home, not as a parlor ornament for William's house but to be buried beside Father and Mother in the Mt. Auburn Cemetery. "So that we shall not be myths, as Harry suggests we might otherwise become," I say.

Next, we move on to the afterlife of my money and possessions. I tell Katherine I wish to redo my will, leaving out all who have offended me since my last. (If you want to know, I shall leave a third of my estate to William, a third to Henry, and a third to Katherine. Bob, married to a rich man's daughter, does not require anything from me.) Katherine writes to the American Consul in Birmingham, who informs her that the documents must be signed in his presence. Since I am incapable of traveling, the Consul will condescend to travel to me. Apparently there is a need for witnesses who can vouch that I am Alice James and not an imposter, and it is best if they are from Boston. K enlists Elizabeth Putnam, sister of Jim and Charley, who is presently traveling through Banbury. Then there is Katherine, and we call in Miss Leppington, who is British, but how many Americans can you round up in the Midlands on short notice?

On the appointed day the consul arrives, a lean, leathery man from one of our western states who informs us with considerable *gravitas* that he was appointed to his post by the President. Indeed he'd only "accepted the Birmingham place as a special favor to President Harrison." I refrain from telling him that my brother and I were deeply stricken by President Harrison's election and I devoted an entire night to tears.

Faced with the consul's august presence, I "go off" almost as soon as he arrives and take to my bed, spending most of the time in a half-faint. As through a mist I make out five black figures filing into my bower. The consul, all gesticulation and grimace, plants himself at the foot of my bed and while stroking my knee begins a long harangue to the effect that he and his wife "had both laid upon a bed of sickness." This is meant to cheer me, I think. He invokes the president again, implying that they are never far from each other's thoughts.

K informs me later that Nurse, positioned at my head, was wearing her most devoted nurse expression throughout. And the mild Miss Leppington told K afterwards, "The scene will remain in my thought as one of the most pathetic I ever saw and in my imagination as the most picturesque and American!"

"So now," I tell K after the solemn ceremony, "I am packed up and ready to go! I feel a little like George Sand, who writes a long letter to a friend telling him why she is going to commit suicide and says to be sure and have her two mattresses corded."

SIX

1891

EVENTUALLY THE DARK DAY ARRIVES WHEN KATHERINE, LIKE Persephone, must descend to the underworld again. From my point of view, I mean. She assures me it will not be so long this time; that she will be back before I have time to miss her, but, of course, she knows I miss her all the time.

In the vacuum left by her departure, I peg away again at the black future, working it off five minutes at a time. Large wet snowflakes are drifting softly though the dim winter sky, making a vivid contrast to the soot on the chimney pots. The lamplight comes on in mid-afternoon and blurry little globes of light are suspended here and there in the winter gloom. William's French madwoman who sees the world in black and white would feel quite at home here.

My daybed must be pulled right up to the fire now, and I require at least three pillows and four shawls to stay warm. The shawls and pillows are a trial, for they seldom remain in their proper place and if I reach for a book, the whole structure falls apart, and I must call Nurse in for assistance. Or, if she is out, shiver until she returns, quite helpless. Fortunately, I am deep in the memoirs of Massimo d'Azeglio, an Italian politician of the Risorgimento, who has some interesting beliefs—for instance, that the passion of love should be shunned by youth because it involves a course of perpetual lying.

On Tuesday, Miss Percy stops by, bringing devastating news. Mrs. Arnold died last week, of a fever. "I believe it was malaria."

I feel as if I'd been knocked down by an omnibus. I can't get my breath at first. Tears spring to my eyes, and all I can do is mutter, "I thought she was getting better."

"She got better and then she got much worse." After a thoughtful pause, she adds, "I am not certain it *was* malaria. It may have been typhus." This imprecision about the cause of death is maddening! It makes it so much worse when people essentially say, "Oh, she died of something. Who cares what it was?" I suppose I shall die of something vague, too.

"Was someone with her when she died?" I can't stop picturing the noble Mrs. Arnold burning up with fever, perhaps half out of her mind, and no one nearby who truly understood and cared for her. No one to hold her hand and guide her down the sacred Ganges and through the gates of paradise.

"She had a nurse several times a week. I expect the nurse was with her."

"You don't *know*?"

"I didn't think to inquire, Miss James." Her tone implies that inquiring would be the height of bad manners. I suppose it might be in England.

"Do you know of any living relatives to whom I can write?"

"No. I suppose I could try to find out if you like," she says, clearly disinclined to bother. Mrs. Arnold, dead, is of no further interest to Miss Percy. She is longing to talk about living people she knows or about her dogs. I wonder if it would pay to have a long line of ancestry and come out at the end of centuries like Miss Percy.

It makes me wonder, not for the first time, how *I* became this dreary thing—a woman in bed? It seemed to happen gradually at first and then reached a point of no return.

Since my scaffolding began to fall, I have been living like a mouse behind a skirting board, knowing nothing of the world beyond a few dark tunnels and whatever crumbs happen to drop nearby. But something has shifted recently. It is hard to describe. My thoughts drift through my brain like clouds. I watch them come and go; I seem to be the vast, empty sky in which they happen.

For a month or so I read compulsively to anesthetize the pain of loss—the double loss, of Mrs. Arnold and Katherine. To distract myself, I tunnel through Renan's *Saint Paul*, followed by Halévy's *Notes and Souvenirs*, before returning to William's article on Janet. This time a particular passage arrests me:

> *The secondary self enriches itself at the expense of the primary one,*
> *which loses functions as the second gains them. An hysteric woman*
> *abandons part of her consciousness because she is too weak nervously*
> *to hold it all together. The abandoned part, meanwhile, may solidify*
> *into a subconscious or secondary self.*

The word *abandon* seems to stir something deep inside, and I have a sense of being beckoned by something true and important. I write in my diary:

> *William uses an excellent expression when he says in his paper on the*
> *"Hidden Self" that the nervous victim 'abandons' certain portions of his*
> *consciousness, altho' I have never unfortunately been able to abandon*
> *my consciousness and get five minutes' rest. I have passed thro' an*
> *infinite succession of conscious abandonments and in looking back*
> *now I see how it began in my childhood, altho' I wasn't conscious of*
> *the necessity until '67 or '68 when I broke down first, acutely, and had*
> *violent bursts of hysteria.*

Hysteria was what they called it, anyhow, and I won't deny that there were days when I would sit reading, with waves of violent inclination urging me to throw myself out of the window or knock off the head of the benignant pater as he sat writing at his desk. It seemed to me that the only difference between me and the floridly insane was that, in addition to the suffering of insanity, I had the duties of doctor, nurse, and strait-jacket imposed upon me as well. In the wars between my body and my mind, I learned to "abandon" the former—my stomach, my legs, my arms—but never for an instant my consciousness. What if I *had*?

My mind sinks and sinks, like a surgical patient counting backwards while going under ether. I see again the low, brooding skies when I used to wander over the cliffs of Newport, my young soul struggling out of its swaddling clothes. I am back to the summer when everything changed, when my life was split into before and after.

Oh, but here is Nurse with a cup of tea and buttered toast. I thank her and tell her that I am very busy thinking and don't wish to be disturbed for a couple of hours. She seems to find this acceptable, if mysterious. I take a bite of toast and stare out my window at two shiny crows perched on my window ledge, their black beady eyes full of alien intelligence. An insane urge strikes me to run out into the street calling for help. As if I could run!

Every summer at Newport, we run in a pack with our Temple cousins, "discovering" secret places, points, promontories, sandy coves, secret inlets, lily ponds, spouting rocks, apple groves, wind-sculpted trees resembling buzzards or witches in profile, chasms carved by the sea. Like explorers, we claim our discoveries and name them. One fine day in July, I am with brothers William and Bob, and Elly and Kitty Temple in our sailboat, the *Alice*. Bob is at the helm. We are hugging the coastline, with its low bluffs and small inlets. William takes over at some point and Bob minds the mainsail and I the jib. For a while everything is perfect. The rhythmic *chip chip chip* of the wavelets against the hull, the silvery foam of our wake, the sun's toasty warmth on my skin, the raucous cries of gulls, the taste of salt on my lips. I remember thinking, *I am perfectly happy right now.*

The wind stiffens; I feel the tug of the jib sheet in my hands. Elly pleads to "steer the boat," and while Bob observes churlishly that women are bad luck on ships, William cedes the tiller to her. We are headed in the direction of the rocky shoreline. William reminds Elly that she must come about soon. "I know, I know!" she says. A few minutes later, without warning, she panics. She shouts, "Ready about!" and pushes the tiller sharply toward the sail. Wrong! After "ready about" she should have waited a decent interval so we could release the sails and *then* said "Hard-a-lee!" and only then pushed the tiller to make us come about. Now we are in a mariner's worst pickle: the sails close-halt

on the wrong side, and strong gusts knock us over sideways. The lee-
ward rail dips dangerously and water starts to pour in. Now, much too
late, Elly screams, "Hard-a-lee! Hard-a-lee!" William leaps over me,
grabs the tiller from her, and tries to point the bow into the wind. Bob
releases the mainsail and I the jib sheet, and the sails flap wildly. We
barely avert capsizing.

I wait for Elly to apologize or act contrite, but she doesn't.

We are searching for something on the shoreline. Five black rocks
that point toward a cleft in the granite cliff. About five minutes later,
there it is. Elly breaks into gales of laughter. "It looks—it looks like—"
She can't talk for laughing.

"What?" Then Kitty sees it. "Elly, you shameless hussy. You mean
like a vagina!"

William is gazing dreamily at the cleft in the cliff. We hear the
dull roar of the tide rushing in.

"Well, I'm only saying what we're all thinking."

The others—Wilky James (Harry was absent that day) and Will,
Minny, Henrietta, and Bob Temple—wave to us from the small drift-
wood-covered beach. As we approach, I make out a picnic hamper, a
checked tablecloth, a few towels, and flashes of sunlight reflected off
several metal flasks, which no doubt contain whiskey. Drifting toward
shore in a din of luffing sails and clicking halyards, we pull up the
centerboard, lower the sails, and roughly furl the mainsail. That is,
William and I do. Bob nimbly leaps out with the painter and pulls us
in. Elly and Kitty do nothing but chatter like magpies.

Ignoring evidence of corks, bottles, handkerchiefs, and other arti-
facts of civilization, we have on a previous occasion declared ourselves
the discoverers of this place. The Abyss, we call it. Above us the cliff
rises steeply, covered with brambles, wind-bent pines and cypresses,
and narrow deer trails. Down one of these paths the rest of our gang
has come, bearing our picnic lunch.

Our clothes are damp from our near-drowning. Elly peels off
her outer garments and Henrietta follows suit, although she didn't go
sailing. I keep my damp clothes on, shivering in the sun. After eating
our sandwiches, we race around collecting shells and sea glass and

wading in the surf. Between the sun-dazzled sea and the whiskey in the flasks, a wildness begins to crackle in the air. I feel it breaking out in goose-bumps on my skin. Henrietta leaps from boulder to boulder stripped down to her drawers and bodice, the wind whipping her hair like a mare's tail.

After lunch we follow the deer-trail up the hill and gather at the lip of the Abyss (which I think would more accurately be called a chasm), watching the rising tide pour in four to six feet below.

"Let's take off our clothes and jump in!" Kitty says. Elly's eyes widen. "Yes, we'll be mermaids." Will Temple, Wilky, and Bob laugh; I see their teeth. (Two years later the three of them will march off to war; Will Temple will be killed, Wilky gravely wounded, Bob will survive unharmed but will suffer night terrors for the rest of his life.)

"Are mer*men* invited? Do such beings exist?" William asks.

"They *must* exist," says Minny, perched on a flat rock, dreamily pulling off her stockings. "Otherwise the mer-people would die out."

The boys peel off shoes and socks, unbutton trousers; the Temple girls giggle in a froth of petticoats, laying out their clothes on the boulders, with smaller rocks to hold them down. William is staring at the girls, transfixed. Blue eyes flecked with green. I stand with my bare toes on the lip of the chasm, staring down at the roiling green water with its flailing banners of yellow foam. The others start jumping in; their splashes and voices echo off the rock walls. There is a moment when I might have jumped, but I pause too long. I think too much; I already know this is one of my problems.

I step backwards, away from the chasm, sealing my fate.

I shade my eyes with my hand and gaze out at the sea. Black and white ducks bob for fish. They look like clockwork toys. Far away to the left is a wide curve of pale sand roughly the color of naked human flesh.

I must record what happens next, but I shrink from the task. Do I dare disturb the past?

Bob Temple comes up silently behind me, like an assassin, his hand at the nape of my neck. Didn't know he was there. My whole body flinches. "Why don't you take off that dress, Cousin Alice! It looks damp and you're not allowed to just stand around watching." He laughs pleasantly.

"Oh." As the eldest, Bob Temple imposes the rules. He is a grown man, twenty-one years old, with black hair on his knuckles and chest. My stomach flutters and I feel queasy.

"Do you know what our sisters and brothers are doing down there, Alice?"

"Playing. I suppose."

His attention throws me into confusion. Wanting it and dreading it, paralyzed and confused, I stare down at my feet, which seem miles away suddenly.

"Don't *you* ever play, Alice?" His voice is soft, almost caressing.

"Yes." My face grows hot.

"Well? Why aren't you down there with them?"

"Don't want to ruin my clothes." Feeling stupid and tongue-tied, I fix my eyes on a patch of emerald moss on a grey boulder. I don't look at Bob, but I *feel* him staring at me hard. The small hairs on the back of my neck stand up. I can't think why such a worldly and (to me) terrifying young man would have any interest in me.

"Have you heard of 'kissing cousins'? You and I are kissing cousins, Alice."

I can't think what to say to this. Wilting under the burden of my mousiness, my awkwardness, my inability to banter brightly like my cousins, I nudge a pebble with my toe and squint at the horizon with its faint band of citrine. We stand at the edge of America: low bluffs, promontories, islands, and ocean as far as the eye can see. On the other side: Europe. Harry always says that Newport is "midway between America and Europe, culturally" and thus a fitting location for the James family.

I must have drifted off, because the next thing I am aware of is being perched on a boulder, with Bob Temple sitting cross-legged about ten feet away, his back against another boulder, smoking, watching. I feel his eyes burning into me. Then I see that he is naked. I didn't observe him undressing; it is as if his nakedness occurred by magic while my mind was away.

"Little Alice," he says gently, "you ought to let your hair down, you know, or you'll turn into a prune like your mother and Aunt Tweedy.

I'll wager you are a good little daughter, the best little girl in the world. But the world is full of good vanilla pudding daughters who turn into good vanilla pudding wives. There is nothing in it, nothing at all."

He sits waiting and smoking, the smoke unfurling into the wide sky. "May I share a little secret with you, Cousin Alice? A secret between kissing cousins? More than once I have seen Uncle having his way with Aunt. I wish you could have been there. It made me think of the barnyard, jiggling rumps, squeals, grunts and ruffled feathers. Who'd have thought the old people had it in them?" He smiles lazily.

What does he mean? Why is he remaining behind to talk to *me*, anyway? He sits gazing at me for a long time, too long. I try not to look at his thing, a pale rodent in a tangle of black hair. I shut my eyes and feel invisible, like a small child. The sun beats down and the sweat stings my scalp and face. From the Abyss come shrieks of merriment.

I try to think myself back to the verandah at Kay Street, reading magazines while Mother and Aunt Kate sew or embroider. I must have "gone off" again, because the next thing I know, Bob is sitting next to me, his arm thrown fraternally over my shoulder. "How about your parents, Alice? Is there a peephole in their bedroom? There is usually a peephole somewhere if you look well."

"I don't think so." My eyes blur. I want to go home but I can't move. It is like a dream in which you are paralyzed by inaction and words run together and blur and the more you try to get out of the muddle you're in, the deeper you sink into it. A cloud passes over the sun. I shiver, goose-bumps on my skin. Bob is carefully unbuttoning the buttons of my dress. Says he is not a lady's maid, I could help a little. I say, "What?"

His eyes squint at me. He takes my face in his large hands, forcing me to turn toward him. His eyes are obsidian—*a basilisk gaze*, I will think years later, hypnotizing me, pulling me down toward the center of the earth. Suddenly, I grasp why he sought me out: He wields absolute power over me. He is drunk on it; some people are like that. His tongue is prying my lips apart, and my mouth is thick with the yeasty, smoky taste of him, his hot breath. I don't know what to do or think. "You *are* a nervous Nelly, aren't you? If it's about your little flower, cousin, don't worry. I won't take that." His hands are busying themselves inside my clothes, and then I am on my back staring at the sky and the wind lifts my skirt and my petticoats and Bob says, as if from far away. "Be nice, Alice." His voice is rasping and needy, like a giant baby.

His hand is cupped over my mouth, his sweat drips onto my face and eyes, stinging my skin. Glare in my eyes; I shut them. Something is happening, it has been happening for some time, miles away. A tree trunk pinning me down, my tailbone grinding against rock. Perhaps I am caught under a hemlock limb? Can't move. Should I scream? If I called for help, the wind and surf would drown me out.

Moans and a sort of growling, then for a long while nothing, just sky and hot sun and metallic gleam of sea. I hear the cries of gulls and the breeze in the pines, and possibly an animal grunting, nuzzling at my thighs with its snout.

For how long do I "go off"? When I open my eyes next, there is the wide sky, and a tall cumulous cloud that passes, stately as a galleon, and floats off. I cannot feel my legs and wonder if I am dead. I close my eyes and try to feel my way back into my body, into my limbs, bones, skin, and muscles, but I lose myself again. And then Wilky's face hovers above me. "Alice! What are you doing? You'll get sunstroke."

I see the goodness shining from my third brother's face; he appears to me an angel, without sin or guile. Tenderly, he helps me sit up. I feel very old. I see the sea with its rim of white foam, I see the sky, the wheeling gulls, the low bluffs in the distance, the horizon. None of it has any connection with me. Bob Temple has vanished; perhaps he never was there.

I wish I knew what is real and what is not. I *thought* something happened but it may have been a dream. My dress is buttoned all the way to the neck, all the mother-of-pearl buttons fastened, and the faun, the creature, with its hot panting animal breath, is gone. After helping me to my feet, Wilky leads me down the lane, past the wooden houses with green shutters and the painted wooden palings. The squeals and shouts of my brothers and cousins down in the Abyss fade away. My legs are wobbly. A dog barks, a woman in a white frock waves from a pony phaeton, a baby wails out of sight. I tell no one what happened. How should I? I don't understand it.

⌒ SEVEN ⌒

IF I WERE GRANTED THREE WISHES, I WOULD SPEND ALL THREE on making Bob Temple go away or (preferably) die. I do not ever want to see him, his eyes drilling into me. My cousins and brothers go blueberry picking, riding, sailing; they take sea-baths, collect shells, visit the library, walk to the village green in the evening to listen to the band. I tell Mother I am unwell and stay home. I flip through the pages of *Godey's Lady's Book* in the misty mornings and the sparkling afternoons, lying on my stomach on the verandah, bits and pieces of advice sticking to my brain at random.

English waterproofs are all the rage now in Paris and consequently are rapidly gaining favor here.

The earth has been made fruitful, subdued, and embellished by man alone. The ground is tilled by men. The cities are built by men. Nor is there the slightest indication either in Nature or in Revelation, that the work was intended for Woman.

Perhaps because Woman is not a builder or a tiller, the editresses staunchly oppose female suffrage, although they are very keen on the higher education of the fair sex.

Humility leads to the highest distinction because it leads to self-improvement, Study your own character, endeavor to learn and supply your own deficiencies.

The others get used to my being unwell and stop expecting me to join their outings. Aunt Kate shoots me worried glances. I ought to be out in the fresh air, she says, I am looking peaky. In the clarity of vision brought on by misfortune, I have noticed something about my mother and aunt. In middle age, their mouths turn down at the corners, as if frozen in permanent frowns of disappointment. I wonder why, as they are both cheerful, optimistic people. I see them differently suddenly. Has life etched on their faces a dissatisfaction of which they themselves are unaware? Aunt Kate's eyes brim with sadness when she is not being busy and cheerful. Is their habitual cheerfulness a form of resignation? Is that what it is to be a woman?

> *We women have a world of our own, in which we reign supreme. It is the Kingdom of Home. To teach, to console, to elevate, to train in all goodness and nobleness, to concentrate around ourselves the purest and most intense joys.*

Since teaching, consoling, and elevating do not fall within my scope, I don't see how I will ever attain successful womanhood. As for "the purest and most intense joys," what do the editresses have in mind? From day to day I watch life pass through veils of helplessness. My brothers are growing brown as summer progresses. Wilky's hair is bleached the color of straw. They all go barefoot, as do the Temple girls. Their feet will turn into hooves, says Aunt Kate, who frequently refers to the girls, half critically, half affectionately, as "wild Indians."

> *Home is a sort of Heaven on earth and occupies the same relation to the world that the Sabbath does to the rest of the week.*

Every day dawns with a gnawing in the pit of my stomach. My skin is clammy, my throat parched, my heart races. I try to blot out the horrid dreams I have been having every night. I will have to see Bob Temple someday; it cannot be avoided. There is something wrong with me. I feel it inside me, a strangeness, an otherness, growing like a tumor.

One morning I wake up to find blood on my nightdress and bed-sheets. For a moment I think I have been stabbed in my sleep; then I remember the pamphlet Mother gave me a few months ago, informing me that, whether you are a scullery maid or a queen, Nature requires you to bleed for days; that all women walk around with this incurable wound, which has something to do with Eve's disobedience. And it is so much worse than I imagined! Mother and Aunt Kate congratulate me, but I am mortified and see nothing to celebrate. The long dresses and corsets that make running and climbing difficult, when it was easy before? That my legs must be called *limbs* and hidden away, as if I har-bored something scaly and fishlike under my skirt? That I must bury my true self under a mask of cheerful servitude?

Why cheer the sorrows of womankind?

One day Bob Temple appears in our parlor with several of his sisters. There is no time to escape. I press my back against the wall and wait in dread like a fly caught in a spider's web. But Bob pays no attention to me except to say, in a bored tone, "Hi, Alice." No secret smirk, no spark of interest, nothing. What happened on the rocks must have been a kind of dream. I decide to forget the whole thing and go on as before.

But it is not so easy to find my way back to "before." There is a strange laxness in my knee joints. My legs quaver as if they were made of custard. Since my legs always worked properly in the past, I wonder if this has something to do with puberty, which is shocking me daily with new and startling manifestations. It covers me with shame and sets me apart from my brothers. One evening Father is ranting about the vileness of a memoir written by a Frenchwoman. The look he casts in my direction makes me feel that I, too, am in some obscure way cov-ered with filth, or might become so shortly.

Mother, meanwhile, attempts to prepare me for my future as a woman with random pearls of wisdom drawn from her experience. "Marriage requires adjustment in the beginning," she will say. "The wife needs to cultivate patience, knowing that a man's animal spirits may impel him toward all sorts of dangerous situations." I briefly wonder what dangers Father rushed into in his youth. In my own case, none of Mother's advice is helpful. But there is nothing for it but to try to embrace the awful mysteries of femininity and accept that my Realm is Home and my Fate to Do for Others. My parents pretend (and may actually believe) that I am a household angel, but I know better. To be a proper woman I shall have to kill my spirit.

The Emerson children come to visit toward the end of August, and Ellen and Edith remark on how grown-up I have become; they hardly recognize me. Edward Emerson is shaken by the ferocity with which our family argues at the dinner table. I'd always thought it perfectly normal for members of a family to launch *ad hoc* rants, spew colorful insults, stand on their chairs to make a point in a debate, waving knives and forks at each other in a cutthroat manner. "Don't worry, Edward," Mother says, "The boys always do this. They won't stab anyone." Father encourages his sons to argue; he *wants* them to rebel, and keeps poking at William, especially, to train him to be a credible philosophical adversary. But it is taken for granted that I am meant to be a "comfort" to my parents. My views on any question are rarely solicited, and I almost never speak up at table.

With Ellen and Edith Emerson, who are years older, I visit wounded soldiers in a hospital tent in Portsmouth. We are supposed to cheer the boys up by making charming conversation and distributing magazines, handkerchiefs, and warm socks. I don't know what I was expecting but it was not this. Empty sleeves, bloody bandages over faces, flies buzzing everywhere, terrible smells, a suffocating atmosphere of pain, fear, and horror. I kneel next to a cot and try to make conversation with a boy who looks no more than sixteen. He tries to respond to my question about where he is from, but he is missing much of his jaw. I can see his tongue through a hole in his cheek. Hell is real, after all. I don't see how cheerful conversation or a magazine will remedy this situation. While Ellen and Edith go about being angels of mercy, I have to run outside and sit heaving under a tree until I get my breath.

Toward the end of August Bob Temple is seen walking out at twilight with the Grissoms' hired girl, and then we learn that the Grissoms have forbidden her to walk out with him. A week later their terrier is mysteriously dead, bleeding from the mouth. A few weeks later, Bob vanishes, and Father says he has gone to New York State. He says that Bob is an "operator and a swindler" and will end up in prison. (Some years later, Bob Temple *will* go to prison, for swindling; he will write pathetic letters to his aunt and uncle Tweedy, which they won't answer.)

Here, on my desert isle in the English Midlands, it all comes rushing back: Bob Temple's scorn for "the Hatter," as he always referred to Uncle Tweedy. How much we had to hear in those days about the Temples' famous "pride" and "spirit" and "aristocracy." Harry, especially, was star-struck by their blood ties to a distinguished Temple family in England, or perhaps Ireland, but none of this prevented their living at the expense of anyone who took on the job of providing for them.

Our house on Kay Street has a steep staircase, with treads of varnished oak. I stand at the top and imagine my body tumbling, my neck neatly snapped at the bottom. When I do fall, it happens so fast I am not sure how it started. I land badly bruised, but no bones are broken; the bruises start out the color of a storm-cloud and fade to greenish yellow.

"Alice thinks she can walk on air," someone jokes.

One evening Mrs. Tappan (who rents a house in Newport most summers) is reading our fortunes with the Egyptian tarot. I close my eyes and draw a card. It is the eight of swords, a despondent female figure with her face buried in her hands, weeping. Mrs. Tappan tries to tell me it is not bad, but then why is the lady crying and lamenting? All the portents are wrong now.

That night, as I am undressing for bed and brushing out my hair, I hear Mother, Aunt Kate, Mrs. Tappan, and Aunt Mary Tweedy playing cards in the parlor. Outside my window a warm rain is falling. Mother's voice has the hushed, solemn tone she reserves for Female Matters, but most of her words are drowned out by the rain. When the rain subsides a little, I hear Mrs. Tappan say, "brutally violated on her wedding night." What is "violated"? Whatever it is, it happened to a woman Mrs. Tappan knows, in the private car of a train.

"How were they able to go forward with their wedding trip?" I hear Aunt Kate ask.

"I suppose they came to some arrangement," Mrs. Tappan says, in her omniscient way, adding that, years later, the couple is still living together in Washington. The husband is a powerful senator, and they have a daughter. After the child was born, the husband lost all interest in the wife and turned his attentions elsewhere. The wife, much relieved, told Mrs. Tappan, "What a luxury it is to have possession of my own body."

Never having imagined that it was possible *not* to possess my own body, I am horrified by this tale. A great war is being waged over slavery now. Father believes the abolition of slavery will usher in a more blessed society, but a woman who marries the wrong man can end up as a sort of slave and there is little she can do about it, apparently.

Mother says something else, which is blotted out by the rumble of thunder outside.

Then I hear Mrs. Tappan say, "The only power a woman can have is to live by her wits and manage her husband." Apparently, Mrs. Tappan manages hers very well; he is rarely seen with her.

In September, William leaves us to study natural history and chemistry at Harvard, and his long letters home are laced with homesickness and funny anecdotes. Father always opposed college for the boys, claiming it would corrupt their innocence and implant other people's dead ideas in their minds. But he wants William to be a scientist and for this it is necessary to attend the Lawrence Scientific School at Harvard. I am stunned that my parents have consented to this rent in the family fabric, for up till now we have been like a small, isolated clan living in a remote place, with our own specialized vocabulary and *Weltanschauung* (a word William taught the rest of us).

The Cambridge life Will describes sounds as exotic as Lapland to us, and he enjoys shocking the family with the curiosities of science.

> It will probably be a shock for Mother to learn I yesterday destroyed a
> handkerchief—but it was an old one and I converted it into some sugar
> which though rather brown is very good.

Perhaps I am a bit of a seeress after all, for even that far back I had a melancholy glimpse of the future: all my brothers gone and I alone left in an empty, echoing house to "be a comfort" to my parents.

HENRY JAMES
11 HAMILTON TERRACE, LEAMINGTON
AUGUST 14TH 1891

TO WILLIAM JAMES
Alice has relapsed and collapsed a good deal. She is too ill to be left; & the difficult question of doctors (owing to A's extreme dread of them) & her absolute inability to take tonic doses, drugs &c;—they put her in a fearful nervous state—remains. Her little "improvements" now discourage her more than the relapses; she wants to have done with it all, to sink continuously. At any rate, KPL will not leave her while she is in the present condition. She said it would be "inhumane."

— EIGHT —

YOU DON'T FEEL IT AT FIRST, AND YOU CAN'T PUT YOUR FINGER upon it, but as the days go by you unfold it with the *Telegraph*, in the morn. It rises dense from the *Pall Mall Gazette* and the *Evening Standard* in the evening; it creeps through the cracks in the window frames like the fog and envelops you throughout the day.

I asked Henry how it struck him from his wider view. He said he did not think it could be exaggerated. British phariseeism. The way they believe that they alone of human races massacre savages out of pure virtue.

But I really must avoid wide-ranging pontification *à la* Norton.

I am weak and getting weaker for no particular reason. At summer's end this great prostration. Clinging to my little nurse like a drowning creature to a straw. Henry, with his grave grey eyes, summoned from Vallambrosa to my squalid indigestions. Listens so well, like a priest. Holds my hand in silence, later reads to me from Zola's *Thérèse Raquin*. 'Tis a cruel fate that he should have my troubles fastened to him like a burr.

"Your nerves are my nerves," he says. "Your stomach is my stomach. We two are one." Was there ever such a brother? My tears overflow at his goodness. I have given him endless care and anxiety, but notwithstanding this and the fantastic nature of my troubles, I have never seen an impatient look upon his face.

I think we ought to call in a doctor, Alice.

Oh please, no more Great Men. I shall soldier on by myself, thank you very much.

Has the *Pall Mall Gazette* come yet? The English continue to be upset with Mark Twain over his frivolous treatment of Arthurian legend in *A Connecticut Yankee in King Arthur's Court*. They had a little time of being interested in Americans, Henry says, and now they are dreadfully sick of us.

Shall I bring the tea now, Miss? Shall I rearrange your shawls?

The doctors steer clear of the hopeless cases, I believe. I laugh, remembering the one in London who said to Henry, "Your sister will not die but she will never be well." I said, "Well, doctor, it is nice to hear that I am immortal, anyhow."

Henry distracts me with tales of London, his friends, the racy exploits of the Prince of Wales and his crowd. He says he saw Stanley Clarke receiving his orders from the Prince, and his manner was precisely that of Smith, Henry's servant, before Henry, and the manner of the Prince was that of kind master. One day he brings along a sympathy note from Grace Norton, written in *such* Nortonese. I must be very unwell for the Ancient Houri of Kirkland Street to write to me.

A cable brings Katherine across the waves on the Umbria, a stormy passage. My Rock of Gibraltar. Shocked by my pallor, my shrinkage of flesh. "Why didn't you say it had got so bad?" I suppose I had to get a little worse in order to lose all conscience about absorbing Kath as my right.

K is better than the *Transcript* for Boston news. The Annex women still must fight Harvard for every crumb, she says. Tells me all the foolish things said by the president, the overseers, reactionary professors, the male sex in general.

Girls have no natural capacity for classical languages. Latin or Greek places too great a strain on the female nervous system.

Philosophy is inimical to the fair sex.

The female mind is unfit to tackle the higher realms of mathematics.

It is a great waste of Harvard's precious resources to teach women, who will never contribute meaningfully to society or the world of ideas.

I ask K, "Didn't you write me that President Eliot told Mrs. Howe and her group that 'the monotony of women's lives has been greatly exaggerated'?"

"Yes, and the women laughed at him! I wish you could have been there. He looked quite cowed for a few minutes."

One day K is taken to visit a beautiful old house at Mortlake, a private school to prepare infants for Eton, and she describes to me all the luxuries provided for the pampered young ones. A few days later Nurse goes to the Wadsworth Infirmary, where a friend of hers is nursing. She describes a girl of twelve dying of consumption, so thin and shriveled that she seems only five or six. Her mother is in a madhouse from drink and her father died the week before in a drunken fit, and there she lies trying to smile over some biscuits just given her. There was also a little boy with a crooked spine dying of cancer, and many other unfortunates. This is indeed a land of contrasts.

I expected to get better with Katherine here, but there's no denying that I am weaker, thinner, and yellower every day. I see K's anxious looks, hear her whispering with Nurse when she thinks I am dozing. Why, then, do I feel like a child who has been taken to the seashore? A vast holiday stretches before me all the way to the horizon. I see my footprints in wet sand filling with water, reflecting jagged pieces of sky. What is this joy that overflows my heart?

Worn down by the pathetic pleas of K and H, I finally relent and allow the Primrose Knight to present himself to me again. I refer to Dr. Wilmot, who being a fox-hunter and the treasurer of the local Primrose League, cures me by local color more than by his medicines. After listening attentively to my chest, he pronounces a "severe distress of the heart." My heart may give out at any moment, he says, or I may linger on for some time.

K and H decide it will be more practical to move me to London, and I see no reason to object. It doesn't really matter *where* I am; I am always on the island of me! Ten days to pack up our household—me, Katherine, Nurse, and little Louisa, formerly under-parlormaid, now our maid-of-all-work—and whisk us away forever from Miss Clarke and the Mind Cure ladies and the Marie Antoinette wallpaper. Miss Clarke sheds a fountain of tears. "I shouldn't say so, Miss, but there never was nobody like you." I shall miss her, too, her indefatigable spirit and boundless goodness.

Thus my three and a half lonely years in Leamington draw to a close. In an invalid carriage of the great Western Railroad we travel to dark carboniferous London, and take rooms in the South Kensington Hotel in Queen's Gate Terrace, not far from Henry's flat in De Vere Gardens. A fine hotel, but Australian children run constantly through the corridors, screaming. Apparently Australians do not believe in suppressing the child.

Our little maid Louisa asks, "Is this the Jack the Ripper part of London?"

In this hotel the servants gather in the Steward's Room, and Nurse tells us everything that transpires there. She is allowed to report all mental eccentricities of the Lady's Maid, the Chef, the Steward, the Waiter, et cetera, but the line is rigidly drawn at all gossip about the "lydies." The Lady's Maid, however, likes to gossip on ladies' shortcomings, and thus a wider social range is opened to us.

Katherine smiles indulgently at the manner in which I turn up and rake the thin soil of Nurse's substance. I tell her that Nurse has just revealed to me those hitherto mysterious but powerful factors in life, a 'sense of authority' and a 'sense of your betters,' by letting me know that I possess both.

"Do you mean to say you have a sense of your betters?"

"Oh no, Kath. Apparently I *am* a Better as well as an Authority, whose quoted word carries finality in the arguments of the steward's room. Isn't that wonderful?"

Mrs. Sidgwick comes to call, bearing a volume of verse by a Persian poet called Hafiz Shirazi. His words strike me like lightning. Especially a beautiful poem about *the ten thousand things that do not matter.*

"That's it! That's it exactly!" I say to Katherine. "Being so absorbed in the ten thousand things that do not matter, we miss the one thing that does."

"What is that, darling?"

"*Being*, Katherine. This becomes rather obvious when you are stripped to the bone by illness."

"Hmm," she says indulgently, ever tolerant of my "gypsy" ways.

Waves of illumination pass through me now. Some queer magic is afoot. For example, I often come across in my reading just what I'd been thinking about. Yesterday I was remembering a mustard-yellow gown with a bustle I wore to a ball in 1875—only to read in the newspaper a few hours later that the bustle has been declared dead. And my reading so haphazard!

Would you like to hear the Pall Mall Gazette?

Only if there is a good murder.

Here is a letter from Fanny Morse. Shall I read it to you now or later?

Fanny encloses a little pamphlet, "How to Help the Poor." I suppose it is all right for America, but I believe the poor here can improve their lot only by rising up and chopping off some heads.

Harry says people continue to talk about Jack the Ripper, and there is speculation that the killer is a real-life Mr. Hyde, whose consciousness (or part of it) has become inaccessible to himself. Something up William's alley, I should think.

As my dissolution advances, the plan is for me to be carried to H's flat, it being considered unaesthetic here to die in a hotel. Harry, meanwhile, like the buttony-boy, has broken all out in stories. I adore "The Modern Warning," and feel as if I were the heroine.

Abrupt change of plans: Seeing no glimmer of improvement in me—indeed, quite the opposite—Katherine has found us a house in Campden Hill, all covered with Virginia creeper. A cook, a Mrs. Thompson, comes with the lease, and on spring afternoons we hear the rooks in Lord Holland's park. A glimpse of sky and feathery green and Katherine laboring with a hoe and a spade in our scraplet of a garden, planting American seeds sent over by Fanny Morse. I wonder if they will take root in English soil.

Louisa tells K, "You have to be happy when you're young because afterwards you *never can be.* Because then you will be married and how can you be happy with a man at your back all the time?" Nurse and Cook are engaged in a religious war over Louisa's soul. Anglican Nurse gives her a bonnet; Baptismal Cook retaliates with an apron. "She keeps talking about Our Maker," Nurse explains to me, "and that is Chapel, not Church." Meanwhile, upstairs, the cold Unitarian fish (Kath) and the votary of natural religion (your humble servant) look on in amusement. Mrs. Thompson's taste for tawdry jewelry is distressing to behold.

Nurse takes me to the window. Carries me, really. I stick my head out and drink in a long draught of spring. Golden daffodils, swelling twiggery of old trees, relentless housecleaning of rooks, gradations of light, the mystery of birth in the air. I hope as the season advances I may occasionally be carried by my slaveys through the tangled bloom.

A great peace wells up in me these days. Whence does it come?

Please, the curtain, half-way. Yes, like that, exactly.

Sometimes I think I am reliving my life in reverse. Like unwinding a string that has been wound around your finger. One year undone and then the next, and the next, each with a rush of memories like the debris of an exploding planet. And I am not *doing* anything! I only observe.

Is that the teakettle shrieking?

So many things pass though me now, weightless. The skies of Newport. Commonwealth Avenue with its mall of spindly trees. The stone gargoyles in Paris, with their lapping tongues and bulging eyes. The year Father was dying. Harry sleeping in Father's study, keeping the accounts, I keeping house. Reading together in the evenings, both of us unspeakably bereft. H. asking what I thought of his stories, seeming to value my poor opinion.

Calling cards on a silver tray. Lady someone. *Shall I say you are too ill, Alice?*

Yes, too ill.

A draft slips through the cracks in the window frame. I freeze at the first chill even under five blankets. For the others it is warm, Nurse all flushed. How subjective the world is, as William points out in his Psychology. Rain splashes like hail against the glass. Later the sun comes out and rainbows shimmer everywhere.

Although K's venturings into the world are sadly curtailed by my unbridled demands, she did go out yesterday to see "The Dancing Girl" with Mrs. Clough. In the play, a wicked duke rehearses his villainies and says how much better are the lower orders than such as he, whereupon Mrs. C. exclaims, "I am so sorry to hear him say that; it is hard enough as it is to keep people in their place, and it does them a great deal of harm to hear that sort of talk."

As I am still wasting away, K and H feel moved to call in Sir Andrew Clarke, another great man. Physician to Mr. Gladstone no less! Arriving late, he announces himself as "the late Dr. Clarke." It is the same joke he made to an acquaintance of Katherine's seven years ago. Imagine making the same pun for seven years!

My heart troubles me now, I tell the good doctor, skipping beats and sometimes kicking me in the chest like a mule. I also suffer pains, alternately stabbing, burning or grinding, around my ribcage and clavicle. The pains are getting worse, as is the sense of suffocation. Dr. Clarke listens and palpates and then informs me—on May 31st, in the year of our lord 1891—that I have a tumor of the breast. He has me feel it: a stony lima bean under the skin. He says I may die in a week or so, or I may live some months. Or possibly the tumor is not malignant at all.

All things come to her who waits! My aspirations may have been eccentric but I can't complain now that they have not been brilliantly fulfilled. Farewell to hysteria and nervous hyperaesthesia, to spinal neurosis and suppressed gout. The late Dr. Clarke seems shocked I am not more dismayed, probably assumes my queerness springs from being American. But what a relief after all this time to suffer from something real! Dr. Clarke says the pain and distress of the breath is a sign. It will cease to be painful near the end.

In the evening the shadow of a huge moth darkens the pages of my book. For a minute I think it is the angel of death. Katherine tells me I cry out in my sleep, sometimes speak long passages. I tell her I wish she'd take notes; I might learn something from my subliminal.

They have strange ways here of shutting all the windows and doors as soon as a person dies. Nurse says that the corpses turn black if exposed to the air. I wonder if that is true.

A word about my brother Henry. With everything I have put him through, he has never remotely hinted that he expected me to be well at any given moment. He and I have decided not to tell William (knowing his keen sympathy for suffering) until the end, which I hope will not be too long in coming.

Of course, it is impossible to hide the facts from William. I write to tell him, and he writes me a very tender letter, addressed to *My dear little sister*, in which he never pretends that I won't die and shows that he understands my feelings. It is all very deep, beautiful, and William-esque. How could I have thought of hiding my diagnosis from him?

The idea of my post-mortem existence thrills me, wrapped as it is in the eternal mystery. I write to William,

> *It is the most supremely interesting moment in life, and death is as*
> *simple in one's own person as any fact of nature, as the fall of a leaf or*
> *the blooming of a rose & I have a delicious consciousness, ever present,*
> *of wide spaces close at hand & whisperings of release in the air.*

How queer to look ahead on the calendar and know the world will go on without you. Somehow the mind can't grasp its own extinction!

Facts keep disappearing, streaking across the night sky of my mind like meteors and extinguishing themselves. The other day I spent most of the morning trying to recall if the man in *The Ambassadors* was called Strether Lambert or Lambert Strether. They seemed equally plausible. "It is as if someone inside knows that this information will be of little use soon," I tell Katherine.

Last night I dreamt I was dead, and Henry, having found my diary, had given it to Charlemagne to "edit." I find him, looking very cross, going through it with a blue pencil, crossing things out until only a few of my words remain. Looking over his shoulder I make out the notes he scribbles in the margins: *Unsuitable! Distasteful! Inaesthetic!*

"Inaesthetic? Is that even a word?"

"It is now. *I* make the rules."

Covered with shame, I plead with him to give me back my journal, promising to burn it immediately in the fireplace. He shakes his head. "Do not think I refuse because you are an execrable writer, though, of course, you are. I do it because you were my rival."

"What do you mean?"

"You think I didn't see what was happening under my nose? Under my *table*? It is imperative that Sara's name and several others be expunged from this ghastly document."

Death feels very close at hand. It hovers around me like a great lover, my mind prostrate before it.

I tease the Nursling to explain to me by what hocus-pocus my soul is to enter Paradise, as she ardently if inarticulately assumes it will. I think it is all covered for her by that word "American." When she tends my couch of pain, I ask her to remove her cross, claiming it bumps against my nose, but really because it offends my philosophy. But she is the best little creature in the world, and has fitted herself with exemplary patience to all my acute angles.

A new volume of Anatole France is out, which never will be read by me. A small joke I made about a cuckoo and some clocks, Kath tells me, is in Dr. Holmes's *One Hundred Days in Europe*. So I have left some mark on the world after all.

Sara Darwin comes to call, more wan than ever. I almost feel I ought to offer her my bed to lie in. Although obviously very downcast about my prospects, she makes an effort to be cheerful. We discuss Lizzy Boott, who died mysteriously while carrying her unborn babe. "Nobody says what she died of," I say. "What have you heard?"

"Everyone's lips are sealed. But from something Nanny said I got the impression it was suicide. Nanny won't say—if she knows. But *why* would Lizzy kill herself at such a happy time?"

"Maybe it *wasn't* a happy time. The husband is a very difficult, moody person, they say. An artist. Not unlike Francis Boott."

"Oh, Arthur says women *always* marry their fathers!"

Still quoting Arthur. Well, don't I quote my brothers?

"Whatever the cause—and we'll probably never know—the thread of Lizzy's life was certainly cut abruptly."

***

My dying seems to be taking its time. I'd hoped it would go more quickly. One day H. brings to my bedside his friend Dr. William Wilberforce Baldwin, an American physician who lives in Florence. Dr. Baldwin palpates the lima bean, which has grown larger, harder, and more painful of late. Says it is definitely a carcinoma and foretells my death. Such a kind man, kind eyes, kind diagnosis, the kindest of all.

(It is amusing how K reduces doctors to impotent paralysis. Andrew Clarke faded visibly in her presence, but Dr. Baldwin has fared well so far. We continue to like him very much.)

I wonder if I shall have to forgive all those who have wronged me.

Aunt Kate at Niagara saying, "Don't look down, Alice, you'll get vertigo." So overcome by this phenomenon of nature that I longed to wrap myself in the silver foam and jump. One of my most beautiful experiences. After Mother's death Aunt Kate tried to mother me. After Father died, wanted us to set up a household together, two old maids, but I could not. "She is heartbroken," Harry said, "that you close your door to her."

Do not skimp on the morphia, William writes. Meant for times like these. But it means clouds in the brain and a mouth as dry as the Sahara. And my thoughts turning into a dream every minute.

Thought I would die on the voyage over, carried off the ship like a plank by three stout sailor lads. Sun glimpsed through the fog like a pat of butter melting.

Childhood rushes at me now like a rising tide, nursery joys and miseries passing in waves. The women go into the bathing machines and come out wet and laughing. Our maids in Paris hanging Mother's and Aunt Kate's nightdresses on the clothesline in the inner court. Drip, drip on the flagstones. *Monsieur has two wives like a Mohammedan.* So many things stripped away, as the great millstone grinds my bones. Worldly things shrivel and fall away, and then there is this faint hum, a delicious thrumming. Doors are flung open, great vistas coming into view.

NINE

1892

THE ROOM IN WHICH I WILL DIE HAS A PRESSED-TIN CEILING, which I have ample time to study whilst lying on my back. The frieze of pineapples turns out on closer scrutiny to be a frieze of palm fronds, and the tiny angels in the four corners of one tile only look (for a day or two) like the Four Horsemen of the Apocalypse. As my dying progresses, the tiles begin changing from day to day, from silver to slate blue to pistachio green to gunmetal grey to old gold to Pompeiian red. Never know what I'll see. My aunt's profile cleverly concealed among some shrubbery, my cousin Minny Temple romping through a field of tasseled corn, a finger of God pointing to a cluster of grapes with a bee orbiting it.

Katherine says the "bee" is a flyspeck and I would do well to ignore it.

William comes from over the sea, sits by my bedside, visibly shaken by my decrepitude. Such delicious company. When you are soon to die, you see other people in their wholeness. You could sit and watch them all day like your favorite exhibits in a museum.

We discuss Henry's play, which is chiefly what I think about these days. *The American* has been performed in the provinces and now moves inexorably toward London. The best actors are French, H. says, but for *mise-en-scène* the English are second to none.

I told Nurse that when Henry's play comes to London, she ought to go and have a seat in the stalls. She said, "I think, Miss, I would rather go in the gallery, and I could get some of the maids to go with me, and I would be sure not to tell them before that it was written by Mr. James, and then if it did not succeed it wouldn't be any matter."

Hearing this, William roars with laughter.

"William, when I 'pass over,' please promise you won't unleash your Mrs. Piper on my defenseless soul."

Laying his hand over his heart, he says, "The name Alice James shall never pass my lips in her presence. But I'm afraid I can't control Bob."

"No one can control Bob!"

We laugh together as the afternoon stretches out, endless as a summer in early childhood. The curtains billow, and I breathe in the sweet smells of grass and earth. We are in a state in which everything strikes us as funny and we can't stop laughing. And this is the last time we will see each other in life!

William is describing his "experiments" with nitrous oxide gas, "the most mystical of drugs," according to him. Alice stays up with him all night, writing down everything he says in case there is anything important.

"What drugs have you *not* taken, William?"

"Didn't you ever want to take something stimulating, Alice, so you felt yourself just going off and grasping for a second the unity of the universe?"

"Funny you should say that. That seems to be happening fairly often of late."

"What do you mean?"

"Oh, well, I go off all on my own. I don't need drugs."

"You may be interested to know, Alice, that your friend Dr. Weir Mitchell"—he grins mischievously, knowing how I have loathed this man since meeting him years ago at the Fieldses—"sent me peyote recently, promising me I would be in 'fairyland.' I took some while I was in New Hampshire. I retched for hours and felt no other effect."

"William! You ought to know better than to take *that man's* medicine. And that horrid Rest Cure. It does no one any good; it's perfectly obvious."

Probably not, he concedes.

"Poor little Winnie Howells. You must admit it's shocking, William. And these doctors so sure of themselves! By the way, the other day I was remembering Weir Mitchell's gruesome story in the *Atlantic Monthly*—about a soldier who lost all four of his limbs. It gave me nightmares."

"Ah, yes, the Human Stump. It made a deep impression on me as well."

"Wouldn't the man have bled to death, though?"

"Well, I suppose Weir Mitchell must know, being a neurologist."

A fly zigzags insanely around the room. William picks up a newspaper to whack it and I say, "No, William, let it be."

"If you want a fly buzzing around the room—"

"To that fly you and I are as gods, and today I shall be a merciful deity. How long do flies live, anyway? A day or two?"

He doesn't know. I thought he would.

"You know," I say, "I always pictured the Human Stump rolling along end over end like a ball, didn't you?" He nods, and we both break up laughing again.

"How is Charlemagne these days, William? I hear that he gets the bequest of Lowell's manuscripts and so on. He is his—what do you call it?"

"Literary executor. The way Charles gets his name stuck to every greatness is fabulous, isn't it? Dante, Goethe, Carlyle, Ruskin, Fitzgerald, Chauncey Wright, and now Lowell."

"Someone, I forget who, told Katherine that Charles goes around boasting that he has burned some of the sweetest love letters ever written, to make sure that 'no eye but mine should ever see them.' Can you imagine?"

We sit companionably in silence for a while. Well, William sits; I remain supine. The state of dying opens up all sorts of beautiful silences no one feels compelled to fill. A day could be an eternity; before long, a minute may last forever.

"Your essay 'The Hidden Self' interested me very much, William. I was quite taken with Marie, the woman with a fever, delirium, and chills—all hysterical, I gather. It was a buried memory of something, wasn't it?"

"Yes, Janet found that she had immersed herself in a cold bath years before, trying to bring on a miscarriage."

"Do you think everyone has one? A hidden self?"

"Definitely."

"I am flooded these days with old memories and new illuminations. It is like a river rushing through me. I believe your doctor Janet would find me of interest."

"I daresay he would."

"I wish I could describe it properly, William. It is as though parts of myself have been living as captives in the basement while I tried to live on the upper floors of the house. From time to time I'd hear groans or a rattling of chains down there and I'd do my best to ignore it and think of something pleasant. Remember Mother saying, when we went to the dentist, 'Just think of something pleasant, dear'?"

"If only it were so easy."

"But it's curious, William. I am no longer afraid of the captives in the cellar."

To live one's whole life in a cruel world wherein the heart's desire is never attained, and then to discover it was there all along! I want to tell William about this, but I can't find the words.

He has been trying to describe the "moving pictures" he saw recently, taken of the Paris Exposition, blurry people waving from a blurry moving walkway.

"I still don't see how a picture can move, though."

He explains that it is projected on a screen like a magic lantern show.

"Oh! Like the rats jumping into the man's mouth," I say, referring to the magic lantern shows we took in as children in London, where itinerant performers dazzled us with the wonders of science. "If life gets any more modern, what will become of us? Oh, William, you will live into the twentieth century!"

Sorrow flickers across his face. For a minute he looks as if he might cry. Dear William. Persists in believing I should have had a salon, a fuller life, even a whole country at my feet. If he only knew, the paralytic on his couch has a wider experience than Stanley slaughtering savages. But maybe you have to be a terrible invalid to know this.

"I wonder if women will ever get the vote," I muse. It has become a matter of mere curiosity to me.

This inspires William to tell me about his students at the Annex, whom he seems to prefer on the whole to the young men, but then he would, being such a flirt. "It took me months to talk Eliot into letting Mary Calkins into my graduate seminary, held in *my house*. She is a professor at Wellesley College, a brilliant psychologist. He refused at first. I had to badger him for months. We men need to be put in our place, and the women will do it, I hope. It's about time."

"Well, Katherine goes on storming the barricades in her polite but stubborn way."

"I hope she succeeds."

"Think of it, William! In the past year and a half, Henry has published *The Tragic Muse*, brought out *The American*, and written another play, *Mrs Vibert*. Combined with your massive *Psychology*, not a bad show for the family! Especially if I get myself dead, the hardest job of all!"

William goes back to America. Bidding each other good-bye, we pretend we'll see each other again, because how do you say good-bye forever? The strange thing is that now he is always with me. So is everyone I have ever known.

I try sitting up at table. Lean my head against the table, shut my eyes, feel the hum of the gas. I hear the stitches made by Katherine at her sewing. I swear I can even hear a spider spinning its web. Makes a web out of its body, then goes and lives in it. Just like Henry with his fiction—making a world and living back into it.

I cannot go back now to what I dreamt I was.

It appears that I was born a few years too soon. When the morphia I was taking for pain caused insomnia and nervous distress, K and H stumbled upon an article on hypnotism in *The Fortnightly Review* by a Dr. Tuckey. They somehow prevailed on the man to come here to instruct Katherine in his dark arts. To my surprise, the mild radiance of Dr. Tuckey's moonbeam personality has penetrated with a little

hope the black mists that enveloped us. Knew at a glance how susceptible my nerves were and said, "It is dangerous to put her to sleep all the
way." Did not say what would happen.

Katherine performs the hypnotism skillfully. It does little for the
pain, by which I mean the ceaseless grinding of my bones, the vise
tightening around my skull, the blinding spasms in various mysterious internal organs. But, as I wrote to William, what I do experience is
a calming of my nerves and a quiescent passive state, and I fall asleep
now without the sensations of terror that have accompanied that process for so many years. The first time I was hypnotized I floated into
the deep sea of divine cessation, and saw all the dear old mysteries and
miracles vanish into vapor.

A miracle! The snakes stilled at last. The inner watchdog worn out
with its ceaseless vigil. As a child I absorbed from Mother and Aunt
Kate that it was the job of women to worry. Is the laundress consumptive? Will the boys put someone's eye out with a stick? Is there dust on
top of the armoire? Is Alice taking her nap? Is the air too damp? Are
the children learning profanities? Will everyone's clothes be ready for
the season? Is Father becoming fatigued?

I had my own worries. What if you forget me when we move?
What if you sell me to the gypsies? What if my heart stops? What if
I fall through the ice? What if my head gets cut off in a train-wreck?
What if Françoise puts a sleeping draught in our soup and we fall asleep
for a hundred years? What if Father goes away and doesn't come back?
What if he prays for me to die and God hears?

And then your heart finds peace and you learn to love the world.
Should probably have been hypnotized as a babe in swaddling.

I watch Nurse pull the shade to half mast and reposition a vase of
flowers gathered from our garden. How perfect she is. In the worst periods of my neurasthenic youth I used to cry out to Mother and Father in
the infernal nights what would become of me when I lost them. Here was
the answer—a little girl then toddling about in a Gloucestershire village.

Half a dozen times a day I think, "I must ask K about that," or "I
must find out about this," thinking that someday I may need the knowledge. Then I laugh, remembering that "somedays" are over for me.

Constance Maud comes to bid me farewell before she sails to America. A tide of homesickness sweeps me under. Reading *Godey's Lady's Book* in Newport. Those namby-pamby tales. "An Old Maid's Story." *Every woman must be married; it may not be happiest at first but it is later.* Stuck to my mind for some reason, although I don't believe it.

Someday the rights of women will be respected, I suppose.

My ashes to go in a small box, only six guineas and another for a parson. So convenient.

Do you wish to dictate something in your journal?

Not in front of Henry, for no one is to know, only you. You will know what to do when the time comes.

They will want to burn it, I think. Your words into ashes.

Perhaps just a private printing. For the family. Nearly everyone has a crazy aunt in the attic. Could you find someone with a typewriter? I would like to see my thoughts in type; it might give them more *gravitas*.

She smiles broadly. "I was so hoping you'd say that."

"Then, who knows, it might be published someday. Or perhaps not."

William's little Peggy—Billy teases her dreadfully, Alice writes. "When I speak to Billy, it makes my stomach tremble," Peggy said. Heaven forbid a portent of heredity!

Long, long ago in Newport when I first died. Sun beating down, heatstroke, dog dead, bleeding from the mouth. Wilky in the parlor, so grievously wounded. Out of his mind. Don't let the flies.

Standing above the chasm, toes curled over the edge; ten toes, each with its toenail, the baby toenail nearly microscopic.

Sara and her laughing eyes, the Perseids streaking through the heavens.

Creakings on the stair. Aunt Kate opening the bedroom door in Mt. Vernon Street. We never knew if. Life-interest in a shawl. What you bequeath to a servant.

This granite substance in my breast. Gruesome way to pass through the Valley of the Shadow. Great weakness now, like a boulder pinning me down.

The old Swedenborgian lady dressed in black taffeta, her jiggling arms. *What lovely manners your children have.*

When the father takes it off at night there is a stump. A dead fish, white and purple. The mother rubs it with oil. The father lies on his back and sighs, "Never was a man so blessed as I am with my Mary."

House in St. John's Wood 1855. Overlooking a green where elegant ladies and gentlemen practice archery. Like characters out of Robin Hood.

In Paris I see my reflection in the gleaming floors. Robbie says he can see my drawers, and I say, no, you can't, and he says, yes, yes, I can. Grown-ups tower above us like redwoods.

Such good boys, I have such good boys.

Boulogne. On the beach Robbie and I holding our breath as long as. Spinning like tops to make ourselves dizzy. All fall down! Our footprints in the wet sand filling with water and pieces of sky.

Who will help me cross the river Lethe? What is the ferryman's name? Katherine will know.

Madame parle français comme une vache espagnole.

Don't you ever have fun, Cousin Alice?

Dream one night of Clover Hooper. Well, call it a dream. Wearing a white lace dress, sitting on the lip of a baroque fountain, feeding pigeons from her hands. I sit down next to her.

She looks up, startled. "Alice James! I *thought* maybe you'd gone and done it, too. It's not a sin, you know."

"I know that."

"You may still."

"If it gets worse I shall ask K for the lethal dose. Morphine. Dr. Baldwin kindly told us. But you—why did you drink potassium cyanide? I thought you had the perfect life!"

"Not at all. We could not have children and there seemed no point in going on. I am very occupied with the children here." I look down at the pigeons and see that they have changed into street urchins with smudged faces. "But the clergy, Alice! Scurrying around with their horrid rat faces." She shudders. "No, Alice, the real story is this. Henry, *mi caro sposo*, fell in love with Mrs. Cameron. Do you know her? Her husband is a Senator. The love was all in his mind but Henry's sensual organ *is* his mind. The rest of him hardly matters."

"Do you mean to say—?"

"Yes, Alice. He wrote a depressing novel called *Esther* in which a woman bearing a striking resemblance to *moi* falls into a hopeless melancholy after her father dies. Henry wrote it *before* Papa died. A queer case of precognition, no? I can take a hint, you know!"

"Is that so?"

"Yes, and then he wrote a second novel, also anonymous. Most people thought *I* wrote it. But that's not it, either. What *was* it? Oh, yes, my mad dead Aunt Susie kept invading my dreams. Said I would have to kill myself eventually, so why put it off? Her voice in my head all the time, all the time. Do you know what that's like? To blot it out, I had to drink a poisonous chemical used in photography. Did you know I took up photography? Anyway, I died and two years later Ellen had to throw herself in front of a train. Then Ned. The whole family—a chain reaction!"

"But Ned is still alive. In Cambridge, Massachusetts."

"Wait. In a few years' time he'll throw himself out of a window."

They take turns at my bedside, K and H. Is it Sunday? Oh yes, the bells. Nurse at her religious debaucheries all day.

K reading aloud from Miss Woolson's story "Dorothy" in *Harper's New Monthly Magazine*. Stops to hypnotize me every twenty minutes.

Where did my hysteria go?

My feebleness extreme. Can no longer sit up, so many things behind me now. From the supine position I dictate something for my diary. Strange dream this afternoon, woke up choking. Lizzy Boott and Annie Dixwell standing up in a boat in a stream, passing through a cloud into golden sunlight. Look back toward shore, beckoning to me. Both dead.

"The welcoming committee," Katherine says.

Katherine reading aloud again, hypnotizing me every twenty minutes.

Father dying. *Oh, this disgusting world!* Did he not see his only daughter? Was I not there by his side?

Nothing ever happened really. Once I was a small person in a big world. Now the world abides in me. Stars explode. Kingdoms rise and fall, turn to dust, seven layers of Troy, library of Alexandria in flames. Periclean Athens, Napoleon I and the other Napoleon, the one we saw in Paris. Try to tell Katherine and Henry but words become garbled passing through my lips. Time for talk over, I suppose.

I have always been the same: lively and sad, I have loved God my father and liberty. Madame de Staël, as quoted by Mademoiselle Danse. Feeding a goat a scrap of paper through the palings of a wooden fence. Bob Temple goes to prison for his crimes. Governesses depart in tears. God does not haggle. Henry James has kept the secret.

Please, Alice, do take some liquid.

This year my happiest ever. Enfolded in the love of friend and brothers.

La Revue des Deux Mondes. Says it will rain?

H writes W about my progress toward deterioration.

Nights long. Dreadful coughing. Breathing agony. Bones on fire.

I shee it! I shee it!

What, Alice? (Henry)

Typewrii .. fee—fee woman.

Horrible wracking cough. Nurse wipes my mouth tenderly and props me up against a firm pillow so I can breathe. Clots of bloody tissue on my nightdress, Katherine changes me into a clean one. I attempt speech.

Try to rest, dear. Save your strength.

For *what*? (Attempt to laugh; produce a witchy cackle.)

Bi-shycle, bi-shycle.

What's that about a bicycle, Alice? (Henry)

Fee women. Becush closhe. Rub a bit of my nightdress between my thumb and index finger. Henry works it out. "Women who ride bicycles must wear functional clothing?"

Yesh! Yesh!

So women will be set free by the typewriter and the bicycle? (Katherine.)

Yesh. You will shee! Coming. Coming soon.

How nice to have friends and brothers who know me so well they can decode my gibberish.

Pain lifting now. If you squint you can see it. Like space, like the silence between words. A wave of emptiness washes over my mind. My hard core melting, melting. The emptier I get the fuller I am.

To William. A telegram, whispered into Henry's ear. *Tenderest love to all farewell am going soon Alice.* How did people say good-bye before the telegraph?

Who has been dreaming the dream of Alice James?

Alice I can't hear you, you're whispering.

Sun through the mist. Pat of butter melting, melting. Carried off the ship like a plank. Alice James takes her bow, exits stage left. Look!

Please, Alice, try to take some—

Lock eyes with K, squeeze her hand, I think she receives. The pain that consumed me is gone. Please don't ask me, oh please don't, to stay another day.

HENRY JAMES
11 ARGYLL RD., KENSINGTON W.
JANUARY 12, 1893

TO WILLIAM JAMES
Her lungs, her heart, her breast are all in great distress, constant fever, a distressing choking retching cough. . . . She could not sleep. She is perfectly clear and humorous and would be talking if doing so didn't bring on spasms of coughing.

March 6th, 1893—All through Saturday the 5th and even in the night, Alice was making sentences.

> —*Written by Katherine Peabody Loring*
> *at the end of Alice James's diary.*

CABLE FROM HENRY JAMES TO WILLIAM JAMES
MARCH 6. 1893

ALICE JUST PASSED AWAY PAINLESS

KATHERINE PEABODY LORING
11 ARGYLL RD., KENSINGTON W.
MARCH 8, 1893

TO FRANCES ROLLINS (FANNY) MORSE
I cannot give you any idea of the beauty of that last night, those last hours, when Alice knew that she was free at last, though she was too weak to say much.

Ed essa da martiro
E da essilio venne a questa pace
("From martyrdom and exile to this peace")

—*inscription on Alice James's funeral urn, from Dante*

~ TEN ~

1894

THE SOUP COURSE IS STILL IN PROGRESS, AND ALREADY TWO quarrels have erupted among the Jameses of 95 Irving Street. Billy is warming to his favorite sport of tormenting Peggy, calling her a "harridan" and a "frump," words Peggy is too proud to admit she doesn't know. She takes refuge in being dictatorial toward Aleck, the last-born in a family as quarrelsome as the Balkans. Will they have to have another child so that Aleck will have someone to lord it over? No, William thinks, no more! They can scarcely manage the four they have.

The doorbell rings.

"Who could that be, this time of night?" Alice's mother, Eliza, wonders.

"Go answer it, Harry," Alice tells her eldest. "I hope it's not one of your melancholiacs, William—but don't they come by in the morning?" Then she catches the look on his face. "*Oh, no*, William! Please tell me you didn't schedule your office hours during our dinner hour!"

"It was the only time I was sure of being here. I didn't think anyone would come."

Alice rests her forehead on the heel of her hand.

Two voices, one male, one female, echo in the vestibule, and Harry can be heard taking their coats and hats with a bonhomie worthy of a valet at a gentlemen's club. When the students come round the corner to find the James family sitting at dinner, they freeze like deer in a forest. The young woman actually takes a step backwards.

"Miss Stein! Mr. Solomons! Marvelous to see you! Do join us. I hope you haven't eaten." He moves some chairs around and places Miss Stein on his right and Mr. Solomons on his left. Mrs. James smiles from the other side of the table, a little wearily, before ringing for the servants and telling them in excellent French to bring out two more plates.

The students have come to consult Professor James about their research paper, "Normal Motor Automatisms." Dr. Münsterberg told them last week that it was good enough to publish, but as his English is not fluent, he suggested they have Professor James look it over as well.

It summarizes a series of laboratory experiments in automatic writing, designed to find the exact point at which a personality splits and "releases" a secondary personality. The experimental design is Professor James's, but he has abandoned laboratory work since Dr. Hugo Münsterberg of Berlin came to Harvard. Although Miss Stein is only an undergraduate, Professor James granted her special permission to take Dr. Münsterberg's graduate seminar, where she'd be the first to admit she has no business being. She admires Dr. Münsterberg but she *idolizes* Professor James.

Leon Solomons, the most brilliant of the current crop of graduate students in psychology, takes the paper out of his case and proceeds to discuss fine points of experimental design with Professor James. Miss Stein, uninterested in methodology, looks across the table at the little girl and finds her staring back.

"*Lots* of students come to our dinners," the girl says. "We know practically everyone at Harvard. We know Professor Royce and Professor Cummings and Professor Palmer and Professor Child. Do you know about our aunt who died? Her name was Aunt Alice and I never met her. But we put her ashes in a vase!"

"It's an *urn*," says Harry in a tone of amused contempt.

"Peggy, please focus on eating," says the elderly lady, evidently her grandmother, "and let the grown-ups talk."

In her laboratory notes, Miss Stein noted at first that she had "no subconscious reaction." But after performing the experiments for a while, she found that when someone read a story to her at the same time that she wrote down the words dictated by another person, something odd would happen and her hand would begin to write *unconsciously* and go on writing for a long time, in a sort of trance.

When there is a break in the conversation, Mrs. James asks both students where they are from and whether they are enjoying Cambridge. They chat about their respective boarding houses, and about Leon's plans to go to Europe next summer.

"I break down every two or three years and have to ruin myself by going to Europe," Professor James tells them. "Last year, on my sabbatical, the whole family came, and an entire Swiss village was condemned to witness the quarrels and tantrums of the James family on our balcony. Later, in cold damp stony Florence, the children were sick with catarrhs all winter in a freezing house. My brain shut down completely and by the time we came back I'd lost all memory for psychology."

The students are unable to think of an appropriate response to this.

"When you have been over there for a long period, and you come back here, you see all too starkly the American over-strained seriousness, our narrow horizons, our jerky angular unsmiling ways and manners. You become partially dissociated. But maybe that is just me." He smiles graciously.

Miss Stein mentions that she lived in Vienna briefly as a small child and saw the emperor Franz Josef stroll through the Volksgarten while a band played patriotic songs.

"Ah, that would explain why your mind is so—capacious, Miss Stein. Early influences! Which reminds me"—addressing both students—"Have you ever heard of this man Sigmund Freud? Viennese. I have just been reading the most extraordinary article in the *Neurologisches Centralblatt*. The title is *Über den Psychischen Mechanismus Hysterischer Phänomene*. Do you know German?"

Mr. Solomons does; Miss Stein does not. "Well, it begins rather strangely. *A chance observation*—oh, hang it, I've forgotten exactly." He abruptly pushes back his chair and strides out of the room. Peggy has not taken her eyes off the young woman across from her, and tells her now, "You needn't worry about boring us. We are used to intellectual conversations. Except Aleck." With her elbow, she indicates the small boy next to her. "He used to be called Francis Tweedy, but now he's Aleck."

"Was not!" says the boy.

"You were, too! You just don't remember."

From the head of the table, Alice scans the faces, mentally making a place for her dead boy. In her mind there are always five children, not four. Herman would be ten now, filling in the gap between Billy and Peggy.

To get Peggy to close her mouth, she says, "Peggy, dear, do eat your asparagus."

All the Jameses have beautiful voices, Miss Stein notices. She feels as if she were dining with the gods on Mt. Olympus.

"It's too . . . stringy," Peggy says. "I wish I *did* meet Aunt Alice. Now I'll have to wait until I die, and that will be a long, long time." She heaves a dramatic, world-weary sigh.

"You don't *know* that, Peggy," smirks Billy, across the table. "You could be dead as a doornail tomorrow, and we'd have to talk to you through Mrs. Piper." He rolls his eyes up in his head, fluttering his eyelids, and drones in a low voice. *I am Peeeeeggggy Jaaaaames. Reeeecently deceeeeeased.*

Harry, normally more mature, laughs.

"Billy, stop teasing your sister," their grandmother says.

But after sticking out her tongue, Peggy ignores him, apparently riveted by the sight of Miss Stein.

"How old are you?" Miss Stein asks.

"As old as . . . the pangs of old age." Peggy heaves another dramatic sigh.

"She's seven," says Billy. "Seven *months!*" He laughs maniacally, and Peggy pushes out her lower lip in a pout.

Professor James returns with a journal offprint in his hands, and scans it. "Ah, here it is. I'll translate into English. *A chance observation has led us, over a number of years, to investigate a great variety of forms and symptoms of hysteria* . . . What the deuce do they mean by a 'chance observation'? They never *explain*, you see. Later they refer to a 'complicated case of hysteria' dating from 1881 but give no details. Why do you suppose it took them so long to publish? Thirteen years! It's very odd."

It is typical of Professor James to solicit students' opinions, as if they were equals. Neither Mr. Solomons nor Miss Stein can shed any light on the Viennese case.

"Toward the end of the article they write, *Hysterics suffer mainly from reminiscences.* A lovely phrase, *nicht wahr*? But I don't care for this word they use—*das Unbewusste.* That's the unconscious, Miss Stein. I don't believe it is *unconscious.* I prefer the word subliminal. Janet speaks of the *subconscious*, and Dr. Morton Prince of Boston has begun to talk of *co-conscious* selves. Eventually we shall have to agree on terminology!"

"I was very surprised to hear Professor Münsterberg say the other day that he does not believe in the existence of the subconscious mind," Mr. Solomons volunteers.

Professor James looks deeply shocked. "How extraordinary."

At this point the smallest boy's milk splashes onto the tablecloth and his sister's plate. "Bad boy!" Peggy says, taking his small hand and slapping it. The little boy wails, and his grandmother gathers him onto her lap. Peggy is sent to her room and flounces out of the room like an enraged *prima donna.*

After the dessert dishes are cleared, and the rest of the family disperses noisily, Professor James goes over the students' article point by point, asking a few technical questions, and says, "I agree with Dr. Münsterberg. This paper is certainly publishable. I would be glad to send it around to a few editors I know."

Two hours later, sitting before the looking glass of her vanity, rubbing cold cream into her skin, Alice says, "William, was it really necessary for your students to be *minutely* informed about the James family's temper tantrums in Switzerland?"

"Oh, it's all right. They are graduate students. Mr. Solomons is, anyway."

Alice rolls her eyes at the non sequitur. "The young man has a lovely, shy smile, doesn't he? And the stout girl has such a compelling and direct gaze. Such as the goddess Athena might have had." Then, setting down her hairbrush, she gives her husband a sharp glance. "So, how long are you planning to put it off, William?"

"What, darling?"

"Reading your sister's diary. At least do it for Henry's sake. So you can talk to him about it sensibly and calm him down."

"Poor Henry! All those years sitting by Alice's bedside feeding her gossip, never dreaming she was taking notes."

For the past two weeks, stricken letters have been arriving every other day.

I am almost sick with terror. A woman in Venice said to me 'I hear your sister's letters have just been published & are so delightful,' which almost made me jump out of my skin.

Henry wondered, and William does too, whether Alice herself had wanted the diary printed or if it was a "pious inspiration" of Katherine Loring's.

"But didn't Miss Loring just make the four copies for the family and herself?" Alice says. "I don't see the problem."

"Darling, think how famous Henry is, and I suppose I am a bit as well. Things leak out. So far, I've been able to persuade Katherine not to send a copy to Bob while he is floridly insane!"

Various nightmare scenarios have been spooling through Henry's mind and his, he explains. Scenario #1: Crazy Bob gets hold of his copy and allows it to fall into the wrong hands. Scenario #2: The "two Marys"— Bob's wife and daughter—pass it around Concord and alert "the fearful American newspaper lying in wait for every whisper" (Henry's words). Scenario #3: Katherine Loring herself shows it to some reporter or suffragist sob-sister, either here or in England; or Scenario #4: Katherine allows the diary to be published in its entirety as a book.

"Oh, I can't imagine Alice would have wanted that."

"Well, we don't really *know*, do we?"

Much of the distress could have been averted, he says, if Katherine had only substituted blanks or initials for names. William sympathizes with the distress of his emotionally private brother and worries, too, about what Alice may have written about *him*. He still hasn't read the diary and is not sure why he keeps putting it off.

Henry has read it and believes it to be a work of genius. Although he ascribes the vehemence of Alice's opinions of the British to her extreme seclusion, he has found

an immense eloquence in her passionate 'radicalism'—her most distinguishing feature almost—which, in her was absolutely direct and original (like everything that was in her). It would have made her, had she lived in the world, a feminine 'political force.' She felt the Home Rule question as only an Irishwoman (not anglicized) could. It was a tremendous emotion with her. What a pity she wasn't born there—or had her health for it.

For now, they are keeping the diary secret. William has said nothing to Bob, and Alice has kept it secret even from her mother and sisters. "You can't just lock it up forever," she says now. "*I* want to read it. If it is half as good as Alice's letters, it ought to be very good indeed."

"Ah! And this from the person who once referred to Sister Alice as an 'unnatural woman'!"

"I said no such thing, William."

"You did, darling. The winter Father was dying and I was in London. You wrote me that you went over to Mt. Vernon Street one evening and found Alice and Katherine dining *à deux*, and the whole atmosphere gave you the strangest feeling. You wrote: 'Katherine is faithful to Alice and that means that she too is a very lonely woman. And I am finally sure of this: she is not made as other women—our ways of feeling are not hers so we have no right to decide.'

"Your habit of quoting verbatim from my old letters is *very* irritating, William. It would be so much better if you remembered where you put the letters I gave you to mail yesterday."

"I'm sure they'll turn up."

"Perhaps I did say something of the sort. Everything felt wrong then, William. The way your father turned his face to the wall and willed himself to die, casually deserting his children. Poor Alice, above all. In his last weeks she seemed to have completely left his mind. He never spoke of her and when she appeared he treated her like a stranger.

It was shocking and terribly sad. Anyway, as you know, I changed my mind about Alice and Katherine. I am glad they had each other."

"Poor little Sister Alice!"

"Remember how she used to *glare* at me as if she could will me to vanish?"

"I am glad she was unsuccessful."

"It took me years to forgive her for ruining our wedding. I can still see your poor parents, barely managing to smile. It made our wedding a hurried and furtive affair. Not until we were on the train to New York did I grasp that we were really married."

"Sister Alice felt everything acutely and could not put her emotions in perspective. She would go into terrible rages sometimes."

"So a bit like you, darling?"

"I thought you would say that."

With a hairpin in her mouth, Alice says, "That Miss Stein is an unusual girl. No corset, that was obvious, and as she went out the door she was wearing a hideous straw bonnet with a soiled blue ribbon. In March!"

"She always wears that. She doesn't pay attention to fashion."

"You and your strays, William! But I liked Miss Stein. There is something about her."

"Depend on it, dear. Gertrude Stein will go far!"

The diary was not Sister Alice's first postmortem appearance. Some nine months after her death, she "came through" Mrs. Piper. This occurred during one of Bob James's sittings with the psychic in Boston and he wrote up an account, copies of which were circulated to his siblings, children, estranged wife, various friends and acquaintances, spiritualists, and other interested parties. It did not escape William's notice that Bob's problems were the central focus of the communication.

NOTES ON A SITTING WITH MRS. PIPER
December 28, 1893

At the sitting Father, Mother, Alice, and Wilky were said to be present. Alice comes and wishes to know if I am present and then says they

are all in trouble about me and that if they could take me out of my
surroundings they would, but that they cannot do. They have been in
trouble about me for a good while, that Father is never absent from
me, that he is in reality my guiding and guardian spirit. Alice wants to
know if my resentment about her will still exists, to which I assure her it
does not. When I said to Alice, "How is it you speak now, whereas you
on Earth threw discredit upon spiritualism and didn't believe it was
possible or wise for the dead to talk with those who were on Earth?" She
answered, "We all think differently now. You must not think of us as
we were but as we are. Father, Mother, Wilky, and I are always together.
We will try and impress Mary in her sleep." Phinuit predicts, "Some fine
morning you will have a peculiar feeling and then you will see a ball of
light and out of it your father will come just as you knew him in life."

William sighs. How dreary the dead are, how inarticulate, dull and blundering—in the séance room, at any rate. While he still champions Mrs. Piper, and absolutely believes she is not a fraud, it is a fact that most messages from the beyond are astonishingly banal. "The photograph . . . which sat on the mantel . . . is now in the spare bedroom. It needs dusting." A man returns from the dead and has nothing better than this to say to his wife?

He thinks, *If that is my sister, I'll eat my hat.* Sister Alice would never become invested in Bob's train-wreck of a marriage or devote all her postmortem efforts to sorting it out. Nor would she have consented to be channeled by Mrs. Piper in the first place.

Bob is presently in the Danville Sanatorium (again), drying out, and thus for the present unable to trouble the departed. He does trouble the living, however, and frequent screeds have been arriving by mail.

William wanted to invite Bob as a guest speaker in his Philosophy 20b seminar, on mental pathology. The course began with hysteria, and proceeded through double personality, trance states, the history of witchcraft, the classic types of insanity, and the criminological litera-ture. "Beyond—or perhaps it would be more accurate to say *below*—the separate islands of consciousness we call our minds lies the infinite, the Mother Sea," William told his class. This much he has learned from his self-experimentation with drugs and from interviewing ordinary people who have had mystical experiences.

Apart from his induced coma at Somerville, he has never had a full-fledged mystical experience and keeps hoping. Nitrous oxide comes closest. As he told his class recently, at the institution formerly known as the Annex and recently incorporated as Radcliffe College, "Depth beyond depth of truth seems revealed. The truth fades out, however, at the moment of coming to." In the sober light of day his utterances, written down by his wife, never fail to sound silly. Nevertheless, the sense of a profound meaning having been there persists.

Bob's letters from Danville are monuments of self-absorption and self-sabotage. William believes his students could learn more about systematic delusions from one hour of Bob than from days of some alienist prattling about his theories.

"You *can't*, William!" Alice had told him.

"Why not?"

"You can't put your insane brother on display at Harvard. They think you're half mad already."

"Really? Do they say that?" He is amused by the periodic rumors of his madness, Alice less so. In the end he listened to his wife, the wisest person he knows, and arranged to treat his students to a tour of the Worcester Lunatic Asylum instead.

Soon after the box containing Alice's ashes arrived—brought over the ocean by the faithful Miss Loring, along with (as they would learn later) the two notebooks containing Alice's diary. William shook out the contents of the box onto the pages of the *Boston Evening Transcript* and sat contemplating a pile of fine grey powder laced with hard bony bits. It was impossible to conceive of this mound of grit as Alice. Maybe the crematorium sweeps out a handful of ashes from numberless carbonized bodies, sprinkles some into an urn, and says, "Here's your loved one." But it makes no difference because it is not Alice.

The box sat on a shelf in his study, where it remained until the marble gravestone he ordered in Florence arrived.

He chose the epitaph from Dante. When he saw it chiseled in stone, he broke down—in gratitude for his sister's final release, in grief that she was gone. Henry wrote him that the inscription was so right that *it was as if one sunk down on one's knees in a kind of anguish of gratitude before something for which one had waited with a long, deep ache.*

He and Alice took the urn containing the ashes to the family plot in the Mt. Auburn Cemetery. Harry, Billy, and Peggy came along and were uncharacteristically quiet and solemn. He had not pictured how hard the ground would be in December, and barely managed to scrape out a hole, while the snow fell around them. The flakes floated slowly through the air and made a downy quilt on the ground. The far shore of the river was curtained in mist, and the boughs of the hemlock branches bowed under their dollops of white frosting. There was a sense of holy presence, as Alice deserved.

"Is Aunt Alice sorry she never met me?" Peggy asked.

"I am sure she is, dear," her mother said.

We are trees whose roots grow deep and intertwine in the dark, William thought. Life is a passing dream, and then we enter into our deeper life. To Sister Alice, as to Father, death seemed truer, more complete, than life. One thing he knows: Normal waking consciousness is but one special type of consciousness, whilst all about it, parted by the flimsiest of screens, lie forms of consciousness altogether different.

That night, William falls asleep and sleeps soundly for an hour, then awakes, lucid and alert. He knows there is no chance of going back to sleep. This is probably the beginning of a period of exaltation—one of his "jiggle" states, as Alice calls them, when he is full of electric energy and his leg jiggles nearly constantly. Eventually he will feel as if he'd ridden a roller-coaster fifty times in a row, but right now life is murmuring to him, communicating its intricately woven patterns. With his fingertips tingling and his heart on fire, he pads downstairs in his carpet slippers and sits in silence in the dreaming house. His father's portrait (by Francis Boott) regards him levelly, almost sternly, as if to say, "What are you afraid of?"

It is chilly in his study, and he makes a fire. Then he unlocks the desk drawer, and pulls out Alice's typewritten diary, surprised by its thinness. Sitting in his favorite armchair, he reads. The first entries are tentative, almost apologetic. Then she seems to gain traction and the power of her mind kicks in. As he reads on, he has an impression, almost palpable, of being inside his sister's head, reading about the Parnell case in the newspapers, talking to Nurse about the Bachellers and Brookses, receiving a visit from a couple of Mind Cure crones. Being inside her mind is an intimate thing, and he is moved in ways he cannot put into words.

Soon he is reading ravenously. About the drunk and reckless "chair-man" who nearly dumped Alice out of her bath chair into a pasture. About the new baby who was an "excrescence" upon its sister's body. About Henry Morton Stanley's activities as reported in the newspaper. The oleaginous "clericule." Nurse's and Miss Clarke's views of life. Miss Leppington, Miss Percy, the identical twin sisters who say, "We have such a headache." Henry's visits and his gossip. Miss Loring coming and going. Ireland and Home Rule. The follies of England's "tinsel monarchy." The American consul from Birmingham who had "laid upon a bed of sickness." The crushing poverty of the masses and the haughty insouciance of the rich.

Here is Alice's sharp tongue, her sarcasm, the hilarious epithets she invented for the Great Men and others she scorned. But, above all, he is struck by passages of deep discernment and insight. She had so little to feed on, and so much loneliness and pain, yet her diary has a fierce beauty that makes him think of fantastic spiny plants abloom in the desert. He finds his name scattered throughout. He is quoted on various topics, his wit contrasted to Miss Clarke's lack of same, his children's memorable quotations noted, and, of course, he appears in *the somewhat devastating episode of July 18 when Henry presented himself doubled by William.* Of his next appearance, after the Physiological Congress, she writes, *William is simply himself, a creature who speaks in another language as Henry says from the rest of mankind and who would lend life and charm to a treadmill.*

His little sister's love for him, despite his being so often a clumsy, judgmental, insensitive clod, brings tears to his eyes. She thought of him far more frequently than he thought of her. He and Alice and

the children were always on her mind; any scrap of information confided in a letter lived a second life through her. And Henry's visits are
described like the visitations of a prince; everything he tells her takes
up residence in her mind.

It is painful to read that she considered herself a "Barnum monstrosity" and that after Henry left her side, *I could cry for hours after he
goes, if I could allow myself such luxuries, but tears are undiluted poison.*
Recalling her loneliness after Father's death, she wrote of

> *those ghastly days when I longed to flee to the firemen next door and to
> escape from the 'Alone, Alone' that echoed through the house, rustled
> down the stairs, whispered through the walls, and confronted me, like
> a material presence, as I sat waiting, counting the moments as they
> turned themselves from today into tomorrow.*

He and Alice should have reached out to her! Why hadn't they?
She could have moved in with them for a while. At the time he thought
that Katherine Loring was the only person she wanted near her. Aunt
Kate had assumed that she and Alice would form a household together,
but Alice would have none of it. In tears, Aunt Kate complained to him
that Katherine was poisoning Alice's mind, that she had a "Svengali-
like effect" on her.

Now that he considers it, Sister Alice probably would not have felt
comfortable living in a nest of Gibbenses.

He takes in, deeply now, how it was to be the youngest in the James
family and the only girl—alternately doted on, overlooked, petted, taken
for granted, stifled, sacrificed to others. At the mercy of four teasing older
brothers, subject to the iron rule of Mother and Aunt Kate, on the one
hand, and the impenetrable conundrums of Father's Ideas on the other.
To possess her gifts and be told that the only way to be a successful female
was to be sunny, self-denying, and receptive. (He, too, once believed that
females were intended to be lovely, selfless angels devoted to the happiness of men, but he has been capable of change, thank heavens.)

He comes to the terrible summer of 1878, which Alice refers to
as *the time when I went down to the dark sea, its dark waters closed*

over me, and I knew neither hope nor peace. The summer of his wedding. Alice's rudeness toward his fiancée made him want to wring her neck but at times, catching sight of her pale, haunted face, he would feel overwhelmingly sorry for her. He had an obscure sense of having wronged her. As if he'd abandoned her somehow. Deep waters there. Screams in the night. Mother, Father, and Aunt Kate taking turns sitting up with her. The way she looked at him as if she would reel him in with her drowning eyes. It was, as their mother put it, "a genuine case of hysteria." Was it? And what *is* hysteria *au fond*?

So many things he does not understand. Why did she decide in early adolescence to *clothe myself in neutral tints and walk beside still waters*? What prompted her urge to *knock off the head of the benignant pater*? What did she mean when she wrote, *How thankful I am that I never struggled to be one of those 'who are not as other ones are,' but that I discovered at the earliest moment that my talent lay in being more so*?

He cannot ask her now.

She wrote: *I am not rebellious by nature, having learned early in life that surrender, smiling, if possible, is the only attainable surface which gives no hold to scurvy tricks of fortune.* How he wishes he had her here to argue with. He would tell her, "You *were* rebellious, Alice, but your attempts were stifled. What a loss!" A year or two before she died, he recalls, she wrote to tell him of finding an old letter in which Father confided to a friend of the family that he, William, was the only one of his children with any intellectual gifts. She wrote: *And me among the group who, all unconscious, constantly gave birth to the profoundest subtleties, and am 'so very clever.' Arm yourself against my dawn, which may at any moment cast you and Harry into obscurity.* He savors the droll Aliceness of the last sentence.

He reads of her long struggles with her body, her mind and, above, all, her subliminal. When she spoke of parts of her body being "insane," or of harboring violent inclinations, it was the subliminal she meant, though she probably was unaware of this.

Although bedridden so long, her mental atmosphere was altogether that of the *grand monde*, and the information about people and public affairs she absorbed through the air was extraordinary. Henry, bereft without her, insists that if she had not been ill she would have presided over a great salon. Or that if she'd been born into different circumstances (Ireland, for example), she might have been a heroine of her people. But these are but the fancies of grief-stricken brothers. Her life was as it was. It was as if fate had contrived to present the greatest possible contrast between her contracted life and the breadth and subtlety of her mind and heart. In its peculiar way her life *was* a triumph.

He finishes the diary at 5:45 AM. His mind wanders to his last conversation with his sister. He was to leave in two hours, to catch the train to Liverpool. She fell asleep and he sat beside her, studying her face. She was not quite skeletal, but getting there. He was struck by how many different little bones and pieces of cartilage made up her nose, her cheekbones. It seemed a work of art, part of the unique human masterpiece that was Alice. She had finally gotten her wish and he tried to feel happy.

She moaned in her sleep from time to time, and tossed and turned. When she woke up and caught sight of him, she smiled beatifically. "Oh, William, I forgot you were here!"

He helped her sit up against the bolster and tried to feed her some of the broth that her nurse brought up from the kitchen while she slept. She licked a minute amount off the spoon with a flick of her tongue—it was like feeding a tiny kitten with a dropper—and, grimacing, waved the spoon away.

"Now I understand how Father felt. This is not the food I need now. It only feeds the cancer, anyhow."

"Shouldn't you eat *something*, Alice?"

"*Why*, William? I won't be wearing this costume much longer." Gesturing toward her body. She laughed, triggering another fit of coughing that lasted about three minutes and alarmed him, though he tried not to show it. When it subsided, she scanned the room and then whispered conspiratorially, "I am ready to go, William. My trunks are all packed. I *can't wait* to see what's behind the curtain!"

After a pause she added, with a playful smile, "Don't worry; I shan't haunt you."

"It might be nice if you did! Wouldn't you like to be published in *The Proceedings of the American Society for Psychical Research*?"

She smiled and closed her eyes. After a moment, she said, in a barely audible voice, "I hope that due to Father's Ideas, we aren't doomed to wander in a, in a—" she paused for so long he wondered if she'd fallen asleep—"Swedenborgian fog for all eternity. I should dislike that very much." Her voice was so faint he had to bring his ear close to her mouth.

"Yes, but your traditional harp-playing angels don't appeal much either."

She laughed until her face turned mottled and she began to cough into her handkerchief. Then she said, "Ah, the harp. Such a heavy instrument. It hardly seems . . . worth it."

After finishing the diary, William sits at his desk in a state of meditation, not wanting to break the spell. As the birds begin to warble and the rim of the sky turns pale pink he stares out his window at Kirkland Street. Who is that waddling away from Grace Norton's house? As the man gets closer, he recognizes the studious figure of Professor Blocher. So old Grace has taken a lover! He is reminded of Sister Alice's references to Grace Norton's "dissolute pruderies." Last month, at dawn, from this same window, he caught a glimpse of Theodora Sedgwick, heavy and large-hipped now, making her way home from Shady Hill and Charles. The aged voluptuaries of Kirkland Street! How he wishes he could write to Sister Alice about this; there is no one else who could appreciate it so well.

He dashes off a note to Henry saying that the diary "sank into me with some strange compunctions and solemnity. It produces a unique and tragic impression of personal power venting itself on no opportunity. And such very deep humor." One day it should be published; "it will be a new leaf in the family laurel crown."

He glances at the clock. Just past six, thirty minutes before he can reasonably expect coffee or hot water for a shave. He hopes he heard the oven being lit a half hour ago. To while away the time, he picks up the article by Freud and Breuer and reads it again. He reads that "external events determine the pathology of hysteria to an extent far greater than is known and recognized." The precipitating event could be an accident or merely a painful emotion, but the *symptoms* of hysteria are always related to what happened back then. Interesting. He wonders what Sister Alice's atrophied legs signified. Was this hysterical symptom related to Father's missing leg, that overwhelming fact of their childhood? He will never know.

Hysterics, Freud and Breuer claim, include "people of the clearest intellect, strongest will, greatest character and highest critical power . . . but in their hypnoid states they are insane, as we all are in dreams." Sister Alice was anything but weak-minded, yet she suffered (apparently) from hysteria. But whereas William sees the "subliminal" as a vast starry vault opening onto infinity, Freud's "unconscious" seems somehow hot and wet and seething with primitive desires. He is a little afraid of it.

He decides to write a triple review of Janet's new book, *L'État Mental des Hystériques,* Fred Myers's latest tome, and the Freud–Breuer material. The field of the subliminal is heating up grandly! And tomorrow he'll give his wife Alice's diary to read.

As he shaves at his basin, squinting into the little beveled mirror, he notes the fine webbing around his eyes, the horizontal lines in his forehead (crisscrossed now with vertical lines as well), the droop of his eyelids, the white bristles in his eyebrows. Good God, how has he become so antique? Age creeps up on us gradually but we notice it all at once. Not such a great leap from his present age, fifty-two, to the hallowed ground of the Mt. Auburn Cemetery.

He recalls Sister Alice's words when she wrote to tell him she was dying:

> *When I am gone, pray don't think of me as simply a creature who might have been something else, had neurotic science been born. Notwithstanding the poverty of my outside experience, I have always had a significance for myself—every chance to stumble along my straight and narrow little path, and to worship at the feet of my Deity, and what more can a human soul hope for?*

EPILOGUE

ALICE JAMES'S DIARY LAY UNPUBLISHED FOR NEARLY FORTY years. William James and his brother Robertson (Bob) died in 1910, Henry James in 1916, after destroying his copy of the diary. (Garth Wilkinson James, known as Wilky, had died in 1883.) To the world beyond the family and a few friends, the diary's existence remained a secret. In 1923 Katherine P. Loring gave one of the remaining copies to William James's eldest son, Henry James III, and this copy ended up at the Bancroft Library of the University of California. Katherine's own copy was purchased and donated to the University of Virginia's Alderman Library.

Katherine Loring kept the two notebooks containing the original, handwritten diary.

In 1933 Bob James's daughter, Mary James Vaux, wrote to Miss Loring to say she'd like to publish the diary in a book devoted to the younger and less famous members of the James family. Miss Loring gave her permission to use the diary, which she said Alice had wanted published. Mary Vaux hired a writer, Anna Robeson Burr, to put together a volume about the family.

This news sent shock waves through the other Jameses. All of William James's four children violently opposed publication. Henry James III informed his sister, Margaret James Potter (Peggy), that he was trying to persuade Edward (Ned) James, son of Bob, to "restrain" his sister. Ned, however, considered his aunt's diary "one of the most important pieces of literature that have been produced by any James." The diary, edited and cut, with proper names indicated by initials, was incorporated into a volume called *Alice James: Her Brothers—Her Journal,* published in 1934. It was published again thirty years later in an edition by James family biographer Leon Edel called simply *The Diary of Alice James.*

Appalled by the specter of publication of a diary of "neurasthenic and unadmirable character," Peggy James Potter wrote that Henry James's autobiographical work

> gives all the family biography that should be for public consump-
> tion. Why parade the failures, neurasthenias, and depressions of its
> younger members, as does Mrs. Burr? The book is an exposure, in the
> worst possible taste. Though I never knew Aunt Alice, I did know and
> adore Uncle Henry and that is probably why I shrink and shudder so
> over this publication.

Katherine Loring wrote to Mrs. Potter, explaining that, originally, she'd had four copies printed.

> I gave one to your Uncle Henry, which he tore up and said was not
> worth while for anyone to read; I gave one copy to your father, which
> I believe you have and which I understand you have shown to many
> friends. When your brother gave the James papers to the Harvard
> library, I sent him the third copy to deposit with the other papers. . . .
> As far as I can remember, your father never thanked me for his copy—
> simply acknowledged the receipt of it and certainly never made any
> suggestion as to its being read or not. I respected your Uncle Henry's
> wish not to have it published; knowing him . . . I appreciated his hor-
> ror of having any responsibility about himself or his friends.

> Mary Vaux and her brother Edward [the children of Robertson—
> "Bob"— James] and his wife are the only grandchildren who have ever
> taken any interest in me . . . and asked me about my relations with the
> James family. Mary Vaux and her mother have been my intimate and
> valued friends and when Mary asked me to tell her about her Aunt
> Alice I gave her the journal, which, you will understand, belonged

absolutely to me . . . and told her to do what she liked with it, all of the persons mentioned having died.

Alice had asked her to have it typewritten before her death, according to Miss Loring, and while she never said so, "I understood that she would like to have the diary published."

To Mrs. Potter, she added, "I think your criticism of the impression that the diary would make is unjust, absurd and altogether unwarranted."

The wider world agreed. Alice James's diary was a literary sensation, earning rave reviews in the *New York Herald Tribune*, the (London) *Times Literary Supplement*, the *New Republic*, the *Nation*, and *The New York Times*, among other publications. The Sunday *Times* noted that "in character and intellect she was the equal of her distinguished brothers and a daughter, beyond all question, of her pungent and iconoclastic father," while the *New Republic* cheered: "In some of her insights, some of her assessments of nineteenth-century humbug, Alice James went beyond either of her eminent brothers."

In a thoughtful appreciation in 1943, Diana Trilling wrote, "There is a common [James] family store of perception, imagination, and, above all, gifts of style. Alice, too, can write that wonderful educated James prose with its incandescent accuracy and then its sudden flights of homeliness." She compared Alice James to Emily Dickinson. In his group portrait *The James Family*, the biographer F.O. Matthiessen treated Alice James as an intellectual and a writer in her own right, observing that "Alice James, contemplating the world from her sanatorium, had come to a more incisive understanding of some of the forces in modern society than either of her brothers."

⟨ AFTERWORD ⟩

What was wrong with Alice James?

LET'S START WITH WHY ALICE COULDN'T WALK.

A year ago a friend of mine developed a condition with the somewhat Victorian-sounding name of Benign Paroxysmal Positional Vertigo (BPPV), a benign and ultimately self-correcting inner ear condition. Suddenly, she literally could not sit up or raise her head from the horizontal without being hit with waves of nausea and vertigo. It was like being seasick on dry land. This struck a chord and I wondered if BPPV might explain what happened to Alice James on her voyage to England in 1885, unraveling the mystery of her baffling inability to walk (when, just days before, she walked perfectly well).

Even today, when the mechanism is understood and exercises have been devised to correct it, BPPV can last for weeks or months. (After doing the exercises, my friend's vertigo disappeared after four weeks.) In 1885, it might have lasted forever. If Alice stopped walking long enough, her muscles would atrophy—and her brothers' descriptions of her "pitiful, shriveled" legs suggest this was the case—and she would be bedridden for the rest of her life. As Alice was.

THE INNER EAR OF WILLIAM JAMES

The sense of balance and equilibrium is primarily controlled by a maze-like structure in the inner ear called the labyrinth, at one end of which sit the semicircular canals. These fluid-filled loops allow the brain to read our position in space. One of the first physicians (if not *the* first) to describe the role of the semicircular canals was William James. It would be fair to say he was obsessed, writing two articles on the subject for the *New England Journal of Medicine*. When his sister and Katherine and Louisa Loring sailed to England in 1885, William saw them off with a special going-away present: "blistering patches" to wear behind their ears to prevent seasickness.

Katherine used the patches and did not get seasick. Alice very likely did not (she had a skeptical attitude toward the fads her brother took up), and was massively seasick. By the time she reached Liverpool she could not walk at all. We don't know about Louisa.

William James understood that the ear's semicircular canals played a vital role in providing feedback about one's position in space and that a disturbance of this part of the vestibular system could play a role in seasickness. In letters to friends about to sail to Europe he'd discourse at length about these canals and the calcium carbonate grains floating in gel that act like a carpenter's level to inform the brain which way is up. He was fascinated in part because he was a martyr to seasickness.

Thus perhaps part of Alice's bedridden condition might be explained. But what about the rest?

WHAT WAS "GOING OFF" ALL ABOUT?

Since adolescence at least, Alice James had been "going off," i.e., suffering spells of fainting or loss of consciousness. A remark of Katherine's (reported in Alice's journal) tells us that during her years in England Alice "went off" every day before noon. There are sometimes hints of "fits," and her episodes of "going off" were often linked to the hyper-emotional states to which she was susceptible and which any jarring piece of news could set off.

In Alice's day there were no X-rays and few blood tests; the endocrine system, like the brain, was terra incognita; microorganisms were not known to cause infectious diseases. Antibiotics lay in the distant future. Diseases were believed to result primarily from aspects of climate—bad airs and such—and could be remedied by a spell in a better climate and/or a spa with beneficial waters. Before drug and food safety laws, doctors dispensed medicines that were useless at best and often harmful, containing arsenic, mercury, or other toxins. (Small wonder that Alice's medicines always made her worse.) Add to that the damage done by tight corsets and by common toxic household products, such as paint or wallpaper containing arsenic.

In short, there is no way to arrive at a definitive diagnosis for Alice, who suffered from blinding headaches, "rheumatic" pains in all her joints, perpetual cold, as well as inability to walk. If she suffered from hypothyroidism, to take but one example, no one would have been the wiser, and her extreme fatigue and other symptoms would have been ascribed to weak nerves. That said . . .

The snakes in her belly

Let's take a closer look at what was for Alice herself her most troubling symptom, a churning sensation in her stomach area ("like snakes coiling and uncoiling"). It afflicted her just as she was falling asleep and was associated with overwhelming anxiety and/or panic.

The worst kind of melancholy is that which takes the form of panic fear, William James observed in "The Sick Soul" chapter of *The Varieties of Religious Experience* (1902), and then went on to quote a first-hand account by an unnamed Frenchman, which he claimed to have translated.

> *I went one evening into a dressing room in the twilight to procure some*
> *article there; when suddenly there fell upon me without any warning,*
> *just as if it came out of the darkness, a horrible fear of my own existence.*
> *Simultaneously, there arose in my mind the image of an epileptic patient*
> *whom I had seen in the asylum, a black-haired youth with greenish skin,*
> *entirely idiotic, who used to sit all day on one of the . . . shelves against*
> *the wall, with his knees drawn up against his chin, and the coarse grey*
> *undershirt . . . drawn over them inclosing his entire figure. He sat there*
> *a kind of sculptured Egyptian cat or Peruvian mummy, moving nothing*
> *but his black eyes and looking absolutely non-human. . . . That shape*

am I, I felt, potentially. Nothing that I possess can defend me against
such a fate, if the hour for it should strike for me as it struck for him. . . .
I became a mass of quivering fear. . . . I awoke morning after morning
with a horrible dread at the pit of my stomach, and with a sense of the
insecurity of life that I never knew before . . . this experience has made
me sympathetic with the morbid feelings of others ever since.

. . . I remember wondering how other people could live. . . . My mother
in particular, a very cheerful person, seemed to me a perfect paradox
in her unconsciousness of danger. . . . I have always thought that this
experience of melancholia of mine had a religious bearing.

After William's death, his eldest son, Henry James III, told a
biographer that his father had written the passage; there had been no
Frenchman. (For James connoisseurs, the word *potentially* is a clue;
William used the term—not then in wide circulation—so frequently
that Clover Adams joked about it in letters.) And the mother of the
"Frenchman" clearly bears a marked resemblance to Mary James, as her
children viewed her.

For William, as for his father, the religious sense was awakened
by a searing experience of panic-fear, and the "Frenchman" passage
in *The Varieties* carries a footnote: "For another case of fear equally
sudden, see *Henry James: Society, the Redeemed Form of Man*, Boston
1879, pp. 43 ff."

This, of course, was on account of Henry James Senior's Vastation,
which occurred in 1844. Sitting one evening at the family dinner table
after the meal, gazing at the fire, he experienced

a perfectly insane and abject terror, without ostensible cause, and only
to be accounted for, to my perplexed imagination, by some damned
shape squatting invisible to me within the precincts of the room, and
raying out from his fetid personality influences fatal to life.

With this footnote, William implicitly (and privately) acknowledged the kinship between his father's horror of *some damned shape*

and his own of the green-skinned epileptic boy. Alice's "snakes," coiling and uncoiling in her stomach since childhood, were equally horrifying for her and arose most likely from the same familial weakness. She who lost consciousness daily and suffered severe pain with little complaint was utterly undone by this white-knuckled, pure-adrenaline fear centered in her gut. Only at the very end of her life was her panic dispelled by Dr. Tuckey's "moonbeam radiance" and his hypnotism.

Toward the end of his life, Henry James Jr., too, was completely derailed by a panic so desperate it prompted him to submit to a crude form of psychoanalysis at the hands of family friend James Jackson Putnam, M.D., who had become a Freudian. (Who wouldn't like to be a fly on *that* wall?)

Whatever their other illnesses, many of the Jameses clearly suffered from panic disorder, the anguish of which can be inferred from the fact that ten percent of its victims commit suicide. If left untreated, panic disorder almost inevitably leads to agoraphobia. Even if she had not lost the use of her legs, Alice might have become a shut-in.

But that is not all that lurked in the James "blood."

Henry James Senior had several peculiar and/or mad relatives, including his niece, Kitty James (Prince), who ended her life in the Somerville asylum (the precursor to McLean Hospital). In her own letters and those of her relatives, Kitty appears to be a textbook case of severe bipolar disorder. So was Alice's fourth brother, Robertson (Bob) James, who was in and out of sanitariums and whose terrible mood swings and alcoholic rages alienated his extended family and wrecked his marriage. Henry James Senior may well have been bipolar as well (which might explain why he took so many mysterious trips and why Aunt Kate saw fit to burn the family letters after his death) but the evidence we have is inconclusive. He was undeniably an unusually emotional and tempestuous man.

Then there is William James, whose life is minutely documented. His diaries and letters and the letters of those close to him paint a picture of recurring cycles of mania (sleeplessness, flights of ideas, et cetera) alternating with intractable melancholia, which nearly drove him to suicide several times. His struggles made him exquisitely sympathetic to the suffering of others, and, throughout his life, he went out of his way, professionally and personally, to befriend troubled souls and seek a cure for mental illness.

Was Alice bipolar? Possibly, but her diary and letters, while highly original and definitely Jamesian, do not necessarily (in my admittedly unprofessional opinion) strike a manic note. The fact is, we just don't know. Our task of diagnosing people beyond the grave is complicated by the fact that late nineteenth-century psychiatry did not recognize our diagnostic categories. Melancholia, mania, and what was called "cyclical mania" were described in Alice's lifetime, but schizophrenia was unknown. Schizophrenics were herded into the catch-all category of Hysteria, which embraced everything from florid hallucinations, hysterical blindness and paralysis, dissociative and fugue states, to vague female discontents. At various times Alice's doctors diagnosed her with hysteria, neurasthenia (an equally vague term meaning "weakness of the nerves"), "suppressed gout" (a disease unknown to modern medicine), "nervous hyperaesthesia" (presumably, extreme sensitivity or nervousness) and, implicitly, with not being a proper female.

The late nineteenth century was very keen on nerves. In the most advanced medical centers, patients with "nervous" complaints—i.e., just about everybody—were hooked up to batteries and soothed with gentle currents. Dr. James Jackson Putnam, William James's good friend and former lab partner, held the prestigious post of Electrician at Massachusetts General Hospital, and often treated William and kept him supplied with batteries, which William carried to Europe when he traveled, electrifying himself diligently. Alice appears to have been less than enthusiastic. Like everything else, electricity seemed to make her worse.

Whatever ailed her, Alice James herself did not consider her life tragic or wasted, as she explained to William in a letter not long before her death:

> Notwithstanding the poverty of my outside experience, I have always
> had a significance for myself—every chance to stumble along my
> straight and narrow little path, and to worship at the feet of my Deity,
> and what more can a human soul hope for?

⟿ BIBLIOGRAPHY ⟿

SPECIAL THANKS TO THE FOLLOWING

LIBRARIES AND SPECIAL COLLECTIONS:

The Amherst College Archives & Special Collections for access to the letters of Katherine (Kitty) James (Prince) in the Julius Hawley Seelye Papers, 1824–1898

The Houghton Library at Harvard University for access to:

- The letters of Henry James Sr. and Mary Walsh James to various correspondents; letters from other James family members, 1858–1906; letters of Alice James; letters of Henry James; the William James 1842–1910 papers
- The E.L. Godkin Papers, BMS AM 1083, containing letters of Ellen Sturgis Hooper Gurney

The Massachusetts Historical Society, The Adams-Thoron Papers; letters from Marion (Clover) Hooper to various correspondents

ABOUT OR BY ALICE JAMES

Edel, Leon. *The Diary of Alice James.* Dodd, Mead & Co, 1964.

Moore, Rayburn S. *The Letters of Alice James to Anne Ashburner,1873-78, The Joy of Engagement Part 1 & 2.* www.researchgate.net/publication/249913735. Originals in the National Library of Scotland in Edinburgh.

Strouse, Jean. *Alice James: A Biography.* Harvard University Press, 1980.

Yeazell, Ruth Bernard (edited). *The Death and Letters of Alice James.* Exact Change Books, 1981.

About or by Henry James

Edel, Leon. *Henry James*. (5 volumes). Harper & Row, 1953–72.

Horne, Philip (ed.). *Henry James: A Life in Letters*. Penguin, 1999.

James, Henry *The American*
The Bostonians
Roderick Hudson
A Small Boy and Others
Notes of a Son and Brother
The Portrait of a Lady
Transatlantic Sketches

Matthiessen, F.O., and Kenneth B. Murdock (eds.), *The Notebooks of Henry James*. Oxford University Press, 1961.

About or by William James

Blum, Debra. *Ghost Hunters: William James and the Hunt for Scientific Proof of Life After Death*. Penguin, 2006.

James, William. *The Principles of Psychology*. Dover Publications (1890 by Henry Holt). *The Varieties of Religious Experience*, 1902.

Richardson, Robert D. *William James: In the Maelstrom of American Modernism: A Biography*. Houghton Mifflin, 2006.

Skrupskelis, Ignas K. and Elizabeth M. Berkeley (eds.). *William James: The Correspondence*. (10 vols.) University Press of Virginia, 1995.

Taylor, Eugene. *William James on Exceptional Mental States: The 1896 Lowell Lectures*. University of Massachusetts Press, 1984.

Wilson, Gay Allen. *William James*. Viking, 1967.

About the James family

Fisher, Paul. *House of Wits: An Intimate Portrait of the James Family*. Henry Holt and Company, 2008.

Lewis, R.W.B. *The Jameses: A Family Narrative*. Farrar Straus Giroux, 1991.

Skrupskelis, Ignas K., and Elizabeth M. Berkeley (eds.). *William and Henry James Selected Letters*. University Press of Virginia, 1997.

Matthiessen, F.O.. *The James Family: A Group Biography*. Vintage Books, 1950.

On late 19ᵀᴴ century psychiatry

Breuer, Joseph, and Sigmund Freud. *Studies on Hysteria*. Translated and edited by James Strachey with the collaboration of Anna Freud. Basic Books (reprinted from Volume II of the standard edition of the *Complete Works of Sigmund Freud*. Hogarth Press, 1955).

Ellenberger, Henri F. *The Discovery of the Unconscious: The History and Evolution of Dynamic Psychiatry*. Basic Books, 1970

Janet, Pierre. *The Mental State of Hystericals: A Study of Mental Stigmata and Mental Accidents*. G.P. Putnam's Sons, 1901.

Jones, Ernest, MD. *The Life and Work of Sigmund Freud, Vol. 1: The Formative Years and the Great Discoveries, 1856–1900*. Basic Books, 1953.

Masson, Jeffrey Moussaieff (translated & edited). *The Complete Letters of Sigmund Freud to Wilhelm Fliess 1887-1904*. The Belknap Press of Harvard University Press, 1985.

On Boston and Bostonians

Chapman, John Jay. *Memories and Milestones*. Moffat Yard and Company, 1915

De Wolfe, M.A. *Memories of a Hostess: A Chronicle of Eminent Friendships* (drawn chiefly from the diaries of Mrs. James T. Fields). The Atlantic Monthly Press, 1922

Friedrich, Otto. *Clover: The Tragic Love Story of Clover and Henry Adams and Their Brilliant Life in America's Gilded Age*. Simon & Schuster, 1979.

Gregg, Edith E.W. *The Letters of Ellen Tucker Emerson*. Kent State University Press, 1982.

Holmes, Oliver Wendell. *The Autocrat at the Breakfast-Table: Every Man His Own Boswell*. Akadine Press, 2001.

Homans, Abigail Adams. *Education by Uncles*. Houghton Mifflin, 1966.

Smith, Richard Norton. *The Harvard Century: The Making of a University to a Nation*. Harvard University Press, 1986.

Thoron, Ward (ed.). *The Letters of Mrs. Henry Adams*. 1865–1883. Little Brown & Company, 1936.

⌒ ACKNOWLEDGMENTS ⌒

A FEW KEY PEOPLE EARLY ON SAW THE VALUE OF A NOVEL ABOUT
a nineteenth-century invalid who spends a very long time in bed
thinking. My wonderful agent, Michael Carlisle, believed in Alice and
showed me what to throw away and where to start (my original chapter
20). Masie Cochrane, a wizard at structure and pacing, provided valu-
able advice and helped lead me out of confusion.

Pat Strachan was the first person to read the fictional Alice and
utter encouraging words, which meant a great deal.

Thanks to Jack Shoemaker, Counterpoint's editorial director, for
his perspicacity, wisdom, and humor, and to Jane Vandenburgh, whose
gifted editing touches helped make *Alice* a better read.

I am indebted to Mary Bisbee-Beek for being exactly on the right
wave-length with this book; to Matthew Hoover, whose organized
thoughtfulness made the succession of galleys practically painless;
and to Irene Barnard, who saved me from my worst mistakes (and in
French, too!); and to Sharon Wu and Claire Shalinsky for their excellent work, and everyone at Counterpoint who worked on this book.

Pam Petro, Praseela Feltenstein, and my son, Jake Teresi, were
brave enough to read and appraise the manuscript in a larval stage.
I am also grateful to a number of special people whose insightful
readings of intermediate drafts kept me going: Bayard Cobb, Rachel
Hooper, Thad Carhart, Marion Abbott, Gomila Garber, Cam Mann,
David Gillham. Much of *Alice* first surfaced in writing groups led by

the multi-talented Nerissa Nields; thanks also to my fellow groupies, too numerous to list here. Dorothy Firman, Ludmilla Pavlova-Gillham, Gail Kenny, Christina Platt, and Ellen Story helped by reading Alice carefully (in our book group), and hatching diabolical schemes to make it a bestseller.

And, finally, special thanks are owed to my nonfictional husband, Dick Teresi, for living with Alice these long years without complaint— or almost without complaint.